Christmas

BE
THE
MISTLETOE

Two bestselling authors deliver two
emotional yuletide stories

BENEATH THE MISTLETOE

Make-Believe Mistletoe
GINA WILKINS

Christmas Bonus, Strings Attached
SUSAN CROSBY

MILLS & BOON®
Pure reading pleasure™

*This collection is first published in Great Britain 2008.
Harlequin Mills & Boon Limited,
Eton House, 18-24 Paradise Road, Richmond, Surrey TW9 1SR*

BENEATH THE MISTLETOE
© Harlequin Books S.A. 2008

The publisher acknowledges the copyright holders of the
individual works, which have already been published in the UK
in single, separate volumes, as follows:

Make-Believe Mistletoe © Gina Wilkins 2003
Christmas Bonus, Strings Attached © Susan Crosby 2003

ISBN: 978 0 263 86113 6

064-1108

*Printed and bound in Spain
by Litografia Rosés S.A., Barcelona*

Make-Believe Mistletoe

GINA WILKINS

GINA WILKINS

is a bestselling and award-winning author who has written more than sixty-five books. She credits her successful career in romance to her long, happy marriage and her three "extraordinary" children.

A lifelong resident of central Arkansas, Ms Wilkins sold her first book in 1987 and has been writing full-time ever since. She has appeared on various bestseller lists. She is a three-time recipient of the Maggie Award for Excellence, sponsored by Georgia Romance Writers, and has won several awards from the reviewers of *Romantic Times*.

For the volunteers in the Rebsamen Hospital
Auxiliary, who do such a tremendous service in
our community and have been so nice to me.
Thank you and Merry Christmas.

Chapter One

Lucy Guerin had never quite understood the appeal of a white Christmas. After all, the holidays were traditionally a time for travel, and snowy weather had a way of seriously impeding travel plans. When Bing Crosby crooned about glistening treetops, he had probably not had anything like this in mind, Lucy thought glumly, staring out the rapidly icing windshield of her small car.

She had asked Santa for a man for Christmas, but she hadn't meant Jack Frost.

Ice storms happened fast and sometimes without much warning in the Ozarks. The weather guy Lucy had listened to had said that, depending on the temperature, there would be rain or snow or maybe ice. His own guess had been rain changing to light snow with little accumulation.

He had been wrong.

The ice on twisting, rural Highway 65 through north central Arkansas was growing thicker by the moment, causing Lucy's car to slide perilously. It was rapidly getting dark at 5:00 p.m. on this December 23. Between the heavy clouds and early sundown of winter, little natural light remained to guide her way. The beams of her headlights splintered off the falling ice. She was still several miles from the nearest town, and the only sign she saw warned that the next five miles of road were winding and steep. Great.

She wasn't going to make it much farther. Her back tires skidded, and it was all she could do to keep the car from sliding off the road. Though this highway was usually well traveled by Branson-bound tourists, the combination of the weather and the approaching holiday had the road almost empty now. Only one other vehicle was visible, an ancient pickup truck following at some distance behind her, also headed north.

Maybe all the other would-be travelers had listened to better weather forecasters.

It was quite a relief when she spotted a driveway ahead—a long gravel road leading to a rock and redwood house set at the foot of a rocky hill. She slowed her car to little more than a crawl to study the place. Evergreen and hardwood trees surrounded the area, but a fair-size yard had been carved out of the woods. The yard was surrounded by a chain-link fence with a gate that crossed the driveway.

A single security pole lamp sat beside the house, casting a dim glow over the place. There were no Christmas lights or other decorations visible, and the windows seemed to be heavily draped or covered with blinds, so Lucy couldn't tell if there were any lights on inside. For all she knew, no one was home. But she could at least park in the driveway and get off this dangerously slick road before she smashed her car into a mountainside.

She skidded again as she made the turn into the gravel driveway. Holding her breath, she brought the car to a stop in front of the chain-link gate. The old pickup truck slid in behind her, its driver obviously coming to the same conclusion she had about the hazards of traveling farther.

Now what? Lucy drummed her fingers on the steering wheel, staring at the house and wondering if the gate was locked. She could see now that there was another large building behind the house, a workshop, perhaps. No lights in those windows, either. She couldn't call for assistance from here; her cell phone wasn't picking up a signal. This, she thought, must be the very spot people referred to when they said "out in the boonies."

It was getting darker by the minute, and the freezing rain and sleet were falling harder. She heard the distant crack of a tree branch snapping beneath the weight of accumulating ice. She had to do something.

A tap on her driver's side window made her start. She looked around to see an elderly African-American man huddled beneath a black umbrella that was having little effect against the pelting ice. She rolled down her window and he asked, "Are you okay, miss?"

He looked as though the strong winds would topple him right over—or carry him away by the umbrella like Mary Poppins. "I'm fine, but you should get out of this weather."

"You think that gate's locked? Maybe if we blow our horns, someone in the house will come out to let us in. My wife wants me to keep driving, but I don't think I can get much farther in this."

"Absolutely not." He shouldn't have driven this far. Lucy reached for her door handle. "You go back to your wife. I'll see if I can get someone in the house to help us."

She slipped a little when she stepped out of her car, clutching at the door for balance. Ice bombarded her head and slid down the inside collar of her inadequate leather jacket. She had a heavy parka but it was in her trunk, as she hadn't expected to be out of her car long enough to need it before reaching her destination.

After making sure the older man was safely back in his truck, Lucy moved carefully toward the gate. The gravel driveway provided a bit more traction than a smooth surface would have, but the hard-packed rocks were still slick and wet. Thank heaven she had worn hiking boots with slip-resistant soles. She had selected them more because they completed her outfit of a heavy hand-knit green sweater and boot-cut jeans than because she had expected to do any hiking, but she was grateful for them now—not that even boots helped much in this weather.

The gate was latched but not locked, she discovered in relief. Cold seeped through her thin leather driving gloves when she lifted the latch and pushed the gate open far enough to allow her to slip through. Literally slip through. She nearly fell on her butt before she caught her balance.

Her curly red hair was wet and icy, and her face was so cold it hurt. She wouldn't have been surprised if an icicle formed on the end of her nose. Huddling into the fashionable leather jacket, she carefully climbed two slick rock steps to the covered porch that ran the length of the single-story house. It felt somewhat better to be under cover, but no less miserably wet and cold.

She was shaking so hard she missed the doorbell the first time she aimed for it, jabbing her finger into the redwood siding, instead. The second attempt was more successful. She heard a chime echo inside the house. And then she rang it again, hoping this wasn't the secluded hideaway of a paranoid, gun-toting, bigoted survivalist.

The door finally opened to reveal the most gorgeous man Lucy had ever seen in person. Around thirty. Thick, dark hair, navy-blue eyes, chiseled features, body to die for. What little breath the cold had left in her lungs escaped in a long, appreciative sigh.

Thank you, Santa.

She blinked ice-tipped lashes to clear her vision, just in case she was imagining this apparition of masculine perfection. But no. He was still there, and still fabulous— even if he did wear a less-than-welcoming frown.

"What is it?" he asked, and his deep voice was as beautiful as his face—if a teensy bit grouchy.

"We're stranded," she said simply, motioning toward the two vehicles in his driveway. "We need shelter."

He looked glumly at the ice growing thicker on the ground by the moment. "There's a motel about fifteen miles down the road," he offered without much optimism.

"We won't make it fifteen more feet. It's treacherous out there—and the old couple in the pickup need to come in out of the cold. Surely you and your family would allow us to come in for a little while?"

"No family," he muttered. "It's just me."

Maybe there really *was* a Santa Claus. Pushing a long, dripping curl out of her face, Lucy gave him a smile that stung her frozen skin and tried to look less like a wet stray cat. "We would certainly appreciate your help."

Even as she spoke, another northbound car—this one a beige sedan—skidded into the driveway, gravel spewing as the driver brought the car to a sliding stop only inches from the tailgate of the pickup truck. There was just enough light for Lucy to see that the car held a woman and two children.

The man in the doorway let out a resigned sigh. "I guess you can all come inside."

His enthusiasm was underwhelming, but Lucy forged on. "We'll probably need your assistance getting everyone in safely. The ground is as slick as a skating rink, and that's an elderly couple in the truck. Looks like two small children in the back seat of the sedan. It's going to be tricky."

He nodded morosely. "I'll get my coat. You can come in, if you want. You're hardly dressed to be traipsing around in an ice storm."

"I have a hat and a heavier coat in the back of my car. You'll need my help, I think."

His eyes swept the length of her five-feet, two-inch, 105-pound frame, making it clear he didn't know how much help she could offer. But he merely shrugged and turned to fetch his coat.

Lucy frowned at the man's retreating back. The guy might have the looks of a Tom Cruise, but he apparently had the heart of an Ebenezer Scrooge.

Maybe Santa hadn't been quite so generous to her this Christmas, after all.

When Banner had opened his front door in response to the completely unexpected chime of the doorbell, his first thought had been that a lost Christmas elf had somehow wandered onto his front porch. The top of her wet red head came barely to his chin. She had enormous green eyes set into a pixie face with a ridiculous excuse for a button nose, a full mouth that looked incongruously sexy in the center of all that cuteness, and a curvy little figure that made him rethink his former appreciation of tall, busty blondes.

When he had learned that she was the first wave of an invasion of strangers into his cherished privacy, he had been tempted to close the door in her cute little face. But even he wasn't quite that mean, despite what some people might say to the contrary. His ex-wife, for example.

The weather was vicious. Gusts of wind slapped him across the face with icy hands. He pulled his Sherpa collar more snugly around his jaw. His wide-brimmed hat kept his hair dry, but the freezing rain blew sideways, getting him pretty wet everywhere else. He thought wistfully of his warm, dry, peaceful living room, where he had just been sitting with a crackling fire and a good book.

So much for the quiet, lazy winter evening he had been anticipating.

The elf seemed to be taking charge of the rescue. She stopped by her car, where she quickly swapped her stylish leather jacket for a heavier hooded parka. Then she slung the shoulder strap of a bulging duffel bag over one shoulder before slamming her trunk and stuffing her keys into her pocket.

"Dry clothes," she shouted over the storm. "We're all going to need them."

He nodded and picked his way cautiously to the pickup. The driver's door was already open and a skinny, rather frail-looking man climbed out. "My wife needs help walking," he called out.

Banner nodded. "Hold on."

He and the elf looked toward the beige sedan, in which the woman driver was stuffing two young children into coats, hats and mittens. "Can you give her a hand while I help the other couple in?" Banner asked the redhead.

"Yes," she called back. "You go ahead. We'll be fine."

A hiss of air brakes, the skid of tires on ice, and the unmistakable sound of crumpling metal made Banner whirl toward the highway. A large, southbound delivery truck had missed the curve just before his driveway, the cab plowing into the shallow ditch.

Hissing a curse, Banner started to run toward the truck, but he slowed when he saw the driver climb out of the cab, obviously uninjured. Enveloped in a heavy coat, with a broad-brimmed oiled-leather hat pulled low over his face, the mountain of a man trudged toward them.

"You okay?" Banner called out.

A booming bass replied, "Disgusted but undamaged."

Banner nodded. "I'm trying to get everyone inside," he said as the large man drew nearer. "Got some women and kids and an old couple here. I could probably use your help with some of them."

"You bet." Banner caught a glimpse of sandy beard as the man moved closer, one big foot sliding on the ice but quickly regaining traction.

Turning back to the parked vehicles, Banner saw that the elf and the mother had the children out of the car. The redhead hovered protectively over the little ones while their mother dragged a couple of suitcases out of the se-dan. The large man moved toward them to offer assistance.

Banner turned his attention to the elderly couple. The old man was standing inside the open passenger door of the pickup, helping his wife unfasten her seat belt. Moving closer, Banner saw that the woman was even more fragile than her husband. She had snowy-white hair and a wrinkled face that had faded to a soft caramel color. The shapeless cloth coat she wore wasn't heavy enough for the weather, and Banner wasn't sure how much her visible tremors were due to age and how much to the cold.

"She uses a walker," the old man explained, nodding to the silver contraption folded and stowed behind the seat.

"That won't do any good on rocks and ice." Banner moved closer, noting that the woman probably didn't weigh a hundred pounds soaking wet. "Why don't I just carry you in, ma'am? I won't drop you."

"He looks like a strapping young man, Mother," the woman's husband said. "Let him carry you inside where it's warm."

"All right." Her voice was thin yet surprisingly strong. "But don't you go throwing your back out, son."

As if she weighed enough to make that a concern, Banner thought, moving in to slide his arms beneath her. He'd hauled bags of dog food that weighed more. She put her arms around his neck and held tightly as he lifted her, his feet solidly planted beneath him.

The older man pulled a blanket out of the cab and draped it over his wife's head, providing some protection from the falling ice. Banner tucked it snugly around her. The old man reached for the walker. "I'll bring this. And we have suitcases under the tarp in the back."

"Leave it. I'll come back for those things," Banner said, worried that the man wouldn't be able to keep his balance if he tried carrying anything. It was going to be a tricky enough walk as it was. "Let's just get inside."

He could feel the wind biting through the blanket and into the woman's coat and thin, knit pantsuit as he moved carefully toward the house. She shivered when the downpour gained strength again, and Banner instinctively hunched around her, trying to protect her as much as he could.

He worried that she would catch pneumonia on the way in, and he worried that her husband would fall and break a leg or a hip or something. He was relieved when the big truck driver rejoined them halfway to the house, having already deposited the others inside. The truck driver took the old man's arm, supporting him for the rest of the walk.

With the couple safely inside, Banner and the truck driver made a second hasty trip outside for more bags and the walker. It was almost completely dark now, and the ice was building thickly on every surface. The woods echoed with the sharp cracks of breaking tree limbs, and Banner cast a frowning glance at the overhead power lines. He figured it was just a matter of time before they were brought down by a falling branch, cutting off the electricity. Fortunately he had laid in a good supply of firewood, candles and batteries.

By the time he finally closed his front door against the storm, he was wet, cold, tired and grouchy. At least no more cars or trucks had arrived. He assumed the roads were so bad now that anyone who had been on them had found shelter elsewhere. He would be willing to bet the state police had closed the mountainous highway by now.

He only hoped the temperature would warm during the night, melting the ice and letting his stranded travelers be on their way. In the meantime, he seemed to have a houseful of unexpected guests.

He stood in the doorway of his big, wood-paneled living room, gazing rather helplessly at the chaos taking place there. Once again the young woman he had dubbed the elf seemed to be in charge. She had found his linen closet and distributed towels and was busily making sure everyone was getting dry and warm. As her hair dried, it curled even more riotously around her face, the red-gold color mimicking the fire crackling in the big stone fireplace.

The mother and two children were close to the hearth. Mom was a somewhat mousy-looking, average-size brunette with purple-shadowed brown eyes and nervous hands. Banner guessed her age to be midthirties, a few years older than himself. She was towel drying the hair of a little girl of maybe five years, a brown-eyed, pink-nosed duplicate of her mother.

A brown-haired boy whom Banner guessed to be around seven stood nearby, staring in fascination at Banner's enormous, dumb lump of a dog. The multicolored mutt sat on his favorite scrap of rug, studying the roomful of strangers with his usual unflappable acceptance of circumstances.

The truck driver had shed his big coat, but that hadn't reduced his overall size by much. Broad-faced, bearded and barrel-chested, he might have been forty, and he looked as though he'd have been as at home panning for gold in the Old West as behind the wheel of a big truck. He rubbed a towel over his bushy, sandy hair, leaving it standing in spikes around his ruddy face.

The older woman Banner had carried inside huddled beneath a thick, dry blanket also retrieved from his linen closet. She sat in a Windsor rocker pulled close to the fire, and the firelight flickered over her lined face, highlighting the fine bone structure that was still beautiful. She looked so fragile it scared him now to think he had carried her in; what if he'd dropped her or fallen?

Her husband hovered around her chair, his wispy gray hair already dry, his bent hands patting his wife as if to assure himself that she was all right. Banner doubted that either of them was younger than eighty.

What on earth was he going to do with all these people?

Lucy noticed that their host was standing in the doorway, looking rather dazed. She supposed she couldn't blame him. Judging by the nice fire and the mystery novel sitting open beside a cooling cup of coffee on the table next to a big recliner, he had just settled down to ride out the storm in comfortable solitude. Except, of course, for the company of his dog—the shaggiest, oddest-colored, laziest-looking mutt Lucy had ever seen.

At least the dog didn't seem to mind the company—which was more than she could say for its owner, who was definitely showing signs of stress.

Someone needed to do something to put him more at ease. Never one to wait around for others to take care of things she could handle herself, she gave him a big smile. "Thank you so much for taking us in. You've been very kind, Mr...?"

"Just call me Banner," he said, lifting a hand to massage the back of his neck.

She nodded. "Mr. Banner."

"Just Banner," he corrected, letting his hand fall to his side.

"Oh." Strange, but anyway... "I'm Lucy Guerin. I'm on my way to Springfield, Missouri, to spend Christmas with my family. Why don't the rest of you introduce yourselves?"

She knew she sounded like a too-perky cruise director, but the man who called himself "just Banner" was making her nervous, lurking glumly in the doorway like that. She turned to the mother and children behind her. "What are your names?"

The woman's face paled, as if she had been asked to make an impromptu speech in front of a large audience. The shy type, apparently—which Lucy had never been.

"I'm, um, Joan Gatewood," the woman finally murmured. "These are my children, Tyler and Tricia. We're going to my mother's house in Hollister, Missouri, for the holiday."

"I'm Cordell Carter," the older man said, smoothing a

spotted hand over his mostly bald head. "Everyone calls me Pop. This is Annie, my wife of sixty-two years. We're on our way to Harrison to our grandson's house."

"Sixty-two years of marriage," Lucy repeated in wonder. "Mrs. Carter, you must have been a child bride."

The old woman's weary eyes brightened with her smile, which still held hints of the mischievous grin that had likely captivated her husband sixty-two years ago—and apparently still did. "I was twenty-three. And you can just call me Miss Annie. Everyone always has. 'Mrs. Carter' reminds me of my mother-in-law, and I never cared much for her, God rest her contrary soul."

Her husband chuckled and patted his wife's shoulder indulgently, seeming to take no offense to the slight to his late mother. After so many years, Lucy figured he must have gotten used to it.

"I'm Bobby Ray Jones," the big truck driver volunteered. "I was headed the opposite direction from the rest of you—s'posed to be in Little Rock by tonight. I'd hoped I could beat the storm, but I guess I miscalculated. My boss is going to be ticked off that I put the rig in a ditch, but that's just too bad, I guess."

Lucy noted that Joan Gatewood was eying the big, bearded man with the same wariness she displayed toward Banner's huge dog. Apparently Joan was intimidated by large, hairy critters. As for herself, Lucy thought Bobby Ray seemed very pleasant. Everyone here seemed nice—with the possible exception of their glowering host.

"Okay," she said, wiping her hands on her jeans. "Now that we know who everyone is…."

"What's the dog's name?" Tyler asked, pointing to the mutt.

Lucy looked questioningly at Banner.

"That's Hulk," he said, speaking to the boy. "He answers to Hulk or Get-Out-From-Under-My-Feet-Stupid."

The unexpected quip took everyone by such surprise that there was a brief hesitation before they laughed. Though Lucy smiled, she wasn't entirely sure Banner had been joking.

Returning to the task at hand, she said, "Now, we all need to get into dry clothes and—wait a minute."

She whirled back to their host, her hands on her hips. "Your name is Banner and the dog's name is Hulk? I don't suppose your first name is Bruce?"

"No." He looked at her without smiling. "You haven't wandered into a comic book."

No kidding. Despite the joke he had just made, she hadn't seen this guy crack a smile since they had arrived. He obviously had a warped sense of humor, but he did a good job of hiding it.

Shaking her head, she turned back to the others. "We need dry clothes and a telephone so we can call our families and let them know we're safe."

"Mommy, I'm hungry," Tricia said, tugging at her mother's damp blouse.

"I'll start a pot of soup or something," Banner said, and once again he sounded glumly resigned. "The telephone is on that table. Make yourselves at home."

As he turned away, Lucy thought she heard him add beneath his breath, "It's not as if there's any other choice."

Chapter Two

Following the scents of food, Lucy wandered into the kitchen a short time later. She had changed into a dark-red sweater and dry jeans, and her feet were clad in thick red socks. She'd left her boots by the fire to dry.

Still wearing the damp jeans and gray sweatshirt he'd worn earlier, though he had kicked off his rubberized boots, Banner stood at the stove, stirring something in a large stockpot.

"That smells delicious. What is it?"

"Vegetable-beef soup," he answered without turning around. "I hope no one's a vegetarian. If they are, I'll rustle up something else."

She peered over his shoulder into the pot. "That looks homemade."

"It is. I had a couple of containers stashed in the freezer. All I had to do was thaw and heat." A timer dinged, and he reached for an oven mitt, then bent to pull a large pan of corn bread from the oven. It smelled as good as the soup.

Lucy stared at Banner in astonishment. "You made all of this?"

He shrugged. "I like to eat, and I'm the only one here to do the cooking."

"I see."

"Where's everyone else?"

Just as he spoke, a heavy gust of wind threw ice pellets against the kitchen window. The lights flickered but remained on.

Relieved that they hadn't been plunged into darkness, Lucy released the breath she had been holding. "Pop and Miss Annie are changing clothes in your bedroom. Joan and the children are using the guest room. Bobby Ray waited while I changed in the bathroom, and now he's in there."

"I'm surprised he fit."

Lucy laughed. The bathroom was rather small and Bobby Ray was notably large. But Banner wasn't smiling. Did he ever?

One half of the big country kitchen served as a dining room. A double trestle oak table filled most of the area on the other side of a sit-down bar fitted with two oak stools. The table was surrounded by six ladder-back oak chairs—a lot of seating space for a man who lived alone, she mused. "Would you like me to set the table?"

He pointed. "Dishes are in that cabinet."

Lucy carried an armload of functional brown stoneware to the dining area. She paused to run a hand appreciatively over the smooth surface of the table. Bending, she studied the solid but graceful pedestals, then took a moment to admire one of the beautifully contoured chairs. She glanced up to find Banner watching her, and she smiled a bit self-consciously.

"I have a thing for nice furniture," she admitted, "and you have some beautiful pieces. This dining set is wonderful. And that rocker in the living room is gorgeous. And I couldn't help but notice the tables in the living room and the furniture in the bedrooms. So much nice wood."

"Thanks." He turned back to the stove.

She stroked a hand over the smooth grain of the tabletop again, envying him the opportunity to do so every day. "I really admire the quality of this dining set. Do you mind if I ask where you shop for your furniture?"

"My shop's back behind the house."

"No, I meant—wait a minute. You made this set?"

"Yeah." He tasted the soup, nodded, then set the spoon in the sink.

"And the other furniture? You made all of it?"

"My great-uncle made the furniture in the bedrooms. I built the rocker and tables in the living room."

She rubbed her hand over the back of a chair again, loving the feel of the wood. "Is this what you do for a living? Build furniture?"

"Mostly outdoor furniture. Swings, Adirondack chairs, outdoor rockers. The stuff that's sold in tourist towns like Branson and Eureka Springs and Mountain View."

"You're very talented."

"Thanks. The food's ready. I guess we should bring everyone in."

He cooked and he built furniture. But he didn't make small talk, Lucy decided. Who *was* this guy?

It was a subdued group that gathered around the beautiful table a few minutes later. Bobby Ray had given Miss Annie his arm for the short walk to the table, but she looked so tired that Lucy worried about her. The storm still raged outside, making the lights flicker periodically, and she knew everyone was wondering when they could leave this place. Tomorrow was Christmas Eve, and there were places they all wanted to be for the holidays.

Banner wasn't by any means a jovial, put-everyone-at-ease type host. He sat in silence at the head of the table, eating his soup and corn bread without looking up much. Was it possible that he was shy? Or just not particularly friendly?

Joan and the children sat at one side of the table, opposite Lucy and the Carters. The kids had pulled the bar stools to the table, raising them high enough to easily reach their soup bowls and keeping them close to their mother.

They were quiet, well-behaved children, Lucy mused. Perhaps they took their behavioral cues from their mother, who seemed to take great pains not to call attention to herself. Was she simply shy—or someone who had been beaten down by circumstances until there was little spirit left in her?

It seemed that it was again up to Lucy to try to raise everyone's spirits. "Did you all get through to your families to let them know you're safe?" she asked the table at large.

She was answered with a silent round of nods.

Okay, new tactic. She smiled at Tyler. "How old are you, Tyler? I would guess around seven."

"I'll be eight in February," he replied.

A complete sentence. She was making progress. "So you're in second grade?"

"Yes, ma'am."

"I'm in kindergarten," Tricia supplied, not to be left out.

"Are you? Do you like it?" Lucy asked encouragingly.

Tricia nodded. "My teacher's nice. I like music time best."

"Where do you live?" Lucy looked at Joan this time, hoping to draw her into the conversation.

"We're from Mayflower," Joan murmured. "That's north of Little Rock…"

"I know where Mayflower is," Lucy said with a smile. "I live in Conway, practically next door to you."

"Mother and I have a little place outside of Jacksonville," Pop supplied, patting his wife's hand. "We've lived there more than forty years."

Lucy wondered about the wisdom of a man in his mid-eighties making a three-hour drive in an old pickup truck, especially in weather that had promised to be cold and rainy at best. What was his family thinking to let him make that trip?

Because that was really none of her business, Lucy spoke to Bobby Ray. "Do you live in Little Rock or was that a business stop?"

"I live there. I was hoping to make it home this evening. But my boss just told me on the phone that the weather guys are saying it could be day after tomorrow before the roads are passable."

"Day after tomorrow?" Tyler's eyes widened in alarm. "But that's Christmas! We can't stay here until Christmas!"

"What about Santa Claus?" Tricia looked at her mother in dismay. "We told him we would be at Grandma's house. He's s'posed to come tomorrow."

Lucy noted that Banner's face was showing new signs of strain in the form of deep lines around his stern mouth. Not only had his home been invaded by a group of strangers, but those strangers were all making it quite clear that they would rather be somewhere else. She couldn't help feeling a bit sorry for him.

"Don't worry about Santa Claus," Joan told her children. "Even if he can't come see you tomorrow night, he'll make a special trip as soon as we've settled somewhere."

The children still looked crestfallen, and Lucy couldn't blame them. Now the general mood around the table was depressed again.

"Banner, this soup is delicious," she said, determinedly cheerful. "You're an excellent cook."

"Thanks."

"Mother's a wonderful cook," Pop said, trying to help Lucy with the conversation. "Barbecued chicken, pork chops, spare ribs. And her pies—best coconut cream pie in the whole world. Her chocolate pie's good, too."

"Don't cook as much as I used to," Miss Annie murmured, glancing at her gnarled hands. "I still like to cook fresh vegetables in the summertime, though."

"We used to grow all our own vegetables," Pop added. "Had a big ol' garden back behind the house. Can't do it much anymore, now that the arthritis has gotten so bad. Still put some tomato plants in every spring, though."

Miss Annie gave him a sweet smile. "Pop loves his fresh sliced tomatoes."

Lucy watched the exchange between the couple with a wistful envy. Sixty-two years of marriage, she thought. Children, grandchildren, companionship and memories.

She wanted that for herself. As her twenty-eighth birthday approached, she found herself thinking about it more and more. She was perfectly capable of supporting herself and taking care of herself, but she wanted the fairy tale. The husband and children who loved her and who she could adore in return. The happily-ever-after. The sixty-second wedding anniversary.

The only thing holding her back was the fact that she was having a great deal of difficulty finding anyone she actually wanted to marry.

"Does anyone want more soup?" Banner asked gruffly, drawing her attention back to him.

Gosh, he was gorgeous, she thought, sighing a little as she admired the way the overhead light gleamed in his thick, dark hair. But good looks alone weren't enough to put a guy on her prospect list, as she knew from several disastrous dates with very attractive—and completely unsuitable—men.

No one wanted more soup.

"Let me clean the kitchen," Joan offered shyly, glancing at Banner and then quickly away. "You've been so generous to all of us. I'd like to help out."

"I'll help," Lucy offered.

"Let me help you back to the living room, Miss Annie," Bobby Ray said, pushing away from the table.

"Actually, I think I'd like to lie down for a few minutes," Miss Annie replied, her smile weary. "Would that be all right with you, Mr. Banner?"

"Just call me Banner, ma'am." Lucy noted that he spoke to the old woman with a respectful warmth that was notably missing in his brief dealings with his other guests. "You're welcome to use my room for as long as you're here. There are plenty of other places where I can sleep."

Miss Annie beamed at him. "Thank you. You're a very kind young man."

Lucy was fascinated to see the faintest touch of red appear briefly on Banner's tanned cheeks. Were compliments that rare for him?

Tricia was growing tired, too, and stressed by the changes in her routines and holiday plans. She began to whine, and when her brother taunted her about it, a squabble began.

Lucy watched as deep lines appeared around Banner's mouth again. Apparently, he hadn't spent much time around children—and judging by his expression, he would have been content to leave it that way.

"Why don't you take care of the children," Lucy suggested to Joan. "They're tired and unsettled. I'll clean up in here."

The harried mother sighed and nodded. "I suppose that would be best."

"There's a TV in the living room," Banner said. "I have satellite. Maybe you can find something to entertain the kids."

Nodding again, Joan ushered her children out of the room, leaving Lucy alone with Banner.

"I can take care of this," Lucy assured Banner when he reached for a dirty bowl.

"I'd just as soon clean the kitchen as go back in there."

She couldn't help smiling at his tone. "You must feel as though your home has been overrun."

"A bit," he agreed.

She wondered again if he ever smiled. She couldn't help imagining what a smile would do to his already spectacular face. For the sake of her peace of mind, it was probably just as well that he continued to glower.

"I'm sorry your peaceful evening was so rudely interrupted," she said as she carried a stack of bowls to the sink.

"Couldn't be helped. Too dangerous out on the road,

which is why none of you should have been out driving. Especially the Carters.''

''I suppose all of us were so anxious to get to our holiday destinations that we didn't pay enough attention to the weather forecasts—even though the guy *I* listened to got it all wrong,'' she added in a grumble.

Without responding, Banner squirted dishwashing liquid into the warm water filling his deep sink. No dishwasher, Lucy noted as he reached for the first bowl. She supposed he didn't need one just for himself and Hulk.

She picked up a dish towel to dry the bowls after he washed and rinsed them. There wasn't a lot of room in front of the sink, so they stood nearly shoulder to shoulder—or rather, shoulder to forearm, since he was a good ten inches taller. Another reason he wasn't going on her prospect list, she reminded herself. When a woman was just under five-three on her tallest days, men six feet and over were simply too tall for a comfortable match.

Because his silence was making her nervous, she asked, ''Do you have any special plans for Christmas, Banner? Or did the weather interfere with your travel, too?''

''I had no plans.''

''Oh. You don't celebrate Christmas?'' Not everyone did, she reminded herself belatedly. She should have thought of that already.

But he shook his head. ''I do observe Christmas—I just didn't have any plans this year.''

''You don't have a family?'' Her admittedly overtender heart immediately twisted. How sad to be alone, especially during the holidays.

''I have family. I simply wasn't in the mood to travel this year.''

''None of them live close by?''

"No." He put another bowl in her hands, seeming to take care not to touch her in the process.

Okay, maybe she was asking too many questions. Not everyone liked talking about themselves, though most of the men she had encountered lately seemed obsessed with the subject. Maybe he would rather hear about her, instead.

"I love Christmas. I always spend it with my favorite aunt and uncle in Springfield—my father's younger sister and her husband and their two sons. My father is an Army major stationed in Texas, and he'll fly in on Christmas day—weather permitting, of course."

A hard wind blew against the window over the sink, and the lights flickered again, staying out a bit longer this time. Lucy sighed in relief when they came back on, though she figured it was just a matter of time before the power went out.

Since that thought made her even more nervous, she chattered on. "My mother died when I was almost thirteen. My father sent me to live with my aunt and uncle after that, so they're almost like parents to me."

"Here." He set the clean, wet stockpot in her hands. "This goes in the cabinet next to the stove."

So maybe he wasn't interested in talking about her, either. "Do you think this ice storm will stop soon?" she asked, seizing on the weather as a last-ditch conversational gambit.

He dried his hands on a paper towel, studying her with a slightly quizzical expression. "You're not one to let a moment of silence slip by, are you?"

Something about his wording amused her. Totally unoffended, she chuckled. "I'm afraid not. I tend to talk a lot, anyway, but especially when I'm nervous."

"You're nervous now?" That seemed to surprise him.

"Maybe a little."

"Because of the storm?"

It seemed an innocuous enough excuse. "Okay."

"You're safe here, you know. Even if the power goes out, I have plenty of firewood and a gas stove to cook on."

She found his somewhat awkward attempt to reassure her rather touching. Darned if she wasn't starting to like him—at least a little—despite his curt manners. "I know we're safe. It's just a little…awkward."

"Tell me about it." He glanced toward the doorway as if he still wasn't particularly looking forward to joining the others.

Lucy glanced at her watch. It was only seven-thirty. What were they going to do for the rest of the evening?

Bobby Ray wandered through the kitchen door, pushing a meaty hand through his bushy hair. "Miss Annie is asleep," he informed them. "I talked Pop into lying down, too. Poor old guy's wiped out, though he won't admit it. Stubborn old bird. Reminds me of my grandpa."

"I had a great-uncle like that," Banner said. "Lived on his own until he was eighty-two, when he died in his sleep of a heart attack. Never would accept any help or advice from anyone."

It was the most Banner had volunteered about himself since they'd arrived. Lucy wondered exactly how much Banner had in common with the great-uncle he seemed to have admired so much.

"I threw some more wood on the fire," Bobby Ray said. "Getting kind of low in the wood box. You want me to bring some more in?"

"I keep a good supply on the back porch, under cover." Banner motioned toward the back door on the other side of the bar.

Bobby Ray nodded. "Good. We're probably going to need it. I just caught a local news report on the TV, and they said electricity's going out all over this part of the state. I imagine we'll be in the dark ourselves directly."

Lucy shivered and wrapped her arms around herself.

Banner looked at her in question.

"I'm not really crazy about being in the dark," she admitted.

"Does it make you nervous?"

She smiled wryly. "Yes."

Banner glanced at Bobby Ray. "At least we won't have to worry that it will get too quiet."

It was another example of Banner's odd sense of humor—and once again he'd said it without even a hint of a smile.

"Very funny, Banner," she muttered.

He gave her a look that might have held a gleam of amusement. And, darn it, she felt her toes start to curl in response to that hint of a smile.

Time to get control again. "Okay," she said, "so what are we going to do with everybody? You have only two bedrooms, right?"

Banner nodded. "The Carters can have mine, and Joan and the kids can have the other. Bobby Ray and I will bunk in the living room and you can sleep on the couch in my office."

"Your office?"

He jerked his head toward a closed door on the far side of the kitchen. "In there."

She nodded. "That will work. What about—"

Someone pushed her from behind. She turned to find Banner's dog standing behind her, taking up most of the spare room in the kitchen. It was the first time she had seen the beast standing up, and he was nearly the size of a small horse. She hardly had to bend over to look straight into his lazy eyes.

"He needs to go out," Banner said. "You're standing in his way."

"Excuse me," Lucy said to the dog, scooting to one side.

The dog made a grumbly sound that might have been a response, then ambled to the door, where he gave Banner a look over his shoulder. A gust of damp, icy air entered the room when Banner opened the door. The dog gazed dolefully out past the covered porch to the wet, ice-coated yard beyond. He gave a deep sigh, then walked out, his shaggy head already hunched in preparation for the elements.

Lucy couldn't help smiling at the mutt's behavior. "He's a very…interesting character."

Banner gave her another one of those looks that wasn't quite a smile. "He's excited by all the company."

"That's excited? How can you tell?"

"He's awake."

She laughed. "I see."

Lucy stood back and watched as Banner pulled a big towel out of a cabinet. He opened the back door, letting dog and cold air inside again. After toweling the mutt off, he gave him a bone-shaped dog treat from a box he kept on the counter near the door. With a low "woof" of thanks, the dog strolled out of the room.

Lucy grinned as she watched the long scraggly tail disappear through the doorway. She was beginning to like that dog a lot.

She was still reserving judgment about his owner.

Chapter Three

Banner couldn't remember this many people being in his house since—well, ever. Having brought in one of the straight-backed chairs from the dining room for himself, he sat uncomfortably in one corner of his living room, studying the others, who were watching a Christmas special on TV.

The Carters were still resting; Banner wouldn't be surprised if they were down for the night. They had both looked exhausted after dinner.

Sprawled in Banner's big leather recliner, Bobby Ray rubbed his bearded chin. His eyes were focused on the television screen, but his thoughts were obviously elsewhere.

Joan and Tricia sat on Banner's brown suede couch, Tricia's head cradled on her mother's lap. Tyler lay on the floor, using Hulk for a pillow. The dog seemed perfectly content to serve in that capacity; his head was on his paws and quiet snores escaped him every so often.

Though he barely knew them, the children seemed subdued to Banner, probably still upset that their holiday plans had been disrupted. They watched the TV, but without much enthusiasm.

Finally Banner turned his gaze to Lucy, who sat in the brown-and-tan-striped easy chair, leaving the Windsor rocker as the only unoccupied chair in the room. Banner had been trying to avoid looking at Lucy, but it wasn't easy. She fascinated him. No matter how hard he tried to concentrate on the others, it was Lucy who kept drawing his attention.

She seemed to be trying to watch the program, but judging by her restless fidgeting, she was having trouble concentrating. Banner got the distinct impression that she would rather be moving around and talking at her usual mile-a-minute rate. There was a lot of pent-up energy in that tidy little package, he mused, letting his gaze drift down her figure.

He and Lucy seemed to be opposites. While he was content to spend days, even weeks, with no company but his own, Lucy probably preferred having lots of people around. She was gregarious, extroverted, impulsive, emotional. He was none of those things.

A woman like Lucy would certainly have no interest in a socially awkward, frequently tongue-tied, oddball loner like Banner. But that certainly didn't make him any less mesmerized by her.

Another strong gust of wind rattled the windows, and the lights flickered again. Once, twice, three times before they stabilized.

Tricia whimpered and Joan comforted her. Banner noticed that Lucy had paled a little and seemed to be chewing on her full lower lip. The prospect of being in the dark made her nervous, and when she was nervous she tended to babble, he reminded himself. She must be making quite an effort to remain quiet so the children could enjoy the television program.

The singing and dancing gave way to a commercial, and Lucy looked away from the screen. Her gaze met Banner's, and she gave him a tentative smile. "You don't look very comfortable over there."

"I'm fine." He didn't know squat about being a host—and even less about running a bed and breakfast, which he seemed to be doing at the moment. He suspected he should be doing more than sitting in a chair staring at everyone like a silent sphinx. "Um, does anyone need anything?"

Apparently, no one did. The room fell silent again except for the sounds from the TV speakers and the storm outside. Banner sat back to watch the show, but his attention kept wandering to Lucy, to his annoyance.

The Christmas special ended at 9 p.m. By that time Tricia, Tyler and Hulk were all asleep, and Bobby Ray looked ready to join them.

"I'd better get these two into bed," Joan said, looking at her sleeping children.

Bobby Ray stirred and rose to his feet. "Want me to haul the boy in there for you?"

Joan glanced at him, then quickly away, and Banner wondered if the timid woman was unsettled by Bobby Ray's size. But then, she seemed intimidated by Banner, too, and he was two inches shorter and a good seventy pounds lighter than the truck driver.

"I can manage," Joan said in the tone of a woman who was accustomed to taking care of herself and her children without assistance.

Bobby Ray yawned again. "Then I'll have a drink of water before turning in. You take the couch, Banner. The recliner's comfortable enough for me."

Banner stood, compelled again to do something host-like. "There are extra blankets in the guestroom closet," he told Joan. "If you need anything else, just let me know."

"We'll be fine," she assured him, her arms around her sleepy children.

He nodded. "I put a flashlight on the nightstand in case the power goes out. If it gets too cold, you and the kids can bring blankets and pillows in here and bunk in front of the fire."

He had a small gas log fireplace in the master bedroom, so even if the power went out, the Carters should be okay. They had an attached bath, which would give them privacy and keep Miss Annie from having to walk too far. He had already carried blankets and a pillow into the office for Lucy.

He waited until Lucy emerged from the face-washing and tooth-brushing line for the bathroom, letting Bobby Ray go in after her, and then he motioned toward the doorway that led to the kitchen and office. "I'll walk with you," he said. "Just to make sure everything's okay."

"Thanks." Slinging her big duffel bag over one shoulder, she went ahead of him, giving him an intriguing view of her tight, compact backside. He lifted his gaze to the back of her head, reprimanding himself for the thoughts running through his head—thoughts she certainly wouldn't approve of from a total stranger upon whom she was temporarily dependent.

The office was a small, single-windowed room stuck onto the far side of the house. It was furnished with a large desk that held a computer, printer, phone and fax machine. A copier on a stand was shoved into one corner, and a faded and rather worn green corduroy couch had been pushed against one wall. A white-cased pillow, clean sheets and two blankets waited on one end of the rather shabby green couch.

"It's not pretty, but it's comfortable," he said, motioning toward the couch. "I've napped on it a few times. So has Hulk, I'm afraid, but I tried to brush off all the dog hair."

"I'm sure I'll be fine." She cast a wary glance at the curtainless window that rattled every time the wind blew. "Maybe you could lower those blinds for me?"

He moved to do so. "You're sure you'll be okay in here?"

She gave him a smile that was just a shade too bright. "I'll be fine," she said again.

He knew she was worried about a power outage. She'd made it clear enough that she didn't like the dark. Opening a desk drawer, he took out a small flashlight and handed it to her. She accepted it gratefully.

"You certainly seem prepared for company," she said, motioning toward the pillow and extra blankets. "Does your family visit often?"

"No. I inherited most of my household supplies from my great-uncle. He built this house."

"The great-uncle who lived alone until he died?"

He had almost forgotten that he'd mentioned his uncle Joe to Lucy. "Yeah. He died four years ago, leaving me his house and workshop."

Lucy was already spreading sheets on the couch, her backside swaying with the movements. Banner stuck his hands in his pockets and half turned away, keeping his gaze focused intently on anything but her. He cleared his throat. "Let me know if you need anything during the night."

"Banner?" She spoke quickly as he stepped through the doorway, his hand on the doorknob. "Would you leave the door open, please?"

He did so, saying over his shoulder, "Keep the flashlight close at hand in case you need it."

"I certainly will," he heard her mutter.

She really was nervous. He wondered if her fear of the dark had a basis in experience or if it was a quirk. Maybe she was afraid because circumstances had stranded her here in an unfamiliar place.

All things considered, he was a bit nervous himself. It seemed odd, though, that of all the strangers camped out in his home, Lucy was the only one who reduced him to the almost inarticulate self-consciousness that had plagued him during his awkward youth.

As Banner had promised, the couch was more comfortable than it looked. Lucy nestled into the covers, trying not to think about the storm outside. At least she couldn't see the creepy, ice-covered branches swaying now that Banner had closed the blinds.

He had left a dim light on in the kitchen, which provided enough illumination to make her reasonably comfortable. She wondered if he always kept that particular bulb burning at night, or if he'd left it on because she had told him the dark made her nervous.

To reassure herself, she slid a hand under her pillow, touching the flashlight he had provided her with. He really was trying to be a good host in his own awkward way, she thought with a slight smile.

She wondered why a young, good-looking guy like him lived alone out here in the back of nowhere. She wondered why he wasn't joining his family for Christmas. She wondered if he had a girlfriend. And as she drifted into the first stages of sleep, she wondered if he wanted one....

The sound of someone breathing deeply, heavily in her ear brought her eyes open in a hurry. She nearly had a heart attack when she saw a big, dark form looming over her, so close to her face she could feel the heat of his breath on her skin.

"Oh, it's you," she said a moment later, not sure if she was relieved.

Hulk laid his shaggy head on her arm. Moving clumsily, she patted him with her other hand. "I know I'm on your couch, but I'm not moving," she said. "You'll have to take the floor if you're sleeping in here."

He sighed deeply, then removed his head from her arm, curled up on the braided rug in front of the couch and was soon snoring.

That dog was downright spooky, Lucy thought, shaking her head as she settled into her pillow again. But then, Hulk's owner wasn't exactly ordinary.

The power went out just as she closed her eyes again. There wasn't a warning flicker this time, not even a hard gust of wind. Everything just quietly went dark. Pitch-dark.

Lucy sat up with a gasp. She couldn't see the doorway into the kitchen now. Without the background noises of the heater and other electric appliances, the house was completely silent. She could hear the wind and ice outside, and occasional sharp cracks that she knew were more tree branches snapping.

She hadn't heard the branch that had taken down the power lines.

Her heart pounded in her throat as she strained to see through the inky blackness. She was growing disoriented, unsure now exactly where the door was. The sounds from outside seemed to grow louder and eerier. Creaks and pops and groans—strange noises in a strange place.

"Hulk?" she whispered, reaching unsteadily for the dog. Even his presence would be comforting now. But he wasn't there. The shaggy mutt had slipped out as stealthily as he had entered earlier, leaving Lucy alone in the dark.

Drawing a deep breath to calm herself, she remembered the flashlight under her pillow. It must have been panic that had driven it from her mind before, she thought sheepishly, making a dive for it. She felt better immediately when her fingers closed around the metal cylinder. And then she cursed beneath her breath when she fumbled to find the button that would turn it on. She should have figured out how to work it *before* the lights went out, she chided herself.

A thin beam of light swept over her, settling on her hands. "Twist the top to turn it on," Banner said from across the room.

Following his instructions, she sighed in relief when her efforts turned the flashlight on. The light hit her full in the eyes, making her squint, but that was okay. As long as she had light, she thought, aiming the flashlight toward Banner's legs. She didn't want to blind him, too.

She saw now that his dog stood close beside him. Surely that beast wasn't afraid of the dark.

"Are you okay?" Banner asked quietly.

"Yes, I'm fine." She wished her voice hadn't quavered.

He moved a few steps closer to the couch. "You don't sound fine."

"No, really, I'm okay. We knew the power would go out."

"It's going to get cold in here. You'll probably want

to bring your pillow and blankets and sleep in front of the fire.''

That sounded like a good plan. Fire gave off both heat and light. She threw off her blankets and swung her legs over the edge of the couch. She still wore her sweater, jeans and socks, so she didn't have to worry about modesty. Awkwardly gathering her pillow and blankets while still balancing the flashlight, she took a step toward Banner—and promptly tripped over one of the blankets.

Banner caught her before she could hit the floor. His arms closed around her, pulling her against him, and she became aware of exactly how strong that slim body of his really was. Woodworking seemed to be very good for building muscles, she thought a bit dreamily.

''You okay?'' His deep voice was very close to her ear as he bent his head over her.

If her hands hadn't been so full, she might have been tempted to let them roam up his chest—to satisfy her curiosity about the definition of the muscles beneath his gray sweatshirt.

Except for his small flashlight, Banner's hands were free—not moving, just holding her. His face was close to her hair, and he didn't immediately move away. It looked as though it was going to be up to her to move first— before she did something stupid. Like dropping those blankets and satisfying her overactive curiosity.

She took a step backward. Banner's hands fell immediately to his side, and he, too, moved to put even more space between them. The dog shuffled out of his way, bumping against Lucy's hip. She certainly didn't want to risk stumbling again, which could very likely lead to her ending up back in Banner's arms.

With a very faint, slightly wistful sigh, she followed

carefully as he led her through the kitchen and toward the living room.

Bobby Ray knelt in front of the fire, slowly adding wood. The flickering firelight danced across his broad face, gleaming in his thick hair and beard. "You doing okay, Lucy?" he asked, looking up from his task.

"Yes, I'm fine. Thank you."

Bobby Ray pushed himself to his feet and adjusted the fireplace screen. "I doubt the power will be back on anytime tonight. It's going to get cold."

Lucy glanced toward the two bedrooms. "What about the others?"

"The bedrooms are more heavily insulated than the office, which was an add-on," Banner said. "There's a gas fire burning in the master bedroom, so it should stay fairly comfortable in there. Joan and the kids are sharing a bed and a pile of blankets, so I think they'll be okay."

Had Banner made the effort to come after Lucy because he thought she would get too cold—or because he knew she didn't like the dark? Either way, it had been a nice thing for him to do.

Bobby Ray leaned back into the recliner and raised the footrest. He pulled a blanket over himself and settled in more comfortably, making the chair frame creak. "Good night, y'all."

Lucy started to lay her blankets on the floor in front of the fire, but Banner put a hand on her arm to stop her. "Take the couch. I'll bunk on the floor."

She shook her head. "I'll be fine here. You go back to the couch."

"No." The firelight played across Banner's mulish expression. "You'll be more comfortable on the couch. The floor's fine for me."

His hand was warm on her arm, even through her

clothes. She could think of plenty of ways to ward off the cold with Banner—but not in front of Bobby Ray. Her cheeks going hot in response to the unbidden thought, she cleared her throat. "You've already made up the couch for yourself. I'll just—"

A loud sigh erupted from the recliner. "Lucy, will you get on the couch? I'm pretty sure Banner's more stubborn than you are, and this argument could go on for a while."

"Sorry, Bobby Ray," she murmured, and gave in— mostly because she suspected the truck driver was right about who was more stubborn.

A few minutes later Lucy was settled on the couch, and Banner and his dog lay on the floor in front of the fire, Banner in the sleeping bag he'd spread on the couch earlier. Bobby Ray snored rhythmically in the recliner, having fallen asleep almost as soon as the room got quiet again.

Even though Banner had taken the pillow he'd used before, Lucy was still too aware that he had recently been on the same couch where she now lay. It was silly, of course, for her to feel as though she could still detect the heat from his body radiating from the thick cushions.

Something about Banner sent her sadly neglected libido into spasms. She didn't know if it was the way he looked—or the way he looked at her. It certainly wasn't his sparkling personality that drew her. But there were other things about him: his awkward attempts at hospitality, his low-key and decidedly offbeat sense of humor, his skill in the kitchen…

She couldn't help wondering about his skill in other rooms.

An exasperated sigh escaped her as she hid her face in the pillow in an attempt to smother that thought.

Banner lifted his head to look her way. "Lucy? Are you okay?"

"I'm fine," she whispered back, squeezing her eyes closed and ordering herself to go to sleep.

Maybe all that ice had given her a case of brain-freeze, she thought. She was quite sure she would have herself completely under control again by morning.

After a restless night Lucy woke early, the tantalizing scent of coffee tickling her nostrils. The fire still crackled steadily, providing warmth and light, but neither Banner nor Bobby Ray were in the room.

She didn't like waking up in strange surroundings. She felt grubby and rumpled and disoriented—her hair a mess, her face pillow-creased, her clothes wrinkled. She snatched up her duffel bag and made a dash for the bathroom, wanting to put herself to rights before Banner saw her—or any of the others, of course, she added quickly.

She took a very quick shower, using as little hot water as possible since there were so many others in the house. She was glad Banner had a gas water heater. She spent barely fifteen minutes in the bathroom, emerging with damp hair and a minimal amount of makeup, but she felt much better. At least her teeth were brushed and she had on fresh socks and underwear and a clean Christmas sweatshirt with the jeans she'd slept in.

Stepping out of the bathroom, she nearly tripped over the motley dog that sat in the hallway, apparently waiting for her. "Did you want the next shower?" she asked him wryly.

He gave her a goofy grin and a flick of his scraggly tail in reply, then followed at her heels as she made her way back into the living room. Someone had opened all the drapes while she'd been in the bathroom. It was still gray and cloudy outside, but at least some light came in through the large windows.

She paused to look outside at the frozen landscape. Ice covered everything as far as she could see, glittering like freshly polished glass. Beneath nearly every tree lay a pile of broken limbs, and the evergreens were bent almost double beneath the weight of the ice. It was like being inside a snow globe.

Christmas Eve, she mused. It certainly looked the part outside. But it didn't feel right, not being with her family today.

Sighing, she turned and walked toward the kitchen.

Pop and Miss Annie sat at the table, both looking much more rested than they had the night before. Banner stood at the stove, skillfully flipping pancakes, while Bobby Ray served coffee for the older couple. Joan and the kids hadn't yet made an appearance.

Bobby Ray and the Carters smiled when Lucy walked in. Banner didn't, but he gave her a nod of greeting. "Pancakes?"

"Yes, please."

He handed her an overfilled plate. "Syrup's on the table."

"Thank you."

So much for little pleasantries like "good morning" or "did you sleep well?" She reminded herself that she'd been confident that seeing him again in daylight, in all his grumpy glory, would put last night's silly fantasies right out of her mind.

So much for late-night confidence, she thought, studying the back of his gorgeous, grouchy head with a silent sigh.

The others welcomed her to the table. "Quite a night,

wasn't it?'' Bobby Ray asked, setting a cup of stove-perked coffee in front of her.

Since the big trucker's enthusiastic snoring was at least partly responsible for Lucy's restless night, she gave him a crooked smile. ''Yes, it was. Miss Annie, did you rest well?''

''Slept like a log,'' the older woman replied. ''I guess I was more tired than I'd thought. I didn't even know the power went out until I woke up this morning.''

Bobby Ray stood at the back door, looking through the glass at the frozen vista on the other side of the narrow back porch. ''I haven't seen this much ice since the winter of '99. Some folks went without power for days—weeks, even—back then.''

''Are the phone lines still working?'' Lucy asked.

Bobby Ray nodded. ''I've already called my boss this morning.''

''Did you get an update on the roads?''

''The temperatures today are predicted to be just above freezing. There could be some melting this afternoon, but any standing water will freeze again tonight. Though it's supposed to be warmer tomorrow, it will be after noon, at the earliest, before it will be safe to travel.''

Lucy thought longingly of her aunt's Christmas Eve open house—the crowds of friends and family, the food and drink, the carols and laughter. It would be the first time she had missed it since she was a child.

She was sure the others were just as anxious to be with their families today—all except Banner, she temporized with a glance across the room at him. What was his story, anyway? Was he estranged from his family? Or just, as he had claimed, in no mood for holiday travel?

''Maybe if we drive very slowly and carefully...'' Pop began, his gaze on his wife's disappointed expression.

"Don't even think about it," Bobby Ray said flatly. "I've been driving these roads for years and they're dangerous enough when they're wet. Add patches of ice and you've got a disaster waiting to happen. You saw me hit the ditch yesterday. First time I've done that in years."

To Lucy's relief, Pop didn't argue. He merely nodded in resignation and patted his wife's hand.

Before anyone else could speak, Joan and the children entered the room. It was obvious at a glance that Tricia had been crying. Her face was red and streaked with tears and her lower lip was still quivering. Tyler didn't look much happier. His head hung and his shoulders drooped as he followed his mother into the kitchen. Joan tried to smile for the benefit of the other adults, but the smile didn't reach her brown eyes.

It was a very unhappy trio, Lucy thought with a surge of sympathy. No child should look so sad on Christmas Eve.

Banner looked at the family, then reached again for the pancake batter. "There's milk in the refrigerator. With the door closed, it stayed cool enough. We might as well drink it before it goes bad."

"We put some of the perishable stuff outside in a big cooler," Bobby Ray added. "It'll probably stay cold enough out there to keep anything from ruining too quickly."

Without saying a word, the children took their seats at the table. Tricia climbed onto the bar stool she'd sat on the night before. Their mother set plates of pancakes and glasses of milk in front of them, and they began to eat without enthusiasm.

Miss Annie studied the children compassionately. "Did you sleep well?" she asked them.

Both nodded without looking up from their breakfasts.

"Yes, thank you," Tyler mumbled after a nudge from his mother.

"You both look like someone licked the red off your lollipops," Bobby Ray commented.

Tyler heaved a deep sigh. "It's Christmas," he said, as if that should explain everything.

"That should make you smile, not frown," Bobby Ray replied.

Tricia's lip quivered again. "We were s'posed to go to Grandma's. Santa was going to come there tonight. But Mama said we can't go 'cause of the ice."

"I still think we could make it," Tyler insisted. "If Mama would drive real slow…"

"Now you sound like me," Pop said ruefully. "The others have convinced me that it would be foolish to even try. Trust me, boy, it's better to celebrate Christmas a day late than not to have the chance at all."

"But there's nothing to do here," Tyler protested. "There's not even any electricity, so we can't watch TV or anything."

"I don't want to stay here for Christmas," Tricia agreed in a whine. "I want to go to Grandma's."

Lucy saw Banner's jaw clench as he took the seat next to Lucy with his own breakfast. Bobby Ray shifted uncomfortably in his chair, the Carters looked anxious, and Joan seemed apologetic for her children's complaining. Unless someone did something very soon, it was going to be a very long day.

Electing herself to be that someone, Lucy donned a bright smile and addressed the children. "You know what I think we should do today?"

They looked at her without much interest. "What?" Tyler asked.

"Banner hasn't gotten around to decorating for Christmas. He's been too busy,'' she added, deliberately not making eye contact with her host. "I think he would really like it if we all helped him decorate today."

Tricia, for one, looked somewhat intrigued. "He would?"

"I would?" Banner murmured so that only Lucy could hear.

Lucy kept her gaze focused on the children. "Of course he would. It's Christmas."

"I, um, don't have any Christmas decorations," Banner said.

The children's budding enthusiasm wilted visibly. Lucy spoke even more enthusiastically. "Okay, fine. We'll just have to make some, won't we? That will be even more fun, won't it, kids?"

"I don't know how," Tricia said uncertainly.

"I'll show you." Lucy found the courage to look at Banner then. "You'd like us to decorate for you, wouldn't you, Banner?"

"Yeah," he said, trying to play his part. "Sure."

His doubtful tone drew a look from her, but she turned quickly back to the kids. "We'll get started as soon as we've finished breakfast, okay? It will be a lot of fun."

Tyler and Tricia began to eat more enthusiastically, and Joan gave Lucy a smile of gratitude.

Banner, Lucy noted surreptitiously, simply looked resigned.

Chapter Four

When the children finished eating, they dashed off to brush their teeth while their mother and Lucy washed dishes in water heated on the stove. Bobby Ray and Banner assisted Miss Annie into the living room, where they settled her in the rocker in front of the fire with an afghan around her and her knitting close at hand. Pop sat on the couch with one of Banner's recent newsmagazines.

Between the light from the windows and the glow of the fire, there was just enough illumination in the room for reading and knitting, though Banner offered to bring in an oil lamp if the light began to fade. Satisfied that the older couple was comfortable, Banner wandered back into the kitchen.

He leaned against the bar, watching Joan and Lucy efficiently clean his kitchen. Well, to be specific, he watched Lucy. His gaze was drawn to her, no matter how hard he tried to concentrate on anything else.

"Just what, exactly, do you intend to use for decorations?" he asked her curiously.

She tossed aside her dish towel and tapped a fingertip against her chin. "We'll need a tree, of course…"

"A tree," he repeated, hoping he had misunderstood.

"A Christmas tree," she clarified, looking surprised that it had been necessary. "Do you have an artificial one, by any chance?"

"No, I don't own one."

She looked disappointed. "I suppose we could get by without a Christmas tree…"

Some insane impulse made him say, "I'll find you a tree."

Had he really volunteered to tromp around out there in the ice, cut down a tree and then figure out some way to stand it up in his house? Her sudden, radiant smile assured him that he had. Looking at that smile, he couldn't even honestly say he regretted the words.

He wondered if maybe the milk had been spoiled, after all. He found it much easier to attribute his uncharacteristic behavior to bad milk than to the charms of a pretty Christmas elf's smile.

"What kind of tree?" Bobby Ray asked, coming back into the room.

"They want a Christmas tree," Banner answered.

"Not if it's too much trouble," Joan insisted, trying to shrink into the woodwork behind her.

Joan was such a mousy, unprepossessing woman, Banner thought. She couldn't be less like Lucy, who was even now using her hands to describe to Bobby Ray exactly what sort of tree she envisioned for their holiday decorating.

The big trucker nodded, then looked at Banner.

"You've got some small evergreens in the woods around your house, don't you?"

"Yeah. It shouldn't take long to find one. The hard part's going to be finding one that isn't covered with ice."

"Maybe if there's one that's been sheltered by bigger trees…"

"So much trouble," Joan fretted, wringing her hands.

"Not if it means making them kids happy for Christmas," Bobby Ray assured her kindly.

Joan's eyes welled. "That's very kind."

Both Banner and Bobby Ray took a few steps backward, discomfited by the sight of tears. "We'll, uh, take care of the tree," Banner said quickly, then turned to Lucy. "What else do you need for decorations?"

She tapped her chin again. "Popcorn, maybe, for stringing. Do you have any art supplies? Paper, glue, markers—that sort of thing?"

Banner turned on one heel. "I'll see what I can gather up."

"Thank you, Banner," she called after him as he left the room.

It must have been the milk, he thought again with a slow shake of his head.

By midmorning Lucy had turned the living room into a Christmas workshop. Banner had provided a generous— and rather surprisingly varied—supply of materials. Colored papers, thin sheets of cardboard, markers, glue, large tubes of silver, red and gold glitter, several colors of ribbon, yarn and fabric scraps. There was also a shoebox filled with buttons of all different shapes, sizes and colors, and a couple of booklets of gold and silver star-shaped stickers.

"Craft supplies?" Lucy asked when he'd carried the big carton of items into the room.

He shrugged. "My great-uncle kept supplies here to entertain his friends' children when they visited—kept the kids from getting into his tools. I used to play with the craft stuff, myself, when I was a kid. Always looked forward to it—until I got old enough to start working with his tools, which I liked even better. I found this carton in one of the storage closets after I moved in, and I thought it might come in handy someday."

She gave him a grin. "Looks like it's 'someday.'"

"Apparently," he agreed with that slight quirk of his lips that she had finally decided was a smile.

Now, warmed by the crackling fire, Joan and the children sat around the coffee table happily making paper chains and ornaments for the tree Banner and Bobby Ray had gone out to find. The dog snoozed beneath the round oak table, seeming to enjoy the company.

Miss Annie knitted contentedly in her rocker, while Pop strung popcorn on fishing line. His hands were a bit gnarled, but he handled the needle skillfully. "I've strung plenty of popcorn in my day," he boasted. "Done my share of sewing, too."

Lucy studied the scene with a touch of smugness. Very domestic. The children were laughing and the adults were all smiling. The appetizing scent of popcorn filled the room, and the flickering of the candles that lightened the shadowy corners added an old-world charm.

What a clever idea she'd had, she thought as she turned toward the kitchen to pour herself another cup of coffee. Now everyone was happy again.

She had just stepped into the room when the kitchen door flew open with a bang and Banner carried Bobby Ray into the house.

Of course, Banner wasn't exactly carrying the much larger man, but he was obviously supporting him as Bobby Ray limped inside, a painful grimace behind his beard. Forgetting the coffee, Lucy rushed forward. "What happened? Bobby Ray, are you hurt?"

It was a stupid question, she realized as Banner lowered the other man into a chair. But Bobby Ray answered patiently. "I'm okay. Just took a spill on the ice, that's all. Bruised, but no real damage."

Having heard Lucy's cry, Joan came in to see what was going on. She took one look at the men and hurried to the percolator. "You both look half-frozen."

Banner and Bobby Ray had peeled off their hats and gloves, revealing faces reddened by cold and fingers that moved stiffly as they reached for the steaming mugs Joan offered them. Lucy bit her lower lip in guilt. She had been so focused on having a Christmas tree for the children that she hadn't given enough thought to the dangers of trudging around on a sheet of ice.

She moved closer to Bobby Ray. "Are you sure nothing's broken? Maybe I should look at your injury to see how bad it really is."

Banner cleared his throat.

Bobby Ray gave a bark of laughter. "I don't think so, Lucy. Truth is, my feet flew out from under me and I landed flat on my—" he glanced at Joan, then concluded "—on my behind. Just bruised my tailbone, that's all. It's sore as he—er, heck, but I'll be all right."

"You should at least take a pain reliever."

Banner moved to the pantry, took out a plastic bottle of ibuprofen, and tossed it to Bobby Ray, who caught it in one big hand. Lucy noted that Banner's expression was shuttered, so that she couldn't read his thoughts. Which, she decided with a grimace, was probably just as well.

He caught her eyes as he moved toward the back door again. "I'll go out and build a stand for the tree," he said, handing her his empty mug when he passed her.

Setting the mug on the counter, she turned to follow Banner out onto the back porch, leaving Joan to see to Bobby Ray. The frigid air hit her like a hard kick, driving the breath from her lungs. It hung in a frosty cloud in front of her. She crossed her arms over her thick sweat-shirt and shivered. "You found a tree?"

Pulling his hat back onto his head, Banner nodded. "A small cedar that managed to miss most of the ice because it was under several larger trees. It's over by my work-shop."

"Do you need any help?"

"No, I can handle it. Looked as if you're keeping things under control in there. Why don't you go back inside? You don't even have on a coat."

"I feel guilty," she admitted. "You've been out here in the cold and ice finding a tree you didn't want in the first place while I've been in your warm house watching the kids make decorations you didn't ask for. Bobby Ray got hurt and you—"

"Wait a minute." He set his hands heavily on her shoulders and looked straight into her eyes. "When those kids came into the kitchen this morning, they were the saddest sight I ever saw. Now they're in there laughing and having a good time getting into the Christmas spirit, and all because you had the clever idea to have them make decorations. There's no reason at all for you to feel guilty."

She looked up at him through her lashes. "But Bobby Ray—"

"Bobby Ray bruised his butt," Banner interrupted in-elegantly. "I saw him fall, and I'm confident he'll be fine.

Just sore. And I'm sure he would risk falling again if it meant making the kids happy. He told me he hated seeing them so sad.''

Banner's reassurances made her feel better. Though she was self-conscious about standing so close to him and having his hands on her, she found herself in no hurry to move away.

"If it hadn't been for you," he went on, "I wouldn't have known what to do with everyone today. The kids would probably be whining and crying and bringing everyone else down, and it would have been miserable. Believe me, you have nothing to feel guilty about.''

She smiled up at him. "Thank you for saying that.''

"I wouldn't have said it if I didn't mean it.''

That statement made her laugh. "Trust me, that's one thing I have figured out about you.''

His gaze dropped slowly to her smiling mouth, then lingered there. She felt her smile fade in response to his expression. They stood so close together their breath mingled into a single hazy cloud—and there was something uncomfortably intimate about that observation.

"You're cold," Banner said after a moment. "You should go back inside.''

Cold? Funny, at that moment, he wasn't at all aware of the cold. She actually felt a bit warm in some places.

But the shiver that ran through her wasn't entirely due to sexual awareness. Reluctantly she took a step backward, and Banner's hands fell to his sides. Suddenly she felt the cold again. "Let me know if there's anything I can do to help.''

He nodded, stuck his hands in his coat pockets, turned and headed toward his workshop, placing his feet with care on the icy path. Lucy watched him for a moment longer, until the cold drove her back inside.

* * *

While the others stayed busy making decorations, Lucy and Joan went into the kitchen at just before one that afternoon to prepare lunch. Even from in there, they could hear the slightly off-key strains of ''Jingle Bells'' being sung in the living room.

Pop, they had discovered, loved to sing, and he particularly loved to sing Christmas carols. Bobby Ray had pulled out a battered old guitar he claimed was never far from his side; he hadn't left it in the truck because he said the damp cold was bad for the wood and the strings. Pop and Bobby Ray had been leading the children in familiar holiday tunes for the past half hour.

''Pop's a sweet man, isn't he?'' Joan asked Lucy as they opened the pantry door. ''He reminds me of my grandfather.''

Lucy smiled. ''That's what Bobby Ray said.''

Joan bit her lip. ''Did he?''

''Yes. Bobby Ray's nice, too. Very funny, and so kind to Miss Annie and the kids. Although he snores like a freight train and can't carry a tune in a bucket,'' she added with a chuckle. ''But he does play the guitar well.''

''He does seem nice,'' Joan agreed hesitantly. ''I have to admit I was a bit intimidated by him at first. He's so large and hairy.''

''Rather like Banner's dog,'' Lucy murmured.

Joan smiled a little. ''Bobby Ray's louder. I haven't heard the dog so much as yip since we got here.''

''He snores almost as loudly as Bobby Ray.''

The other woman laughed, then looked into the pantry again. ''Poor Banner's getting low on supplies. We'll all have to chip in for groceries before we leave.''

''Definitely.'' But Lucy wondered if he would accept any money from them. Banner seemed to be the fiercely proud and independent type. "We could make sandwiches with chips and pickles on the side. I saw some lunch meat out in the cooler. It should probably be used soon."

"Sandwiches sound fine."

Lucy stepped out onto the porch, glancing toward the workshop as she did so. The doors were closed, but a thin plume of smoke rose from a small chimney in the roof, indicating a woodstove of some sort. She wondered if it was really taking Banner this long to craft a simple stand for the tree or if he was busying himself in his workshop to avoid entertaining his guests. She suspected the latter.

It was probably just as well that he was staying away, she decided. She was getting much too intrigued by that man. And with her tendency to tumble into trouble, she was likely to do something stupid if she spent much more time with him—especially as close as she had been to him on this porch earlier, she thought with a touch of pensiveness.

If she had ever seen a heartache waiting to happen, it was Banner—a man so private and reserved that he had only shared one name with her.

She carried the lunch meat back inside, closing the back door on the sight of Banner's workshop.

Working in comfortable unison, Lucy and Joan assembled the ingredients for sandwiches. Lucy's curiosity about Joan was growing, and she had never been very successful at reining in her curiosity. She would, however, try to be as tactful as possible with her prying.

"Your children are very well behaved," she began. "Considering everything, they've been real troupers today."

Joan's brown eyes brightened in response to the compliment. "Thank you. I really appreciate everything you all have done to entertain them."

Lucy shrugged. "It keeps us entertained, too. Are you a single mom?"

She had tried to slip the question in casually, but subtlety had never been one of Lucy's talents. Joan stiffened a bit. "Yes," she replied after a moment. "I'm divorced. The kids haven't seen their father in several years."

"You're doing a wonderful job with them."

"I do my best."

It couldn't be easy raising two children alone, Lucy mused. Which was why a solemn respect for the responsibilities of fatherhood was high on her list of husband qualifications. Lucy definitely wanted children, and it was her intention to provide those children with a good father.

"Have you ever been married?" Joan asked, turning the questioning around.

"No, but I'm looking," Lucy replied cheerfully.

"Um, you are?"

"Yep. I've been on more blind dates than I can count during the past year. None of them has led to anything promising, but I haven't given up."

"So you really are looking."

"Oh, yes. I concentrated on establishing my career first, but now I'm ready to establish a family. I'll be twenty-eight in a few months."

"I was married at twenty-three," Joan confided as she spread mustard on a slice of wheat bread. "Three years later we were on the verge of a breakup when I found out I was pregnant with Tyler. We struggled along for another couple of years, but Roger left while I was pregnant with Tricia. He said he couldn't handle the pressure of a wife and two children."

What a jerk. Keeping that thought to herself, Lucy said only, "I'm sorry."

Joan shrugged. "It was all for the best, I suppose. The kids and I have gotten along fine without him."

More determined than ever to make sure Tyler and Tricia had a nice Christmas, Lucy asked, "Do you have their Christmas gifts in your car?"

"Yes, hidden in the trunk. Why?"

Lucy glanced quickly toward the doorway. She could hear Pop and the children singing "Rudolph the Red-Nosed Reindeer" in the living room, so she felt safe enough saying, "Would you like for Santa Claus to stop here for them tonight? We have a tree—and the rest of us could help you."

Joan turned to face her, obviously intrigued by the suggestion. "I had thought I'd just wait until we reached my mother's house, but maybe—"

"Wouldn't they get a kick out of waking up tomorrow morning to discover that Santa found them after all?"

Joan's smile turned tremulous in anticipation. "They would be thrilled."

"Then let's do it."

Joan nodded. "It's a deal."

Lucy called Banner in from his workshop for lunch, which they ate around the dining room table. Bobby Ray was moving more easily now, the pain reliever having done its job, and everyone seemed to be in good spirits.

After lunch Banner carried in the six-foot-tall cedar he and Bobby Ray had found earlier. Banner had nailed a wooden stand to the bottom of the tree, which he set in one corner of the living room.

"We don't have any twinkle lights," Tricia said, studying the bare branches.

Her brother gave a long-suffering sigh. "We don't have

any electricity, dopey-head. The lights wouldn't work even if we had some."

"I'm not a dopey-head," Tricia protested, lower lip protruding.

"Are, too."

"Am *not!*"

Joan interceded quickly. "It's Christmas Eve, kids. Don't forget who might be listening."

They fell silent immediately. Tricia looked around as if searching for hidden Santa listening devices. Joan and Lucy exchanged conspiratorial smiles.

Joan helped the children drape strung popcorn and paper chains around the tree. A stack of imaginative paper-glitter-button-and-ribbon ornaments waited to be hung from the branches. Pop, Miss Annie and Bobby Ray watched indulgently, offering occasional suggestions.

Lucy remembered seeing a box of cocoa in the pantry. She leaned toward Banner. "Would you mind if I make hot chocolate?"

He made a sweeping gesture toward the kitchen. "*Mi casa es su casa*. At least until the ice melts."

She gave him a sympathetic smile and patted his arm. "You're a very gracious host."

"I'll be even more gracious," he countered. "I'll help you make the cocoa."

"You're just trying to avoid decorating."

He smiled, a very brief flash of white teeth against his tanned face. "You've got that right."

She very nearly melted into a puddle right there at his feet. All it took was a tiny little smile, she thought in bemusement. Amazing…

He took her elbow and led her into the kitchen. By the time they'd reached the pantry, Lucy had herself under control again. Mostly.

"Well, it's almost three o'clock," Banner said, handing her the cocoa and sugar. "It should take an hour—at most—to decorate the tree. Then what?"

"Then...we'll do something else," she said with a shrug. "Games or stories or anything to keep the kids entertained until bedtime."

She cast a quick, furtive glance toward the doorway, making sure neither of the children was within hearing range. "Joan and I were talking earlier. She has the children's Christmas presents in the trunk of her car. We were thinking maybe Santa Claus could visit here tonight so they would have gifts under the tree on Christmas morning."

He nodded. "What do you want me to do?"

She giggled in response to his stoically resigned expression. "What makes you think I want you to do anything?"

"Experience," he answered dryly.

She laughed again. "Poor Banner."

Without responding, he stepped out onto the back porch to retrieve the milk from the big cooler. "There's some melting going on," he commented when he came back in with the milk. "The thermometer on the porch reads a few degrees above freezing."

"Great. Maybe we'll be able to get out of your hair tomorrow. I'm sure you'll be glad to have your house to yourself again."

He didn't answer, but crossed his arms over his chest and leaned one hip against the bar. "So what do you need me to do to help with Joan's kids?"

"I don't suppose you would put on a Santa suit?"

"Not even if my life depended on it," he answered evenly.

"That's pretty much what I thought," she said, amused.

"So, how about if you get the gifts out of Joan's trunk before it's dark and stash them somewhere close until after the kids are asleep?"

"That I will do."

She sighed. "I appreciate it, of course, but I would have dearly loved to see you in a Santa suit."

He reached around her to turn down the heat beneath the bubbling cocoa. His arm brushed against her with the movement, sending a jolt of awareness through her.

"Is this some sort of kinky fetish thing?" he asked in a murmur. For a moment she couldn't think what he was talking about, since his touch seemed to have temporarily emptied her mind.

When she realized that he was displaying yet another example of his quirky humor, she managed a smile. "I've always had a thing for Santa Claus."

"Must be hard for your other boyfriends to compete."

She took the pan of steaming cocoa off the heat, setting it on a cool burner. "So far, no one's been able to."

"So what would it take?"

She could feeling him watching as she ladled the hot beverage into mugs. He wasn't an easy man to banter with—if that's what they were doing. He was too serious, too intense. And his humor was unpredictable, to say the least.

Still, she gave it a try. "He'd have to be generous, of course."

Banner's left eyebrow rose. "Opening his home to stranded holiday travelers, for example?"

"Um, yeah, something like that." She kept her gaze focused on the ladle as she reminded herself yet again that he couldn't be taken too seriously.

"What else?"

She cleared her throat. "He should be resourceful. A good provider."

Banner reached into the pantry and produced a bag of marshmallows for topping the hot cocoa. "How did you like the tree I found?" he asked as he handed her the bag.

Was he really comparing himself to Santa Claus? She plopped a couple of marshmallows into a mug. "It's a lovely tree."

He was standing rather close to her now, his arm making contact with hers again as he set one of the filled mugs on a big tray. "So what else would a guy have to do to compete with Santa for your affections?"

"He would have to be jolly, of course."

Banner had been reaching for another mug. His hand went still. "Jolly?"

"Jolly," she repeated firmly.

Thoughtfully he finished transferring the mugs to the tray. "I don't suppose you would settle for two out of three?"

She smiled at him then, a bit more confident, now that she had decided he really was teasing, in his odd way. "I never settle."

He heaved a somber sigh. "That's what I suspected."

Balancing the tray with the skill of a seasoned waiter, he nodded toward the living room. "Let's go check on the progress of the tree."

She would have liked to remain behind for a moment, just to savor the pleasure of that unexpectedly lighthearted exchange, but he was obviously waiting for her to precede him. Keeping her smile firmly in place, she walked into the living room, knowing the past few minutes would replay themselves plenty of times in her mind.

Chapter Five

Borrowing the keys from Joan, Banner slipped out to her car later that afternoon to retrieve the large plastic bags she had described to him. Stuffed into her trunk, the black drawstring-topped bags held wrapped presents for the children. There were other presents in the trunk, but Joan had instructed him to leave those, since they were for other members of her family.

He hauled the bags to his workshop. It was becoming somewhat easier to walk as the ice slowly melted. Still slippery, though, he mused, placing his boots carefully as he carried the bags to his workshop. The ground had pretty much turned to mud beneath the ice.

Glancing toward the road, he noted several large exposed patches, but no longer frozen asphalt. Ice covered the road in the shaded areas, making travel extremely hazardous, but he'd bet it would be navigable by tomorrow afternoon. His guests would be on their way, which was good for them since he knew they were anxious to be with their families.

The house was going to seem quiet after they left, he thought. It was usually the way he preferred things, but he had to admit—rather to his own surprise—that he had sort of enjoyed the last few hours. Thanks to Lucy, he added thoughtfully. Of all his guests, he knew she was the one who would linger in his thoughts after everyone was gone.

Half an hour later he was still puttering in his workshop when the door opened and a head poked in. Lucy's head, to be specific.

"Banner?" she said. "May I come in?"

He was working at a table he'd pulled close to a back window for light. "Sure," he said, setting down the sanding block he'd been holding. "Come in."

She had donned her warm black parka over her Christmas sweatshirt and jeans, he noted. Black leather gloves covered her hands, and the green knit hat perched on her riotous red curls made her look more like a Christmas elf than ever. Her sparkling green eyes and rosy cheeks only added to the image. But that sexy full mouth…his gaze lingered there for a moment as he wondered just how those perfect lips would taste.

"I hope you don't mind, but I was curious to see where you create that beautiful furniture."

Roused from his inappropriate thoughts by her words, he nodded and swept a hand around in invitation. "This is it."

Standing in the center of the drained concrete floor, she turned slowly in a circle to study the rows of power tools on wheeled stands, the long workbenches above which hung cabinets filled with hand tools and materials, and the neat stacks of wood in racks against the far wall. A woodstove sat in one corner, keeping the temperature comfortable. Banner preferred central heat when the electricity was on, but since he lived in a rural area where power outages were fairly common, he'd left his great-uncle's old stove in place.

Lucy paused to admire a couple of rockers and Adirondack chairs in various stages of completion, and then she wandered over to his table, studying the items he had been working on. Her eyes lit up. "Are these for Tyler and Tricia?"

A bit self-consciously he shrugged. "Do you think they would like them?"

Lucy beamed at him. "Of course they will. They're lovely gifts."

She ran a gloved hand over the smooth footboard of a doll-size Shaker cradle. He had built the cradle out of pine and had stained and buffed it to a rich golden glow. Sitting beside the cradle was an eight-inch-high semi cab, hooked to a foot-long trailer that hauled a detailed backhoe tractor, all crafted of oak and finished to a matte sheen.

The truck-and-backhoe rig represented quite a few hours of work. It was a project Banner had made of scrap wood after seeing the pattern in a woodworkers magazine. He hadn't made it for anyone in particular, but because the project had appealed to him at the time.

The cradle was left over from a batch he'd made to sell in a Branson craft store. It had lacked only a final light sanding with very fine sandpaper, which he had just completed. He would go over it again with tack cloth to collect dust, and the cradle would be ready for play.

Even before he had known that Lucy and Joan were planning a visit from Santa, he had decided to give these toys to Tyler and Tricia. It just seemed to him that kids needed a little extra attention at Christmas. Lucy had come up with the arts and crafts projects, while Pop and Bobby Ray had entertained with music and funny stories. Working with wood was Banner's only talent.

"The detail on this rig is amazing," Lucy marveled, lifting the jointed front-end loader and backhoe with the attached side levers. "I can't imagine how much time went into this."

"I don't watch a lot of TV, and I don't socialize much," he replied, pleased by her compliments. "Working with wood helps me pass the time. This was a pattern I wanted to try just for the heck of it. I didn't know what I was going to do with it, but I'd like to give it to Tyler, if you think he would like it."

"What boy *wouldn't* like it? And what little girl wouldn't love this cradle? Of course," Lucy added, "I suppose I'm being sexist. Tricia will probably enjoy playing with the truck and tractor, too, and Tyler might very well have a favorite stuffed toy or doll that he would enjoy putting to bed in the cradle."

"So which did you prefer when you were a little girl? Dolls or trucks?"

"I played with trucks," she replied, then wrinkled her nose in what he considered to be an adorable expression. "But I really loved my baby dolls."

"I can tell by watching you with Tyler and Tricia that you like kids."

"I love children. I'd like to have at least two of my own—once I find that Santa Claus substitute to father them," she added with a laugh.

Banner couldn't imagine that it would be difficult for Lucy to find someone willing to fill that role. She certainly seemed to have a great deal to offer a man who was interested in marriage and kids. Which didn't include him, of course.

He had tried the marriage thing, and it had been an abysmal failure—something he should have predicted from the start. Considering his history with relationships, he had no desire to risk making a fool of himself like that again.

Not that Lucy would be interested even if he *was*, he assured himself. After all, she was looking for a frigging jolly Santa Claus.

"What's that expression?" Lucy asked him suddenly, studying him with her head cocked curiously to one side. "You're frowning as if someone just stomped on your ingrown toenail."

That comment changed his frown to a slight smile. "I don't have an ingrown toenail."

"So what's the problem?"

"No problem. I was just wondering if I should ask Joan's permission before giving her kids gifts."

"She'll probably be delighted."

"Still, it might be best for me to clear it with her first."

Lucy had wandered back over to the rocking chairs. Banner had noticed that she wasn't the type to stay in one spot for very long.

"These are beautiful. You're so talented. Have you always been a professional woodworker?"

"I've had other jobs but nothing I liked this much. When my great-uncle left me this place, I was able to take over the business he had started. He's the one who taught me everything I know about working with wood."

"It sounds as though you were very close to him."

"I was," he answered with the familiar lump that always came into his throat when he thought of his uncle Joe. He still missed the old coot.

Lucy sat in the one finished rocker and began to rock,

sliding her gloved hands appreciatively over the armrests. "Are your parents still living?"

"Yes."

"Where do they live?"

"Why?"

She shrugged. "Just curious."

He doubted that her curiosity would be satisfied with a simple answer, so he gave her the expanded version. "My father and his wife live in Nashville, Tennessee. They have a daughter who is finishing medical school at Vanderbilt and a son who's in his first year of law school. My mother and her husband live in Lexington, Kentucky, close to their two grown daughters. Both the girls are married, and they each have one child."

She had followed his family details attentively, and he had no doubt that she could quote it all back to him. Lucy was definitely a "people person"—someone who was actively interested in other people's lives and opinions. Again, unlike himself.

"Your siblings aren't much younger than you," she commented. "Your parents must have divorced when you were very young."

He reached out to idly roll the truck back and forth with one finger. "My parents were never married. They split up before I was a year old."

If that shocked her, she didn't let it show. "Did you live with your mother?"

"Part of the time with my mother, part of the time with my paternal grandparents here in northern Arkansas. This is where I preferred to be because my great-uncle was here. He never married and he had no kids, so he and I sort of bonded."

She was studying his face a bit too closely now, obviously trying to read his emotions. Long accustomed to keeping his feelings hidden, he wasn't concerned that she would see more than he wanted to reveal.

"Did you see your father very much?" she asked.

"I spent the occasional weekend and holiday with him and his family. We get along fine, just don't have much in common."

Lucy rocked a bit faster, which Banner figured was a clue to the questions racing through her mind. "Didn't you want to spend the holidays with family? Didn't your parents want to see you?"

He shrugged. "My parents have plenty of family around for the holidays. They both invited me, but I wasn't in the mood this year. I have a furniture order to finish, and I had a hunch the weather was going to be bad. Besides, they tend to get their noses out of joint when I choose one over the other."

"They fight over you?"

"They compete for me," he replied. "Not quite the same thing. Truth is, neither one particularly cares whether I join them as long as I don't choose the other one, instead."

Okay, that was more than he had intended to say. He blamed the slip on his preoccupation with how fetching Lucy looked sitting in his rocking chair with her sexy mouth, rosy cheeks and silly green hat.

Her pretty mouth immediately formed into a sympathetic frown. "I'm sorry," she said. "I tend to ask too many questions sometimes. I didn't mean to pry—"

He shrugged. "It's okay. I can understand why you'd be curious about why a guy with so much family would choose to spend Christmas alone with his dog. Especially when you were willing to risk life and limb in an ice storm to get to your family."

"I don't get to see my father very often. He travels a

lot in his job with the army, even though he's officially stationed in Texas. Christmas is the one time he makes a determined effort to get home. My aunt and uncle are like my second parents, and my cousins are as close as I have to siblings. I'm crazy about all of them.''

Banner would be willing to bet they all felt the same way about her.

She hopped suddenly out of the chair and headed toward the door. ''I'd better go see how everything is going inside. Last I looked your whole living room was being decorated.''

Banner was almost surprised to realize that it didn't particularly bother him to hear that.

The children were pleasantly tired by late afternoon. Tricia fell asleep on the floor beneath the lavishly decorated Christmas tree. Tyler was on his stomach on the rug in front of the fire beside Banner's dog. An open comic book lay in front of them, and it looked for all the world as if both boy and dog were enjoying the pictures.

Joan was reading a paperback in a chair beside the window. Having napped for a short while after lunch, Miss Annie had returned to her rocker and her knitting, her long needles clicking industriously. Pop and Bobby Ray sat on the couch engaged in a low-voiced conversation that seemed to consist mostly of tall tales about hunting and fishing.

Lucy was curled up in Banner's big recliner, her sock-clad feet beneath her and a book lying open and unread in her lap. It was a lazy, cozy scene, and she could appreciate the peacefulness of it, but it bothered her that their host was outside alone while his guests enjoyed each other's company.

She thought about the things he had told her of his

childhood—okay, the things she had pried out of him, she amended sheepishly. She had left him rather abruptly because so many more questions had been bubbling inside her that she had been afraid she would offend him with her nosiness if she didn't hush.

Still, she couldn't help considering everything she had learned about him and reflecting on how his childhood experiences had molded him. He didn't remember his parents as a couple, but both parents had married and started new families while Banner was quite young. He had spent his time being shuttled between his mother and his paternal grandparents, bonding most closely with a great-uncle who had never married.

Had Banner felt like the odd man out in his parents' homes? Their youthful mistake, perhaps? Was that why he always seemed to be off to one side of a room, watching others interact?

She wondered how he got along with his stepparents. Had they accepted him, made him feel welcome in their homes, or had they seen him as an intrusion? Perhaps his stepmother had felt that way, which might explain why he seemed to have spent so little time in his father's home. The occasional weekend and holiday was the way Banner had described his time there.

Not that any of this was Lucy's business, of course. She doubted that he would appreciate knowing she was sitting here engaged in armchair analysis of him. She just couldn't seem to help it. The man simply fascinated her.

As if he had heard her thinking of him, Banner appeared in the doorway of the living room. He entered silently, his gaze skimming the room and settling on Lucy.

He had left his wet boots behind, and his feet in their thick wool socks made no sound on the hardwood floor as he approached the recliner. "Quiet in here," he said, pausing at Lucy's side.

She smiled and nodded. "I think the children wore themselves out. How do you like your Christmas decorations?"

He looked around the room again, and she tried to see it from his point of view. The cedar tree in the corner was very festive now with its strings of popcorn and chains of colored paper. Glitter- and marker-colored paper ornaments cut out in shapes of snowflakes, stars, bells, angels and gingerbread men dangled from the branches on strips of ribbon.

More paper chains draped the mantel, and glittery paper stars had been scattered randomly around the room. Along with the firelight and the candles burning in shadowy corners, the handmade decorations were reminiscent of an old-fashioned Christmas.

"They made a lot of ornaments," Banner commented.

"They really got into it," she answered with a smile. "I think they depleted your craft supplies."

"That's what the supplies were here for."

"We turned the radio on for a little while—we didn't want to run down the batteries too quickly. The latest weather report said that temperatures are expected to remain above freezing tonight—just barely—and to rise into the midforties tomorrow. Some roads are already clearing, and crews are working around the clock to restore power."

"Sounds like a promising report."

"Bobby Ray's boss is sending a wrecker tomorrow to get the truck back on the road. And Pop's grandsons are planning to come tomorrow afternoon. One of them will drive Pop's truck to Harrison. Even though Pop insisted he was perfectly capable of driving himself," she added in a low voice with a glance at the elderly man. "Apparently, his grandsons wouldn't hear of it."

"Good for them. I'll feel better if he doesn't head out on his own without someone to help him in case of trouble."

"So will I."

"What about you?" Banner's gaze was focused on the flames in the fireplace as he spoke casually. "Are you heading out first thing tomorrow?"

"I'll wait until everyone else leaves, if you like. Just to help everyone get underway."

"Yes, that would be helpful."

She had been careful not to suggest a personal reason for lingering, and she heard no particular expression in Banner's voice. She shouldn't feel as if there was some significance to their agreement that she would be the last to leave. So why *did* she feel that way?

She glanced at her watch to distract herself from that line of thought. "It's almost five. I suppose we should be thinking of something to feed everyone."

"I put a lasagna in the oven. It will be ready to serve by six."

Lucy looked at Banner in surprise. She hadn't even realized he'd been in the kitchen prior to joining her in the living room. She knew he hadn't been in there long enough to assemble lasagna. "How—"

"It was in the freezer. I make two at a time when I'm in the mood to cook, and I freeze one for later. It should be enough to feed everyone, along with a couple of side dishes. I usually eat leftovers for two or three days."

"You're a very resourceful man, aren't you?"

He gave a quiet chuckle. "I try to be."

Oh, gosh, she was starting to like him, entirely too much. The darned man seemed to be weaseling his way onto her prospect list—even though he absolutely did not belong there. And certainly wouldn't want to be there, she added glumly.

Candles provided light for the lasagna dinner Banner had prepared. Having grown more comfortable with each other as the day passed, the travelers laughed and bantered during the meal. A newcomer might have thought they had known each other for ages, Lucy thought with a smile.

Though Banner didn't contribute much to the conversation, he seemed to enjoy listening. Lucy was getting the distinct impression that he wasn't quite the crusty recluse he pretended to be. She suspected that there was more to his story than a history of being the family misfit. What was he really hiding from here in his rural lair? And, yes, she was being nosy again, but it was Banner's fault for being so mysterious, she reasoned.

Before the meal was over, something else claimed her attention, something that was no more her business than Banner's secrets. But she couldn't help noticing that Bobby Ray was spending a lot of time watching Joan across the table. His expression made Lucy wonder if the big trucker had become attracted to Joan.

It was an interesting possibility. Lucy wondered if Joan was aware of it, and if so, how she felt about it. Something told her that Joan didn't have a clue. As far as Lucy could tell, Joan had absolutely no vanity. And since she had admitted to Lucy that she was a bit intimidated by Bobby Ray, Joan probably never considered that he might be interested in her.

Lucy didn't consider herself the meddlesome type. But there was no reason they shouldn't all get to know each other better, was there? Wasn't that what casual conversation was all about?

"You haven't told us much about yourself, Bobby Ray," she began, stabbing her fork into a bite of lasagna. "Are you originally from Little Rock?"

"I grew up in Prescott," the trucker replied obligingly. "Moved to Little Rock about fifteen years ago to be closer to my wife's family."

Oops.

"Your wife?" Lucy repeated.

He nodded. "Andrea. She died five years ago of melanoma. She had just turned thirty-two."

"I'm so sorry," Lucy said, and the sentiment was echoed in the faces of their dining companions.

"You would have liked her," Bobby Ray assured Lucy. "She was a pistol. You remind me of her, in a way."

"I'll take that as a compliment," she said with a smile.

"It was meant as one."

Lucy noticed that Joan was looking down at her plate now, though Lucy would bet Joan was paying close attention to the conversation. "You and Andrea didn't have any children?"

Bobby Ray shook his head, his eyes dimming a bit. "We were never blessed with any. We both loved kids and would've liked a houseful if we could've had 'em."

"Children are a blessing," Pop agreed. "Mother and I raised four of our own and more than a few that we took in along the way. I'm not saying we never had our troubles with any of them, but the good times made up for the bad ones, didn't they, Mother?"

"Oh, yes, they did," she concurred. "Hardest part was when we lost our oldest boy in a car accident twenty years ago. We learned then to cherish the moments we have with our loved ones and to never take each other for granted."

"That's the way I've always felt," Lucy said. "Probably because I lost my mother when I was young, I've always treasured my other family members. Even when my cousins made me so mad I could punch them—and I tried once or twice," she added with a laugh.

Tricia wanted to contribute to the discussion. "My brother makes me mad sometimes. He calls me dopey-head, and he hides my dolls."

"Well, you broke my model airplane," Tyler retorted heatedly, always game for a squabble. "And you are a dopey-head."

"Am not!"

"Are, too."

Joan cleared her throat, and both children fell into silence, turning their attention quickly back to their dinners.

Bobby Ray laughed. "That's the same sort of sound my own mama used to make when I was acting up. She didn't have to say a word, just gave my brother and me a look, and we knew we were in for it. That little bitty woman could sure swing a mean hickory switch."

Tricia's eyes rounded. "What's a hickory switch?"

"A little bit of history, missy," Bobby Ray answered with a chuckle. "It's been replaced with other methods now, but it surely was effective in its time."

Pop grinned. "I can testify to that. My grandma was the switch swinger in my family, and we learned right quick not to get on her bad side."

"My teacher gives us frowny-face stickers if we're bad," Tricia said, still eager for attention. "Three frowny faces means we can't go out to recess. I've only had one frowny face all year," she bragged, "and that was because Kevin Perkins pinched me and made me yell at him when we were supposed to be listening to a story."

Lucy couldn't help smiling at the little girl's disgruntled expression. "Kevin Perkins sounds like a brat."

"He's okay," Tricia said. "I told him to be nice to me and he could be one of my boyfriends, so now he doesn't pinch me anymore."

That made the adults laugh, except for Joan, who groaned and shook her head.

"Looks like you're going to have your hands full with this one," Bobby Ray told Joan sympathetically. "Going to have to beat the boys away with a stick."

"Maybe I should find a hickory switch, after all," Joan agreed.

When Joan and Bobby Ray shared a smile, Lucy silently congratulated herself for getting the conversation started. Who knew where this could lead? Bobby Ray and Joan both seemed like nice people. Bobby Ray loved children, and Joan had two who needed a father figure in their lives. It seemed like a great match to Lucy, who had always had better luck matching up her friends than herself.

Maybe she could drop a few hints in Joan's direction when they were alone again....

She happened to glance toward Banner right then. He was sitting next to her, looking at her in a way that made her wonder if he had guessed what she was thinking. Was that disapproval or merely curiosity she saw in his eyes before he masked his expression and looked back down at his plate?

"Perhaps you'll play your guitar for us again after dinner," Miss Annie suggested to Bobby Ray. "You play beautifully. Doesn't he, Joan?"

Joan looked a bit surprised, but nodded agreeably. "Yes. I enjoyed listening earlier."

Lucy smiled brightly at Miss Annie, sensing a compatriot. "We'll all look forward to hearing him again."

Bobby Ray looked almost shy when he promised that he would play whatever they would like to hear. Lucy was amused to see the faintest tint of pink beneath his bushy beard.

Knowing it took a bit more persistence to get Joan to talk about herself, Lucy turned her attention to the other woman. "You said you live in Mayflower, Joan. Do you work there?"

"No, I work at a bank in Conway. It's less than fifteen miles from my house, so I don't have far to commute."

"My mom's a loan officer." Tricia looked proud of herself for knowing the title.

"Think she could lend me a dollar?" Bobby Ray asked with a grin.

Tricia nodded seriously. "But you would have to pay her back."

"With interest," Tyler added, proving that he, too, was knowledgeable about his mother's career. "Like seventy-five cents, maybe."

"Whew, that's high interest," Bobby Ray said, grinning at Joan.

She smiled tentatively back at him. "The rates aren't quite that high."

"Glad to hear it."

Probably uncomfortable at being the center of attention, Joan turned to Lucy. "I don't think you've told us what you do, Lucy."

"I'm an assistant professor of mathematics at the University of Central Arkansas in Conway. I just finished my first semester there, and I enjoyed it immensely."

For some reason everyone at the table, with the exception of the children, perhaps, looked surprised by her reply.

"You're a math professor?" Bobby Ray asked after a moment. "You seem awfully young for that."

"I'll be twenty-eight soon. I was always in a hurry to finish the next stage of my education, so I earned my bachelor's degree by the time I was twenty and my Ph.D. when I was twenty-five. This is what I was anxious to do—teach in a university setting."

"You're a doctor!" Miss Annie said. "Isn't that something."

"You must have students who aren't much younger than you are," Pop commented.

"I have several who are older than I am," Lucy replied. She glanced at Banner, who was studying her closely again, and she couldn't begin to read his thoughts.

She didn't think her profession merited quite the amazement the others had shown, but she did wonder if he was as surprised as they were. She was used to people being startled upon hearing her profession, of course. She knew she looked younger than she was, and she was aware that she didn't fit any particular stereotypes of a mathematician or a professor.

As far as she was concerned, her career was no different than truck driver or loan officer or woodworker—she had simply found a way to support herself doing something she enjoyed.

So what did Banner think about her career? And why should it matter to her, anyway?

She started to say something to him—she wasn't sure what it would have been—but he turned away, reaching for Tricia's empty plate, which he stacked with his own. "Anyone want dessert?" he asked. "The ice cream is melted, I'm afraid, but I have some thaw-and-serve carrot cake that should be ready to eat."

"I like carrot cake," Tricia told him eagerly. "Can I have the little frosting carrot on the top?"

"Tricia," her long-suffering mother admonished. "Take what you are served."

Bobby Ray was chuckling again, Lucy noted in satisfaction. He seemed quite taken with the kids, which boded well for Lucy's matchmaking scheme.

If only there was someone as interesting to go on *her* prospect list, she thought with a silent sigh. And then found her eyes turning to Banner again as he served a slice of carrot cake topped with a bright orange frosting carrot to little Tricia.

Chapter Six

As promised, Bobby Ray played his guitar again after dinner. Miss Annie was back in the rocker and Pop was in the big recliner now. Bobby Ray sat on one end of the couch with Joan at the other end. The children and the dog were on the floor in front of the fire.

Lucy sat in the striped wing chair. She'd half expected Banner to pull his dining room chair close to her side, as he had before, but instead he'd placed it just inside the doorway, where he could watch without really being a part of the group.

She tried a time or two to catch his eye, to share a smile, but he seemed to avoid looking at her. Or was she simply imagining that? She couldn't think of anything she might have done to annoy him.

The evening passed slowly, but pleasantly. Pop sang for them again, urging the children to join him. Miss Annie asked if anyone would like to hear her read the Christmas story from her battered, well-used Bible. "I used to read it every Christmas Eve for my children," she added with a nostalgic sigh. "I would've read it for my great-grandchildren tonight."

Everyone, of course, assured her that they would be delighted to have her read to them. She held the Bible close to her faded eyes, and her hands shook a bit, but her voice was strong as she began, "And it came to pass…"

Lucy had a lump in her throat by the time the elderly woman finished the reading. She saw Joan surreptitiously wipe a tear. Even the children had been spellbound. Bobby Ray cleared his throat, and Pop leaned over to kiss his wife's cheek, which only made the lump in Lucy's throat grow bigger.

From her sprawled position on the floor, Tricia sighed. "That was pretty, Miss Annie."

"Thank you, sugar pie."

"Do you have a book with 'The Night Before Christmas' in it? My grandmother promised to read that to me tonight."

"I'm afraid I don't have that one."

The little girl looked disappointed. "We always hear it on Christmas Eve."

"Doesn't matter," Tyler muttered. "This isn't like real Christmas Eve, anyway. We won't even have Santa Claus tonight."

Banner shifted in his chair, drawing attention his way. "I could say the poem for you, Tricia, if you want me to," he added in a mumble.

Tricia sat up straighter. "You have the book?"

"Well…no."

The child looked confused. "But you said you would read it to me."

"I said I would recite it for you," he corrected, and Lucy thought he looked as though he regretted that he had ever spoken at all.

"You have the poem memorized, Banner?" Pop asked encouragingly. "Is that what you mean?"

"Um, yeah. I don't know that I would win any awards for dramatic recitation, but I have a knack for memorization. I learned that poem when I was just a kid, and it has stayed with me ever since."

Tricia scooted closer to Banner's chair, her expression eager. "Say it for us," she urged. "I want to hear about the reindeer."

He cleared his throat and glanced somewhat sheepishly toward Lucy, who nodded encouragement at him. And then he began, his voice deep and rich as the words rolled fluently from him. The logs in the fireplace crackled in accompaniment, and Lucy didn't think she had ever heard a more perfect telling of the beloved poem.

A love of literature was one of the criteria for a man to be placed on her prospect list. How frustrating that Banner met so many of her requirements—"jolly" being a notable exception—yet still set off every emotional alarm she possessed.

"'Merry Christmas to all, and to all a good night,'" he finished, causing Tricia to break into delighted applause.

"Well now, I've played guitar, Pop sang for us, Miss Annie read from the Bible and Banner's quoted poetry," Bobby Ray said. "Lucy, do you or Joan want to entertain us now?"

Joan blushed. "I'm afraid I don't have any talents."

"Sure you do, Mama," Tyler argued. "You sing all the time at home, and Grandma said you could have been a real music star."

Joan blushed even more brightly. "My mother tends to exaggerate."

"Sing for us, Mama," Tricia urged. "Bobby Ray can play guitar for you, won't you, Bobby Ray?"

"I would be delighted." Bobby Ray cocked his head toward Joan. "What do you want to sing?"

She sighed, apparently realizing that her children wouldn't stop pressing her until she gave in. "How about 'I'll Be Home for Christmas'? Maybe that will be a good omen for the roads tomorrow."

Bobby Ray strummed the opening chords of the song. Lucy was pleased that Joan really did have a lovely voice. Her slight country drawl made Lucy think of Reba McEntire. Joan's mother might have been right about Joan having a career in music had she chosen to pursue it. Lucy wondered if that was a dream that had been abandoned for Joan's unfortunate early marriage.

Everyone applauded when Joan finished singing.

"That was lovely," Miss Annie enthused.

"Very nice," Pop seconded. "We should try a duet."

"I agree with your mother," Bobby Ray said. "You have a beautiful voice, Joan."

Joan's eyes glowed in the firelight, showing her pleasure with the compliments. "Thank you. But that's enough, please."

Bobby Ray turned to Lucy with a mischievous grin. "Well, Miss Lucy? What are you going to do for us?"

She wrinkled her nose. "I don't suppose you would be interested in hearing some advanced math calculations?"

"Not hardly. Why don't you sing us a song?"

She laughed. "Trust me, you would rather hear Hulk sing than me."

Tricia scooted closer to Lucy's chair. "What can you do, Lucy? Besides math, I mean?"

"I play a little piano, but we don't have one of those available. It isn't exactly a portable instrument like Bobby Ray's guitar."

"What else?" Tricia seemed confident that Lucy had talents she hadn't yet revealed.

"I can wiggle my ears," Tyler announced, and proceeded to do so.

Tricia sighed. "We're talking about Lucy, not you."

Lucy turned to Banner. "Do you have a deck of cards?"

He stood, reached into a cabinet beneath a built-in bookcase beside the fireplace and produced a card deck that he tossed to her.

"You do card tricks?" Tyler asked, moving closer on his knees, and making Lucy wonder how many pairs of jeans he had worn out that way.

"I read minds," she corrected him.

The boy snorted. "Yeah, right."

"I suppose I'll have to prove it." She shuffled the cards, then fanned them in front of him. "Pick a card."

Keeping his eyes suspiciously locked with hers, Tyler slid a card out of the middle of the deck. He looked at it quickly, then held it pressed against his chest. "You didn't see it, did you?" he asked.

"No. I'll close my eyes while you place the card back in the deck." She made a production of squeezing her eyes tightly shut, laughing when Tricia placed a soft little hand over her face, just to make sure there was no cheating.

After Tyler had replaced the card in the deck, Lucy dramatically hummed and swayed, keeping her eyes locked with his while she slowly shuffled the cards in her hands. And then she pretended to psychically receive inspiration.

"Voilà," she said, sweeping a card in an arc and then turning it toward Tyler. "You drew the three of clubs, didn't you?"

His eyes widened. "How did you know?"

"She read your mind," Tricia said in exasperation. "Weren't you listening, dopey-head?"

Tyler reached out to give his sister a push. "It was a trick, stupid."

"I'm not stupid! Mama, he pushed me."

"Did not."

"Did, too. Everyone saw you."

"You know, I would have sworn I heard jingle bells outside a minute ago," Pop murmured to his wife, making sure the children heard him.

Tricia perked up. "You did?" she asked, forgetting the quarrel.

"Could've been the wind," he answered. "But you never know on Christmas Eve."

Tricia ran to the window to look out into the cold darkness. Tyler sighed gustily. "Santa doesn't know we're here, remember?"

Bobby Ray shook his head. "Oh, I don't know. Santa's a pretty smart guy."

"That's right," Pop agreed. "Remember the song?"

He launched into the opening of "Santa Claus is Coming to Town," urging the others to join in. Despite her warning to the others about the quality of her singing, Lucy sang along. She wasn't really awful, she figured— just not solo quality. She noticed that Banner even sang a few lines, though so softly she couldn't hear if he could carry a tune or not.

She knew he had planned to spend this evening alone with his dog, but she suspected that he wasn't particularly sorry his plans had changed.

After another couple of songs, Joan announced that it was time for her children to brush their teeth and get ready for bed. Carrying flashlights to guide their way, they told everyone good-night and headed out of the room.

Tricia paused in the doorway, turning to say in her clear little voice, "Merry Christmas to all and to all a good night." And then she giggled and turned to run after her family.

"Isn't she a precious little thing?" Miss Annie murmured.

"She is a cutie." Pop turned back to Lucy. "Let me see that card trick again. I don't think I watched closely enough the first time. Didn't see how you managed it."

"Watch as closely as you like. You won't see how I do it this time, either," she bragged, shuffling the deck as she walked toward his chair.

"I want to see this, too." Bobby Ray walked over to stand behind Pop's chair, his gaze focused on Lucy's hands.

By the time she had performed the trick twice for Pop and once for Bobby Ray, the men had to concede that they had no idea how Lucy knew which card they had chosen each time.

"I read your mind," she teased, quoting Tricia. "Weren't you listening, dopey-heads?"

Everyone laughed—except Banner, who stood and turned toward the kitchen. "I think I'll go out to the workshop and bring some things onto the back porch."

Lucy knew he meant the children's gifts. They would be easily accessible on the back porch once they knew the children were sound asleep. "I'll help you," she said, laying the deck of cards on a table.

"You need me to come with you?" Bobby Ray asked.

"No, we can handle it," Banner replied, already on his way.

Bobby Ray picked up the cards and looked at Pop. "Want to join me in a game of candlelight gin rummy?"

"I believe I will," the older man said, scooting his chair closer to the coffee table.

Miss Annie's knitting needles were already clicking again when Lucy left the cozy room in Banner's wake.

Lucy had donned her coat and cap, but she still shivered when she stepped outside. She knew the temperature was only in the low thirties, but it felt colder. It was pitch-dark outside without the security lamps, and she had to aim her flashlight carefully to guide her steps.

"You okay?" Banner asked over his shoulder.

"Just lead the way."

It was dark in the workshop, of course, but a little warmer than it was outside, since there was still some heat radiating from the woodstove. Banner turned his flashlight to one side of the door, where he had left the children's gifts. "There they are. You grab one bag, and I'll take the other. I'll come back for whatever is left over."

"This is sort of fun, isn't it? I've never done the Santa Claus thing before."

She didn't know how to interpret the grunt he gave her in reply.

She tried again to draw him into a conversation. "I think everyone had a lovely Christmas Eve. The children seemed happy when they went off to bed."

Banner hefted bags, choosing the lightest one to hand to Lucy. "I think they were kept entertained."

"I was really impressed by the way you recited the poem. I've tried to memorize it a couple of times, but I can never remember all the reindeer names."

"Yeah, well, I can't do card tricks. Or advanced math calculations."

Something in his tone made her frown. Did it bother him that she was a mathematics professor? She had met a few guys who were intimidated by her degree, but she wouldn't have thought Banner was the type. He seemed to have plenty of self-confidence, but she didn't doubt that he was a master at hiding any insecurities he might have.

It seemed the more time she spent with him, the more questions she had about him.

She wished she knew exactly why he had become so reticent. She missed the camaraderie she had shared with him earlier, what little there had been. But he seemed to have started drawing back even before the discussion about careers.

Had her growing attraction to him been so obvious? Was he pulling back because he didn't want to risk sending the wrong signals—didn't want her to think he was interested in her, too?

To be honest, that was exactly what she had started to believe. She thought there had been a spark between them—not necessarily suitable, but genuine. Maybe she had been mistaken. Or maybe she hadn't, and he was simply being sensible in applying the brakes to an attraction that probably wouldn't lead anywhere.

He opened the workshop door again, motioning with his flashlight for her to precede him so he could close the door behind them. "Watch your step."

It wasn't easy manipulating the big bag of gifts and the flashlight. Though she tried to be careful, Lucy found herself slipping once or twice on the path back to the house. Since Banner's hands were also full, there wasn't much he could do to help her, but he stayed close just in case. She was relieved to make it to the porch with both the gifts and herself in one piece. Banner set his load down beside the door, and she placed hers beside it.

He immediately turned to walk back down the steps. "I'll get the rest of the stuff."

Remembering the size of the cradle and the wooden truck and trailer rig, Lucy took a step after him. "I'll help you."

"That's not necessary," he said without looking back.

"No, really." She moved a bit faster, the beam from her flashlight swinging in front of her. "I can carry the cradle for you."

He half turned to face her. "Go back inside where it's warm. I can—"

There must have been an icy patch beneath his foot. Or perhaps it was mud. Whatever, it was slippery—and Banner's foot shot out from beneath him, his arms flailing as he tried to regain his balance.

Lucy threw herself at him, bracing him until he regained his footing. His arm went around her waist, probably an instinctive move.

After a moment Lucy asked, "Are you okay?"

"Yeah. Just slipped."

She noted that he didn't immediately move his arm. Had the temperature risen or was it the fact that she was pressed so snugly against him that made her feel so warm? As if she didn't know. Nor was she in any hurry to move away.

She looked up at him. Their flashlights were pointed downward, so she couldn't really see his face. The moon gave enough illumination to show a gleam in his eyes as he gazed back down at her. And still he didn't move.

"Um, Banner?"

"Yeah?" His voice sounded gruff.

"What are you doing?"

"Just wondering if you really do read minds—or if it was only a card trick," he murmured.

Caught off guard, she asked blankly, "Why?"

"Because if you read minds, you would know that I've been wanting to do this ever since you showed up on my doorstep."

"Do wha—"

His lips were on hers before she could complete the syllable.

The kiss didn't last very long, barely long enough for her to note the details of the way his lips tasted, the way they felt and moved against hers. Yet she knew those details were being filed away inside her mind and that she would replay this kiss countless times in her head. Just as she knew that when the kiss ended, she would no longer be able to pretend that she was only casually interested in Banner.

She could no longer ignore the fact that his name had slipped to the top of her prospect list.

Who was she kidding? His name was the only one on her list now, even if he didn't fit all the criteria she had once believed a man must have to be a suitable match for her.

In just over twenty-four hours, Banner had gone from total stranger to someone she wanted very much to get to know better.

Brief, but powerful—that was the way she would have described the kiss if pressed. Banner lifted his head but didn't immediately step away, his face still close enough to hers that their breath formed a single frosty cloud between them. She cleared her throat.

"No," she said, "I definitely did not know that was on your mind."

"So it was a card trick."

"Yeah. Just a trick."

He dropped his arm and moved away, being very careful with his footing this time. "And that," he said, "was just a kiss."

She frowned. "Which means…?"

"Nothing." He turned toward his workshop. "It meant nothing."

"Banner, wait a minute—"

"I'll get the rest of the gifts. You'd better go back inside before you freeze."

He didn't wait around for whatever she might have said in response.

Banner remembered his earlier suspicions that bad milk was making him behave strangely. Now he figured it had to be something much stronger affecting his behavior. What on earth had possessed him to kiss Lucy Guerin?

Sure, she was pretty, in her elfish sort of way. And, yeah, she had the most kissable lips he had ever encountered. And, okay, he liked being with her, enjoyed her unpredictability. But as for doing anything about any of that…no way.

She was a mathematics professor, for crying out loud. Even if they had anything else in common, that was enough to convince him he should stay well away from her. He could hear his father laugh at the very thought of Banner hooking up with a college professor.

Hell, Banner's father didn't think there was any woman alive who could put up with Banner for very long. "You're just like my uncle Joe," Richard Banner had said on more occasions than Banner could remember. "He never could find anyone willing to take him on, either."

Banner had always wondered if he had married Katrina mostly to prove his father wrong about that. If so, it had been a futile effort. The marriage had been over almost as soon as it had begun.

After that disaster he'd thought maybe his father had been right, after all. Maybe Banner was too much like his reclusive, somewhat eccentric great-uncle.

Joe had never had time for social games and hadn't known how to play them if he had wanted to. Like Banner, Joe had liked other people, but he had never known quite how to behave around them. He had confessed to Banner that he'd always felt as if he was on the outside looking in at other people's interactions. Banner had identified strongly with that sentiment, since it was exactly the way he had always felt in his own family—or rather, families.

He had sure as hell never fit in with extremely extroverted, highly educated, compulsively inquisitive women like Lucy Guerin.

Even if he and Lucy had been getting along surprisingly well so far, they had only spent a day together. He had no doubt that she would get sick of him soon enough. Katrina sure had, and she had professed to love him. Probably the biggest problem between them had been that he simply hadn't been capable of loving her in return.

He should never have kissed Lucy. He certainly didn't want to give her the mistaken impression that he had anything to offer her—even if for some incomprehensible reason she would be interested.

He couldn't say he entirely regretted it, though. Kissing Lucy had most definitely been a memorable experience.

The children were sound asleep when the presents were arranged beneath the tree. Joan was delighted with Banner's handmade toys, assuring him that the children would love them. Bobby Ray and Pop both seemed thoroughly impressed with the truck-and-tractor rig, and Lucy was amused by how long Bobby Ray played with the backhoe.

After seeing the cradle, Miss Annie sent her husband to their borrowed bedroom to fetch her knitting bag. She pulled out a lap-size afghan crafted from a soft, cream-colored yarn and finished with fringed ends. "Put this in the cradle," she ordered. "It's just the right size for Tricia to tuck her dolls into."

"Miss Annie, that's lovely," Joan said, visibly touched. "But I can't—"

"It's not for you, it's for Tricia," the older woman interrupted indulgently. "And don't worry about me not having plenty more. Knitting is about all I can do these days without wearing myself plumb out."

The afghan added the perfect touch to the charming little cradle. The women all admired it while the men continued to study the intricately detailed truck rig. And then Miss Annie reached into her bag again, pulling out a thick, warm gray knit cap. "Do you think Tyler would like this? I make them for my great-grandsons, and I always have a couple of extras around."

"He would love it, if you're sure it's an extra." Joan's voice was thick now, as if she were speaking around a lump in her throat.

Lucy had her own gifts to contribute to the cause. She had brought a shopping bag in from her car a little earlier and had set it in a corner behind the couch. She reached into it now, pulling out a handful of paperback children's books.

"I buy these on sale all year and take them to my cousins' children. I'm known as Aunt Lucy the book lady—I just love books. Please pick a couple you think Tyler and Tricia would like."

"I've got a little something for them, too," Bobby Ray

said, looking thoughtful. "I'll give it to them in the morning."

Joan's eyes were wet now, her voice even thicker. "You're all being so kind."

After sharing a smile with Miss Annie, Lucy replied, "You're giving us a chance to enjoy Christmas through the eyes of children. That always makes the holiday more special."

Joan wiped her eyes with her fingertips. "Thank you. All of you. This could have been a miserable Christmas Eve, stranded away from our families, but it has been lovely."

"Well, I, for one, am ready to call it a day," Miss Annie said, putting her knitting bag aside.

Bobby Ray moved immediately to assist her out of her chair and escort her to the master bedroom, with Pop tagging behind. A chorus of good-nights followed them.

"I think I'll turn in, too," Joan said. "It's been a long day, and I'm sure the kids will be up early in the morning."

Thanking them again, she headed for the guest room where her children were sleeping.

Lucy turned toward Banner, looking at him through her eyelashes, that kiss still haunting her memories. "So..." she began.

He turned away. "I need to let the dog out. C'mon, Hulk."

The agreeable mutt pushed himself upright and strolled out of the room at Banner's heels.

Banner, Lucy decided, was obviously regretting the impulsive kiss. As for herself, she had thought it was pretty spectacular, considering its brevity.

She could only imagine how amazing it would be if he really put some time and effort into it.

"Lucy?" Bobby Ray's voice sounded panicky when he appeared in the living room doorway. "You'd better come quick. Something's wrong with Miss Annie."

Chapter Seven

Lucy rushed toward Bobby Ray. "What do you mean? What's wrong with Miss Annie?"

"I was telling her good night and she just sort of collapsed. I caught her and helped her onto the bed, but it scared the stuffing out of me."

Lucy followed him to the master bedroom, where Miss Annie lay against the pillows of the bed while her husband hovered close by. "Miss Annie? Are you okay? Pop, should we call an ambulance? Surely some sort of emergency vehicle can get to us here, even with all the ice on the roads."

Miss Annie shook her head against the pillows. Her voice was weak, but determined. "That's not necessary, dear. I just had one of my spells."

Not particularly reassured by the comment, Lucy looked at Pop. "She's done this before?"

He looked concerned, but there was no panic in his

grave expression. "Every so often. She takes medication, but sometimes she gets dizzy, anyway. There's really no need to call an ambulance tonight."

Stepping to the side of the bed, Lucy looked down at the older woman. "Is there anything I can get for you, Miss Annie?"

The older woman looked slightly embarrassed at having caused a fuss. "No, thank you. I'll be fine after a good night's sleep."

Looking to Pop for confirmation, Lucy hesitated in indecision about what to do. He nodded to let her know everything would be all right. "We'll both be fine," he said. "Just need some rest. It's been quite a day, hasn't it, Mother?"

"Good night, then," Lucy said a bit uncertainly, still worried about leaving them alone.

Pop escorted her and Bobby Ray to the hallway. "Good night. See you both in the morning."

He closed the door firmly in their faces.

"Well," Bobby Ray said as he and Lucy walked back into the living room, "I guess Pop would be more worried if there was anything seriously wrong."

"I'm sure you're right." Lucy wished she felt more confident about that. Miss Annie had looked so frail and tired lying there against Banner's pillows.

Sensing Lucy's anxiety, Bobby Ray threw a meaty arm around her shoulders and gave her a bracing squeeze that nearly emptied her lungs of air. "Don't you worry, Lucy, we'll take good care of Miss Annie while she's here."

She smiled up at him. "I know. She's become very dear to me in the past few hours."

"She's a dear lady," he agreed. "Funny how we've all gotten to know each other so well in such a short time, isn't it?"

"I would like to think we've become friends," she replied. "And speaking of which…"

Banner's dog nosed between them, as if to participate in a group hug. His shaggy tail thumped roughly against Lucy's hip. She laughed as his cold nose burrowed into the hem of her waist-length sweatshirt, touching the sensitive skin beneath.

Stepping away from Bobby Ray, she pushed against the mutt. "Your nose is freezing, you silly dog, and I'm not letting you warm it against me."

Looking over the dog's head, she spotted Banner standing in the doorway, scowling rather fiercely as he gazed at her and Bobby Ray. "Y'all ready to get some sleep?" he asked, his voice more curt than usual.

"I sure am." Bobby Ray scratched his beard. "I don't usually turn in this early, but we've stayed busy today."

"You'll want to sleep on the couch again, Lucy," Banner said in the same impersonal tone he had used before. "It's too cold in the office."

Not to mention that it was dark and lonely in the office, Lucy added silently. "The couch will be fine, thank you."

Lucy and Banner found themselves alone again one more time that evening. Bobby Ray was in the bathroom, taking a quick shower by candlelight. Lucy had already dressed for bed in a pair of navy knit yoga pants with baby-blue piping down the side and a snug-fitting, long-sleeved baby-blue T-shirt. She wore white socks on her feet to keep them warm. While still modest, this outfit would be much more comfortable than the jeans and sweater she had slept in the night before.

Banner had changed into gray sweatpants and a matching sweatshirt. Like Lucy, he wore white sport socks. His dark hair was tousled, and his jaw was stubbled with dark whiskers that did nothing to detract from his brooding good looks. Quite the opposite, actually.

Lucy studied him in silent appreciation as he knelt in front of the fire, feeding logs into the flames, his endearingly ugly dog at his side. The firelight played across Banner's face, highlighting the planes and shadows of his features. It wasn't difficult for her always-active imagination to picture him sitting there without his shirt, that same firelight playing over tanned skin and rippling muscle. The image was clear enough to almost make her salivate.

"You're looking at me," he said.

Since he hadn't glanced away from the fire, she wasn't sure how he had known, but she said agreeably, "Yes, I am. Does it make you uncomfortable?"

"A little."

"Sorry, but since the television isn't working…"

He didn't smile at her quip. "I've done all the tricks I know. Unless you want to hear 'The Charge of the Light Brigade.'"

"No, that isn't necessary, thank you." His wry comments always amused her, whether he intended them to or not.

"I suppose you could always pull a coin out of my ear."

"I don't do coin tricks. Only card tricks. And, to be honest, I only know the one."

"I see." Poking one last time at the fire, he pulled the screen back into place and brushed off his hands.

"Tricia and Tyler are going to be so excited to see all those gifts under the tree. Are you sure you won't put on a Santa suit?"

"Only if you put on a bikini."

That made her raise her eyebrows. "What?"

"Hey, you have your kinky fantasies, I can have mine."

She was still laughing when Bobby Ray ambled into the room. He looked from Lucy to Banner in surprise. "You in here telling jokes, Banner?"

"Just talking nonsense. Ready for me to put out the lights?"

Lucy lay down on the couch and pulled the blankets to her chin.

"Good night, Banner. Good night, Bobby Ray."

Bobby Ray settled into the recliner with the now-familiar creak of springs. "G'night, Miss Lucy. Don't you be running off with Santa Claus during the night now, y'hear?"

Lucy looked automatically at Banner, who was looking back at her with that not-quite-smile of his. "Good night," he said, then turned off the lantern and blew out the candles.

It occurred to Lucy as she nestled into the blankets that Banner had spread out his sleeping bag close to the foot of the tree, not far from the presents piled there. A good-looking, but probably unattainable, bachelor under the Christmas tree.

She sighed wistfully, thinking that Santa definitely had a warped sense of humor where she was concerned.

Lucy must have been more tired than she had realized. Not even Bobby Ray's snoring disturbed her sleep that night. She didn't awaken until a high-pitched shriek penetrated her slightly salacious dream about Banner in the firelight beneath the Christmas tree—without the sweat suit.

Jerking upright, she blinked and pushed a tangle of red curls out of her eyes. Her heart was racing, but she wasn't sure if that was due to her abrupt awakening or the after-effects of her dream.

Illuminated by the firelight and the early sunlight streaming through the living room windows, Tricia stood in the doorway, staring at the presents piled beneath the Christmas tree. "He was here," the little girl said in stunned disbelief. "Santa Claus found us."

Bobby Ray made a production of knuckling his eyes and staring at the tree. "Well, I'll be. Where did all them gifts come from?"

"Santa Claus brought them," Tricia said, hopping up and down. "He found us! Tyler, come look! Santa found us!"

Her brother and mother, both still groggy from sleep, appeared in the doorway behind her, Joan looking apologetically at Lucy, Bobby Ray and Banner for waking them so early.

Banner had climbed out of his sleeping bag and was moving it out of the way to clear a path for Tricia and Tyler to reach their gifts. Lucy couldn't even look at him without blushing as she remembered that dream.

"Sweet," Tyler breathed, moving slowly toward the piles of packages. "Presents. Are they really for us?"

"Looks like it," Bobby Ray said, lowering the footrest on the recliner and tossing his blanket aside. "Don't just stand there, kiddos. Dive in."

"Wait a second. Don't touch a thing." Joan disappeared back into the bedroom, then returned carrying a small camera. "Okay, now we're ready."

Tricia dropped to her knees in front of the pile of wrapped presents. "These have my name on them. See, it says 'To Tricia, from Santa Claus,'" she read, pointing out the words with pride.

''These are mine.'' Tyler gazed at his gifts almost as if he was afraid they would disappear if he looked away.

Joan sat cross-legged on the floor with her camera. Roused by the noise, Miss Annie and Pop entered the room, looking eager to watch the children open their presents. Bobby Ray jumped up immediately to assist the older couple, who greeted everyone with a warm ''Merry Christmas.''

Lucy was relieved that Miss Annie seemed much stronger this morning. Pop and Bobby Ray escorted her to the rocker, tucked a blanket around her, set her walker within easy reach, then settled down to observe the festivities.

Banner had left the room after stowing his sleeping bag. The scent of perking coffee drifted from the kitchen, explaining his absence. Lucy thought of going in to help him, but she was reluctant to leave the room yet. She simply loved watching children on Christmas morning.

She couldn't wait until she had children of her own with whom to share such special occasions.

Finally given the signal by their mother, Tyler and Tricia tore into their presents. They oohed and aahed over video games and dolls, die-cast cars and board games, a football for Tyler and a soccer ball for Tricia. Every time they opened a gift, they turned to display it for their smiling audience, who all made appreciative noises over each item.

Lucy noted with interest that Joan hadn't spent a great deal of money, but had provided a nice variety of toys designed to last awhile. Tyler seemed particularly pleased with his football and a kid-size helmet painted to resemble the ones for the St. Louis Rams. Tricia had obviously fallen instantly in love with a life-size newborn-baby doll that came with several adorable outfits.

The doll was the perfect size for the cradle Banner had made, which, along with the tractor rig, was waiting at the back of the tree, not yet noticed by the children. Lucy couldn't wait until they saw them, but she hoped Banner would return in time to watch.

Banner came back into the room then, carrying a tray crowded with mugs of coffee for the adults and glasses of orange juice for the kids. He set the tray on the coffee table and distributed the mugs. Lucy was impressed when she realized that he had remembered everyone's preference as far as cream and sugar and had prepared each serving accordingly.

Banner might claim to be a surly recluse, but Lucy didn't completely believe him. He had been an ideal host to this group of stranded former strangers. Whether he believed it or not, he had a great deal to offer others—if he chose to make the effort.

He handed her a mug of extralight coffee, no sugar. Just the way she liked it.

"Thank you," she said, then patted the couch beside her. "Have a seat."

Hesitating only a moment, he settled on the couch, almost as far as he could get without falling off the other end.

"I really don't bite," she murmured, just loud enough for him to hear her. And then she couldn't resist adding wickedly, "Not in public, anyway."

He gave her a look over his mug. "Drink your coffee."

Chuckling, she turned to watch the children again.

"Look at what we got, Banner," Tricia urged, holding up her doll. "Santa brought us a whole bunch of stuff."

"I'd say so," he replied. "You both must have been very good this year."

"Well...mostly good," Tricia said with a quick glance

at her mother. And then she prudently changed the subject. "Didn't *any* of you see Santa when he brought these presents in last night? You were all sleeping right here."

Bobby Ray had excused himself from the room for a few minutes, so the question was addressed to Lucy and Banner. They swapped a brief look, and Banner's expression was amusingly baffled. Lucy got the impression that "let's pretend" was not a game he felt comfortable playing.

She answered for them both. "I don't know about the guys, but I was so tired I didn't hear a thing last night. I'm sure both Santa and the Easter Bunny could have come into the living room and danced a polka across the floor and I never would have stirred."

Tricia laughed. "The Easter Bunny doesn't come at Christmas. He only comes at Easter."

"Lucy knows that," Tyler said, rolling his eyes. "She was just making a joke, weren't you, Lucy?"

Lucy nodded gravely. "Yes. I was making a joke."

"I wonder why Hulk didn't bark when Santa came in?" Tricia mused, still preoccupied with the logistics of Santa's visit.

"Hulk's not much of a guard dog," Banner explained with a resigned shrug. "He tends to accept all newcomers with a yawn and a wag of his tail. I guess Santa and the Easter Bunny could have stolen all the silver and Hulk would have opened the door for them to carry it out."

As if he knew he was the topic of conversation, the dog made a snuffly sound and laid his head on Banner's knee. Everyone laughed, both at the dog's actions and Banner's attempt at embroidering on Lucy's imagery.

Bobby Ray came back into the room then, and from the ruddy flush on his face it was obvious that he had been outside. Lucy remembered his comment that he had something in his truck for the children, and she assumed he had been out to get it. He had one hand behind his back, so she couldn't see what he was holding.

"It's already warming up out there," he announced. "Bet those roads are clear by noon."

"That's good news," Joan said, and then turned back to the tree. "Kids, you have a few more gifts back here."

"More?" Tricia perked up in interest. "Santa left us more presents?"

"These aren't from Santa." Her mother pulled out the cradle and tractor rig. "Tricia, Banner made this beautiful cradle, and Miss Annie knit the pretty blanket inside it. And Tyler, Banner made this truck and trailor and the backhoe on it, and Miss Annie made this nice warm cap that is just your size. Wasn't it nice of them to give you these lovely things?"

Tyler pounced on the large wooden rig, his eyes huge and excited. "Oh, wow. This is so sweet," he said, using his favorite adjective. "It looks just like those big machines that have been building the new gas station down our street. You made this, Banner? Really? What does this scooper thing do? Why's it got bucket things on both ends?"

Banner set his mug on the coffee table and moved to kneel beside the boy. "This is a backhoe. It digs, or trenches, with this end. And this other end is a front-end loader that can be used for moving or scraping dirt. See, you use these levers to raise and lower the…"

Ignoring the guys, Tricia had already put her doll to bed in the cradle and was rocking it gently. "She's sleepy," she told her mother. And then she smiled sweetly at the others. "I'm going to name my doll Annie Lucy. Is that okay?"

Both Lucy and Miss Annie solemnly agreed that they were honored to have such an adorable namesake.

When the children had finished admiring those gifts and had politely thanked Banner and Miss Annie, Joan pulled out the books Lucy had contributed. At Lucy's urging, Joan had selected two books for each child, and they seemed very pleased with her choices. They thanked Lucy without being prompted, so sweetly that she was touched—and very glad she'd had the bag of books in her car.

"I've got something for you, too, kiddos," Bobby Ray said. He brought his left hand around from behind him to display two brightly colored and beribboned boxes of Christmas chocolates. "Your mom said it was okay for you to have these."

"Oh, wow. Candy." Brown eyes gleaming, Tricia licked her lips in anticipation. "Thank you, Bobby Ray. Can we have some now, Mama?"

"Not for breakfast," she replied, smiling as she shook her head. "You can have some later."

"Speaking of breakfast…" Banner rose, leaving Tyler to play with the truck rig on his own. "I'll go get something started. No, stay with your kids," he added when Joan automatically moved to help. "I can handle it."

Lucy sprang to her feet. "I'll help."

"That's not—" Banner abandoned the argument when he saw her expression. Probably because he didn't want to lose an argument in front of the others, Lucy decided. And he *would* have lost.

Bobby Ray was on the floor playing with Tricia and Tyler and their toys when Lucy followed Banner into the kitchen. "That was fun, wasn't it?" she asked as they headed for the pantry.

Banner shrugged a little, keeping any emotion out of

his voice when he replied, "The kids seemed to enjoy it."

She refused to be discouraged by his lack of enthusiasm. "It really made my Christmas. I loved the look on Tricia's face when she saw the presents under the tree. She was so surprised. And so thrilled."

"I could have done without the shriek. I nearly jumped right out of my skin."

Lucy laughed. "She was excited."

"No kidding. D'you think she would be as excited by instant oatmeal made with boiling water? Because that's about all I've got left for breakfast."

"I don't know if you'll get a shriek, but I'm sure she'll eat whatever we prepare. Neither Tyler nor Tricia seem to be picky eaters."

"If there's anyone who doesn't like oatmeal, I've got some canned fruit in the pantry. Maybe they would rather have that."

"Anything will be fine, Banner. I'm sorry we've emptied your food supplies."

He shrugged. "That's due more to the power outage. I have plenty of canned goods, but the perishables are running low."

"The kids love the toys you made," she said as she began to take bowls out of the cabinet. "They'll treasure them for years, maybe pass them down to their own children."

"I'm glad they like them. I didn't really have anything else to do with the things."

She looked at him from beneath her lashes as he started the water to boil and set boxes of instant oatmeal on the counter. "Do you ever picture yourself making toys like that for your own children at Christmas?"

"I don't have any children."

"I didn't mean now. I mean in the future."

His characteristic shrug told her nothing about his feelings. "Don't expect to have any. Why don't you get out a couple of cans of fruit?"

She moved slowly to the pantry. "You don't want children?"

"Not particularly."

"I'd like to have at least two."

"Figures."

"What does that mean?" she asked, setting the cans of fruit beside the oatmeal packages.

"Just that it didn't surprise me. Hand me that roll of paper towels, will you?"

"Why doesn't it surprise you that I want children?" And why *would* it surprise him? Certainly not every woman wanted children, but almost all of Lucy's friends and acquaintances planned to start families at some point in their lives.

"It just confirms my belief that you and I couldn't be more different. The can opener's in the drawer left of the sink."

It occurred to her then that Banner was sending her a not-so-well-buried message within the casual conversation. If he had known about her prospect list, he would be telling her flat-out that he didn't belong on it.

As if she hadn't already figured that out. And as if she hadn't already put him on the list, anyway.

Banner might have written off any chance that there could be more than a passing acquaintance between them, but Lucy wasn't so sure.

It looked as though it was going to be up to her to take the initiative. Because she seemed to have missed inheriting the shy gene altogether—at least when it came to something that was of particular importance to her—she moved a step closer to him, rested a hand lightly on his chest and smiled up at him through her lashes. "There's one holiday tradition we've forgotten."

He immediately looked suspicious. "What?"

"The mistletoe."

"We don't have any—"

"Pretend we do," she advised him just before rising on her tiptoes to place a kiss on his lips.

He didn't respond at all at first, and she wondered if she had made a miscalculation. And then his arms went around her and she found herself pressed against the counter as he kissed her with a barely contained heat that almost singed her eyelashes. Even as she was a bit startled by the emotions she had unleashed, she was gratified to confirm that Banner wasn't nearly as disinterested as he had tried to act.

His lips were hard and hungry against hers, moving with a rough skill that drew an equally powerful response from her. She felt her heart pounding against her chest, and she was pressed so tightly against him that he could probably feel it, too.

She could certainly feel the signs of his arousal, which only made her heart slam harder against her rib cage.

A burst of laughter from the other room intruded on the moment, catching Banner's attention and causing him to lift his head. Without releasing Lucy, he closed his eyes in an expression of self-recrimination. "Damn it."

Hardly the most romantic conclusion to a spectacular embrace, Lucy thought with a soft sigh. But from Banner, maybe it was more revealing than any other man's flowery compliments.

"I thought it was a great kiss, too," she murmured with a shaky smile.

He hesitated a moment, studying her face intently, and

then he stepped back. "The water's boiling," he said. "We should call everyone in for breakfast."

He was right, of course. There were still too many other people around. There would be time for Lucy and Banner to explore their attraction later, after the others had gone.

Proving that she could be patient when the incentive was important enough, Lucy decided to enjoy every moment of this unexpectedly magical Christmas morning.

Chapter Eight

Temperatures warmed rapidly during the morning, and by lunchtime the ice was all but gone except for in the most deeply shaded areas. Traffic was beginning to move on the highway again, the number and speed of passing vehicles increasing as Christmas day progressed and the roads dried.

Banner raided his kitchen one last time for lunch, opening cans of soup, which he served with crackers and cheese and the canned fruit that had been left over from breakfast. Lucy noted that the entire group was a bit more subdued than they had been before, perhaps because they knew their time together was coming to an end.

Everyone seemed ready to proceed to their original destinations, she decided, but they had enjoyed being here more than they had expected. She was pleased to know they would all have some pleasant memories of this Christmas morning to carry with them.

Tyler and Tricia pretty much dominated the lunchtime conversation, talking about the gifts Santa had brought them and anticipating the ones they would be getting at their grandmother's house. Tyler was expecting a highly touted new game for the video game system he had received for his birthday in September. Though his mother warned him about not being too confident of what his grandmother had gotten him, something about her tone let Lucy know the boy wouldn't be disappointed.

Lucy couldn't help noticing that Joan and Bobby Ray were doing quite a bit of quiet talking at the other side of the table. She overheard Bobby Ray say something about giving Joan a call after the first of the year. Lucy hoped that meant Bobby Ray was planning to ask Joan out and that he had not been referring to something less promising.

The more Lucy had thought about it, the more she believed that Bobby Ray and Joan made a great couple.

She smiled as she visualized Banner and Bobby Ray sitting beneath the Christmas tree, a big shiny bow on each manly head. Maybe Santa had arranged a pleasant little surprise for both Lucy *and* Joan.

"What does that smile mean?" Banner leaned over to ask her, studying her expression with a curious frown. "It looks sort of…wicked."

She laughed. It was a good thing he couldn't read her mind. If he knew what she had been thinking, or how prominently he had appeared in last night's dreams, he really would think she was wicked.

"I don't think I should say just now," she told him, which only made him look more suspicious.

Joan and Lucy insisted on cleaning up after lunch since Banner had done so much for them already. They had barely finished clearing the kitchen when someone knocked heavily on the front door. The promised wrecker had arrived to pull Bobby Ray's truck out of the ditch and get him back on the road for his impatient employer.

It didn't take all that long to get the mostly undamaged truck out of the shallow ditch. Barely half an hour after the wrecker arrived, Bobby Ray was ready to go.

He drew Lucy aside. "Banner won't take this from me, but I want you to make sure he gets it before you leave— even if you have to slip it into his cookie jar," he said in a low voice as he pressed a hundred-dollar bill into her hand. "I tried to tell him I wanted to repay him for his food and hospitality, but he kept telling me to forget about it."

"I'll make sure he gets it," she promised with a smile, "and I'll be adding a bit to it. We pretty well cleaned out his supplies."

"Yeah. We were all lucky that he took us in."

"Most definitely. So, you're on your way?"

"Looks like. They've got the truck ready to go, so there's really no reason for me to hang around any longer."

She squeezed his hand. "It was very nice to meet you, Bobby Ray. I enjoyed spending Christmas Eve with you."

"Same here, Miss Lucy." He leaned way down to plant a smacking kiss on her cheek. "Maybe we'll see each other again sometime."

"Maybe we will. And, um, maybe you'll be seeing Joan again?" she asked in a broad hint she simply couldn't resist.

He chuckled, catching her meaning. "If it's up to me, I will. What do you think?"

"I think you should definitely call her."

"Guess I should listen to the doctor," he said with a grin. "You've had some pretty good ideas so far."

Lucy watched Bobby Ray take a warm leave of Miss Annie and Pop, and then he said his goodbyes to Tyler and Tricia. It was so obvious to her that he had already grown fond of the children. Joan needn't worry about her kids being a barrier to a possible relationship with this big, kind-hearted man.

Way to go, Santa, Lucy thought with a mental thumbs-up. Now, if only he had come through as well for her....

It seemed much quieter in the house without Bobby Ray's deep voice and booming laughter. Joan was particularly preoccupied after his departure, obviously distracted by her own thoughts. Less than an hour after he left, at just before two that afternoon, she deemed the roads clear enough for her to continue her journey to her mother's house.

"You be very careful," Lucy cautioned her. "And have a wonderful Christmas with your family."

"I will. Thank you." Joan gave her an impulsive hug. "We're going to get together for lunch in Conway soon?"

"Definitely. I'll look forward to hearing from you."

Lucy felt a tug at the bottom of her sweater. "Merry Christmas, Miss Lucy," Tricia said, copying Bobby Ray's nickname for her. The little girl was already swaddled in her coat, hat and scarf, and had her new doll tucked protectively into the curve of her left arm. "Thank you for the books. I like them a lot."

Reaching down to hug the child, Lucy replied, "You're very welcome, Tricia. I hope you enjoy them."

"Thank you for my books, too," Tyler said after a subtle nudge from his mother.

Lucy knew better than to embarrass him with a hug, but she gave him a warm smile instead. "You're welcome, too, Tyler. I hope you have a wonderful Christmas with your grandmother."

The children then thanked Banner again for the wooden toys and Miss Annie for the knitted gifts. They hugged Pop when he held out his arms to them—Tyler with a macho show of reluctance that he didn't really seem to mean—and both told Pop how much they had enjoyed singing Christmas carols with him.

Tyler took his fondest farewell of Banner's dog—the only one the boy really seemed to have trouble leaving, Lucy thought in amusement. Going down onto one knee, Tyler hugged the shaggy dog with an affection he hadn't allowed himself to show the others.

"'Bye, Hulk," Tyler said. "You be a good boy, okay?"

The dog woofed softly and wagged its tail lazily in farewell.

Joan paused shyly in front of Banner. "I don't know how to thank you for all you've done," she said. "You've been so kind. Are you sure you won't let me repay you at least for…"

He cut in before she could say any more, his voice gruff, his expression embarrassed. "That's not necessary. I enjoyed having company for Christmas. As for the food, it would all have spoiled, anyway, with the power out. I'm glad it went to good use."

Joan held out her hand to him, obviously accepting that his male pride would not allow him to take money from a single mother. "Then I'll simply say thank you, and merry Christmas."

He shook her hand. "Merry Christmas to you, too. Drive carefully."

Lucy sighed a little in response to the awkward kindness in Banner's voice as he spoke to Joan. He was so darned appealing.

Almost as if on cue, the Carters' grandsons arrived just

as Joan backed her car carefully out of Banner's driveway. Two handsome, strapping young men who obviously adored their grandparents thanked Banner effusively for offering safe shelter to the stranded couple. They, too, offered reimbursement, but once again Banner refused to even consider accepting.

Lucy made a mental note to make sure he didn't have a chance to refuse the money from herself and Bobby Ray. She would leave it somewhere where he would find it after she was gone. He would be annoyed, but he would realize that he would have done the same had the situation been reversed.

Both Pop and Miss Annie kissed Lucy's cheeks as affectionately as if they had known her for ages rather than hours. And then Miss Annie pulled Banner down to her so she could kiss him, too.

Lucy was delighted when Banner blushed as vividly as a schoolboy.

Pop lingered behind after his grandsons escorted Miss Annie out to the car. His expression was somber when he turned to Banner and Lucy.

"My wife isn't well," he said, his voice quiet. "This is likely to be her last Christmas on this earth. She wanted to spend it with people she cared about."

Banner looked almost stricken and at a loss, as Lucy was, about what to say in response to Pop's poignant words. "I'm sorry your plans didn't work out," he said finally.

Pop smiled then. Gently. Sweetly. "You don't understand. I'm trying to thank you for making her wish come true. Everyone was so kind to her—especially the two of you. You went out of your way to make sure it was a pleasant holiday rather than an unfortunate string of circumstances, and I appreciate your efforts more than you'll ever know."

Now Lucy was blushing. "It wasn't just us," she said, knowing she spoke for Banner, too. "Bobby Ray and Joan—"

"Yes, I know everyone pitched in to make it nice," Pop cut in indulgently. "And I thanked them as they left. Now I must be going. Mother and I have another Christmas celebration waiting for us with even more people that we care about."

There was an enormous lump in Lucy's throat as she watched the old man shuffle outside, where he was joined hastily by one of his grandsons. She watched until the two vehicles left the driveway, leaving her little car sitting there looking a bit lonely.

She would miss them all, she mused. As much as she looked forward to seeing her own relatives, she felt almost as though she had adopted a second family during the past couple of days.

Even knowing that they had shared the superficial camaraderie of enforced circumstances, she thought the warmth between them had been sincere. She had genuinely liked each one of her fellow travelers, and she hoped to see them all again. She thought she had made a new friend in Joan, and she always welcomed new friends.

As for Banner...

She turned to face him, suddenly, intensely aware that they were now alone in his house. She was free to leave at any time—but she didn't want to go just yet. She only wished she knew how Banner felt about her.

Banner didn't want Lucy to go. Even though he knew it was time for her to move on, time for her to return to a life that didn't include him, he dreaded the thought of saying goodbye to her. The requisite niceties, the patently false assurances that they would see each other again sometime, the polite offer and rejection of compensation, the expressions of gratitude he didn't want.

It had been bad enough from the others, but that wasn't at all the way he wanted to part from Lucy.

Problem was, he didn't want to part from Lucy at all. At least, not yet, he corrected himself.

But because he saw no point in delaying the inevitable, he drew a deep breath and turned to her. "Thanks for helping me see everyone off. I know you're eager to join your father and your other family members."

"Yes. But there's no reason for me to rush away. It's just a little more than a two-hour drive from here, and it's not even three o'clock yet."

Was she telling him she was in no hurry to leave? Remembering the way she had kissed him in the kitchen earlier, he wondered again if she was seeing something in him that wasn't really there, if she was perhaps mistaking simple—if powerful—physical attraction for something more lasting.

He cleared his throat. "It'll be nice to have my house to myself again. I'm not used to having a lot of people around. I get a lot more done when Hulk and I have the place to ourselves."

Amusement warmed her pretty face and gleamed in her emerald eyes, as if she were savoring a joke she wasn't ready to share with him. "I'm sure Hulk is excellent company."

"Ideal company," he replied, studying her smile with some suspicion. "He doesn't expect me to entertain him or cater to him. He isn't offended when I spend all day in my workshop or if I'm not in the mood to talk or play. It doesn't bother him that I don't know when his birthday is and he has no interest in mine. He's happy with a simple life—plain food, a warm bed, an occasional tummy rub. He's never asked for more from me than I was willing—or able—to give.''

"That's quite an endorsement, Hulk," she murmured, patting the dog's shaggy head. "You should be very proud. What breed is he, by the way?"

Realizing that she was talking to him again, Banner cleared his throat. "Beats the hell out of me. I found him on my doorstep when he was a pup about three years ago. I figured he was so ugly someone just dumped him.''

"And because you identified with him, you took him in and made him your friend," Lucy murmured. And then she laughed at his expression.

"I don't mean you identified with the ugly part," she assured him. "You've got enough mirrors around here to know you're just the opposite of ugly. But perhaps there were other things about him that reminded you of yourself.''

How had she possibly known how strongly he had been drawn to the gawky, oddball, unwanted stray pup he'd found huddling defensively in his yard? And when she had said he was the opposite of ugly, did that mean she found him...?

Shaking his head impatiently, he half turned away. "I'm sure you're eager to get on the road."

"You seem awfully anxious for me to leave." She reached out to rest a hand on his forearm. "Maybe I was mistaken, but I thought we had a few things to say to each other before I go."

His first instinct was to move away from her, but her touch felt too good to shake off so easily. Instead he resorted to cynicism. "The professor and the woodworker? I can't imagine we'd have much to say to each other.''

He'd expected either hurt or anger in response to his dismissive tone. He wasn't prepared for her laughter. The low, husky sound of it went straight to his loins, even as it baffled him. What the hell was so funny?

Her hand slid slowly up his arm to his shoulder, and his imagination kicked into overdrive, so that he could almost feel little pops of electricity everywhere she touched him. "I think we can find something to talk about," she murmured, looking up at him through her wickedly long lashes.

He swallowed heavily. "You, uh, should realize that we didn't meet under normal circumstances. The holiday mood probably influenced you, and I've made an effort to be...well, more charming than usual. I'm not really like—damn it, would you stop laughing at me?"

"I can't help it." Her smile was nearly blinding, her eyes glittering with firelight and appreciation. "You're just so sweet when you're all panicky and noble."

Sweet, panicky, noble. Not one of those adjectives pleased him. "I am not panicky," he informed her, choosing the one that bothered him most. "I'm trying to keep you from doing something you'll regret."

"I'll worry about my regrets. Do you want me to leave now, Banner? Because if you do, I certainly don't want to overstay my welcome."

"No." He had answered without having to think about it. "But—"

Lucy moved a little closer to him. "You know that make-believe mistletoe in the kitchen?"

"Yeah?"

"It just moved into this room," she said as she rose onto her tiptoes.

Oh, hell. Who was he to resist mistletoe—even the make-believe kind?

He dragged her against him and closed his mouth over hers, tasting the smile that had been taunting and tempting him.

Had her mouth not been otherwise occupied, Lucy might have been tempted to sigh with relief. She had been so sure that Banner didn't really want to send her away, but she knew the mutual attraction that had developed so quickly between them made him very nervous.

She couldn't blame him; she'd felt the same way initially. But then, Lucy had always been the type to make up her mind quickly. Banner, apparently, took a bit more persuasion.

And this kiss, she thought, sliding her hands up to lock behind his neck, was a heck of an argument in her favor.

His arms were around her now, and the strength she felt in those woodworker's muscles thrilled her. It would take no effort at all for him to literally sweep her off her feet. He'd already done so figuratively, and as far as she could tell, he had made no effort at all.

He lifted his head just far enough to break the kiss, though he didn't drop his arms. ''Why aren't you on your way to Springfield?''

Her hands still clasped behind his neck, she allowed her fingertips to play with the back of his hair. It was lushly thick and surprisingly soft and she would have liked to dive into it with both hands—but that could wait. ''I will be. Eventually. But I'm not quite ready to go yet.''

''If you're staying because of me…''

''Well, I'm not staying to spend more time with your dog—no offense, Hulk.''

The dog snuffled a lazy acknowledgment, making her smile before she turned her attention back to Banner.

He was frowning at her, though she noted that he still

held her quite closely. "You should think about what I said—about how the last few hours haven't exactly been normal circumstances."

"Yes, I know. You're worried that I've been so dazzled by your suave charms that I've succumbed to a fleeting infatuation."

He had the grace to color a bit in response to her wry comments about his awkward insinuations. "Okay, I'm aware that I'm not exactly the social type, but I did make more of an effort than usual these past couple of days."

"Why?"

Her simple question seemed to confuse him. "Why? I don't know. Because it's Christmas, I guess. The kids...and Miss Annie...it just seemed like the thing to do."

"You were extremely kind to the children and Miss Annie. And to the rest of us, for that matter. Sharing your home and your hospitality, giving up your bed and letting us decorate your living room...you turned a terribly timed ice storm into a pleasant holiday interlude."

Frowning fiercely, he shook his head, finally letting his arms drop from around her. He took a step backward, moving away from her touch as he spoke flatly. "That's exactly what I mean. I didn't really do anything except open the door. You were the one who came up with the ideas to entertain the kids and keep everyone else busy and content. I'm not a particularly kind person. In fact, I've been accused of being rude and boring and antisocial."

Now she was the one who frowned, hearing undertones of old pain in his voice. "Who would say such things about you?"

"My family," he said with a grim shrug. "And my ex-wife had a few extra adjectives to apply to me, but none I'm comfortable repeating in mixed company."

Ex-wife. That revelation made her blink a couple of times, but it was the mention of his family that twisted her heart. He tried so hard to pretend it was his own choice to distance himself from his parents and half siblings, but she suspected the distance hurt him—maybe because no one else ever bothered to try to bridge it.

"Has it occurred to you that maybe I see you more clearly than you think I do?" she asked him gently.

That possibility seemed to scare him worse than his theory that she was overromanticizing him. "I, uh—"

He didn't seem to know what else to say.

Banner had been kicked around so much he'd learned to expect nothing better, Lucy decided. His ex-wife had obviously been all wrong for him. Maybe it was his experience with her that made him worry that Lucy was trying to turn him into something he couldn't and didn't want to be.

He had lost confidence in his ability to form relationships with other people—and it was going to take patience and understanding on Lucy's part to convince him there was a chance that something special had developed between them during the past two days. Something that might last a lifetime, if they gave it a chance.

Just as Lucy didn't take long to make up her mind about someone, she saw no need to waste time once she had. "I'd like a chance to get to know the real you, Banner, if you're interested in getting to know the real me. Because, you see, I've been using 'company manners' myself the past couple of days. I'm not really perky and cheerful all the time. Sometimes I'm downright surly."

That brought a reluctant smile to his lips. "I find that hard to believe."

"Trust me. Or better yet, ask some of my students. They'll tell you that I can be a pain when I'm in a rotten mood."

His smile died. "Since the chances are slim that I'll meet any of your higher math students, I doubt that opportunity will ever arise."

It still seemed to bother him that she was a math professor. Though she didn't quite understand that little hang-up, she figured she would find out the reason eventually. She would deal with it then. If he let her get that far.

She thought she had made it clear enough that she would like to stay a while longer. She had done everything short of tackling him, actually—and she wasn't entirely opposed to that measure, if necessary.

If Lucy had been the shy type who wasn't willing to go after what she wanted, she wouldn't have gotten as far as she had in her career this soon. But she would give him a little more time to make a move toward her first, she thought with a secret smile.

She didn't consider that she was being arrogant. Their last kiss had left little doubt that Banner wanted her.

There was an honesty in his kisses that reflected the innate frankness of the man himself. He wasn't a game player, and he had no patience for the type of insincere flattery other men might use for seduction. He was simply Banner, and to Lucy that fact alone was more captivating than any other man's flowery words had ever been.

This was certainly the first time she had thought about a lasting relationship within forty-eight hours of meeting anyone.

Yet there was still that battle-scarred skittishness to contend with. "Why don't you offer me a cup of tea?" she suggested casually.

The abrupt change of subject seemed to take him aback. "Um, you want some tea?"

"Thank you, I would love some," she said promptly, as if he were offering rather than merely parroting. More than the tea, she wanted him to relax and stop worrying about what she might expect from him.

At the moment, she wanted nothing more than she had said—a chance to get to know him better. And the best way to get started seemed to be over tea and conversation.

If that didn't work, well, there was always the option of pouncing on him.

The kitchen table seemed bigger somehow with only Banner and Lucy sitting at it. The room itself was notably quiet without the chatter of the departed guests.

Banner was intensely aware of the silence, and self-conscious about his ability to fill it with anything interesting. His ex-wife had expressed her doubts that he would ever develop conversational skills. She had told him once that talking to him had been like trying to carry on a conversation with a block of the wood he worked with.

That had been toward the end of their brief marriage, when she had criticized everything about him, from his lack of ambition to his disinterest in social activities to his thoughtlessness about her happiness. She had taken off not long afterward, and last he'd heard she'd found herself a dirt-track race car driver who liked to party when he wasn't risking his neck at more than a hundred miles an hour. In other words, she had chosen someone who was exactly Banner's opposite—the opposite of the settled, dependable security she had once claimed to want. From all accounts she was much happier now, and so was he, for that matter.

He didn't want to make any more stupid mistakes that would result in anyone else being hurt—himself included.

Lucy seemed perfectly content to sip her tea and wait for him to speak when he was ready, which surprised him since she had claimed a tendency to babble when she was nervous. He supposed she wasn't nervous now, which made him wonder why *he* was.

He racked his brain for something to say. "So, um, how's your tea?"

She smiled over her cup. "It's delicious, thank you."

His gaze lingered on her moist, up-curved mouth. And his mind went blank again. Every time Lucy smiled at him, every time she licked a drop of tea from her lips or tossed back her cascade of soft red-gold curls, he went completely tongue-tied.

It was a condition that was familiar to him, since he had never been comfortable making small talk—which made him one lousy date, as he had been informed on a few memorable occasions. But it was even worse with Lucy, because with her—as with no one before her—he actually wanted to be witty and charming and interesting. It was precisely because he couldn't be any of those things that he should be urging her to leave, to join the family that was waiting so impatiently to spend the rest of this Christmas day with her.

He was generally a selfish person, but not even he could feel right about keeping her from that loving family when he couldn't even seem to carry on a conversation with her.

Seeming to sense that he was at a conversational loss, Lucy spoke up. He should have expected her to say something completely unexpected, and she did. "Let's play a game."

"A game?" he repeated somewhat blankly. "Like what?"

"Twenty questions. Only I'm making a few new rules."

He felt decidedly wary when he asked, "What new rules?"

"I can ask twenty questions about you, and you can ask twenty questions about me. And no matter what you're asked, you have to answer honestly."

"And the point of this would be...?"

"It's a very efficient way of getting to know each other. That's one of our goals, isn't it? Exploring the attraction between us? Assessing the potential for more?"

She made it sound as logical and prosaic as if they were considering a financial investment. Must be the math professor in her. Not that he wanted her to start waxing poetic on him, of course. He had already decided that he should be convincing her how incompatible they would be in a long-term relationship—his fault, of course, since there was certainly nothing lacking in Lucy.

Maybe a few blunt answers to her questions would make the futility of any romantic expectations clear to her. Labeling it a game seemed an odd way to determine their fate, but he had learned not to be overly surprised by anything Lucy suggested.

Chapter Nine

"What question do you want to ask me?" Banner said, injecting just enough resignation in his tone to let Lucy know what he really thought about this exercise—which should be her first clue to their incompatibility, he mused.

His reluctance to participate didn't seem to bother her in the least. She reached for one of the cookies he had set out to accompany their tea when she replied. "Question one. Hmm. What's your birthday?"

Hardly a question of deep importance, he thought, which meant he could answer without weighing his words, "April 3. I'll be thirty-one."

"That's two answers for one question," she observed cheerily. "I should get extra points."

"I didn't know we were awarding points."

"I'll fill you in on that part later. Your turn to ask a question."

The woman wasn't quite normal, which, Banner had to

admit, if only to himself, was one of her charms. "I can't think of anything to ask. You go ahead."

She sighed heavily. "Banner, you have to play the game correctly. Surely you can think of something to ask me."

He shrugged. "Okay. What's your birthday?"

"July 25. I'm a Leo. Since you're an Aries, that makes us a very interesting combination."

He cleared his throat, feeling the need to derail that train of thought before it got a good start. "Yeah, whatever. I've never been particularly interested in astrology. You don't really believe in that stuff, do you?"

"No cheating, dude. It's my turn to ask a question."

He couldn't help chuckling at her wording. "So it is."

She lowered her teacup and picked up her half-eaten cookie. "I like it when you laugh. You don't do it often enough."

"That wasn't a question, it was an observation. Doesn't count." But he liked that she liked it when he laughed. Which only demonstrated how much she messed with his mind, he thought in exasperation.

She seemed delighted that he was participating in her game, however reluctantly. "Okay, question two. What's your favorite color?"

He didn't know how she figured she was going to get to know him with such superficial questions—nor did he know how he was going to convince her of how different they were if all she asked were trivialities—but he gave her an answer, anyway. "Blue, I guess."

"Most men say blue. Did you know that?"

"Is that another question?"

"No, just an observation." She swallowed the last of her cookie and reached for another. "What's your next question?"

"I don't know—what's your favorite color?"

She frowned at him. "You aren't giving this enough thought. You're simply asking the same questions I am."

"So maybe I really want to know your favorite color. What is it?"

"You know that pinky-purple color that a clear blue sky turns to just before sunset? That's my favorite color."

Of course it was. He certainly shouldn't have expected her to give a simple, predictable answer like red or green or yellow.

She propped her elbows on the table and studied him. "What sort of music do you like?"

Question three, he thought. Only seventeen more to go. "Alan Jackson's in my CD player right now. Last week I was in the mood for Celtic tunes."

"Ah. An eclectic listener. So am I—though I suppose I listen to classical recordings more than anything else."

That was no surprise to him, either. Hadn't he read somewhere that there was a strong connection between mathematics and Mozart? "I didn't ask you what sort of music you liked."

She chuckled. "Consider that a freebie. You still have eighteen questions."

Oddly enough, he felt much more relaxed now than he had earlier. Had that been her intention with the whimsical game? He decided it probably had been her plan, since her questions weren't exactly thought provoking.

He tried to think of another question for her. There were a few things he wouldn't mind knowing about her, but most of them seemed too personal to ask. So he asked, instead, "What's your favorite snack food?"

"That's a good one," she said with a nod of approval. "You can tell a lot about a person from their favorite foods. Have you ever had a deep-fried Twinkie?"

"I can't say that I have. That's your favorite snack?"

"No, but I had one at the state fair last year. I'm a fiend for chocolate-covered malted milk balls. I love the way they dissolve in your mouth when the chocolate is gone."

Banner cleared his throat and shifted a bit in his chair. Something about the sensuous look on her face aroused him all over again. "I see."

"Aren't you going to tell me your favorite snack?"

"You haven't asked," he reminded her.

The way her full lower lip protruded when she pouted was enough to raise his blood pressure by a few dozen points. He dragged his gaze away from her mouth and reached for a cookie as she said, "Okay, if you have to be picky about it, I'll make it a formal question. What's your favorite snack food?"

"Moon pies."

"Chocolate or banana?"

His left eyebrow rose. "That's question number five?"

"No. It's four-A."

His mouth twitched with a wanna-be smile. "I'm not sure that's in the rules."

"I make the rules," she reminded him airily. "Chocolate or banana?"

"Banana."

"Yuck."

"No editorializing, please. That happens to be my favorite."

"I don't remember seeing any moon pies in your pantry."

"I'm out. Finished them off a couple of days ago and haven't been back to the store since. I'll stock up with a half-dozen boxes next time I go to town."

She looked him up and down in a leisurely manner that

made his heart start to pound. "Sure doesn't look like you eat half a dozen boxes of moon pies at a time. Not an extra ounce on you."

Damn. He could almost feel himself starting to blush. Because she had embarrassed him, he blurted his next question without thought, grabbing randomly for another cookie at the same time, even though he hadn't taken a bite of the first one yet. "Have you always been afraid of the dark?"

Lucy didn't seem to find the question too personal. Nor did she seem to mind answering. "I think it started when I was ten or eleven. That's when my mother got sick, and she seemed to always be worse at night. Several times I woke up and found a baby-sitter in the house after my father had taken my mother to the hospital. It got to where I was afraid to go to bed because I didn't know what would have changed in my world by the time I woke up."

She sighed a little and gazed down into her teacup as she continued, "I woke one morning to be told that she had passed away during the night—just as I had always predicted, I suppose. I've given a lot of thought to my neurosis during the past few years, and that's the best answer I can come up with. It's not that I'm so terrified of the dark that I turn into a screaming hysteric or anything like that—I just don't like not being able to see."

Because he didn't know what to say in response to that heart-wrenching explanation, and being so lousy at expressing sympathy, Banner changed the subject. "Are you cold? We can move back into the living room in front of the fire, if you are."

"No, I'm fine. This sweater's warm and the hot tea tastes wonderful. And I'm enjoying our game. It's a way for me to get to know the real you."

That was the problem, of course. He wasn't sure how to show anyone the real him. He just…was.

Still looking at him much too knowingly, Lucy said, "My turn to ask a question. What's your first name?"

That made him frown. "Haven't I told you that already?"

She smiled again. "No. You said to call you Banner."

"Oh." Embarrassed, he shrugged. "Habit, I guess. It's Richard. Richard Merchant Banner."

"You don't care for the name Richard? And that's question 6-A, not a new one."

He shrugged again without protesting her fast-and-loose rule making. "It's my father's name. I answered—reluctantly—to Ricky as a kid, but I outgrew that by the time I was in high school. Never really liked any of the other nicknames for Richard and my middle name is my mother's maiden name, not exactly one I'd want to answer to. Banner just seemed to suit me."

"Richard Banner. It's a nice name."

"It's my father's," he repeated. "I'd have preferred a name of my own."

She seemed to consider that response as she slowly chewed a bite of cookie, and then she swallowed and prodded, "Your turn."

"Er—what's your middle name?"

"Jane, after my maternal grandmother. My aunt Janie was named for her, too."

He really couldn't think of anything else to ask about her that seemed safely impersonal. Wasn't she tired of this game yet? Did she really intend to ask him fifteen more inconsequential questions? He didn't see what she thought they were accomplishing, other than killing time by making small talk.

She certainly wasn't getting to know the "real" him with such trivialities.

But Lucy's next question turned out to be far from innocuous. "What was your ex-wife like?" she asked, her gaze focused intently on his face.

Banner's response was a startled, "Why?"

"I'm just curious. We're trying to get to know each other better, remember? I'll tell you about my last serious relationship, if you like, and you don't even have to use one of your questions. Not that there's much to tell. I thought I had found a partner, and he thought he had found a second mommy. Wanted me to take care of his needs without giving much consideration to mine. Needless to say, it didn't last long. How about your marriage?"

Deciding to think about what she had told him later, he concentrated on her question. "It lasted less than a year."

"Did you love her?"

It was an extremely personal question, of course, and he had every right to decline to answer. Some things didn't belong in any sort of game. Instead, he scowled and said flatly, "I thought we were suited. I was mistaken. I was trying to prove that everyone else was wrong about my ability to maintain a meaningful relationship with another person, but all I succeeded in doing was proving that they had been right after all."

Lucy shook her head in exasperation. "You decided that from one failed relationship? Didn't it occur to you that perhaps you simply ran your experiment with the wrong partner?"

He shrugged. "I know exactly what I proved. And that was your seventh question, by the way."

Her hands wrapped tightly around her teacup, she ignored the reference to the game. "You're afraid to try again to have a real relationship with anyone."

"I'm not afraid," he countered instantly. "Just realistic."

"So the kisses we've shared have been…?"

She let the quiet words fade off, waiting for him to complete the sentence.

"They were nice," he said after a moment. "But I know you'll have to leave soon."

He was making it clear that he would do nothing to detain her. "Nice," she repeated with a lifted eyebrow. "That's the way you describe our kisses?"

A faint flush crept up his neck from the open collar of his sweatshirt. It seemed that he had accidentally tripped over her feminine ego. "They were, uh, really nice. Great."

Without warning, Lucy rose and rounded the table toward him. He rose instinctively to meet her.

Stopping directly in front of him, she reached out to stroke a hand up his chest. "I really think I can do better than 'nice.' Why don't you give me a chance to prove it?"

He really tried to resist her. But then her other arm went around his neck, and his willpower crumbled just like the cookie he'd been mutilating only moments before.

His arms went around her and his mouth met hers.

The spectacular kiss—*much* better than nice—was interrupted by the ringing of the telephone. It wasn't a sound Banner heard much, so it took him a moment to identify the sound. Dragging his mouth from Lucy's, he released her and snagged the receiver from the kitchen extension. His voice was gruff when he barked, "Hello."

After only a slight pause, a man's voice asked, "Is Lucy Guerin there?"

"Yeah. Hold on." Banner motioned with the phone toward his guest. "It's for you."

He moved aside as she took the phone, giving him a smile that made his chest tighten again. Lucy's high-voltage smiles were definitely dangerous, especially when they followed one of her mega-watt kisses.

Hulk was sitting at the door, patiently waiting to be let outside. As Banner moved to open the door, he heard Lucy say into the phone, "Daddy! Merry Christmas. Are you at Aunt Janie's house?"

He wasn't eavesdropping, Banner assured himself. But he couldn't help overhearing a little of her conversation as his dog ambled out through the open door. The affection in Lucy's voice was obvious, indicating that she loved her father despite having lived away from him since she was very young.

He wondered if Lucy's father had made a special effort to stay in touch with his daughter despite the distance between them. Had he called regularly on the phone, sent her cards or letters, made sure she had a gift from him for every birthday? He wondered if Lucy's father had been there for any concerts and dance recitals and sporting events she might have participated in.

Banner would bet Major Guerin had done all those things when his military career had allowed—unlike Richard Banner, who had always been much too busy to regularly remember the son he had fathered with his high school girlfriend.

Maybe if Richard had made the effort occasionally, Banner himself would have turned out differently—or maybe not. And it was too late to dwell on such things now, anyway.

Disgusted with himself for his uncharacteristic bout of self-pity, he tuned out Lucy's warm, happy voice and stepped onto the porch, ignoring the cold that seeped through his sweatshirt and jeans. His breath hung in front of him as he stood at the top of the steps, watching Hulk halfheartedly give chase to a fat squirrel.

Banner stuck his hands in his pockets to warm them and studied the damage the ice had done to the surrounding trees. Broken limbs littered the ground and hung precariously from the tallest branches. Most of the ice had melted into splotches of mud, though frozen patches still gleamed in some of the deepest shadows where the sun hadn't yet penetrated.

The sky was clear, the almost blinding blue of a crisp winter day. He could smell the tang of bruised evergreens and the wood smoke that drifted lazily from his chimney.

Hulk seemed to be in no hurry to go back inside, having been cooped up for the past couple of days. Banner knew the feeling. He wouldn't mind going for a long run, himself. He seemed to be in need of some heavy physical activity to take his mind off…well, other things.

He was lucky no limbs had crashed through his roof, he thought as he surveyed the mess on the ground to distract himself from what had gone on inside the house. He had a lot of cleaning up to do in the next few days. Damage control, he thought.

He would be wise to limit the damage to broken limbs, rather than risk any personal scars left behind by a certain kissable Christmas elf. He just wasn't so sure he had any more control over that than he'd had over the weather.

Lucy was watching the back door when she hung up the phone. Banner had gone outside almost ten minutes earlier and he hadn't been wearing a coat. He must be half frozen by now.

If he'd left to give her privacy, it hadn't been necessary.

She hadn't said anything to her father that she would have minded Banner overhearing.

She opened the door quietly, catching her breath when a gust of cold air rushed inside like an impatient visitor. Banner must not have heard the door open. He had wandered into the yard and was studying a small tree that looked to have broken nearly in two beneath the weight of the ice.

Lucy would have been shivering like crazy out there in a sweatshirt and jeans, but Banner seemed indifferent to the temperature. Was he really that tough or just that good at blocking his feelings?

As if he had sensed her standing there, he looked around, his eyes meeting hers. Even with the distance between them, she felt the impact of his intense gaze like a physical touch.

"Aren't you cold?" she asked after clearing her throat. "Would you like me to bring you your coat?"

"No. I'm coming in. C'mon, Hulk, leave that squirrel alone and let's go get warm."

Lucy moved out of the way as Banner and the dog came back inside. Banner passed almost close enough to brush against her, and she could feel the cold radiating from him. What had driven him outside so impulsively that he hadn't even stopped for his coat?

She followed him into the living room, where he threw another log on the fire and then stood there soaking in the warmth. "Looks as though there was a lot of damage to your trees," she said to start him talking again.

"Yeah."

"Was there any damage to your house? Are all your water pipes okay?"

"They're well insulated. I think everything is fine."

The dog gave a huge yawn, turned around a couple of

times and settled down for a nap on the hearth rug. Banner looked down at the beast as if he were considering joining him.

Lucy settled into the rocker where Miss Annie had spent so much of the past two days. It was amazingly comfortable, the slat back and solid oak seat carved to cradle her. An easy push of her foot set it in motion, probably giving her an appearance of relaxation she didn't feel just then.

The afternoon sun streamed through the windows, shining on the glittery stars Joan's children had left behind. The scent of cedar wafted from the corner, drawing Lucy's attention to the cheery little Christmas tree, and the fire popped and sputtered merrily, as if trying to do its part to lighten Banner's tense mood.

It didn't seem to be working. He just stood there, staring moodily into the fire, apparently oblivious to the decorations…and to her. It seemed the game she had so impulsively initiated was over, ended by her switch from casual, impersonal questions to a more personal—and more painful—subject.

Maybe she should go. In Springfield, she would be welcomed with smiles and open arms, unlike the strained atmosphere of this room.

She had never been one to hang around where she wasn't wanted—and she did eventually take a hint, though sometimes she was a bit slow to give up when she had set her sights on something. Maybe this was one of those times when she should throw in the towel.

There was only one way to find out how Banner felt about it. Placing her hands on the arms of the rocker, she pushed herself to her feet. "I think it's time for me to let you have your privacy back. I'll just get my things out of the bathroom, and I'll be on my way."

He reached out unexpectedly to catch her arm when she would have walked past him. "Wait."

She looked up at him with a renewed hope. "Something else you want to say?"

"Something else I want to do," he corrected after a rather lengthy hesitation. And then he drew her against him.

"You're really not one for conversation, are you?" she murmured, smiling as she slid her hands up his still-chilled chest.

"Sometimes it's better not to talk," he muttered in return, and proceeded to demonstrate.

Okay, this was definitely promising, she thought, letting herself sink into his kiss. Maybe Banner had trouble with words, but he communicated beautifully this way.

Standing on her tiptoes, she clung to his neck and allowed her mind to shut down. To paraphrase Banner: sometimes it was better not to overthink things.

Once again it was the shrill ring of the telephone that brought an end to the kiss before it flared out of control.

Aroused and somewhat disoriented, Banner glared at the insistent instrument. Damn it, he hadn't had half a dozen calls in the past month. And now the stupid phone rang twice in one afternoon, each time interrupting a very interesting interlude?

It was probably an omen that he should heed. Instead, he heard himself urging, "Just let it ring this time."

Lucy rolled her eyes and motioned toward the table where the telephone sat. "We can't do that. It could be an important call."

He shoved a hand through his hair and tried to regain control of his raging hormones as he reached reluctantly for the receiver. "Hello," he said, frustration making his voice even more curt than usual.

"Hi, Rick. I just called to say merry Christmas."

He recognized his paternal half sister's voice after only a momentary hesitation. "Thanks. You, too. How's it going, Brenda?"

"My sister," he mouthed to Lucy, who was hovering close by in case the call was for her again.

She nodded, then turned to leave the room, obviously to give him privacy.

Banner turned his attention back to the call, hearing his sister say, "Everything's fine, I suppose. We wish you could have joined us for Christmas, of course. We missed you at the dining table."

Banner doubted that was true. As little as he usually contributed to one of the lively, and most often political, mealtime discussions at his father's table, he couldn't imagine that his presence had been missed. His sister was simply being polite. "Tell everyone I said hello," he said.

He wasn't particularly surprised that his father hadn't called. Richard Banner wasn't exactly supportive of his eldest son. He had never approved of Banner's decision not to attend college and to attain limited success as a woodworker rather than in the higher-profit and higher-profile careers Richard's two younger offspring were pursuing.

Banner's mother hadn't called, either. That, too, was no surprise to him. His mother was sulking because he hadn't attended her Christmas dinner, even though she usually wasted their time together criticizing his appearance, his lack of interest in social skills and his decision to live in rural Arkansas "like some backwoods hillbilly." Her words, not his. She had always been miffed that he preferred the simple existence of his great-uncle to the social-climbing lifestyle she and her husband maintained so frantically.

As different as they were, Banner's parents still shared one thing in common. They were both disappointed in the son they had produced together.

He supposed he would call his mother in a little while. A call from him would appease her somewhat—at least until the next time he didn't live up to her expectations, which would come along soon enough.

"You know, Rick, you could try to get along better with Dad," Brenda said, the argument an old and tired one as far as Banner was concerned. "You are a member of this family. I don't know why you pretend you aren't."

"I know exactly where I stand in the family. And I get along fine with the old man. He talks, I pretend to listen, and then we both go back to our own lives. I guess you could say it works for us."

"But Tim and I hardly know you. You don't let us get to know you."

It wasn't that Banner didn't care at all about his half siblings. He simply didn't have much in common with them. Couldn't imagine that they had very much to say to each other on a regular basis.

Brenda shouldn't take it personally. He didn't interact any more with his two other half sisters, as his mother frequently pointed out. Not that his mother wanted him to have any undue influence over her well-connected daughters, but she would have been royally perturbed if she thought he was closer to his father's offspring than to her own.

Banner's family—both of his families—were basically nice people. His parents were hardworking, successful, upstanding citizens, and all his siblings seemed to be following that same path. He didn't dislike any of them.

He simply didn't fit in. He never had. He couldn't imagine that he ever would. It had taken him a lot of time and a lot of anguish before he had finally accepted that fact.

Because he didn't want to deliberately hurt his sister's feelings, he made an effort to sound interested when he asked, "So, how are you and Tim? Everything going okay for the two of you?"

The resignation in her voice when she responded told him that she knew exactly why he had asked. "I'm fine. Very busy, of course, but that's just part of the career I've chosen. Tim—well, I guess he's fine, too."

"Something wrong?"

"I don't know. He's seemed unusually distracted lately. A little subdued. Probably the natural stress of a first-year law student."

"Probably. Well, tell him I said hello, will you? And, uh, merry Christmas."

"Sure. I'll tell him. Goodbye, Rick."

He hung up knowing that he had disappointed her. It was something he seemed to do to other people on a regular basis without even trying.

Which, he reminded himself, was why he had chosen to isolate himself from other people to a large extent, learning to be content with his own company and his own pursuits.

It still seemed like a good plan to him. One he would probably be foolish to change at this stage.

After a moment he went into the kitchen to rejoin Lucy. She was sitting at the table reading a woodworking magazine he'd left lying on the bar. She seemed oblivious to the chill in this room that did not benefit from the heat of the fire in the living room.

Hulk padded into the kitchen, moving without hesitation to his empty food bowl, where he stopped to look hopefully at Banner. Banner reached into the pantry to pull out a bag of dry dog food, which he poured into the big stainless steel bowl.

"Your sister called to wish you a merry Christmas?" Lucy asked, looking up from the magazine.

He nodded as he turned to replace the dog food bag in the pantry. "Yeah. She must have been the designated caller from Dad's family."

"Did I hear you call her Brenda?"

"Right. My father's daughter. The medical student."

"She probably missed seeing you today."

"She said she did."

"Don't you miss seeing her? And your other siblings?"

He shrugged, keeping his eyes on the stainless steel water bowl he was washing and filling with clean water. "I think I've told you before that I'm not really close to my half siblings. Not much in common with them."

"But you love them, of course. After all, they're your family."

"Yeah, I guess." He reminded himself that Lucy couldn't understand what it had been like for him, belonging to two families but not really being a part of either of them.

Sometimes Lucy had a way of looking at him as if she could read his mind. As if she really could understand, after all. And that, too, was a dangerous way for him to think, tempting him to believe they were more alike than they really were. To harbor a faint, foolish hope that, with Lucy at least, he was more than just a misfit.

Turning away from that gaze that looked entirely too perceptive, he set the dog's water bowl next to the food dish. "I'd better call my mother," he said gruffly. "She'll be annoyed if I don't call her today."

There was nothing like a chat with his mother to bring him back to harsh reality, he assured himself.

Chapter Ten

The afternoon wasn't going exactly as Lucy might have hoped. Banner was more distant now than he had been before their latest kiss. She supposed she shouldn't have been surprised. This seemed to be a classic panicky-male retreat, the behavior of a man who had gotten closer to someone than he had intended.

If she looked at it that way, it was almost a compliment, she mused.

Of course, it was just as likely that Banner regretted what had developed between them and was now trying to think of an excuse to send her on her way as gently as possible.

Because that possibility depressed her, she decided she would stick with the first explanation. She wanted to believe he was starting to care for her, but he was afraid of his feelings. Knowing his family background, and considering his broken marriage, it was an entirely credible possibility, she assured herself.

Lucy still believed Banner belonged at the top of her prospect list. Now it was just a matter of convincing him.

She was sitting in front of the fire, rubbing the dog's ears, when Banner rejoined her after his conversation with his mother. She studied his face from beneath her eyelashes, trying to guess how the call had gone. She found no clue in his expression, which was absolutely emotionless.

He looked at her for a moment, then managed a faint, polite smile that didn't soften his face in the least. "Looks like you've made a friend for life."

His dog was sprawled beside her, eyes closed in ecstasy as she rubbed the sensitive areas behind his ears. Had he been a cat, he would have been purring. As it was, he gave an occasional groan of pleasure. "He's a very sweet dog. I can see why you love him."

Banner's smile faded. He shrugged, apparently trying for the appearance of nonchalance. "He's okay—for a dog."

He wouldn't even admit that he loved his pet, Lucy thought with a ripple of sadness. Would he—or could he—ever admit that he loved anyone else?

Determined to get him talking again, Lucy plugged on. "You spoke to your mother?"

"Yes."

"She and the rest of your family are well, I hope. Enjoying their holiday."

"Apparently."

"I'm sure she appreciated your call."

"I guess."

Lucy was getting frustrated—and a bit annoyed. Banner

knew how to carry on a conversation. He was just being stubborn.

What, exactly, was he trying to prove?

When he did finally speak, his words weren't exactly encouraging. "You really should get on the road. The pavement could get slippery again when the temperatures drop after dark."

Giving Hulk one last pat, Lucy rose. "You seem in a hurry to see me off."

"It isn't that. But I know your family is anxious for you to join them. And you do want to see them, don't you?"

She did, actually. It was Christmas, after all, and Christmas was meant to be spent with family. It had been several months since she had last seen her father, and she knew he was impatient for her to arrive. But it was still harder than she might have imagined to leave Banner.

How could she have imagined two days ago when she'd set off on her drive to her aunt's house that she would fall hard for a stranger on the way? Because whatever this was that had developed between her and Banner, it was much more than a fleeting infatuation, at least on her part.

"Why don't you come with me?" she asked on a sudden rush of inspiration. "I hate to leave you here with no electricity. My family would welcome you. Aunt Janie's a fabulous cook, and my cousins are always fun."

Banner was shaking his head before she'd even finished speaking. "Thanks, but I'm not much for family gatherings—not even my own family, obviously. Besides, I have work to do here, remember? A full order that I've barely gotten started on."

She hadn't really expected him to accept, but it had been worth a shot. Torn between going and staying, she pushed a hand through her tumbled curls. "Will we see each other again?"

There was a long pause before Banner said, "You know where I live. Maybe you could stop by and visit sometime on your way to your aunt's house."

She supposed she should be encouraged that he left an opening for them to continue seeing each other, though it hadn't exactly been a formal invitation. As obvious as it was that he considered them an unlikely pair—and, yes, she had understood exactly what he had tried to tell her during their twenty-questions game—he still couldn't deny the attraction between them.

"Maybe I will," she said.

He nodded. His expression shuttered. "Fine."

Pushing her hands into her pockets, she said reluctantly, "Then I guess I'd better get on the road."

"I'll help you take your things out to the car."

He could have sounded a little less eager to help, she thought with a frown.

Lucy glanced around the living room as they prepared to step out a few minutes later. "Are you sure you don't want me to help you take down these decorations before I leave?"

"No. I'll do it."

She gave one last look at the funny little tree, the scattered stars and paper chains. And then, with a tiny sigh, she turned and walked out, promising herself that she would see this room again.

Banner waited until she had tossed her belongings into the back of her car, and then he opened the driver's side door for her. "Drive carefully."

"I will."

"Have a nice Christmas with your family."

"Thank you. For everything, Banner. You've been incredibly generous."

Her expression of gratitude made him scowl. "Forget it. You'd better go now before it gets dark."

She bit her lip for a moment, then turned toward the car, growing increasingly depressed by his rush to see her off. "Merry Christmas, Banner."

He laid a hand on her shoulder, turning her back to face him. "You forgot something."

She looked up at him expectantly. "What?"

He pointed upward with his other hand.

Following the gesture, she frowned in question, seeing nothing but deepening blue sky above them. "I don't—"

"The mistletoe," he cut in to remind her. "I believe it has followed us out here."

The unexpected flight of whimsy made her smile in delight—and remember exactly why she had begun to like him so much. "I believe you're right."

He kissed her lingeringly, more tenderly than he had before. There was a lot of emotion in this kiss, but she was afraid she also sensed a finality that she didn't want to accept.

Maybe Banner really believed this was goodbye, she thought as she climbed into her car and started the engine. But as far as she was concerned, it was just the beginning for them.

That thought made it a bit easier for her to steer her car out of his driveway and onto the road that led her away from him.

Banner watched Lucy's car until it was out of his sight. Only then did he turn and walk back into his dark, chilly house. Hulk was still sleeping on the rug in front of the fire, and the silence was both absolute and very familiar.

Had it not been for the handmade decorations scattered around his living room, it would have been as if the past couple of days had never happened.

For a moment he stood in the center of the room, picturing Miss Annie in the rocker, Pop and Bobby Ray on the couch, Joan in the wing chair and the children playing on the hearth rug. And Lucy, flitting around the room like the lady of the house, making sure everyone was happy and comfortable. Oddly enough, he had enjoyed most of the interlude with his unexpected guests.

He wondered if he would ever see any of them again. Most specifically, he wondered if he would ever see Lucy again.

Sure, she had said she might stop by again sometime. But he wondered if she would still feel the same way after a few days away from him, back with her family. Once the rosy, romantic glow of their holiday adventure had worn off, she would probably see him more clearly, and perhaps wonder what she had briefly seen in the reclusive, divorced woodworker who couldn't even maintain a close relationship with his own family members.

He shook his head impatiently and moved toward the Christmas tree. Might as well get rid of all this stuff now that everyone was gone. He still had a few packages to open in his bedroom—the usual shirts, books and food gifts from his family. He had mailed his customary gifts to them—Internet-ordered gift certificates for everyone. Easy, efficient, and guaranteed to fit.

Maybe he would warm some apple cider in a little while and drink it in front of the fire, he decided. The perfect Christmas celebration, in his opinion. Just himself and his faithful dog enjoying the peace and quiet together, as he had intended when he had declined his parents' invitations to spend the holidays with them.

When he looked around the room this time, those echo images of his guests were gone. Except for Lucy. Something told him he would be seeing her in his mind for quite some time.

"So tell me about this man who opened his home to a group of stranded travelers," Janie McDonald urged Lucy late Christmas evening. "What was he like?"

The two women had escaped to Janie's sitting room while Janie's husband and Lucy's father sat in front of the big-screen TV in the den to watch a war-themed DVD one of them had received as a gift. Janie had decorated her room as a feminine retreat, with thick-cushioned love seats and rockers, bookshelves filled with fiction and knickknacks, a small-screened TV and a sizable collection of classic movies.

A big basket beside Janie's favorite chair was stuffed with crocheting supplies for the thick, warm afghans Janie crafted while she watched those films. The multicolored skeins of yarn reminded Lucy of Miss Annie.

But it had been Banner that her aunt had asked about, she reminded herself. How on earth could she describe Banner?

"He's interesting," she said, then shook her head at the inadequacy of the adjective. "He's a very talented woodworker who makes beautiful furniture. He has an understated sense of humor that's not always readily apparent, and he's much nicer and kinder than he gives himself credit for. He thinks of himself as a misfit, a bit of an outsider—because his parents and stepparents have made him feel that way, I think. He lacks confidence in himself and his people skills, but he really isn't the loner he tries to convince everyone, including himself, that he is."

"He does sound interesting," Janie murmured, studying Lucy speculatively. "How old did you say he is?"

"He'll be thirty-one on April third."

"Sounds as if you got to know him fairly well in a short time."

Remembering several heated kisses, Lucy had to make a determined effort not to blush. "There wasn't much to do except talk," she said evasively. "With the electricity out and all, I mean."

"You said he was a nice-looking young man?"

"I didn't say what he looked like," Lucy corrected, not being fooled for a moment.

"But he is nice looking?"

"He's gorgeous," Lucy admitted with a sigh. "Pretty enough to frame and hang on a wall."

Janie laughed. "He sounds more interesting all the time. Are you going to see him again?"

"Absolutely." After all, Banner had left that choice open, she reminded herself with characteristic optimism.

"Sounds promising."

"Definite potential," Lucy agreed. "But the man is skittish."

Janie waved a hand in dismissal. "Honey, they all are."

"Yes, but trust me, this one's the champ."

Her aunt shrugged. "That just means you have to be a bit more persistent—or devious, as the need might be."

Lucy laughed. "As much as I appreciate the confidence you show in me, I wouldn't be planning any wedding showers yet. As determined as I can be when I set my mind to something, I'm not sure even I'm a match for Richard Merchant Banner."

Janie only smiled at the niece she had raised as her own daughter for so many years. "If it comes down to a battle of wills between you and this Richard Banner, my money is on you.''

Lucy wasn't making any bets herself. But it was nice to know she had at least one supporter firmly in her corner.

Banner woke to the rumble of central heating on the morning after Christmas. An overhead light burned directly into his eyes when he opened them. In the background he could hear the hum of his refrigerator and the other electric appliances that provided the generally unnoticed noise of modern life. They sounded unnaturally loud after the absolute silence.

Yawning, he rolled over in his sleeping bag, dislodging Hulk, who had been sleeping with his head on Banner's stomach. Even though his bedroom had been free, Banner had slept in the living room again last night. He just hadn't been in the mood to sleep alone in his big bed.

He had taken down all the Christmas decorations before turning in, so his house looked normal again. He wondered how long it would be until he felt the same as he had before meeting Lucy.

She had been his last thought before falling asleep, and his first upon awakening this morning. How could someone who had been in his life less than forty-eight hours have made such a powerful impact on him?

Because the house seemed unusually quiet, even with the appliances making their sounds, he turned on the television for noise while he cooked and ate breakfast. He was going to have to make a grocery run this afternoon to replenish his supplies, he thought with a glance into his nearly empty pantry. And then he intended to lose himself in his work, keeping himself too busy to think and too tired to lie awake that night mentally replaying ill-advised kisses.

Four-month-old Nicolas McDonald kicked happily in Lucy's arms, his wet, toothless baby smile making her melt in response. She leaned over to nuzzle his chubby cheeks, which gave him the perfect opportunity to grab a fistful of her red curls.

Carefully disentangling herself, she wrinkled her nose at him. "You are adorable," she said.

He gurgled in smug agreement.

This was her cousin Tony's youngest child, and Lucy was crazy about him—as she was his three-year-old sister and their eight- and six-year-old cousins. She had always loved children. Never in her life had she considered that she wouldn't have any of her own, though motherhood had been one of her back-burner goals, something that could wait while she pursued her education. Now that her twenties were slipping so quickly away from her, she was becoming more aware of passing time.

Oh, sure, she was still quite young. She knew plenty of women who were putting childbearing off until their thirties, even beyond. But Lucy felt that she was at a prime point now, both physically and emotionally.

Sure, she could have a child on her own, do the single-mother thing—and she had no doubt that she could be good at the role. But she wanted it all—husband, partner, children, dog and picket fence. And Lucy had never been content to settle for less than everything she wanted.

"You're so good with children," Tony's wife, Hannah, said, as she watched Lucy play with the baby. "I've always wondered why you chose to be at the university instead of teaching younger children."

"Because I prefer the university setting," Lucy replied.

"I like discussing mathematics on a higher level. That doesn't take away from my enjoyment of children, though."

"So, are you seeing anyone special?"

Lucy wondered if Hannah's ultracasual tone was intended to make the segue less obvious. If so, it didn't work. Hannah was obviously wondering if Lucy had prospects for marriage and children of her own.

Hearing the echo of her own thoughts made Lucy clear her throat and keep her gaze focused on the baby. "Not at the moment."

She had no intention, of course, of mentioning the new name at the top of her list. But that didn't mean she wasn't thinking of him as she continued to play with her cousin's tiny son.

Banner found the money hidden in his bread box when he was putting away the supplies he'd bought that afternoon. The bills had been tucked into a folded sheet of white paper. Frowning, he spread the page to study the neatly slanted handwriting, which he knew instinctively belonged to Lucy, even though there was no signature.

"Banner," the note said, "your kindness and your hospitality have made this a very special Christmas for all of your guests. None of us will ever forget you. Thank you."

He sighed as he looked at the money. He had told them not to do this. It wasn't as if he couldn't afford to feed a few houseguests for a couple of days—even though it wasn't something he did very often. Okay, ever.

Kindness and hospitality. He gave a short, humorless laugh. Wouldn't his family be surprised to read those words in connection with him? None of them would have believed he knew how to offer either one.

He found himself tracing the letters of his name, imagining Lucy writing them. "None of us will ever forget you," she had said.

He was rather afraid that he would never be able to forget her, either.

"So, how's my little girl?" Major Les Guerin asked as he and Lucy wandered arm and arm down Janie's winding garden path. The garden was dormant for winter, but bird baths and feeders provided entertainment as a variety of birds scrambled for the best seeds.

Lucy and her father, bundled against the cold, had slipped out of the house a few minutes earlier to spend a little time alone together. It was something they tried to do whenever they found themselves in the same place at the same time, something that happened all too rarely these days with their busy schedules.

Lucy leaned comfortably against her father's arm. When she was a little girl, she had thought he was the strongest, wisest, most handsome man on the planet. Now that she was an adult, she had no doubt that he was.

She had never blamed her father for sending her to live with his sister and brother-in-law after her mother's death. Les had had no interest in remarrying after the loss of his longtime sweetheart, and his military career had been too demanding to allow him to give her the time and attention an adolescent girl deserved. Janie had been able to offer those things as well as a woman's perspective, and Lucy had never lacked for love and attention.

Her father had called her almost every evening to ask how her day had gone and had visited as often as his schedule allowed. It hadn't been a traditional father-daughter relationship, perhaps, but it had worked for them.

"I'm hardly your little girl anymore, Daddy."

He chuckled and patted her gloved hand, which rested on his arm. "I don't care how many advanced degrees you get, you'll always be my little girl."

It was an old, familiar exchange, and as always it made Lucy smile. She rested her head against his shoulder. "I love you, Daddy."

He responded with a characteristic mumble, then quickly changed the subject. "I hope you learned your lesson about taking off in your car when an ice storm is threatened. You were lucky you didn't spend Christmas Eve in a ditch somewhere, you know. Or worse."

"I didn't know there was going to be an ice storm. The weather forecaster said he thought there would only be snow, if that. If I had known about the ice—"

"You probably would have tried to make it, anyway," her father said with resignation.

"Maybe," Lucy agreed ruefully. "I wouldn't have liked the thought of not being with everyone for Christmas. As it was, I missed the big Christmas Eve shindig."

"Sounds like you had an interesting time where you were."

"It was definitely interesting. Everyone was so nice. I really enjoyed watching the children find their gifts from Santa Claus." She had told her family all about Tyler and Tricia and the lengths the adults had gone to so the children would have a special Christmas.

"You were just darned lucky you had a safe place to stay. Could have been stranded alone in your car. Or the guy in the house could have been a dangerous nutcase. Anything could have happened to you."

"Yes, Daddy," Lucy said, tolerating his lecturing because she knew he really did worry about her. "I promise I'll be more careful in the future, but this time everything worked out fine."

"And now you're humoring me."

"Yes, Daddy."

"Should've spanked you more when you were a kid," he muttered.

Not believing a word of it, she laughed and rubbed her cheek against his shoulder as affectionately as a kitten. The major might intimidate most other people, but Lucy knew that where she was concerned, at least, the man was a marshmallow.

"So this guy who took you in—you going to be seeing him again?"

She wasn't particularly surprised by the question. Her father had always had a sixth sense about her. It had been particularly spooky when she was a teenager hundreds of miles away from him and somehow he had still known everything she was up to, but she had gotten accustomed to it since then. "Yes, I'll see him again."

"Too early to get serious. Two days isn't long enough to get to know someone."

"Are you telling me you don't believe in love at first sight?" Her gently mocking tone was deliberate, since she had heard the story about her father meeting her mother and immediately saying to himself, "Here is the woman I'm going to marry."

The Major had the grace to flush a little. "I didn't say that," he answered gruffly. "Are you telling me you already fancy yourself in love with this man?"

"All I'm saying is that I like him quite a lot, and I hope to have a chance to get to know him better. Maybe you'll meet him before long. I think you would like him, too, even though he's a little...well, different."

This time it was her father who chuckled. "I wouldn't have expected anyone who caught your interest to be anything but different."

That made her lift an eyebrow. "I'm trying to decide if that's a compliment or an insult."

Patting her hand again, he led her onto a new pathway. "I'll let you think about it for a while. And, by the way, I do want to meet this Banner guy. Sooner, rather than later, if things start getting serious."

"Yes, Daddy."

Apparently satisfied that he had made his point, Les changed the subject to family matters, and Lucy willingly went along.

She had said all she intended to say about Banner. More than he would have liked, probably, considering how obsessively private he was. But nothing had changed about her interest in seeing him again.

Chapter Eleven

It was funny the way thoughts of Lucy popped into Banner's mind at random moments that seemed to have no connection to her. Even five days after she had left, on December thirtieth, he still found himself thinking of her frequently, hoping she had made the remainder of the trip safely, wondering if she was enjoying her visit with her family.

Wondering if she thought of him even half as often as he thought of her.

Probably not, he decided as he ran a length of white pine through his planer. After all, she had plenty of other people now to distract her and divert her. If she had spoken of him at all, it had probably been to describe him as an oddball who lived alone with a scraggly dog and had been grudgingly gracious enough to allow a few stranded travelers to stay with him for a couple of days, though he had done little to entertain them while they were there.

Maybe he could have been a little friendlier. A little more social. Or maybe…

But no. He'd been himself, pretty much. And while Lucy might have found him a novelty while she was here, he wouldn't be surprised if the novelty had already worn off.

The planer whined shrilly as he fed another board into it, though the high-decibel sound was muted by the hearing protectors he wore along with safety glasses. Banner protected himself as assiduously in the workshop as he did in all the other areas of his life.

A tap on his shoulder made him jump and nearly drop the board he'd just planed smooth. Turning off the machine, he spun with a glare. "Damn it, Lucy, don't sneak up on me in the workshop. I could have taken a hand off or something."

She somehow managed to smile and look penitent at the same time. "Sorry. I didn't mean to startle you."

"The machinery I work with is dangerous. You could get hurt yourself if you aren't careful. From now on, when you come out here, make sure I see you come in so I can turn off anything…"

He fell silent as it occurred to him what he was saying. From now on? What made him think Lucy would be coming back into his workshop on a regular basis?

For that matter, what was she doing here *now?*

"Uh. Hi," he said, pulling the hearing protectors off his head and tossing them aside.

Her musical laughter was a much more pleasant sound than the machine he had just silenced. "Hi, yourself. And I promise I'll be more careful from now on."

Making it sound as if she planned to visit his workshop regularly. He cleared his throat. "I wasn't expecting to see you."

"You said I should drop by again—is this a bad time?"

He couldn't imagine a bad time to see Lucy—but he would keep that thought to himself. "Let's go inside," he suggested. "I'll make you some tea."

"I'll take you up on that." She turned to precede him out of the workshop.

She looked great, he couldn't help noticing as he followed her across the backyard to his house. She wore her black parka with the emerald knit cap and an emerald scarf. Jeans and sneakers completed what he could see of her outfit. Not exactly fancy dress, but he liked the way it looked on her. He suspected she would carry off sequins and diamonds with the same sort of carefree panache.

The thought of her dressed in her doctoral robe and sash made him scowl. Hardly a fitting match to his flannel shirt and worn jeans—but that was no revelation to him.

Hulk was at his food bowl when they entered the kitchen. The dog looked up from his kibble, spotted Lucy and ambled over to greet her, his feathery tail lazily sweeping the air as she removed her scarf and jacket and tossed them over a chair.

Admiring the way her cream-colored sweater emphasized her slender curves, Banner murmured, "He's excited to see you."

Patting the dog's head, which she didn't even have to bend down to accomplish, Lucy looked around with a smile. "He shows it about as well as you do."

Was she actually comparing him to his dog again? Just to prove that he was at least somewhat more demonstrative than his four-legged roomie, he reached out to tug her into his arms. "Maybe I can do a bit better."

Her smile deepened. "I'm sure you can."

His mouth was on hers almost before she finished speaking.

He had fantasized about kissing her again ever since the last time. Had dreamed of doing so again ever since she had driven away. And he had wondered if he would ever have another chance to hold her.

Without releasing her, he finally lifted his head a couple of inches. "I wasn't sure you would come back."

Her fingers locked loosely behind his neck, she raised her eyebrows. "Didn't I tell you I would?"

"Yeah, well, people say things like that and then change their minds."

"I don't," she said, and pulled his mouth back to hers.

He had kissed plenty of women before, though perhaps not as many as some men his age could claim. What was so different about kissing Lucy? Why was the taste of her lips so memorable, the feel of her body so perfect against his? If simply kissing her was this good, he could only imagine how spectacular making love with her would be.

"The electricity is back," Lucy murmured when Banner finally lifted his head for oxygen.

"Oh, yeah," he muttered, still feeling the energy coursing through his veins.

She laughed. "I meant that your power lines have been repaired."

Banner blinked and cleared his throat. "I knew what you meant."

The look she gave him then was a bit too knowing. "Maybe you could make that tea?"

Feeling as awkward and nervous as a randy schoolboy, Banner let his arms fall to his sides. "Yeah. Sure. Uh…"

Still smiling, she moved to the sink to fill the kettle.

Lucy had been a little nervous when she had pulled into Banner's driveway, a bit concerned about what she would see in his eyes when he spotted her. Operating on a hunch, she hadn't even bothered knocking on his front door, but had walked straight to his workshop.

She had been somewhat disconcerted when his first words to her had been a lecture about shop safety. But when he had suddenly, rather humorously, realized she was back, his expression had been gratifyingly dazed. And when he had kissed her...well, suffice it to say those kisses had left no doubt in her mind that he was glad she had returned.

It was just as obvious that he had no idea what to do with her.

He sat grimly silent across the table as they sipped their tea. Even though the house was centrally heated now, the hot beverage still felt good in comparison to the crisp cold air outside. Lucy cradled the warm mug between her hands and studied Banner through her lashes.

"How's your work coming?" she asked. "Have you finished the order you were working on?"

"Almost. A few minor things left to do."

"Then what?"

"Then I start working on another order."

"It sounds as if you're doing well."

He shrugged. "I have my regular customers who keep me busy."

They had talked about his work before, of course. Lucy could think of nothing new to ask him about it just now, which meant that line of conversation had come to an end.

Banner made an effort to find a new topic. "How was your visit with your family?"

"It was great. I really enjoyed seeing everyone."

"Your father is well?"

"Yes, thank you."

"I'm, uh, happy to hear that."

She couldn't help but laugh then. He was trying so hard

to make innocuous small talk—and he was so very bad at it.

Her amusement made him scowl. "You're laughing at me."

"I'm laughing at us," she corrected him. "We're being so very proper and polite."

His frown deepened. "I told you I'm not good at this. Talking to people, I mean."

"Maybe we should go back to twenty questions. I think it's your turn. You have—what?—thirteen questions to go?"

"Fifteen," he replied automatically. "The last one I asked you was your middle name. You're the one with thirteen to go."

She lifted an eyebrow. "You do have a good memory."

"Yes," he replied simply. "I do, actually. I remember every question we asked—and the answers."

Which meant he was fully aware that she had been asking about his ex-wife when her impromptu game had ended. She would have to be a bit more careful with her questioning this time, but she still intended to find out as much about him as he would allow.

It seemed to her that the best way to start was to let him take the lead. "So, if you were to ask a sixth question about me, what would it be?"

"Why are you here?" he asked without even taking a moment to think about it.

She set her empty mug on the table. "Is that one of those existential, philosophical questions? Like what is the meaning of life?"

The look he gave her chided her for the deliberate misinterpretation. "You know what I meant."

"Why did I come back?"

He nodded.

"You already know the answer to that one. I came back because I like you and I wanted to spend more time with you. I was rather hoping you felt the same way?"

It wasn't officially a question, she assured herself, but she lifted her voice at the end to encourage him to reply.

Instead, he nodded toward her mug. "Want some more tea? Something to eat, maybe?"

"No, to both questions, which, I assume, don't count toward your official twenty."

He smiled a little at that. "I was just trying to be a good host."

"You *are* a good host, whether you believe it or not. Ask anyone who stayed here Christmas Eve."

As always, the compliment seemed to make him uncomfortable. "Do you have any hobbies?"

She grinned, knowing he had blurted out the first question that popped into his mind as a way to turn the subject away from him again. "A few. I love to read. I enjoy dancing. I play piano fairly well. And I play golf. Badly."

He grunted. "I tried golf a few times. It was bad for my character."

Amused, she asked, "In what way?"

"Ruined my language. I used cuss words I wasn't aware that I knew. How the hell is anyone supposed to put a ball that small into a little hole that far away? Football—now that's a sport. A big ball you can tuck into your arm and run with. Or basketball, maybe. At least the basket's right over your head, not half a mile away."

"Do you play football or basketball?"

"I'm what you might call an armchair athlete. Catch the games on TV."

She couldn't help running a slow, assessing look down his lean, muscular frame. "You must do something physical to stay in shape."

He shifted in his chair, looking self-conscious. "I run a little."

"More than a little, I think."

"Five or six miles a day when the weather's nice. I'm not one of those guys who runs in rain or snow."

"Whatever you're doing, it works for you."

A hint of color crept up from the collar of his flannel shirt. "Could we change the subject now?"

Every time she turned the subject to him, he grew uncomfortable. So many men she encountered couldn't talk about anything except themselves. Did Banner really have so little conceit?

"Of course. Do you like to dance?" she asked him, thinking of how nicely she seemed to fit into his arms—even if he was nearly a foot taller.

"Is that one of your official questions?"

"Number eight, isn't it?"

"Close enough. And the answer is that I don't know how to dance. I doubt that I would be any good at it."

"Surely you've danced a few times."

He shook his head. "Nope. Never found myself in a position where I had to try."

"School dances? Weddings?"

"Never attended any school dances. Only been to a couple of weddings, and neither one had dancing. Mine was in front of a judge at a county courthouse, so there was no reception."

How could a guy get to be thirty years old without ever dancing? "Why didn't you go to any dances in school?"

"I tried a couple in junior high, because my mother made me. Hated 'em. Didn't know what to say or how to act. Basically they bored me senseless. I announced in ninth grade that I would never attend another one, and I didn't."

No wonder he had never developed a talent for small talk. No one had encouraged him to participate in social activities or supplied him with the skills to make sure he enjoyed them.

Honestly, had his parents both been so absorbed with themselves and their younger offspring that they had given no thought at all to Banner's happiness? Had the protective shell he'd developed at such a young age been so tough that they hadn't been able to get through it—or had they given up trying too soon?

Something he must have read in her expression made him defensive. "I had friends in school. Guys like me who were interested in tools and cars and camping and fishing. Dated some, though not seriously until I hooked up with Katrina. I particularly enjoyed the hours I spent in my great-uncle's workshop. I was content with my life."

Content, maybe, but still left feeling like an outsider, she mused. And as far as his ex-wife was concerned, Lucy had already surmised that he had married her because he'd been expected to marry and settle down at that stage in his life. It had been one of the few times Banner had tried to satisfy outside expectations, and that hadn't worked out. Which had only reinforced his reclusive self-image.

She saw nothing wrong with Banner's choice to work at home or to shun artificial social gestures. She simply sensed that he wasn't entirely happy with his solitude. She had watched him with his Christmas guests, and she had seen the pleasure he had taken in the companionship, even if he hadn't known how to express his feelings. And when he had watched the children open their gifts, she would have sworn that he was imagining Christmas mornings with children of his own, just as she had done.

Maybe she was mistaken, but she really didn't think so.

Banner was a man in need of someone to love, and someone to love him in return. She just happened to know a suitable candidate for that position.

Leap-before-you-look Lucy. Her cousin Mark's old nickname for her hovered in the back of her mind as she carried her teacup to the sink, then turned to smile up at Banner, who had followed her. "I'm ready to ask you my next question."

He made a show of sighing in resignation. "Fire away."

"Did you miss me?"

"Yes," he said after a moment. "I did."

Her smile deepening in pleasure at the unexpected sincerity of his answer, she held out her hand to him. "Prove it."

Banner had spread his sleeping bag in front of the fire again. The fleece lining was soft beneath Lucy as she lay beside him in the warmth of the dancing flames. She loved the way the golden light played over his face, gleaming in his dark eyes and glinting in his thick dark hair. Appearance wasn't a priority for her when it came to men, but it certainly was a plus that Banner was so nice to look at.

He reached out to stroke a fingertip down her cheek, his touch gentle, as if he was afraid of hurting her. She felt the calluses on his skin, and she trembled at the thought of those work-roughened hands sliding over her body. It had been quite a while since she had felt any man's hands, actually. She hadn't even been tempted with any of the men she had dated recently in her quest for a soul mate—but oh, was she tempted now.

This had never happened for her before. Not this fast, this strong. And as exciting as it was, it was also a little scary. She'd had her heart bruised before, maybe even cracked a little—but it had never been broken.

Those few other men hadn't had the power to hurt her that badly. She wasn't at all sure the same was true of Banner.

Too fast. Too strong. But it felt real, nonetheless.

"You're frowning," he said. "Have you changed your mind?"

"No." She reached up to brush a lock of hair away from his forehead, an excuse to feel the silky texture. "I thought this might happen when I came back to you. I hoped it would, actually."

His hair felt so nice against her fingers that she let her hand slide into it again. And since she was already there, she applied just enough pressure to bring his mouth closer to hers.

Banner took the less-than-subtle hint immediately. His lips covered hers as his arms closed around her to pull her close. His fire-warmed body was long, lean and hard against hers—the perfect counterpart to her petite curves, she decided on the spot, nestling into his strength. As much as she considered herself any man's equal, she could still savor the restrained power of work-honed muscles and the breadth of masculine chest and shoulders.

Behind her, the fire crackled and popped almost frantically as Banner's tongue slid between her lips. Trying, no doubt, to compete with the heat she and Banner were generating on this sleeping bag, Lucy mused dreamily.

It seemed completely natural for Banner to slip his hand beneath the hem of her sweater, his palm sliding across her back. Taking that move as an implied invitation, she allowed her own hands to wander, parting the buttons on his soft chamois shirt to reveal the white T-shirt beneath.

Another disadvantage to winter, she thought with a sigh. Way too many clothes involved.

Seemingly as impatient as she was to have her hands on him, Banner shrugged out of his shirt, then tugged the T-shirt over his head and tossed it aside. Lucy sighed again, this time in sheer appreciation. Was there any part of this man that wasn't beautiful?

She couldn't wait to find out.

Though she had always been a woman who went after what she wanted, Lucy didn't generally consider herself the wanton or aggressive type. Something about Banner made her behave in ways that might have seemed uncharacteristic to her before she had met him.

As if to illustrate that point, she reached for him. All that sleek, tanned skin was simply impossible to resist.

She pressed her lips to the hollow of his throat, feeling his pulse hammering there. His hand was unsteady when he tugged at her sweater, proving that he was as eager as she was. The muscles in his jaw were clenched, making his face look almost harsh when she glanced back up at him, but his eyes gleamed with a hunger that equaled hers.

Funny, she thought, drawing his mouth to hers again. She had left her home to spend the holiday with people she loved. Who would have dreamed that she would end up falling in love on the way?

Maybe it had happened too fast. And maybe she wasn't destined for a lifetime of happiness with this man. But what she felt for him now was much more than simple infatuation. More than lust. She loved everything she had learned about him, and she couldn't wait to learn more.

Maybe neither Lucy nor Banner had intended to do more than talk or kiss when they had stretched out in front of the fire. Maybe. At least, Lucy hadn't deliberately thought that far ahead when Banner had kicked the sleeping bag open and then drawn her down onto it.

Okay, she thought in a sudden rush of rueful honesty. She had known exactly what she was doing. And she had no doubt that Banner had known, too. Maybe it was just easier to pretend to be swept away by passion than to admit that she had wanted him since she'd first met him, and that she had stayed behind when everyone else left because she had wanted this to happen.

And maybe she didn't really want to know what Banner was thinking right now, especially if he was thinking along the lines of a single night of pleasure.

But still she heard herself saying, "Banner?"

He lifted his head from her throat, which he had reached on his leisurely path downward from her lips. "Yeah?"

"This is...important to you, right?"

He went very still, his eyes searching her face as if seeking the meaning behind her hesitant question. "How do you define *important?*"

"More than a convenient tumble, less than a declaration of undying devotion."

He seemed to be getting used to her way of phrasing things. "Then, trust me, it's important."

She smiled and reached for him. "If I didn't trust you, I wouldn't be here."

He hesitated a moment and then, muttering something she couldn't understand, he crushed her mouth beneath his.

Sweaters and jeans and socks and underthings fell into haphazard piles around the sleeping bag. Firelight bathed their bodies as they explored each other, but they would have been plenty warm even without the fire. The heat they generated between them was enough to bring a fine sheen of perspiration to their bare skin.

Banner disappeared long enough to close his dog in the kitchen, and when he returned, he carried a couple of small foil squares that Lucy recognized as condoms. There would be no unwelcome repercussions of this afternoon—at least, no physical ones. The emotional after-effects remained to be seen.

Confident that she could handle whatever might happen between them because she wouldn't allow herself to expect too much, she gave herself over to pleasure.

Lucy hadn't expected Banner to talk during lovemaking, and he hadn't. She thought he might say something, at least, afterward. Instead he lay on his back, staring at the living room ceiling, his face absolutely motionless except for the dancing of shadows from the fire. He had been active enough earlier. Had he used all his energy?

Lying on her side, she rose on one elbow to study him. His hair was a mess—her hands had done that. There was a small smudge of lipstick on his throat—she had done that, too. She suspected that if she could see his back, she might detect a faint scratch or two.

She had definitely left her mark on him. Just as he had left his mark on her heart—invisible, but real, nonetheless.

"Banner?"

"Mmm?" he responded without looking at her.

"Have you gone comatose?"

His mouth twitched with what might have been a smile. "Maybe."

"How long do you think it will take you to recover?"

"I'm not sure that I will."

She smiled. "I think I'll take that as a compliment."

He glanced at her then, his dark eyes gleaming. "It was meant as one."

Resting a hand on his chest, she spread her fingers and admired the contrast between her fair skin and his tan. "I never expected anything like this when I set out on this trip."

"Kind of took me by surprise, too."

She walked her fingers up his chest to the very shallow indention in his chin. "You make a very nice Christmas present, Richard Merchant Banner."

He frowned, and she wondered if it was due to her words or her use of the full name he didn't particularly like. "I, uh…"

Whatever he had intended to say, he apparently changed his mind. Instead he set her hand aside and rolled to his feet. "I think I'll take a shower. I'll use the master bath, so you can have the front one."

"Okay, thank—"

He was gone before she could complete the sentence. And if Lucy had ever seen a panicky escape, that had been one.

Too much? Too soon?

She knew the feeling. But maybe she was dealing with it a bit better than Banner.

Sighing lightly, she reached for an afghan, pulling it around her as she padded toward the bathroom, her clothes in her hands. She wondered what the odds were that Banner would talk to her about his feelings when he finally reappeared.

For some reason, she wasn't overly optimistic about it.

Chapter Twelve

Banner busied himself cooking as soon as he emerged from the bathroom. He had paused only long enough to ask Lucy if she had to hurry on her way, or if she would be staying the night.

"I'm in no hurry to leave, if you don't mind me staying for a while longer," she replied, watching his face for a clue to his feelings.

He merely nodded. "Then, I'll start dinner."

Lucy knew he liked to cook, but it also gave him something to do to avoid having a meaningful, postlovemaking conversation with her. She wouldn't rush him, she promised herself. She could give Banner as much time and space as he needed, since he didn't seem to be in any hurry to send her away.

"What can I do to help with dinner?" she asked.

"I've got it under control," he replied. "I had already planned to make a pot of gumbo tonight, so the ingredients are already chopped and ready. Uh, you do like gumbo, don't you?''

"I love gumbo or any kind of Cajun food, for that matter. I try to get down to New Orleans at least once a year, mostly for the food.''

"I've been there a couple of times. Lots of fancy restaurants, but the best food I found was in the little dives the locals frequent.''

"I feel the same way. I'd rather have a bowl of red beans and rice from a little mom and pop diner than the fanciest blackened offerings from those five-star restaurants.''

He sent her a look over his shoulder that expressed both approval and mild surprise. "So would I.''

That was certainly no revelation to Lucy. "What were you planning to have for dessert?''

He shrugged. "I haven't really given that any thought.''

"Do you mind if I make something? I'll stay out of your way.''

He motioned toward the pantry. "Knock yourself out.''

Pleased to have come up with an excuse to work side by side with him, she moved to the pantry to take stock of his refurbished supplies.

Lucy felt no real need to fill the companionable silence between them as they cooked. That was a rather new experience for her. Usually when she was with someone, she felt the need to keep a conversation going, to fill the silence if only with trivialities. But she found it enough just to be with Banner, working side by side with only the occasional smiling glance between them. He seemed content, too, and she thought he enjoyed having her there—though, of course, with Banner it was sometimes hard to tell.

She bent to place the chocolate cake she had stirred

together into the oven. Banner was standing at the stove stirring the spicy-scented gumbo, and she brushed against him as she straightened. The contact made a shiver of awareness run through her. The look he exchanged with her then made her aware that he felt much the same way.

She smiled at him. "I like being here with you."

"Why?"

His curious response made her giggle. "I just do. Why does that seem so surprising to you?"

He shrugged, then partially changed the subject. "You pretty much say whatever pops into your head, don't you?"

"If you mean I try to be honest about what I'm feeling, then yes, I do. Trying to guess what other people are thinking or feeling is what leads to so many misunderstandings and uncertainties, don't you think?"

"Maybe."

"C'mon, Banner, you must feel the same way. You don't say things you don't mean, do you?"

"No," he admitted, "but I don't necessarily say everything I'm thinking, either."

"I don't say *everything* I'm thinking," she agreed. "I haven't told you how pretty your eyes are, have I? Or that you have a truly spectacular body?"

The wooden spoon he had been holding hit the floor. Giving her a startled look of reproof that made her laugh again, he bent to retrieve it. "For crying out loud, Lucy."

She couldn't resist teasing him a bit more. He was so darned cute when he was embarrassed—though she had a feeling *cute* was another word that would set him off. "Hasn't anyone ever told you what pretty eyes you have?"

"I can't say they have," he muttered, rinsing the spoon at the sink.

"See? How would you have known if I hadn't told you?"

"I've never met anyone quite like you."

"I'm not so unusual. You just don't get out much."

He laughed then. "Maybe that's it."

She had never heard him laugh before. Had never seen his usually stern face lightened with a full grin. It didn't last long, but oh, lordy, it was amazing. And by the time he sobered again, Lucy was even more convinced that she wouldn't be getting over her feelings for Banner anytime soon.

Leaving the gumbo to simmer and the cake to bake, Banner and Lucy moved back into the living room. Banner was still rattled by her outrageous flattery. He wasn't used to that sort of flirting, and he wasn't sure how to respond. But, oddly enough, he had rather liked it. It was nice to hear that she found him attractive.

Trailing her into the living room, he allowed his gaze to travel down her trim figure. Speaking of spectacular bodies...

All too aware of the sleeping bag still spread invitingly in front of the fire, he cleared his throat and pushed his hands into the pockets of his jeans.

He tried to mask his thoughts when Lucy turned to look at him. "Where's that deck of cards we were playing with Christmas Eve?"

"Cards?" Did Lucy plan to demonstrate her mind-reading skills again? If she wanted to read his mind, she didn't need a deck of cards. She only had to check out the condition of his body, instead.

"We can pass the time by playing gin rummy or something while our dinner cooks."

"Gin rummy." He shook his head as soon as the words

left his mouth; he sounded like a damned parrot repeating everything she said.

"Or some other game," she said cheerfully. "It doesn't really matter."

"For someone who claims not to like games, you sure play a lot of them," he grumbled, digging the cards out of a table drawer.

"I love games—just not the hypocritical ones that people play in social situations," she corrected, settling on the floor in front of the coffee table.

He sank onto the couch and handed her the cards. "How can you survive in the academic world without playing social games?"

She took the cards from the box and began to shuffle them. "Academia has its own set of rules that I follow sporadically. And you'll note that I chose a small, public university as opposed to one of the more structured liberal arts schools. It's a somewhat less political, kiss-up type atmosphere."

"I couldn't put up with all the bull, myself."

"Which is why you choose to be self-employed. I figure putting up with a certain amount of bull is the price of working in a job that I enjoy."

Made sense, he supposed. And he couldn't help noticing that nothing in her words or her behavior seemed to imply that her teaching career was any more respectable than his woodworking. Of course, she probably hadn't stopped to think about the fact that she had a Ph.D. and he'd gotten no further, academically, than high school graduation.

He picked up the seven cards she had dealt to him. "What are we playing?"

"Gin rummy. Do you have any fives?"

He looked at her over the cards. "That isn't the way you play gin rummy."

"It isn't?"

"No. You're playing Go Fish."

"Oh. Well, do you have any fives?"

Shaking his head, he handed her a card. "You don't actually know how to play gin rummy, do you?"

"Apparently not."

Because Lucy was such a proponent of speaking one's mind, he said, "You aren't quite normal, are you aware of that?"

She laughed, which he had to admit was the reaction he had hoped for, since he liked the sound so much. "That's what my father always says. I think the two of you would hit it off."

Himself and the major? Doubtful, Banner thought, looking at the cards in his hand. Not that he expected to meet Lucy's father anytime soon, if ever.

"Got any sevens?" she asked.

"Go fish."

She grinned and reached for a card.

Glancing again at the sleeping bag, Banner sighed and resigned himself to playing a slightly offbeat card game with a decidedly offbeat Christmas elf. But the game was interrupted only a few minutes later by a loud rapping on the front door.

Recognizing the rhythm of the knock, Banner stood and crossed the room to answer.

The man on the doorstep wore a thick gray knit cap topped with a purple tassel, a neon-yellow jacket zipped over jeans that looked ready for a rag bin, and expensive running shoes that had seen a lot of hard use. His brown hair hung in a low ponytail over the collar of the jacket, and his lean face was stubbled with two or three days worth of beard. "Hey, Banner. How's it going?"

"Hey, Polston. What's up?"

"Not the temperature. It's cold as a gold digger's heart out here. Really dumb time to go out for a run, but I was feeling restless. Gonna ask me in or are you being antisocial today?"

"No, come in."

A couple of years younger than Banner, Polston lived in a log cabin a few miles down the road. They had known each other almost two years and had become friends and frequent running partners during that time. At least, Banner supposed they could be called friends, even though he certainly didn't feel as if he knew the other man that well. Kyle Polston was almost as rabid as Banner about maintaining his privacy.

Polston was talking even as he entered the living room. "I was thinking about getting up early in the morning and driving to Springfield to the big sporting goods store there. I'm hoping to find a couple of after-Christmas bargains on some fly fishing gear. Thought you might want to..."

He had spotted Lucy. She still sat cross-legged on the floor, and the firelight danced in her red-gold curls. Lively curiosity gleamed in her big green eyes. Her sensual mouth was curved into a warm smile of welcome. Banner figured there wasn't a man alive who would look at her now and not feel as though he had been body slammed.

The way Polston was staring at her seemed to confirm Banner's assumption. Banner watched as the other man took in Lucy's tumbled hair, shoeless feet and the sleeping bag spread in front of the fireplace. And then he turned to look speculatively at Banner. "I see you already have plans."

"Lucy, meet Polston. My neighbor."

She stood and held out her hand. "It's very nice to meet you, Mr....?"

"Kyle Polston," he clarified, taking her hand and holding it. "You can call me whatever you like—as long as you call me."

Banner cleared his throat. Even to him it sounded suspiciously like a growl.

Polston grinned. "Message received," he murmured, then reluctantly released Lucy's hand. "Have you two known each other long?"

"Not very long," Banner replied. "We're about to have dinner. Would you like to join us?"

He'd felt obligated to make the offer, not wanting Lucy to think him rude, but he wasn't disappointed when Polston shook his head. "I don't want to intrude. Need me to pick up anything for you in Springfield tomorrow?"

"See if they've got a good deal on number-five weight forward-floating fly line and some 6X tippet. I'll reimburse you, of course."

"Will do. Lucy, it's been a pleasure to meet you." He took her hand again as he spoke, holding it long enough to make Banner's scowl return. "I hope we have a chance to see each other again."

Banner motioned toward the door. "You'll probably want to head home before dark. As you said, it's damned cold out there."

Polston grinned. "Here's your hat, what's your hurry? Don't worry, Banner, I can take a hint. I'll let you know if I find a sale on the fishing line and tippet."

"See you, Polston." Banner closed the door behind the other man with a sense of relief he couldn't quite explain.

Lucy was studying his face when he looked around at her. "He seemed nice," she said.

"Yeah, he's okay."

"Have you known him long?"

"Couple of years."

"Is he married?"

He felt his eyebrows dip even further downward. "Why?"

"Just curious about your friends," she said, her expression surprised innocence.

"No, he's not married. Never has been. Like me he's too much the oddball to settle into an average domestic routine. Unlike me, he was smart enough to figure that out before he tried it."

She seemed to digest his words for a few minutes, as though thinking about the not-so-subtle message carried in them. And then she turned toward the kitchen. "I think the cake should be about done. And I'm hungry."

It took him only a moment to switch mental gears and follow her. He was getting better at keeping up with her conversational switches. But that didn't exactly mean he and Lucy were meant to be together, he reminded himself with a hollow feeling somewhere deep in his gut.

"What do you usually do after dinner?" Lucy asked as she and Banner cleared away the dishes. They hadn't had dessert yet, but they'd eaten hearty portions of the spicy gumbo. They'd dined without much conversation, but once again it had been a companionable quiet between them, and Lucy hadn't felt the need to fill it with babble.

Banner shrugged as he bent to place the gumbo pot in a lower cabinet. "Sometimes I work. Sometimes I read or watch TV."

"Do you ever go out?"

"There's a place not far from here where a bunch of guys get together to play pool or darts. I hang out there when I want company—a couple of times a month at the most.''

''Have you dated much since your divorce?''

''Not much,'' he said, closing the cabinet door with a finality that also seemed to close that line of conversation. ''Want me to make a pot of coffee?''

''Only if you want some. I'll wait until we have our cake.''

They moved into the living room where Banner turned on the television and settled on the couch. She wondered if he intended the noise from the TV to serve as a barrier of sorts between them so she wouldn't ask any more personal questions. He should have known her better than that by now, she thought with a faint smile.

Rather than choosing one of the other chairs, she curled on the couch next to him, nestled comfortably against his shoulder. After a moment he shifted to better accommodate her, draping one arm around her.

Her smile deepening, she glanced at the television. The sound was barely turned up loud enough to hear the newscast that had been playing when he turned it on. Since Banner didn't seem particularly interested in the latest news from the Middle East, Lucy didn't hesitate to start talking again. ''Tell me about your siblings.''

Either he had been expecting more questions or he was simply getting used to her unabashed nosiness. He sounded more resigned than surprised when he responded, ''All of them?''

''Of course.''

''Why?''

''Because—''

''I want to get to know you better,'' he finished in unison with her, making her laugh.

And then he sighed. ''I've already told you that my

father has two overachieving offspring—Brenda, the medical student, and Tim, the first-year law student. Brenda's very intense, highly focused, goal oriented. She wants everything in her life to fit into neatly organized slots. Including me, I'm afraid. It bugs her that she can't categorize me as easily as she thinks she should. She's always been so intent on being the perfect daughter and impressing the old man that she can't understand why I don't feel the same way. I think he's an overcontrolling, self-centered stuffed shirt. But maybe she knows him better—after all, she grew up with him, I didn't.''

Filing that seemingly offhand comment away in the back of her mind, she prodded, ''What's Tim like?''

''I can't say I know him all that well. He's always been involved in sports and clubs and fraternities so he was usually gone more than he was home when I was around. To all outward appearances, he's pretty much a clone of his father.''

His father. Another telling little slip. ''Is your father a lawyer, too?''

''No. He owns a successful real estate firm. Spends more time at the office than with his family, but his motto is still Father Knows Best.''

Lucy didn't think he was quite ready to talk directly about his parents or stepparents, so she focused on the slightly less sensitive, but still revealing, subject of his siblings. ''Tell me about your other sisters. Your mother's daughters.''

''I know them a little better, since I spent more time with them growing up, but we're not particularly close, either. Eileen's a dental hygienist married to a dentist, and they have a son they call Sammy, after my stepfather, Sam Osborne. Jenny's a full-time homemaker and aspiring children's book writer, married to a defense attorney.

They have a daughter and they're expecting twins. Jenny's heavily into liberal politics and community service, and it annoys her that I have no interest in either.''

Lucy tried to decide if she was imagining a hint of warmth in Banner's voice when he talked about his sisters. She decided after a moment that it was there, just masked. Despite his unemotional facade, Banner was fond of his siblings in his own way. She was convinced that it was primarily his feeling of not truly belonging to either nuclear family that kept him apart from them.

"They all sound nice.''

"I never said they weren't.''

"You just didn't want to spend Christmas with any of them.''

"I simply wasn't in the mood to deal with my parents' competitive games this year. Or to listen to my father's lectures about how I'm wasting my life, or my mother's criticism of my social life—or lack of one.''

For the first time it occurred to Lucy that maybe Banner had actually wanted to spend Christmas with family. That he had chosen to stay away more to avoid any potential conflict than because he really wanted to spend the holiday alone. He would rather spend the holiday by himself than cause more trouble in the families he had spent his life shuttling between.

Looking uncomfortable again, he cleared his throat, glanced at the television, then reached for the remote. "I don't suppose you're interested in college football.''

"Are you kidding? I've followed the games all season. I love watching the bowl games.''

His hand stilled. "Yeah? Who are your favorite teams?''

"Lots of them. But I do have a soft spot for the Georgia Bulldogs and the Florida State Seminoles, since I attended both those universities while I pursued my degrees. Who are your favorites?"

"Since I never went to any college—much less two of them—I have no loyalty to any one particular school. I just like the game."

Once again the difference in their educational backgrounds seemed to be bothering him. Because she didn't want him dwelling on that again, she snuggled closer to him and said, "Which team's the underdog in this game? I'll cheer for them with you."

They had their dessert and coffee at half time.

"Good cake," Banner said, seeming to savor each bite.

"Thanks. It's my aunt's recipe."

He insisted on carrying the used dishes and coffee cups back into the kitchen, since he had to let the dog out, anyway. She heard the water running and the dishes rattling as he cleaned and put them away.

She was getting to know him a little at a time—mere glimpses into his life, she mused, thinking of his friend's visit earlier. Still, they were moving forward, if only in tiny steps. And she hadn't learned anything yet that made her less interested in him.

She was smiling in welcome when he came back into the room. Something about her expression must have caught him off guard. He paused just inside the doorway, his gaze locked on her mouth. She felt her smile fading as a ripple of response ran through her, leaving a shivery longing behind.

Lifting his gaze to lock with hers, he moved toward her. As if pulled by an invisible string, she rose to meet him. His arms opened, and she stepped into them, tilting her face upward. He kissed her with a hunger that was every bit as intense as it had been before they had made love.

After what seemed like a long time, he broke off the kiss. Laying his cheek against the top of her head, he muttered something she didn't quite catch, though she thought she heard the words, "too much."

Lucy wasn't sure what he was referring to, but as far as she was concerned there hadn't nearly been enough between them yet. She drew his mouth back down to hers.

By the time this kiss ended, they were moving toward the bedroom. She couldn't have said which one of them took the first step in that direction, but the decision to head that way was obviously mutual.

It occurred to her as they entered the oak-furnished, earth-toned bedroom that she still tended to think of it as the Carters' room. There was so little of Banner's personality displayed that it could have been anyone's bedroom.

Thoughts of decor fled her mind when Banner paused beside the bed and turned to look at her. He seemed to be trying to think of something to say. To save him the trouble, she wrapped her arms around him and lifted her face to his for another kiss. She had decided that he communicated quite well without words.

Lowering her to the bed, he proceeded to demonstrate just how right she was.

"Banner?"

He had been lying on his back in the deepening darkness for some time, not quite asleep, but not fully awake, either. Lucy lay beside him, her curly head snuggled into his shoulder, her warm body draped bonelessly against his. As much as he had enjoyed the sated, companionable silence, he had known it was only a matter of time before Lucy would be compelled to speak.

Though making conversation wasn't his strong suit, he didn't mind so much with Lucy. Never knowing what she was going to say next made things much more interesting, to say the least, than his usual stilted exchanges with others. And because he felt as if she would never judge him for being less than eloquent or lose patience with him for his lack of tact and polish, he was more comfortable talking to her than to most people.

In some ways she reminded him of Polston, who had become his friend precisely because Polston was one of the least judgmental and most laid-back people Banner had ever met. In other very significant ways, of course, Lucy was very different from Polston. More educated, more ambitious, more gregarious—and a hell of a lot more attractive, he thought with a faint smile.

"What?" he asked without looking down at her.

"How many questions do I have left?"

Her game again. "You've asked so many that I've lost count. Let's say you have five left."

"Not many," she said, and she sounded as if she spoke through a pout.

His lazy smile deepened. "Better make them count."

"Okay, where do you see yourself in ten years, when you're forty?"

His smile disappeared. Trust Lucy to verbalize a question that had been nagging at the back of his mind for some time now. "I'll probably be right here, making furniture and watching my hair turn gray."

"Alone?"

He shrugged the shoulder she wasn't lying on. "Hulk could still be around in ten years. He'd be pretty old, but probably no lazier or more useless than he is now."

After a pause Lucy said, "Is that what you really want from your future?"

It was what he expected, not necessarily what he wanted. Based on the choices he had made before now, he imagined his life would change very little in the next decade—even if having met Lucy made everything look different for the moment. As impetuous and free-spirited as Lucy was, he doubted that she would stay around for the next ten days, much less a full ten years.

He had missed her after she'd left on Christmas Day. He could only imagine how empty he would feel the next time she went away.

Which meant, he decided as he rolled to face her, that he shouldn't waste any of the time he had with her. "I don't want to talk about the future right now," he said.

"Oh?" Her hands slid up his forearms. "What do you want to talk about?"

He spoke against her lips. "I don't want to talk at all."

Tangling her legs with his, she murmured, "That works for me."

Chapter Thirteen

Banner had never been a late sleeper. He woke with the sunrise the next morning—the last day of the year. Propped on one elbow, he spent several long minutes enjoying the novelty of watching Lucy sleep.

She slept the way she did everything else, he mused. Enthusiastically.

Her red-gold hair lay in a heavy mass on the pillow, tangled by the burrowing movements she made in her sleep. Long eyelashes fluttered against her flushed cheeks as she dreamed.

He wondered if he played a role in those dreams.

With a sound that was a cross between a sigh and a growl, he rolled out of the bed, careful not to wake her. He needed a shower. And he had better make it a cold one.

Dressed in jeans and an untucked blue-plaid flannel shirt, he was in the kitchen twenty minutes later when someone pounded on the door. Glancing at the clock, he noted that it was barely 8:00 a.m. Way earlier than Polston usually dropped by, though he couldn't imagine who else it might be.

He opened his front door to find a younger version of himself standing on the front porch.

"Tim? What the hell?"

Tim Banner nodded past his half brother's shoulder. "You going to invite me in?"

"Uh, yeah, sure." Banner stepped out of the way, allowing the younger man to enter. He checked to make sure no other family members were lurking outside before he closed the door, but apparently Tim had come alone.

Tim stopped in the middle of the living room, shoving his hands in his pockets. Already curled on his favorite rug, Banner's dog lifted his head, glanced at Tim, sniffed the air for a moment, then dropped his head down on his paws and went back to sleep.

Banner studied the younger brother he still thought of as a boy, though Tim had recently turned twenty-two. Tim's conservatively cut, usually neat hair was tousled, he hadn't shaved in a couple of days, and there were dark circles beneath his eyes, as if he hadn't slept in a while. He wore faded jeans, a wrinkled cotton shirt unbuttoned over an equally wrinkled T-shirt, and grubby sneakers. No coat. His cheeks were red from the frigid morning air.

It didn't take a particularly perceptive observer to figure out that something was wrong. "What's up?"

"Maybe I just dropped in for a visit."

And if Banner believed that, Tim would probably try to sell him some oceanfront property while he was here. But before he could express his skepticism, Tim jerked his head in the direction of the kitchen. "Do I smell coffee?"

"Yeah." Resigned to playing host until his brother decided to reveal the reason behind his unexpected appearance, Banner headed for the door opening. "C'mon. We'll both have some."

Following Banner into the kitchen, Tim looked at the counter. "You were about to have breakfast?"

"Pancakes. Have you eaten?"

"No."

"Hungry?"

Tim sounded almost surprised when he replied, "Yeah. I am."

Setting a mug of coffee on the table, Banner said, "Sit. I'll get the pancakes started."

Tim sat in silence while Banner put slices of bacon in a skillet, then poured pancake batter onto the griddle. Maybe the boy would be more talkative on a full stomach, he figured. "Want some orange juice to go with that coffee?"

"I'll get it."

"Glasses are in that cabinet, juice in the fridge. I'll have some, too."

"Make that three," Lucy said as she entered the kitchen.

She had showered, Banner noted. Her hair, which she had pulled back with a barrette, was still damp. If she wore any makeup, it was minimal—not that she needed any, he thought, studying her porcelain-fair skin. Her chocolate-brown sweater fit snugly over her slender curves, ending at the band of her hip-riding jeans. Had Tim not been standing there watching them with such startled curiosity, Banner would have demonstrated for her how delectable she looked this morning.

It seemed as if there was almost always someone else around when he wanted to be alone with Lucy, he mused.

Funny, for a guy who had spent so much time alone during the past few years, he'd sure had a lot of company lately.

His life hadn't really changed the day Lucy knocked on his door, he assured himself. Not permanently, anyway. It only seemed that way at the moment. He couldn't help wondering how long it would take him to be content with his solitude again after everything went back to the way it had been.

Without pausing for introductions, Lucy gave the stranger in Banner's kitchen one of her warm smiles. "I'm Lucy Guerin. And you must be Tim."

Both Tim and Banner looked surprised by the instant identification. "How did you know that?" Tim asked.

She laughed, studying his young, handsome, undeniably familiar face. "Are you kidding? The two of you look so much alike, anyone could see that you're brothers."

Tim looked speculatively from Banner to Lucy. "So Rick's told you about me?"

Though she found the nickname a bit disconcerting, she didn't let it show. "Yes, he has. It's very nice to meet you."

"You, too—even though Rick's never mentioned you," Tim added with a sideways look at his brother.

"I'm sort of new around here," Lucy replied lightly, moving to the coffeemaker. She would let Banner explain their relationship—whatever it was—if he chose to do so.

But Banner said nothing as he set the crisp bacon to drain on a platter covered with paper towels, stacked the first batch of pancakes on a plate and poured more batter onto the griddle. Tim carried three glasses of orange juice to the table, then stood somewhat self-consciously beside his chair until Lucy urged him to sit.

Ten minutes later they all sat at the table with their breakfasts. Following the smell of bacon, Hulk joined them, sitting hopefully beside Banner's chair. Banner slipped the dog a piece of the crisp meat, then said, "That's it, dog. You get the rest of your breakfast later."

Hulk sighed in resignation. Licking his lips to get the last taste of the treat, he ambled out of the room to return to his rug, leaving his owner scowling down at his plate as though wondering what to say next.

Not surprisingly, it seemed to be up to Lucy to start a conversation. Figuring that Banner would join in if she got things rolling, she smiled encouragingly at Tim. "Your brother told me you're in law school. How's everything going?"

Tim swallowed a big bite of syrup-covered pancakes, then reached hastily for his orange juice to wash it down before speaking. "I, uh, quit law school. I'm not going back for the next semester."

That certainly took Banner's attention away from his breakfast. "You did what?"

Tim's expression took on a grimly stubborn quality that made him look even more like his older brother. "I quit."

"Why?"

"Because I hated it."

Lucy glanced at Banner, who was studying Tim with a quizzical expression that told her he was trying very hard to figure the younger man out. "I guess you've told the rest of the family?" he asked.

Tim's jaw muscle clenched. "Yeah."

"How did that go?"

"Dad threw me out of his house."

The stark words made Lucy set her fork down, her appetite gone, even though half her breakfast remained on her plate. Banner and Tim seemed to feel much the same way, since neither of them was eating. Banner took a sip of his coffee, but Lucy thought he did so mostly to give himself time to think of what to say.

She felt compelled to try to fill the tense silence. "I'm sure your father is simply disappointed," she offered. "He'll come around."

Tim turned to look at her, his navy eyes almost black with emotion. "Rick hasn't told you much about our father, has he?"

"A little. I know he has high expectations for you and your sister."

With a little snort, Tim shook his head. "My father has had our lives mapped out since Brenda and I were toddlers. He chose our friends, our hobbies, our colleges. After that he gave us two choices—medical school or law school. Brenda seems to be content enough with medicine, but I've always known that wasn't for me. I thought I could learn to like the law, but it's just not going to happen. There's no need for me to waste any more of my life trying."

"You graduated cum laude from the university," Banner reminded his brother. "You were accepted into some of the most prestigious law schools in the country. Why on earth would you want to throw that away?"

Tim's eyes narrowed. "I would have thought that you, of all people, would understand."

"I don't know what you mean."

"You've never let Dad run your life. You do exactly what you want, when you want. You always have."

Banner shook his head. "My situation is different."

"Only because you didn't live with him full-time. I know he tried to talk you into going to college, maybe following him into business, but you wouldn't let him control your choices. From now on, neither will I."

"So what are you going to do?"

"I don't know, exactly. I've never really had the chance to explore my options. I'll probably spend the next year or so doing that."

"You couldn't do that while you're finishing law school? At least you wouldn't be burning any bridges that way."

Tim seemed genuinely surprised by Banner's reaction to his announcement. "I can't believe this. You sound just like Dad."

Lucy watched as a tinge of red stained Banner's cheeks in response to the unwelcome comparison. Temper sharpened his reply. "I'm not trying to control your life. Hell, I don't care what you do. But I assumed you wanted my opinion. Why else would you show up here this morning?"

"You know, that's a good question," Tim snapped, pushing his plate away and rising. "I don't know why I thought you would understand—or care. Maybe I thought for just once in my life I could count on my brother to be on my side."

Lucy gave Banner a look of exasperation when Tim turned to storm out of the room. "Aren't you going to stop him?"

"I can't make him stay," Banner replied.

Because she knew him well enough to understand he meant that he didn't know how to talk Tim into staying, she sighed and set her napkin on the table. "I'll talk to him."

Banner nodded and began to clear away the breakfast dishes.

Lucy caught up with Tim just as he reached the front door. "Tim, wait."

"Why?"

"Because your brother doesn't really want you to leave," she assured him.

His short laugh held no humor. "He doesn't care. You just heard him say so."

"He said he doesn't care what career choice you make. That's a lot different from not caring about you."

"If he doesn't care about my career, why did he sound like Dad with that 'throwing it all away' comment?"

"Maybe because he does care about you," she replied gently. "Didn't you hear how proud he sounded when he talked about how well you've done in school? With your brother it's sometimes necessary to read between the lines, because it's hard for him to say how he really feels."

"And you're his interpreter now?"

She hesitated. "I, um…"

Tim sighed and shook his head. "I'm sorry, Lucy. I shouldn't have snapped at you. It's just…well…"

She smiled and rested a hand on his arm. "Banner could try the patience of a saint. I understand."

He looked at her hand, then up at her face. "Just how long have you known my brother?"

"Less than a week," she admitted after only a momentary pause. "But I think I've gotten to know him fairly well during that time."

Tim's mouth twisted. "I've known him all my life, and he's pretty much a stranger to me."

And that, Lucy realized, was a painful admission for Tim. He had a big brother he barely knew, a brother he had tried to turn to in a difficult time, and it hurt him that he hadn't been able to make that connection. And because she was starting to understand Banner—or at least she wanted to believe that she was beginning to figure him out—she suspected he was in the kitchen right now berating himself for not knowing how to meet Tim halfway.

This family needed help, and there was no better time to start than the present, she decided. While it was true that she was no expert in family relationships, she was the only one here at the moment to give it a shot. Tightening her fingers on Tim's arm, she gave a slight tug. "Come on. We're going back in there to talk to your brother."

Tim shook his head. "It wouldn't do any good. You heard us in there. We barely speak the same language."

"Then what you need is a translator. And I happen to speak a little Banner. Come on."

Tim resisted for a moment, making her give him one of the looks she usually reserved for class disrupters. "Don't make me pick you up and carry you in there."

That drew a reluctant laugh from him. Though an inch or so shorter than Banner, Tim still pretty much towered over Lucy. "Why do I get the feeling that you might try that?"

"Because I would," she told him cheerfully. "So you might as well come willingly."

Lucy and Tim had just taken a step toward the kitchen when Banner entered the living room. He looked first at Lucy, who still had her hand on Tim's arm. "What do you want me to do?"

"You could try listening," she replied. "Maybe Tim would like to tell you why he came here today."

"All right. Let's talk." Banner sat on one end of the couch and motioned toward the remaining chairs. "Sit."

"Maybe it would be best if I leave the two of you alone," Lucy offered, moving toward the bedroom.

"No!" The brothers spoke in perfect unison, both looking a bit panicky at the prospect of being alone together now.

"Please stay," Tim added, giving her a look that was just short of beseeching.

She was the one who had initiated this, she reminded herself. Nodding, she took a seat on the couch next to Banner. "All right. But feel free to ask me to step out of the room if you decide you want to discuss private family matters."

Tim responded to that with a short, bitter laugh. "Rick has less interest than you do in family matters."

"You could be right about that," Banner snapped. "I've always minded my own business and let the rest of you do the same."

"Did it ever occur to you that we wanted you to be part of our lives?" Tim retorted.

"And let Dad try to control me the way he does you and Brenda? I'll pass."

"You would never let that happen. You've never let him push you around."

Was that a touch of hero worship in Tim's voice? Lucy studied his young face, seeing just a hint of vulnerability in his eyes, though he was obviously trying to emulate his older brother's inscrutable mask. It wasn't hard to imagine him as a young boy, both impressed and intimidated by the older brother he saw so rarely.

Banner shrugged. "By the time he paid enough attention to me to try to control me, I was already old enough to be set in my ways. Nothing I did seemed to please him, so I stopped trying. You, on the other hand, seemed to be exactly what he wanted from a son."

"I've spent my whole life trying to be...maybe I didn't have your guts to be able to tell him to back off."

Looking uncomfortable with the comparison, Banner shrugged. "Maybe you had to reach a point where you'd had enough."

Tim didn't look particularly reassured. "Maybe."

The two men fell silent, apparently lost in their own glum thoughts about their father.

After several long moments, Lucy decided it was time to get them talking again. "How did your mother and sister react to the news that you're quitting law school?"

Tim shrugged. "Mother had hysterics and went to bed. Brenda told me I was being an idiot, then left to go back to the hospital, which is where she spends all her time, anyway."

"Brenda really enjoys her work?"

He nodded. "She told me she can't imagine doing anything else with her life. I never felt that way about the law. And I sure never had any interest in medicine—it was all I could do to get through the basic biology classes with grades my father would accept."

"Then you have to find something that excites you as much as medicine excites your sister," Lucy told him firmly. "The way your brother loves working with wood."

Tim threw a quick glance Banner's way, then looked at Lucy again. "What do you do, Lucy?"

"Dr. Guerin is a mathematics professor," Banner surprised her by saying before she could respond.

"*Dr.* Guerin?" Tim's eyes widened. "You're a college professor?"

"Yes." Lucy sighed a little and shook her head. "I really don't know why that seems to stun everyone who hears it."

"I think Tim is surprised that I have a friend who finished college, much less teaches it," Banner drawled.

A friend. Lucy stashed that description away to mull over later.

Tim sounded defensive when he said, "I didn't say I

was surprised that you have a friend like Lucy. She simply seems too young to have a Ph.D.''

''I'll take that as a compliment.'' Lucy smiled at Tim, then gave Banner a look that silently requested he behave himself.

Banner cleared his throat ''So, uh, Tim—do you need any money or anything?''

Lucy supposed Banner considered his offer to be a show of supportiveness, even though Tim immediately turned defensive again.

''No,'' he said. ''I didn't come here for money.''

''Then why did you come?''

Tim rubbed his palms on the legs of his jeans before answering, ''Maybe I was hoping to find one person who would tell me I did the right thing.''

Lucy held her breath until Banner finally spoke. ''You're sure this is what you want to do?'' he asked Tim.

Tim nodded, no trace of uncertainty in his voice when he replied, ''I'm positive.''

Banner shrugged. ''Then you did the right thing.''

The expression that flashed through Tim's eyes made Lucy's chest ache.

''Thanks,'' he murmured.

''So what are your plans now? Tonight?'' Banner asked.

Pushing a hand through his hair, Tim replied, ''I guess I'll find a place to crash tonight, then start looking for a job and an apartment somewhere. Dad's been paying my rent while I've been in school, but that's over. I told him I didn't want him supporting me any longer.''

''That's the only way you're ever going to get out from under his control,'' Banner commented.

''I know. I've got some savings stashed away to live

on until I find a job. Although I'll have to find one pretty quickly.''

"I'm sure your brother wants you to stay here until you find another place," Lucy hinted broadly, nudging Banner sharply with her elbow.

"Uh…yeah, sure." He rubbed his rib cage as he spoke.

Tim's drooping shoulders straightened. "Really? I mean, I was sort of hoping I could bunk here for a day or two, but if you'd rather I didn't…"

He glanced at Lucy as he spoke, making it clear that he worried about having crashed a romantic idyll. It had to have been obvious to him, of course, that Lucy had spent the night here and had just crawled out of Banner's bed when Tim arrived.

"Of course you should stay," she said firmly. "After all, the closest motel is fifteen miles away. And it's New Year's Eve. We'll have a party."

Banner frowned. "Does this party involve decorations? Am I going to have to chop down another tree?"

She laughed and leaned over to kiss his cheek, causing him to blush again. She simply loved seeing this ultra-controlled, habitually gruff man rattled enough to flush. He wasn't nearly as stern and detached as he pretended to be, but she knew it was a facade born of self-protection.

She wanted Banner to understand he could be free to be himself with her, without fear of judgment or criticism. Perhaps that simple level of acceptance had been all too lacking in his life.

Tim's life, too, apparently, she thought, glancing at the young man who was studying her so curiously.

"No tree this time," she promised Banner. "But we must have champagne. Do you have any?"

His mouth twisted. "That's not exactly something I keep on hand."

Not at all surprised, she nodded and rose. "Then I'm off to do some shopping for party supplies. Is there anything else you need me to pick up while I'm out?"

Banner pushed himself to his feet. "I'll do the shopping. Just make a list of what you need, and I'll—"

"No, I'll go. You stay here with Tim." Which was, she thought, exactly what he was trying to avoid. "Do you have black-eyed peas to eat tomorrow for good luck in the new year? If not, I'll have to buy some while I'm out—though it might be hard to find them this late. I waited until New Year's Eve last year, and the shelves were almost empty of black-eyed peas."

"I have them...and a ham hock to season them with," Banner replied, making it clear he followed at least one local holiday tradition. "But, really, I don't mind making the grocery run."

She patted his cheek in a breezy manner that made his eyes narrow. "Talk to your brother, Banner," she murmured in his ear. "He needs your support."

Because he was a man who clearly knew when to surrender, he nodded and stuffed his hands into his pockets. "Be careful."

"I will." Giving Tim an encouraging smile, she headed off to find her purse and shoes.

She had champagne to buy.

Banner and Tim were left staring at each other in Lucy's wake, both of them at a loss for words. Knowing Lucy would tell him that it was his place to get the conversation rolling, Banner cleared his throat. "So, uh..."

Maybe he should have had something in mind to say before he started speaking, he thought with a grimace, falling silent again.

Tim took up the effort. "Lucy seems really great. How did you meet her?"

"She was stranded here during the ice storm last week, along with several other travelers."

"Really?" Tim looked intrigued. "She's been here ever since?"

"No. She left to spend Christmas with her family in Springfield, then came back yesterday. She said she, uh, wanted to get to know me better," he added, still occasionally amazed that Lucy had actually returned.

"And then I show up." Looking apologetic, Tim shook his head. "Sorry, dude, it's obvious I'm in the way here. I'll clear out before she gets back."

"No. She'd have my head if you're gone when she returns. She's all set for a New Year's Eve party—and trust me, when Lucy sets her mind on something, you might as well just nod and ask what she wants you to do."

Tim's smile was a bit quizzical. "I didn't think you would let anyone boss you around, not even someone as pretty as Lucy."

"Lucy doesn't boss anyone around. She just sort of guides people into cooperating with her."

"And you're okay with that?"

Banner shrugged. As much as he admired and desired her, he wasn't blind to Lucy's flaws, just as he was quite sure she was aware of his. Sure, she had a tendency to take charge of things, but he figured he could hold his own with her if it concerned something that particularly mattered to him. He just didn't expect her to hang around long enough for it to become an issue.

Deciding a change of subject was in order, he tried to remember the name of Tim's girlfriend, who he had met at a very stilted and uncomfortable Thanksgiving dinner with his father's family. "So how's...Jessica?"

"Jennifer. She's history."

Studying Tim's morose expression, Banner asked, "Did you dump the girlfriend along with law school?"

"Actually, she dumped me. She really wanted to marry a lawyer."

Banner winced. "Uh, sorry."

"Don't be. It stung a bit, but I couldn't have spent the rest of my life pretending to be something I'm not just to try to keep her happy. And to be honest, it didn't hurt as badly as it probably should have. So maybe she and I weren't right for each other, after all."

Because Banner could identify all too well with those sentiments, he studied his half brother from a new perspective. Truth be told, he had never paid a lot of attention to Tim.

Banner had been nearly eight when the boy was born, and he had already become aware of the estrangement from his father's family. He still remembered hearing his father bragging about his "boy" and knowing that Richard hadn't been referring to him. Just as he remembered the way his perpetually nervous stepmother had hovered nearby every time Banner had attempted any interaction with baby Tim, as if she feared he would do something to harm the younger boy. As Banner had gotten older, choosing to spend even less time with his father, the rift had grown wider, until he'd hardly known his paternal half siblings.

Banner had thought of Tim as brilliant, social, ambitious, driven—all the adjectives their father valued so highly, which Banner could simply never apply to himself. It had never occurred to Banner that Tim could have more in common with him than with their old man.

Which, he reminded himself, was not necessarily a good thing. He would hate to see young Tim end up living alone, isolated from his family, feeling as if he had failed at every relationship he had attempted. And Tim didn't even seem to have a passion he wanted to pursue, the way Banner had always enjoyed his woodworking.

The extent of his concern about Tim rather surprised him. He wouldn't have expected to care what the kid chose to do with his life.

Because he didn't know how to express his misgivings, he said only, "You can crash here as long as you need a place to stay. But your parents are going to hate it. They'll probably figure out a way to blame me for corrupting you. Accuse me of being a bad influence or something, not that I had anything to do with your choices."

"Maybe more than you think," Tim murmured.

Banner was almost relieved when his dog interrupted the conversation before he had to pursue that particular comment. With a big, noisy yawn, the animal rose from his rug, stretched dramatically, then wandered over to Banner. The dog butted the hand that had been resting on Banner's knee, an unsubtle hint that he wanted a head rub.

"No offense," Tim said, "but that is the ugliest dog I've ever seen."

"No offense taken. I'm not blind."

"What breed is he?"

"Your guess is as good as mine."

Tilting his head a bit, Tim eyed the dog curiously. "I'm figuring there are at least ten breeds involved, maybe a little goat and cow thrown in."

That made Banner chuckle. "Anything's possible, I guess."

Tim patted his leg, calling the dog to his side. Reaching

out to rub the dog's long, shaggy ears, he asked, "What's his name?"

"Hulk."

Grinning down at the goofy, good-natured animal, Tim said, "I like him."

"So do I."

Their gazes met over the dog's head. Banner looked away first, reaching hastily for the remote control. "We're missing the bowl games. What teams do you like?"

"I'll watch any game that involves a ball and cheer-leaders," Tim replied.

Thumbing on the power button and raising the volume loud enough to preclude any more meaningful dialogue, Banner rose. "We need snacks. I've got cheese puffs, pretzels, popcorn, beer and sodas."

Tim's attention was already fixed on the screen. "All of the above sounds good."

Nodding, Banner headed off in search of junk food, relieved that the only conversation required from him for the rest of the afternoon would consist of phrases like "Nice catch" or "Bad call."

Chapter Fourteen

Lucy was hit with an immediate sense of familiarity when she walked into Banner's living room a bit later that afternoon. Having grown up in a household with her uncle and two male cousins, she was well acquainted with the sounds of football on the TV and grunts of satisfaction or disgust from the guys sprawled on the furniture. The smells of beer, popcorn and cheese puffs made her smile with nostalgia.

"Who's winning?" she asked, crossing the room and plopping down on the couch beside Banner.

"It's tied at fourteen." Banner draped an arm around her, almost absentmindedly, and she snuggled contentedly into his side. "Did you find any champagne?"

"Sparkling grape juice. You might have told me this is a dry county."

He chuckled. "You were so insistent on going yourself, I figured you knew what you were doing."

Quite cheerfully she punched him in the side. "Thanks a lot."

With a faint "oomph," he shifted his position, gave her a look, then turned his attention back to the TV in time to watch a long spiraling pass fall right into the hands of a defensive player. "Son of a—"

"What was he thinking?" Tim complained loudly. "Didn't he see that sea of opposing color surrounding his receiver?"

"I think he saw those two human tanks coming right at his head," Lucy answered, reaching for a handful of popcorn. "I'd have gotten rid of that ball, myself."

Banner and Tim got into a heated discussion on whether an intentional grounding penalty would have been better or worse than a sack in that play. Delighted that the brothers were communicating in such a basic, male-bonding sort of way, Lucy settled in to watch the rest of the game.

One game had ended and they were engrossed in another when Banner's telephone rang. He looked immediately at Tim, who was looking back at him with a rueful expression. It seemed that both of them had the same premonition about who was calling.

"Ten-to-one that's Dad," Tim muttered.

"Sucker bet," Banner replied, standing to reach for the phone. Maybe they would both be wrong and it would be for Lucy, he thought hopefully.

No such luck.

"Hello, Richard." His father spoke with his usual brusque lack of warmth.

"Sir." Having decided years earlier that Dad was too familiar a term to describe his relationship with his father,

Banner had settled for the more formal appellation. Richard, Sr., had never protested.

"I don't suppose you've heard from your brother today."

"He's been here all day." Banner didn't think Tim had wanted his whereabouts kept secret or he would have said so.

After a momentary pause, Richard sighed. "I shouldn't be surprised."

"Do you want to talk to him?" Banner asked a bit hopefully.

"No. I've said all I know to say to him. But maybe you'll have more luck. You are trying to talk him into going back to school, aren't you?"

"No."

His father's voice chilled several degrees. "Why the hell not?"

Aware that both Tim and Lucy were listening, though they seemed to be watching the game, Banner replied, "Tim's old enough to make his own decisions."

"I should have expected you to take that attitude."

"What attitude is that, sir?" Banner inquired coolly.

"You're frittering your own life away, and now you seem to be encouraging your brother to do the same. I don't know what made me think you would show any responsibility or loyalty to this family now, when you never have before."

"Yeah, well, that's just the kind of guy I am." Even Banner heard the sharp edge to the drawl he had intended to sound merely laconic.

"Your mother did a hell of a job raising you. My wife always warned me about letting Tim spend too much time with you, but I never thought there was a danger that you would have that much influence over him."

"Are there any other criticisms you want to make, or are you about finished?"

"That will do for now. I can only hope spending a few days with you will bring your brother to his senses about the kind of life he could end up leading if he doesn't get back to school."

"I'm sure Tim will be just fine whatever he decides to do. As you've always made a point of telling everyone, he's a smart guy. Smart enough not to let anyone run his life for him—including you."

"All I can say is that both of my sons have been bitter disappointments to me," Richard said stiffly.

Banner kept his own tone rigidly polite. "I'm sorry you feel that way, sir. Maybe you should take some time to ask yourself if maybe you expected too much from us. And whether we might be a bit disappointed with *you*," he couldn't resist adding before he abruptly disconnected the call.

Tim was on his feet by the time Banner replaced the handset in its cradle. His hands in his pockets, his expression young and vulnerable, he murmured, "You said 'we.'"

Confused, Banner frowned. "What do you mean?"

"It's the first time you've acted like we're on the same side," Tim clarified, his cheeks a bit red. "Like we're really brothers."

"Well, we aren't sisters," Banner returned, then almost winced at the lameness of the awkward retort. Uncomfortable with the emotion in the kid's eyes, he cleared his throat and turned sharply on one heel. "I'm going to start dinner. I'm getting hungry."

It was a lie, of course. He wasn't sure he could eat anything at the moment. But it gave him an excuse to get away from all this emotion and drama.

Hell, this was the reason he had done everything he could to avoid getting entangled with his half siblings, he told himself as he stalked into the other room.

Urging Tim to stay behind with the dog, Lucy followed Banner into the kitchen, having given him a few minutes to collect himself after his father's call. She found him with his head stuck in the pantry, his posture stiff enough to be termed ramrod. It took nerve to deal with him in this mood, but Lucy had never lacked for courage.

Some might have added that there were times when she lacked good sense to accompany her recklessness. She hoped this wasn't one of those times.

"How are you doing?" she asked, stopping a few feet behind him.

"Great. How does spaghetti sound for dinner? The sauce would be from a jar, but I can spice it up a little with a few extra ingredients."

He was so determined not to show his emotions, and from what she had heard of his conversation with his father, Lucy could certainly understand why he had developed that habit. But it couldn't be healthy to keep so much bottled inside.

"Spaghetti sounds fine. Do you want to talk about your father's call?"

"Not particularly." Carrying an assortment of bottles and cans to the counter, he set them down and reached for a pan.

"He didn't really blame you for Tim quitting law school, did he?"

"Pretty much. But I really don't want to talk about it right now."

She was nothing if not persistent. "That was terribly unfair of him. But Tim appreciates you sticking up for him. You know that he pretty well hero-worships you, don't you? And that he probably has all his life?''

As she had expected, Banner reacted to her comments with a frown and a growl. ''That's bull. He just came here because he didn't have anywhere else to go where no one would try to tell him what he should do.''

Lucy had a different opinion about that. She suspected Tim had thought that rebelling against their father's manipulations would finally give him something in common with his reclusive older brother. She didn't think Tim had gone so far as to quit law school for that reason—she believed him when he said he'd been pressured into a career he had never wanted to pursue—but he had known where to come for support in that decision.

''He's so young,'' she murmured, looking toward the doorway.

''Not that much younger than you are.''

''Almost six years. And somehow I get the feeling that he's young for his years. Do you think he'll be okay?''

''He'll be fine. It'll do him good to be out on his own for a while.''

''At least he'll have you to guide him a bit.''

Banner frowned at her. ''He doesn't want or need me to guide him. He's a grown man, got a college degree. He can fend for himself.''

Wandering to the refrigerator, she pulled out raw vegetables for a salad. ''You had your great-uncle to turn to,'' she reminded him. ''Tim has you.''

The comparison seemed to startle him. He looked thoughtful as he continued cooking. Knowing he needed time to digest the events of the day, Lucy forced herself to work quietly beside him, leaving the questions and observations for later.

When the meal was on the table a short time later, Lucy

went into the living room to call Tim away from the television. "Dinner's ready."

"Great," he said, almost bounding from his chair. "I'm starved."

Lifting an eyebrow, Lucy looked at the empty snack bowls and soda cans scattered around the room. It hadn't been too many hours since they'd lunched on chili dogs and chips, which both Banner and Tim had agreed made for perfect football food. Tim might have declared himself a man, but he still had the appetite of a teenager, she thought with a shake of her head.

Lucy and Tim kept up a lively conversation during the meal, chatting about everything from sports to movies to music to politics. Banner didn't contribute much, but Lucy knew he heard every word they said.

After dinner, Lucy pulled out the bags of supplies she had purchased for their impromptu New Year's Eve party. Tim watched with curiosity, and Banner with signs of trepidation, as she unearthed an assortment of games, sparkling grape juice, plastic wineglasses, noisemakers and party crackers.

"You really get into the spirit of things, don't you?" Tim asked her with a grin.

"That's what some people would call an understatement," Banner murmured, glancing around his living room as if thinking of the Christmas decorations that had filled nearly every inch of it.

Lucy gave him an exaggerated frown. "At least I didn't ask you to chop anything down for this celebration."

"I should be grateful for small favors, I suppose."

She carried the games to the coffee table. "You are, however, required to participate in the festivities. I bought Yahtzee, canasta and Uno. Which one do you want to play first?"

He might have looked more resigned than enthusiastic, but he went along, settling onto the couch while Lucy and Tim arranged themselves on the floor on the other side of the table. They chose to play Yahtzee first, and it wasn't long before Lucy and Tim were noisily cheering their luck or complaining about their lack thereof.

A football game played on the television behind them, the sound muted but still audible. Banner had started another fire, which hissed and popped, filling the room with cheerful noises, cozy warmth, flickering light and a woodsy scent. Lucy was almost blissfully content.

She already felt almost as comfortable with Tim as she was with her cousins. Banner, however, was a different story. While she enjoyed his company, the constant sexual attraction she felt for him made *comfortable* entirely the wrong adjective for her feelings toward him. There were times during the evening when she simply glanced up at him and was hit with a wave of such intense emotion it was all she could do not to leap at him.

She felt almost like a schoolgirl with her first overpowering crush. But there was nothing girlish about the depth of her yearning for this man, she mused.

Fingers snapped suddenly in front of her face, bringing her out of her latest romantic reverie.

"Yo, Lucy," Tim prompted impatiently. "Your roll."

"Oh. Sorry." She reached hastily for the dice cup, embarrassed to realize she had been staring hungrily at Banner—long enough for him to be looking back at her with an intensity that made more than her cheeks go hot in reaction.

Dragging her gaze away from him, she glanced at Tim, only to find him grinning at both her and his brother with a knowing look that made her gulp and throw the dice so hard they bounced off the table and onto the floor.

As glad as she was that Banner was embarking on a new relationship with his younger brother, there were times when three was definitely a crowd.

With only a little effort, Banner could recall last New Year's Eve. He and Hulk had watched football, shared a pizza and a beer, and turned in at just after midnight, both expecting the new year to differ little from the one that had preceded it.

This New Year's Eve was definitely different.

He glanced at his coffee table, which was littered with empty hot cocoa mugs, scribbled score sheets and the remains of several junk food binges. On the other side of the room, Lucy and Tim were pouring sparkling grape juice into plastic wineglasses. Midnight was ten minutes away, and Lucy had declared it time to begin the traditional celebrations.

She brought him a glass of grape juice, a yellow plastic horn and a silver-foil-covered party cracker. He looked skeptically at the latter. "What do you want me to do with that?"

"Hold both ends and pull," she instructed. "You'll find surprises inside."

Because she was looking at him so hopefully, he let her press the favor into his hands. If he wasn't careful, he was going to find himself following at her heels like a lapdog, he thought with a sigh of mild self-reproach. Still, the brilliance of her smile seemed to amply reward his efforts. Something about Lucy made him care about her happiness more than his own convenience, and that was a new sensation for him. A rather unsettling one, at that.

Pushing his misgivings to the back of his mind, he took hold of the ends of the foil wrapped around a cardboard tube and gave a tug. With a popping sound, the tube opened. He reached inside to pull out a folded purple paper hat, a colorful plastic spinning top and a slip of white paper.

"Read your fortune," Lucy urged.

"'New pleasures await you,'" he read obediently.

She discreetly patted his bottom. "That sounds promising."

He nearly swallowed his tongue.

Lucy had already turned to Tim. "Open yours," she ordered.

"Yes, ma'am," he said, proving himself as susceptible as Banner to Lucy's bewitchery. His cracker contained a yellow paper hat, a plastic parachute man, and a fortune that read, "Your fate rests in your own hands."

Tim looked suspiciously at Lucy. "You didn't happen to know what fortune was in here, did you?"

"How could I?" she responded with a laugh. "It was the luck of the draw. But it's true, you know."

"That's what I've been telling myself for the past few days," he replied wryly.

"Well?" Banner prodded Lucy, finding himself unexpectedly curious. "What's in yours?"

Smiling at him, she pulled the ends of her cracker, giggled at the resulting pop, then dug out a green paper hat and a bracelet made of pink and green plastic beads strung on elastic thread. She promptly put on the bracelet, then read her fortune aloud. "'Persistence pays off.' Hmm. That's always sort of been my motto. Kind of eerie how fitting these were, isn't it?"

Banner shrugged. "They're always vague enough to fit whoever reads them."

Ignoring his cynicism, she grabbed her wineglass. "Let's have a toast before the ball drops. Who wants to make one?"

"You go ahead," Banner said, picking up his own glass. Tim agreed that Lucy should be the one to make the toast.

"Okay." She gave her words only a moment's thought. "To Tim," she began, lifting her glass in his direction. "May you find the path that leads you to happiness and fulfillment."

"Thank you."

"You're welcome. And to Banner," she went on, turning to him.

He felt the muscles at the base of his neck tense with his uncertainty about what she might say next.

"May you learn to see yourself as the generous, talented and unique person that I see when I look at you," she said, smiling at him in a way that made his chest ache as if he'd just been kicked. His throat tightened, making it darned near impossible for him to speak, even if he had known what to say.

Tim watched them with an expression Banner couldn't quite read. Was Tim as surprised as Banner by the way Lucy had described him?

Tim was probably wondering if he and Lucy knew the same guy. Banner, on the other hand, was even more concerned, now, that Lucy had created an image in her mind based on unusual circumstances—a combination, perhaps, of the holidays, the ice storm, and a powerful, and wholly unanticipated sexual attraction.

He gave Tim a look that held a classic, and unmistakable masculine appeal for help. Tim promptly took him up on it, drawing attention away from Lucy's words by proposing one of his own. "To Lucy," he said, lifting his glass. "Thank you for helping me reconnect with my brother, and I hope he knows how incredibly lucky he is to have met you."

Banner wasn't sure that sentiment was any less fraught with emotional landmines than Lucy's had been, but at least she was smiling at Tim now and not waiting for Banner to say anything. To further avoid having to do so, he tipped up his plastic glass and drank deeply, wishing it held something a bit stronger than bubbly grape juice.

Having taken an obligatory sip of her own juice, Lucy pointed to the television screen. "The ball is starting to drop. Quick, everyone grab your noisemakers."

Banner thought about passing on that suggestion, but the look she gave him had him sighing and picking up the plastic horn. Definitely a bossy little thing, he thought...but he supposed he could indulge her for one more holiday.

There was something inherently thrilling about the stroke of midnight at the dawn of a new year, Lucy thought as she began to count down along with the crowd on the screen. There were so many possibilities. So many surprises waiting to be discovered.

"Ten...nine..."

Tim seemed to be as excited as Lucy about the count-down. She figured that he was experiencing many of the same emotions she felt—eagerness, anticipation, hope. A little nervous about what lay ahead for him and whether he had finally found the key to his ultimate fulfillment.

"Seven...six..."

Banner, on the other hand, seemed to be going through the motions of the celebration. As if he was clinging to the safety and familiarity of the old year.

"Three...two...one! Happy new year!" Lucy blew an enthusiastic blast on her plastic horn, echoed almost as heartily by Tim, and very briefly by Banner. And then she rested a hand on Banner's arm and lifted her face expectantly toward him.

"More imaginary mistletoe?" he murmured.

"It's customary to kiss at midnight," she prompted him.

"Is that right?"

She could tell by his expression that he'd known all along. Whether he had been teasing her or simply stalling, she didn't know, but when he bent his head to press a long, firm kiss against her lips, she found she didn't particularly care.

As far as Lucy was concerned, the new year was starting out very well. It looked as though Santa had come through very generously on her Christmas wish this time.

They turned in an hour or so later. Tim took the guest bedroom. He didn't seem to find it particularly surprising that Lucy would be sharing Banner's bed.

Banner closed his bedroom door, then looked a bit uncertainly at Lucy. "Sorry about my brother showing up like this. I hope it doesn't make you too uncomfortable about...well, you know."

"I like your brother very much. I've had a lovely New Year's Eve. And I'm not at all uncomfortable about...you know," she teased him, sliding her hands invitingly up his chest. "Not if you're referring to the fact that you and I are lovers."

Apparently, *lovers* was another hot-button term to Banner. His eyes darkened and his face went carefully expressionless. He motioned toward the bathroom. "I'll let you have first shift at tooth brushing."

"You go ahead. I need to get some things out of my bag."

Banner was already in bed when Lucy emerged from

the bathroom later. He had left the bedside lamp on for her. Lucy was satisfied that the romantically dimmed light was quite flattering to the slinky ivory silk nightgown she had purchased in Springfield for this special night.

At the sight of her, Banner rose slowly to one elbow. The beddings were draped at his waist, leaving his chest bare. His sleek, tanned skin gleamed in the golden lamp light, making Lucy's mouth go dry.

"You are beautiful," he said.

Three simple, well-worn words—and yet they made her knees go weak, and brought a lump to her throat.

She wouldn't expect flowery compliments from Banner. He would never wax poetic or shower her with practiced flattery. What she could depend on from him was simple honesty. Banner thought she was beautiful. How could she not be swept off her feet?

He patted the bed beside him. "What are you waiting for?"

You, she thought. I've been waiting for you all my life.

Without a word, she moved to join him. Banner welcomed her with open arms.

A long time later Lucy listened to Banner's heartbeats beneath her cheek. The sound was steady and reassuring, and she thought she could happily listen to it for the rest of her life.

The bedcoverings were tangled around them. Her expensive nightgown lay tumbled on the floor beside the bed. The bedside lamp was off now, but enough moonlight filtered through the window for her to see Banner's face when she looked up at him.

He looked thoughtful, she decided. As though he was mulling over something very important.

Apparently sensing her gaze on him, he glanced down. "Aren't you sleepy?"

"No." It wasn't a lie. Lucy was wide awake, unwilling to miss one moment of this magical night. "Are you?"

"No."

Crossing her hands on his chest, she propped her chin on them. "You want to talk?"

"About what?"

"Maybe whatever it is that you're thinking about so seriously?"

He lay in silence for a while longer, and she didn't press him, figuring he would talk when—and if—he was ready. After a while he cleared his throat. "When do you have to go back home?"

"I have to be back at work next week."

He waited another few beats and then said, "Maybe you can give me a call next time you plan to visit your family? Maybe you could drop in to see me for a few hours."

Something about that awkwardly worded suggestion made her frown. "I'm not sure I understand…"

"I thought we could see each other again sometime, if you like. I'm pretty much here all the time, and since you have to go right past here to get to your family, any-way…"

Lucy swallowed. Hard. "And perhaps you could come visit me in Conway soon? It really isn't that far, you know."

"I'm not much for visiting," he said without inflection. "You know me. I tend to be more comfortable here, with my own company. But you would be welcome anytime."

"How hospitable of you." She rolled away from him, reaching for her nightgown.

Banner pushed himself to his elbow. "Is something wrong?"

Without answering, she pulled the nightgown over her head, feeling only somewhat less vulnerable when she was covered by the thin fabric.

"You and I live very different lives, you know," he said, as if sensing her disappointment with his suggestion that they see each other only on occasional, fleeting visits. "I can't imagine you would be content to give up your career and the life you've made for yourself to sit around here with Hulk and me."

He spoke lightly, as if expecting her to be as amused by that suggestion as he was pretending to be.

"You're right," she said without smiling. "I wouldn't be at all content with that."

"Of course not. My ex-wife nearly went crazy from boredom before she finally escaped. But maybe I'm not so bad in small doses. So you'll stop in again sometime."

"Like your buddy Polston," she murmured. "A drop-in friend."

"It was just a suggestion." His tone was stilted now, and he obviously regretted that he had said anything at all.

"You know, maybe I am tired, after all," she said, lying down with her back to him. "We'd better get some sleep."

"Yeah, I guess you're right. We can talk tomorrow."

It was going to take a lot more than talk to get through this man's thick skull, Lucy thought as she pulled the covers to her ears and frowned fiercely into the darkness. Somehow she had to figure out a way to overcome the results of a lifetime of rejections and convince Banner that he deserved much more than he was prepared to settle for.

Chapter Fifteen

Lucy was gone when Banner woke the next morning.

It surprised him that she had slipped out of his bed without him hearing her, since he was usually a light sleeper. The bathroom door was open, so he knew she wasn't in there. Maybe in the kitchen?

She wasn't in the kitchen. Nor the living room, nor any other room. Her bags were gone and so was her car.

As incredible as it seemed, at some point during the couple of hours while he had slept, Lucy had gathered her things and left his house.

He found her note taped to the mirror in his bathroom. "Give me a call when you figure out what you really want," it read. "And when you're ready to take the risk of asking for it."

His first reaction was confusion. What the hell did she mean? He'd told her last night what he wanted. He hadn't actually asked her to drop in occasionally, but he'd made it clear that he wouldn't mind if she did.

The second emotion to hit him was anger. Why the hell had she taken off this way without any sort of warning? If she had something to say to him, she should have said it face-to-face, not in some cryptic note.

Most likely this was her way of ending their brief vacation fling without any unpleasantness. Making it sound as though it was his choice rather than hers, she had disappeared without messy scenes or awkward goodbyes. He supposed he should be grateful to her for keeping it so easy for him.

But *grateful* wasn't even one of the many emotions swirling inside him as he glared at her neatly lettered note.

Half an hour later he was back in the kitchen, showered, shaved and dressed. The coffee was already made, and bacon sizzled in a skillet as he cracked eggs into a bowl. This day would be no different from any other, he promised himself. Nothing in his life had changed permanently when Lucy Guerin wandered into his home. It had been nice while it lasted, but he had never expected it to last long.

Following the scent of food, Tim wandered in yawning and finger combing his tousled hair. "Smells good."

"You like your eggs scrambled, don't you?"

"Yeah. How'd you know?"

Banner shrugged. "I've learned a few things about you in twenty-two years."

Tim poured coffee into the mug Banner had set out for him. "Lucy still sleeping off the sparkling grape juice?"

Banner had braced himself for this, of course. "Lucy left this morning."

Obviously startled, Tim glanced at his watch. "So early?"

"Yeah. She had things to do, I guess."

"Since when? Last night she was talking about watching the Rose Bowl with us today."

Belatedly remembering that conversation, Banner shrugged and set a filled plate on the table. "Dig in."

Though Tim took his seat, his attention was obviously not on the food now. "Did you guys have a fight?"

Banner ladled eggs onto his own plate, though he wasn't at all hungry. "No. We didn't have a fight."

Tim laid down his fork, his expression suddenly stricken. "Did she leave because of me? Damn, Rick, I didn't mean to..."

"It wasn't because of you, Tim. Lucy likes you. She told me so. I'm the one she has the problems with."

"So you did quarrel."

Banner sighed gustily. "We did not quarrel. It was just...well, I think she took offense at something I said. Maybe. Though to be honest, I'm not sure what it was that irritated her."

"Surely you have a clue."

"Not really." Sitting on the other side of the table from his brother, Banner picked at his food without enthusiasm. "I said I wouldn't mind her dropping by occasionally when she makes trips to Springfield to visit her relatives. I made it clear, actually, that I hoped she would."

Tim stared at him. "You said it just that way?"

"Well...yeah. Pretty much."

"And you can't figure out why she might have taken offense."

"No."

Shaking his head in apparent disgust, Tim reached for his coffee cup. "And to think I came to you for advice."

Banner deliberately set down his fork. "What's that supposed to mean?"

"Even though I only met Lucy yesterday, I can't imagine she would be satisfied with being an occasional visitor in your life. It was obvious to me that she's crazy about you. She probably needs to believe you feel the same way about her. And I can't imagine that you *wouldn't* feel the same way—she's great. A little bossy, but even that part of her is well intentioned."

Banner's fist tightened around his fork as he forced himself to keep his expression impassive. "Of course she's great. But really, Tim, can you see her being interested in me for very long? She's everything I'm not. I couldn't have found anyone more my opposite if I'd gone looking."

"You thought you had a lot in common with your ex-wife, but that certainly didn't last long. Maybe what you need is someone different from you, have you ever considered that?"

"I don't need anyone," Banner shot back. "I've gotten along just fine on my own."

"You're scared." Tim looked stunned by the realization. "Funny, I didn't think anything ever scared you, but you are. You're afraid to take the risk of a relationship with Lucy."

Because Tim had unconsciously echoed part of Lucy's goodbye note, Banner scowled. "That's bull."

"I don't think so. If there's one thing I recognize it's fear. Fear of failure, fear of rejection, fear of change. I've struggled with all of them lately."

Banner saw no correlation at all between his situation and Tim's. Tim was making sweeping changes because he had been dissatisfied with his life. Banner, on the other hand, was perfectly content with the way things had been for the past couple of years. He had his work, his home, his dog. When he wanted companionship, he had Polston or the guys down at the pool hall. If he ever felt lonely, he reminded himself that solitude was better than being the odd guy out in a crowd.

He wasn't afraid of change, he assured himself. He just saw no need to fix what hadn't been broken. His heart, for example.

And that errant thought annoyed him so much that his scowl deepened even more. "Eat your breakfast," he muttered. "Your eggs are getting cold."

Tim obligingly stuffed a bite of bacon into his mouth, but Banner could tell it wouldn't be long before the interrogation began again. He was rather relieved when someone knocked on the front door.

"Maybe it's Lucy," Tim said after a hasty swallow. "Maybe she changed her mind."

But Banner didn't think so. More likely it was Polston or one of the other guys with an invitation for him to watch the New Year's Day games or shoot some pool or something. Lucy's note had been too firm and pointed to have been written on a quickly regretted impulse.

The way things had been going lately, he shouldn't have been surprised to find another member of his family on his doorstep. At least it wasn't his father, he thought, stepping aside to let his sister enter.

"I don't have to ask if Tim's here," Brenda said, tossing her thick brown bob away from her face to look at him. "I saw his SUV outside."

"He's in the kitchen."

"Dad said you refuse to help us talk Tim into going back to school."

"As I've said to everyone who asked, it's none of my business whether Tim goes back to school. He's a grown man. It's his choice."

"I wouldn't listen if he did try to nag me to go back,"

Tim said from the doorway. "Rick understands that I've made my decision and no one is going to talk me out of it. Not Dad, not Mom, and not you, Brenda. Would you listen if I tried to talk you into quitting medical school?"

"But you can't even tell us what it is you do want," she argued passionately, her blue eyes glinting with a combination of frustration and concern. "What are you going to do? How are you going to support yourself?"

"I'll find a job swinging a hammer or flipping burgers, if I have to," he retorted. "I'm not entirely incompetent, you know."

"And you would be happier doing one of those things than going to law school?"

"I would be happier doing either of those things than going to law school," he said, looking and sounding utterly sincere.

"And what about Mom and Dad? How are you going to make things right with them? You said some very harsh things to them when you walked out."

"All I said was the truth. That they had no right to try to run my life. To choose my career, my friends, my future path. Maybe it works for you, but I need to control my own destiny."

Taking offense, Brenda planted her fists on her slender hips. "I happen to like the career I've chosen. The fact that our parents approve of my choice doesn't mean they pressured me into it."

"Fine. And they aren't pressuring me into anything, either."

"Look, I know Dad can come across as domineering and intolerant, but surely you don't want to give up on your relationship with him."

Tim gave a sullen shrug that was probably intended to

mask any feelings of hurt or loss. "Why shouldn't I? It seems to have worked for Rick."

"Don't pull me into this," Banner said immediately. "I'm no role model. Whatever problems you have with your father have nothing to do with me."

"'*Your*' father," Brenda repeated, turning on him now. "Can't you even acknowledge that he's *our* father?"

Banner shrugged. "He's the one who created that rift, when I made it clear that I make my own decisions."

"And because you felt rejected by him, you've holed up here in your solitude and your surliness. Well, you know what, Rick? Tim and I never rejected you. It was the other way around. You make a big production of being the family outcast, but you're the one who pushes away everyone who tries to love you. Maybe that works for you, but I don't want Tim to end up alone and bitter. And I—"

Her voice broke, but she brought it under control long enough to finish, "I don't want to lose the only brother who ever loved me back."

Tim's young face softened. "You know I love you, Brenda. This has nothing to do with my feelings for you, and I'm not going to let it put a rift between us."

"I want you to be happy, Tim. And I don't want you to do anything you'll regret just to prove something to Dad."

Tim put both hands on his sister's shoulders, looking down at her from his six-inch advantage in height. "I need you to trust me to know what's best for myself, Brenda. And I need you to support me in the choices I make. Just as I'll always support you in whatever you want to do."

She sighed, her shoulders sagging a bit in surrender. "All right. If this is really what you want, I won't nag you anymore about it. But I do hope you try to keep the lines of communication open with the family."

"As long as they give me the freedom to make my own decisions, I can deal with the other baggage. I'm not closing the door on the family, I just need a little space right now. Okay?"

She nodded. "Will you promise to let me know if you need anything? You can always go back to school if you change your mind, you know. Promise you won't let pride stop you from acting if you decide you made a mistake."

Tim gave her a reassuring smile. "I promise—even though I know I'm not making a mistake."

Banner watched as they hugged.

Biting her lip, Brenda turned to Banner after Tim released her. "I'm sorry about snapping at you," she said, her tone stiff. "I was upset."

"Forget it."

She drew a deep breath, her shoulders held with rather defensive dignity. "I promised Tim I wouldn't nag him anymore. I'll give you the same courtesy. If you want me to leave you alone, I will."

"I don't want you to leave me alone," he answered gruffly, shoving his hands awkwardly in his pockets. "You're my sister, too, damn it."

She caught her breath, her eyes suddenly shimmering with a hint of tears. "I think that's the nicest thing you've ever said to me."

He realized too late what he had triggered with his imprudent comment. He braced his feet as Brenda threw herself at him and locked her arms around his waist in a fervent hug. Awkwardly he patted her back.

Lifting her head, she gave him a tremulous smile. "I know you would rather be nibbled by ducks than be hugged by your sister, but I couldn't help it. That was such a sweet thing to say."

Grumbling something incoherent in lieu of thinking of

a real response, he stepped back and pushed his hands into his pockets again. And then he said, ''Are you hungry? Tim and I were just having breakfast.''

''I'd take some coffee.''

''Rick makes really good coffee,'' Tim offered, waving an arm toward the kitchen. ''He's a great cook, actually.''

Something in the young man's voice made Banner remember what Lucy had said about Tim having a touch of hero worship for his older brother. That possibility made him so uncomfortable that he frowned as he led them into the kitchen.

''Good Lord. What is that?'' Brenda asked, staring in disbelief at the beast waiting patiently by the back door.

''That's Banner's dog, Hulk,'' Tim replied as Banner crossed the room to let the dog outside.

''Oh. Well, he's, uh…'' Brenda's voice faded as she was unable to come up with an appropriate adjective.

''Ugly,'' Banner supplied in resignation. ''But he's a good dog.''

''I'm sure he is.''

''Lucy said he's not really ugly, he's just making a fashion statement,'' Tim said with a grin.

Brenda looked at him in curiosity. ''Who's Lucy?''

''Rick's girlfriend. Or, at least, she would be if he'd make half an effort to keep her.''

Pouring a cup of coffee for Brenda, Banner gave Tim a warning look. ''Don't start.''

''What's she like?'' Brenda asked Tim, probably knowing better than to ask Banner.

''She's great. Funny and warm and bossy and cheerful. She has a doctorate in mathematics but she looks like a college student. She looks at Rick the way a chocoholic gazes at a hot-fudge sundae. The way an astronomer studies a newly discovered galaxy. The way an art lover stares at an original Van Gogh found hidden in some old lady's attic. The way…''

"That's enough, Tim," Banner growled, feeling his cheeks warm.

"I get the picture," Brenda assured them. "I'd like to meet her sometime."

"That," Tim said with a look of bravado, "is entirely up to Rick, I think."

"Drink your coffee," Banner ordered with a touch of desperation.

He didn't believe for a minute that Lucy had looked at him the way Tim had described it, of course. Nor did he accept Brenda's accusation that he was the one who had been preemptively rejecting everyone for the past few years, rather than the other way around.

But his siblings had certainly given him some things to think about.

Three weeks into the new year, Banner had settled back into his old routines. He rose early, had his breakfast, headed out to the workshop for a long day's hard work. He ate his meals alone in front of the TV, while his dog snored on the hearth rug. He went running with Polston a couple of times when the weather permitted, making it very clear beforehand that they weren't to talk about Lucy. Because Polston had his own secrets, that wasn't a problem.

Tim called a couple of times. He had found an apartment in Nashville and was working as a substitute high school history teacher until he found a permanent job that appealed to him. He sounded satisfied with his choices and eager to move on to new experiences. Banner believed his kid brother was going to end up just fine, no matter what he ultimately decided to do.

He wished he could say the same for himself.

He wasn't sleeping. No matter how hard he worked, nor how tired he was when he crawled into bed, he managed only a couple of hours of restless dozing a night before he was wide awake again, staring at the ceiling and trying not to think about Lucy. He tried sleeping on the couch, but that didn't help, since he could still picture her sleeping there. Same with the couch in the office. Even spreading his sleeping bag in front of the fireplace held too many memories.

He hadn't missed Katrina this way, he thought with a wince as he almost ruined yet another white pine spindle by letting his attention wander away from his belt sander. How could he miss a woman he barely knew more than he had missed the one who had been his wife? And how much worse would it have been if he'd lost Lucy after becoming even more accustomed to having her in his life?

It was that last thought that made him even more convinced she had done them both a favor by walking out the way she had.

"I think it's time for plan B."

Even though the woman on the other end of the telephone line couldn't see her, Lucy shook her head adamantly. "No. Not yet."

"It's been more than a month. He's not going to call you."

"He might."

"I don't think so, Lucy. He's too guarded. Too shy."

Lucy sighed. "Maybe he's not interested."

"No way," Joan said, sounding absolutely positive. "He was in love with you before Christmas Eve ended. He just needs some pushing."

"Any suggestions?"

"Maybe I should call him. You know, thank him again for taking us in at Christmas. Ask him if he's heard from you. Casually mention that you would love to hear from him."

"Too subtle. It's going to take something far more direct."

"Such as…?"

"I'll probably have to go to him again. I'm thinking about hitting him over the head with a club and dragging him off by the hair."

Joan laughed. "I don't think I'll try that with Bobby Ray—even though he certainly has enough hair to get a good hold on. But he's much too heavy for me to drag anywhere."

"As if you'd have to," Lucy said a bit enviously. "Bobby Ray has no trouble at all making his feelings for you known."

Joan giggled a bit self-consciously. "No, I suppose he doesn't."

"Oh, there's someone at the door. I'll call you later, okay?"

"Sure. In the meantime, maybe you should be buffing your club."

Chuckling, Lucy disconnected the call and headed for the door. She pushed a hand through her tumbled hair on the way, but that was the extent of her primping. She figured her fitted gray T-shirt and gray-piped, black yoga pants looked respectable enough for the delivery guy or friendly neighbor or whoever she would find on the other side of her door.

Of course, if she had known she would find Banner standing there, she might have spent a few more moments in front of the mirror.

"You're here," she said blankly, gaping up at him.

He leaned against the doorjamb, his arms crossed over his chest, the very picture of handsome nonchalance. "You might have mentioned that you have an unlisted telephone number. And that your home address is a well-kept secret. You never told me your aunt and uncle's last name. And the people at the university gave me your office number, but since you didn't work today, that wasn't particularly helpful."

Her heart was doing a frantic tap dance inside her chest, but she managed to speak fairly evenly. "So how did you find me?"

"I had to make a few dozen phone calls. I ended up tracking down your father in Texas."

"You talked to my father?" she said, finding it hard to get past that tidbit.

"Yeah. You mentioned that he was stationed at Fort Hood. He seemed like a nice guy. A little suspicious, maybe, but I guess I can't blame him for that."

She had deliberately left without giving him her number or address, figuring that if he wanted to talk to her badly enough, he should have to work for it a bit. But she had assumed he would call her at her job, since he knew where she worked. She hadn't expected him to just show up at her home on a Saturday afternoon, five whole weeks after she slipped out of his bed.

"It's so good to see you," she said, almost afraid to look away from him, just in case he disappeared.

He straightened and dropped his arms, letting a glimpse of emotion show in his eyes now. "Maybe you could ask me in?"

Quickly moving out of the doorway, she motioned him inside. "Please."

He closed the door behind him, then reached into his jacket pocket. "I brought something with me."

She tilted her head in curiosity. "What is it?"

He pulled out a sprig of greenery. "Does mistletoe still work after Christmas?"

She felt her smile turn radiant. "Absolutely."

She didn't give him a chance to hold the mistletoe over her head. Throwing herself at him, she lifted her face to his to kiss him with all the emotion that had been building in her during the long weeks she had been away from him.

Tossing the sprig to one side, he gathered her into his arms, holding her so tightly she could hardly breathe— not that she would have even considered complaining. This was exactly the way she had dreamed of him holding her.

"I think I like your apartment."

Lucy laughed softly and propped herself on one elbow to study Banner's face. "You think?"

His hard mouth softened with a faint smile. "I didn't get a chance to see much of it."

"Are you saying I dragged you into bed?"

"Something like that."

She gave a satisfied nod. "Plan B," she murmured. "And I didn't even need a club."

He didn't even bother to ask for an explanation. Instead he pulled her face back down to his and kissed her again.

They had a lot of lost time to make up for, she thought, wrapping her arms around him again.

Lucy and Banner didn't leave her apartment for the rest of the weekend. Letting the answering machine take all her calls, she concentrated fully on Banner, so delighted that he had come to her that she didn't want to think of anything else just yet.

When hunger finally drove them from the bedroom, they cooked steaks in her tiny kitchen. Lucy did most of the talking, of course, chattering to Banner about her job and her friends, catching him up on news of Joan and Bobby Ray and the Carters—all of whom she had spoken to since returning home from the Christmas holiday.

Banner seemed content to listen to her chattering without saying a lot, himself, but she was accustomed to that. He did tell her that he'd finished the big furniture order he'd been working on when she'd visited him and that his friend Polston had agreed to look in on Hulk until Banner returned.

"You could have brought him with you—the dog, not Polston," Lucy clarified.

"I wasn't sure you could have pets in your apartment."

"Officially I'm not supposed to, but it probably would have been okay for a visit. Actually, I've been thinking about buying a house so I could get a dog or a cat."

"Buying a house sounds pretty permanent. You thinking about staying here for a while? Not in any hurry to move to a bigger city or a more impressive university position?"

He had asked the question very casually, but Lucy knew he was intensely interested in her answer. "I like it here very much," she said. "I like the school and the students and the central Arkansas area. I think I could be quite happy here for a long time."

"You make it sound as though you're pretty content with your life."

"I am," she agreed. "For the most part."

"Oh? Something missing?"

"Yes. Someone to share it with."

She watched him swallow. Hard. He toyed with the food remaining on his plate, though his appetite was obviously gone. "And if that someone lets you down? Or hurts you, even without meaning to? Or doesn't live up to what you had hoped for?"

"I've never expected to find anyone who was perfect," she answered gently, her throat tight. "Heaven knows I'm far from perfect, myself. The trick is to find someone who can love and accept me, flaws and all. I've always believed that when I found my match, I would know right away. And that I would be willing to risk a great deal to make it work."

Banner kept his gaze focused fiercely on his plate. "I've tried the relationship thing before, you know. It didn't work out."

"How much did you really risk for that relationship?" she countered. "How much of yourself did you really invest in it?"

"Very little," he admitted grimly. "Not nearly enough."

Her hands were shaking when she clasped them tightly in her lap. "And how much are you willing to risk this time?" she asked in a whisper.

He hesitated long enough to almost stop her heart. And then he looked up at her, his expression wrenching. "Everything," he said simply.

Her eyes flooded. "So am I."

He cleared his throat. "You want another glass of tea?"

She didn't switch emotional gears quite as quickly as he did, but she was able to catch up after only a moment. "Sure," she said, her voice still husky. "Another glass of tea sounds good."

"I'll get it." He jumped to his feet with a haste that revealed his eagerness to move away from the emotions that had threatened to overwhelm them.

Smiling through her tears, Lucy figured she still had a long way to go in teaching Banner how to open up to her. But, no matter what challenges lay ahead for them, the potential rewards were most definitely worth any risks.

Epilogue

Lucy made one last check of her dining room, admiring the festive holiday dinnerware, set for six, along with the creamy candles and masses of red and white flowers that decorated the center of the long table. Satisfied that everything looked perfect for the guests she was expecting at any time, she moved into the den, one hand resting on the slight bulge of her tummy.

A fire burned in the fireplace, and Hulk curled lazily in front of it, his snores rumbling softly through the otherwise quiet room. Lucy's requirements for a house had included a big fireplace, a dining room for family dinners, a detached workshop, and plenty of privacy-assuring acreage, yet still within a half-hour drive to the university. This two-story Victorian farmhouse set on five wooded acres in the hills outside of Conway met all her wishes and more.

She smiled when she spotted the man kneeling beneath

the lavishly decorated Christmas tree in one corner of the big room. She loved seeing Banner under the tree, she mused, admiring the way his loden-green shirt clung to his wide, strong shoulders. She could never ask for a more precious gift, she thought as she patted her tummy again.

"Are you still rearranging presents?" she asked, hiding her rush of emotion behind a lightly teasing tone.

"I wanted to make sure the gifts for Tyler and Tricia were at the front where they could find them easily," Banner replied, straightening. "You think they'll like the toys I made them?"

He still needed occasional reassurances, but she never minded providing them. "The wooden motorcycle for Tyler is incredibly cool—or 'sweet,' as he would say. And Tricia's going to love the little high chair for her dolls. I can't wait until they get here. It seems like forever since we've seen them."

"We just saw them at Joan and Bobby Ray's wedding in November. They've been busy since moving into their new home in Little Rock. And speaking of being busy, shouldn't you get off your feet for a while before they arrive? You shouldn't try to do so much."

"I'm not even six months pregnant yet," she reminded him indulgently. "I'm not quite ready to take to my bed."

"Oh, I don't know. Going to bed seems like a pretty good idea to me," he murmured, catching her around the waist for a quick, heated kiss.

"Behave yourself," she said when she emerged, breathless, from the embrace.

"Yes, ma'am. But sit down, anyway."

She moved obligingly to the couch. "Did I hear you talking to Tim while I was changing my clothes?"

"Yeah. He said he's looking forward to seeing us on New Year's Day. He and Brenda both seemed to be pleased that we invited them to spend a couple of days here with us.''

Family had become a big part of their lives together, Lucy reflected happily. She and Banner had spent Thanksgiving with his mother's family, who had accepted Lucy quite warmly into their midst, seeming to give her credit for helping Banner feel more comfortable among them.

She had met his father and stepmother, of course, and while that relationship would never be particularly close, they had managed to be cordial. Maybe, in time, some of the old rifts could be repaired, though not even Lucy expected miracles all the time. At least Banner had grown closer to Tim and Brenda, both of whom Lucy liked very much.

As for her family, they had made Banner feel welcome from the beginning. She and Banner would be traveling to Springfield on Christmas Eve, the day after tomorrow, to spend the holidays with her father, aunt, uncles and cousins. It proved how far he had come in the past year that Banner hardly seemed to dread spending so much time among so many people, though she knew he would be glad to come back home when it was over.

Home. The word made her look around again with another misty smile. Maybe it was hormones affecting her, or maybe the holidays, but she'd felt on the verge of tears all day today. She had never been happier in her life.

She and Banner had been married in May, after he had grown impatient with weekend visits and occasional week nights together and abruptly declared that they might as well get married and save the travel time. It hadn't been the most romantic proposal in history, but it had made Lucy cry, anyway. Especially when he had added gruffly that he loved her and that he didn't want to spend another night away from her for the rest of his life.

Banner had sold the house that had belonged to his great-uncle. Lucy had been reluctant for him to do so at first, assuring him that they could keep it for a weekend retreat or even a place for him to escape to when he needed to be alone, but it had been Banner's decision to let it go. She'd gotten the feeling that he was saying good-bye to more than the house. As much as he had loved his great-uncle, Banner had chosen not to follow in Joe's lonely, reclusive footsteps, after all.

The thought of being a father had caused some early panic for him, but Lucy's absolute faith that he would be wonderful at it was helping him find more confidence. It didn't take any particular skills, she had assured him. It just took a lot of love. And he had plenty of that to give, as he proved to her every day in his own way.

Her husband wasn't an easy man to know, but she found him incredibly easy to love. He would never be one to express himself in flowery phrases, but he would always be faithful and committed. He hadn't given himself easily to her, but once he had, he had held nothing back.

What more could she have wanted? she asked herself again.

She looked across the room, where he was adjusting the gas-log fire to dispel any chill in the room. She knew he was covering his impatience to see their friends by staying busy. "Banner?"

"Hmm?"

"Wanna play twenty questions until our guests arrive?"

He groaned. "What could you possibly have left to ask?"

"Actually, I just have one at the moment."

Heaving an exaggeratedly indulgent sigh, he asked, "What is it?"

''Do you love me?''

All trace of humor disappeared, leaving his expression completely serious. ''That's one thing you should never have to ask. You know I love you.''

She smiled and placed her hand in his as he sank to the couch beside her. ''I know. But it's the only question that really matters to me anymore.''

Banner's lips covered hers in a kiss that adequately illustrated just how sincere his answer had been.

* * * * *

Christmas Bonus, Strings Attached

SUSAN CROSBY

SUSAN CROSBY

believes in the value of setting goals, but also in the magic of making wishes. A longtime reader of romance novels, Susan earned a BA in English while raising her sons. She lives in the central valley of California, the land of wine grapes, asparagus and almonds. Her chequered past includes jobs as a synchronised swimming instructor, personnel interviewer at a toy factory and trucking company manager, but her current occupation as a writer is her all-time favourite.

Susan enjoys writing about people who take a chance on love, sometimes against all odds. She loves warm, strong heroes, good-hearted, self-reliant heroines…and happy endings.

Readers are welcome to write to her at PO Box 1836, Lodi, CA 95241, USA.

To my believers, Georgia Bockoven,
Robin Burcell and Christine Rimmer.
You know what you mean to me.

To Melissa Jeglinski,
editor, advocate and friend.

To Ken, one last time – for the good life,
for the great sons, forever.

One

Lyndsey McCord thought she could listen to him forever. Even the phone book would sound fascinating.

"Let's do a follow-up in two weeks," he said into her ear. "Note to tickler file. End."

Oh, yeah, the tickler, Lyndsey thought, sighing. His rich voice was as decadent as any thousand-calorie temptation. Nate Caldwell was dessert, all right, and she *always* saved him for last.

"You have to do this." His voice lost volume abruptly. Lyndsey could barely hear him. "I need you."

She looked up. It was his voice but definitely not in the recording.

She pulled off her headset, untangling her curly hair from the cord. Maybe she was taking this fantasy thing too far. She freely admitted to an infatuation with the man she'd never met, but she'd *never* imagined him talking to her before.

"You know how I feel about divorce cases, Ar."

It *was* him. Nate Caldwell. Live and in person. He must have come into the building the back way. She didn't know what to do. No one had ever come into the office after midnight before.

"I would if I could, Nate. It's impossible." A female voice grew louder as it neared. "I'm working three cases of my own and I took two of yours already so that you—"

A door shut, silencing the conversation between Nate Caldwell and Arianna Alvarado—two of the three owners of the Los Angeles-based ARC Security & Investigations, and Lyndsey's bosses for the past three months. They must have gone into Nate's office, which was so close to Lyndsey's cubicle she could fly a paper airplane into it.

She had gotten used to the eerie silence of working alone late at night, and now, well, having someone in the building threw her off her routine. What should she do? Print up the case file she'd just typed—her last, fortunately—and sneak out before they saw her? Except...

She had to put all the reports on the various investigators' desks before she left. Including Nate Caldwell's.

She moved to her entryway and listened, able to discern voices but not words. He was definitely upset about something, a tone far different from what she usually heard in dictation, when his voice was smooth, the flow of words easy. Judging by the reports she transcribed, he was smart. Judging by the comments of her friend Julie, who'd recommended Lyndsey for the job, he was thirty-two, charming, quick to smile, attractive, polite and thoughtful. In other words, the perfect man.

Oh, God. Twenty-six years old and she had a crush on a man she'd never met, a fantasy she let herself escape to when her life got dull. She couldn't knock on his door and present him with his report—it wasn't good to tamper with fantasies.

The document finished printing. Do or die, she thought, then stalled by delivering all of the reports but his. Should she interrupt? Their voices were a soft jumble of sound now. Apparently he'd calmed down. She moved closer to his office.

Oh, why hadn't she worn something other than a black sweater and jeans? Why hadn't she taken the time to put on a little makeup?

Why couldn't she lose fifteen pounds in five seconds?

Better to take the coward's way out and leave his report on Arianna's desk along with a note.

Lyndsey tiptoed down the hall, easing past his office. She opened Arianna's door quietly, wrote a quick note then left, backing out of the room and shutting the door soundlessly.

She turned—

"Who are you?" He was right there, no more than a foot from her.

She pressed a hand to her thundering heart. "I'm... Lyndsey McCord."

He glanced at Arianna's door then back to Lyndsey. "What were you doing in there?"

"Working." She tried to act calm. "I...transcribe the investigators' reports." *You might notice that I put yours on your desk, error free, every night, Monday through Friday.*

He looked her over so blatantly that she didn't know whether to feel complimented or harassed, until he walked away without a word.

Well, of all the rude— Lyndsey leaned against the door, stunned. So much for the perfect man. Nate Caldwell might have fooled Julie, but not her—

Oh, come on, Lyndsey. Here you are, creeping around the office. Of course he would question it.

Disappointment settled over her as she made her way

back to her cubicle. Another fantasy bites the dust, which was really frustrating, since she'd learned that one good fantasy could sustain her through twenty harsh realities.

She unplugged the string of twinkling Christmas lights decorating her work area then signed her time sheet.

"What's your name again?"

She jolted around. Her heart went back into overdrive. The man had a penchant for invading a person's space. "Do you make a habit of sneaking up on people?" she asked before she could censure herself. He was her boss, after all. She should bite her tongue.

"I wasn't sneaking. I was following."

"Well, I didn't hear you."

"I only asked your name."

The story of her life. She was one of those people who faded into the background. This time it stung more than usual. He wasn't only her boss, in her fantasies he'd carried her away to some exotic location and read poetry to her. The reality was he couldn't remember her name for fifteen seconds. "Lyndsey McCord," she said at last, resigned.

"Can you cook?"

The question was so out of the blue that she didn't respond at first, barely managing to keep her expression clear. She wasn't about to lose her job because she got snippy with the boss. She needed the position for at least two more months. "Of course I can cook."

"How well?"

"I worked for a caterer for a couple of years."

"Come into my office."

And *she* was worried about being rude?

"Please," she heard Arianna call from within his office.

Nate stopped, turned and looked at her. "Please," he repeated.

"I've already clocked out," she said, trying not to notice how his eyes were deep blue and intent. Never mind that square jaw, the shallow cleft in his chin, and a 2:00 a.m. shadow that only added to his appeal, if you didn't count his personality. His streaky blond hair looked like he spent a lot of time at the beach.

"I have a proposition for you, Ms. McCord." With that, he entered his office, obviously expecting her to follow.

You need the job, she reminded herself, trailing him. You really need the job.

"Come sit down," Arianna said, smiling encouragingly and patting the seat beside her on Nate's sofa. Lyndsey perched there, her hands locked in her lap.

"I need you," he said, hovering over her.

She felt her cheeks heat. Her best fantasy flared back to life. "Excuse me?"

"I need a wife. You'll do."

You'll do?

"For the weekend," Arianna added calmly after shooting Nate a quelling look that Lyndsey appreciated. "You and Nate would pretend to be married domestics. It's a marital infidelity case. I know it's last minute, but we really do need you. I'm sure you've realized from the number of case files this week that we're completely booked over the holidays, particularly for security needs."

Lyndsey liked and admired Arianna, but any job involving Nate Caldwell was out of the question now that he'd so rudely destroyed the fantasy that had kept her entertained for months. It would be one thing had he remained the man of her dreams.

"I'm busy this weekend."

"Doing what?" Nate asked.

She crossed her arms. "I don't believe I'm required to share my personal life. And anyway I'm supposed to work Friday night. Tomorrow."

"My assistant can fill in," Arianna said, making it too hard for Lyndsey to say no.

"Why me?" she asked Nate, suspicious.

"You fit."

"I fit?" What was that supposed to mean?

"It pays three hundred dollars a day," he added, ignoring her question. "Is that incentive enough?"

She managed not to let her jaw drop at the amount. But the advantage was hers. He needed her. She pushed him, not wanting to be in the background anymore. *Pay attention to me.* "I make thirty dollars an hour."

"You make that much because you get a nighttime incentive."

"That's my rate. It calculates to seven hundred and twenty dollars a day, in case you're wondering."

"You expect to be paid to sleep?"

"Would I be on call twenty-four hours?"

"In theory."

"I rest my case."

"Five hundred," he muttered, crossing his arms as well. "That's equivalent to mine."

"You're taking a pay cut?" Arianna asked, shock in her voice.

He sent her a cool look.

Lyndsey contained her excitement. In one weekend she could make enough money to fly her sister home from college for what would have been their first Christmas apart. So what if she didn't like Nate Caldwell?

She adjusted her thinking. She didn't know him, and she had heard good things about him. Surely she could deal with him for a weekend if it meant she and Jess would be together for the holidays. "What would I have to do?" she asked.

"Cook and clean for a philandering husband and his mistress—"

"*Alleged* philandering husband," Arianna interrupted. "Observe and report. Whatever you're asked to do, within reason. We're not sure of all the details yet."

"It doesn't sound like a two-person job."

"You're right," Arianna said, then smiled sweetly at Nate. "If Mr. Caldwell could do more than reheat pizza, you wouldn't be necessary."

Lyndsey debated. She didn't understand why an investigator of Nate Caldwell's stature would take such a basic job. ARC's referral-only clients had one thing in common: they were high-profile, whether their background was in business, politics or entertainment. They demanded and got discretion. A divorce investigation seemed too mundane for the firm, or at least for the owners. She couldn't remember typing up a divorce case for Nate, Arianna *or* Sam Remington, the third partner.

"Well?" Impatience coated Nate's voice.

She was half tempted to say no, just to irritate him a little. She decided not to push her luck. "I'll do it."

"I'll pick you up at eight in the morning." Without another word he walked out the door.

"Yes, sir," Lyndsey said with a little salute to his back, then recalled where she was and who she was doing it to. "Sorry," she said to Arianna. "That was unprofessional."

"He was rude, which is unlike him." Arianna stood. "I won't apologize for him, but I will tell you he has good reasons for not wanting to take this job. I appreciate your agreeing to help out, Lyndsey. We really were in a jam."

"Was it your idea to ask me or his?"

Arianna eyed Lyndsey, her head cocked, her gaze steady. "Does it matter?"

Lyndsey waited.

"His," Arianna said at last. "Come into my office for a minute and choose a wedding band to wear."

"I know it's none of my business," Lyndsey said, "but why did you meet here tonight? It's so late."

"The office was midway for both of us. I couldn't talk sense to him over the phone, and we were both in our cars. In fact, my date is waiting in the parking lot." Arianna flashed a smile. "I do love a patient man." She opened a desk drawer and pulled out a small black case, which she opened to reveal an array of wedding and engagement rings. "Take your pick."

Five minutes later Lyndsey slid into her car. She wrote a mental to-do list: pack, sleep for a couple of hours, shower, tame her hair, go online to check on airfare for Jess from New York to L.A. Could she get a good price only two weeks before Christmas?

After her engine coughed to life, she let it idle. At least it wasn't raining. Wet roads and worn tires weren't a good combination. Maybe there would be enough money left after the plane ticket to get some work done on her car.

You fit, he'd said. Fit what? she wanted to know. She hadn't felt she fit much of anywhere for the past seven years, ever since she put her life and dreams on hold to raise her half sister. She hadn't counted on being mom as well as big sister, but then neither had her mother planned on dying at thirty-eight.

Lyndsey pulled out of the parking lot and headed for home, a fifteen-minute drive. *You fit.* He probably meant she looked like she'd be good at taking care of people. He'd be right, of course. She'd done little else for a long time.

She certainly didn't fit with him, but maybe she could still have fun. They were supposed to look married, after all. She imagined his reaction to her calling him honey. The thought made her laugh. Suddenly he quit being a fantasy and became a man. A person. Just another human being.

She stopped for a red light and glanced at her left hand. From a selection of wedding rings in Arianna's desk she'd chosen one that was two bands woven together, nothing flashy but not too plain, either. On her thumb was a man's matching ring.

She tried to picture how she would act, even though she knew little about what the actual job entailed. She wouldn't fawn over him—she imagined too many women did—but she could establish an intimacy that would look genuine to onlookers, like actors did for their roles.

Nate Caldwell wouldn't know what hit him.

Ms. Lyndsey McCord's little Spanish-style stucco house was nestled in a quiet, old West Los Angeles neighborhood that hadn't been touched by the many revitalization efforts making their way around the city. The lawns were well tended, for the most part, as were the homes. Even in the daylight, Christmas decorations were visible on most houses, although not Lyndsey's. The moment Nate pulled up, her front door opened and she came outside, garment bag and overnight case in hand.

He appreciated that she was ready. No last-minute primping. No adding something to an already bulging suitcase. No asking his opinion of the clothes she was wearing or taking. The novelty was refreshing. They exchanged greetings as he met her on the walkway and took her bags, which he stowed in the car as she locked her front door.

"No alarm?" he asked when she slid into the passenger seat.

"The best kind—good neighbors," she replied.

He watched her buckle her seat belt in the four-year-old sedan. The car was one of several the firm kept for certain undercover work. She looked rested, yet, like him, she'd had only a few hours' sleep, he thought as he eyed her.

Nate enjoyed women, and generally they liked him. It

seemed that Lyndsey did not. He saw it in the way she avoided eye contact and heard it in her short answers as he started to brief her on their assignment. They had to look like a couple, compatible and comfortable, if this operation were to succeed.

Time to undo the damage.

"I apologize for last night," he said. "Nothing was going right."

"Okay." She stared out the windshield. After several seconds of silence, she asked, "Where are we going?"

Did "okay" mean she'd accepted his apology? "To the client's house in Bel Air first, then down to San Diego for the assignment itself. Del Mar, actually."

"Expensive real estate."

"Yeah. Money's no object."

"Money is always an object," she said.

He smiled but she didn't seem to notice. He took a quick survey of her. She looked professional in her blue slacks and crisp white shirt. Her chin-length brown hair wasn't as wildly curly as last night but still got tangled in her trendy glasses with the forest-green frames that matched her eyes. Her curves were…curvy. Temptingly female. No starvation diets for her. She seemed comfortable in her own skin.

He noticed how still she sat, like last night. Her hands were folded neatly in her lap as if she went undercover every day.

"Arianna picked out the rings?" he asked, noticing them on her left hand, irritated and relieved that Arianna remembered. It wasn't like him to forget details. Damn Charlie for calling in his favor.

"I completely forgot." She pulled a band off her thumb and passed it to him. "I chose them, actually. I thought they suited us. The working us."

Ignoring the shards of memories that cut into him, he

shoved the ring on. He would've pocketed the damn thing except he had a job to do, a role to play.

"You started to tell me about the assignment," she said.

"It's fairly routine. Wife found out her big-time corporate husband plans to spend a few days at their weekend retreat in Del Mar with his assistant. Didn't tell her he was going. She's got a spy in the office, apparently."

"Classic."

"It gets better. The wife was previously the guy's assistant. The relationship broke up his first marriage. They've been married almost ten years. She's thirty-five, he's fifty-three. They've got a ten-year bailout clause in their prenup. He's been acting strange lately, and she figures he's about to dump her for the new assistant before he has to shell out millions more. She needs proof of infidelity to secure her financial position."

"There's that money thing."

"As you said. I'm not sure how the wife got to arrange the domestic help, but she worked it out with Charlie Black, the P.I. we're replacing. I wanted to meet the client personally before we started." He gave her a quick look. "Ever done anything like this before?"

She shook her head, sending her curls bouncing. He wondered if they were as soft as they looked.

"I did a little acting in high school. It's kind of the same."

He didn't correct her. There would be no script to follow. The job forced you to think fast on your feet. He'd enjoyed her quickness last night regarding her salary— once he got home and thought about it, that is. And she certainly had no trouble standing on her own feet. He half suspected that if Arianna hadn't been there, Ms. Lyndsey McCord would have given him a piece of her mind. He figured she'd handle her part okay. In a way she reminded him of Arianna before she'd become so sophisticated. One thing that had never changed about his partner was her straight talk. He sensed the same about Lyndsey.

They arrived at the client's Bel Air mansion and were shown into an ultrafeminine sitting room then were joined by the client a minute later. Nate wasn't often wrong about people—anticipating accurately made the difference between a good and a great P.I.—but his expectations of a trophy wife were shattered when she walked in the room. Instead of tall, blond and Botoxed, she was a short brunette with vulnerability in her eyes and wariness in her posture. She introduced herself as Mrs. Marbury.

"You're young," she said, looking from Nate to Lyndsey.

"We're competent," Nate replied.

She sat, then indicated they should, also. "I didn't mean to imply—" She stopped for a moment. "I just want to be sure I get the proof I need. You'll be discreet?" She looked at Lyndsey for an answer.

"Very," Lyndsey said.

"I'll need photographs."

"We'll take care of it," Nate said, drawing her attention back to him.

Mrs. Marbury pulled open a drawer in a side table and withdrew an envelope. She passed it to Nate. "I wrote down as much information as I thought you might need. Needless to say, Michael didn't hire our usual cook, so he won't expect you to know where everything is. He did request certain menus, which I've included. The recipes are in the drawer next to the stove. You'll need to buy groceries before he arrives."

"When will that be?"

"Around dinnertime."

"Does he think we're hired out by an agency?"

"No, his vice president of operations—my friend—raved about a domestic he'd used recently when he took his girlfriend to our place for a week. My friend's praise was part of a test, one my husband failed by asking for the man's phone number. Mr. Black, the other private investigator, took over from there.''

"Does your husband expect a man, then, instead of a couple?"

"No. Mr. Black took care of that."

The woman had backbone yet still seemed fragile, Nate thought. Was it her husband or her comfortable life she was more upset about losing?

"You'll find cash for groceries in the envelope." She stood. "I expect you to check in with me once a day."

"All right."

"I should warn you," she said to Lyndsey. "He thinks women have their place, and it's not in jobs he would consider a man's domain, like private investigator. The more female and distracted you act, the more efficiently you'll be able to work and the less inclined he'll be to be suspicious of you."

She sat back, looking weary. "Can you see yourselves out?"

"Of course. Good day."

Neither spoke until they'd driven out of the neighborhood.

"What's your take on Mrs. Marbury?" he asked. He appreciated how she'd remained silent except to answer the client's direct question. Discretion went a long way in his business.

"Her heart is breaking," Lyndsey said.

Nate almost groaned. This was exactly why he'd wanted to work with Arianna on this case. She didn't sentimentalize anything. "Don't tell me you're a hopeless romantic, Ms. McCord. This job requires objectivity."

"I'm objective. And no one's ever accused me of being either hopeless or a romantic."

Something in her tone made him pay attention. Defensiveness? Ego? Pride? "Why do you think she's so much in love with him?"

"Women in her position usually look perfect. It's part of their job. Yet I don't think she'd even brushed her hair. She's so upset, so depressed, she couldn't pull herself together."

"She's worried about losing the money."

Lyndsey looked at him. "You are so negative. Who burned you?"

Everyone who mattered. He stopped the words from slipping out. "I've seen it all before," he said instead.

"Do they have children?"

"Charlie didn't say." Nate felt unprepared for the job, which ticked him off. He always did his homework first. Being thrust into the assignment without complete background put him at a disadvantage. He didn't like being at a disadvantage. Plus he despised divorce cases. "Why don't you open the envelope and see what's in there."

Lyndsey pulled out the contents. "They eat well. Five hundred dollars for food."

"It's probably to include wine and champagne."

Lyndsey turned over the sheet. "There's no alcohol requested."

"Maybe there's plenty on hand. What else does she say?"

"He'll be using an alias—Michael Martin. He must be famous if he's using an alias, but I've never heard of him."

"CEO of Mar-Cal Industries. And on the board of several corporations and charitable foundations."

"I guess I don't travel in the same circles," she said, smiling at Nate.

It changed her whole face.

She continued. "Our Mr. Marbury/Martin is allergic to shellfish and strawberries," she continued. "He likes his coffee and newspaper brought to him in bed. He's a light sleeper who doesn't sleep through the night and doesn't like to fend for himself, so he'll wake up the help to fix him a snack in the middle of the night.'' Lyndsey looked up. ''See? Twenty-four-hour duty.''

He resisted smiling at her bulldog attitude. ''You're being fairly compensated, Ms. McCord. Anything else?''

''She drew up a floor plan. It's a big place but not that many rooms. A bedroom and an office, a living room with a deck to watch the sunset, she says. Kitchen's roomy but not huge and it backs up to the servants' quarters, which are…um.''

''Which are?'' he prompted after a minute.

She stuffed everything back into the envelope then tossed it onto the dashboard. ''I'm gonna need a bonus.''

He glanced over and saw the bulldog look again. ''Why's that?''

''According to the floor plan, Mr. Caldwell, we'll be sleeping together.''

Two

It was a double bed.

Nate paused, luggage in hand, after he stepped into the servants' quarters at the beach house. Not king-size, or even queen, but an impossible-to-sleep-in-without-touching double. He was six foot two. Lyndsey was about five-seven. He lifted weights. She wasn't petite.

He felt her come to a halt behind him and peek around his shoulder.

"Kind of small," she murmured.

"We'll figure out something," he said, although he couldn't imagine what. The rest of the motel-size room held only a dresser, a small glass-topped table and two serviceable chairs. The floor was hardwood, not carpeted. He hadn't slept on a floor since his army days and didn't intend to sleep on one now. Nor could he expect Lyndsey to.

In silence they put away their clothes. She was done

first and moved into the bathroom with her toiletries. When she emerged a minute later, she met his gaze.

"I'll leave you to come up with a plan," she said, her eyes sparkling. "I'm going to get dinner started."

She breezed past him, a subtle scent drifting in her wake. He breathed it in then carried his shaving kit into the bathroom and stopped short. A clear-glass stall shower dominated the space. He swore it was bigger than the bed. Easily big enough for two.

Her comment in the car about having to share a bed had jump-started his imagination. Reality revved its engine now.

He stowed his kit in the vanity then fingered Lyndsey's flowered travel bag next to his. Her wholesomeness appealed to him. Her buttoned-to-the-neck blouse should have camouflaged any hint of sex appeal but did the opposite. Usually he turned a one-eighty upon meeting a woman like her, one who waved the flag of independence yet also seemed destined for home and hearth. The marrying and mothering kind. Problem was, he couldn't turn his back on her for the next forty-eight hours, even with the other strike against her—she worked for him.

Still, his curiosity was aroused, a rare occurrence. He gravitated toward women who were emotionally undemanding and sexually experienced. He knew where he stood with them and was rarely surprised.

Not this time.

He checked his watch and estimated they had about two hours before Mr. Marbury/Martin arrived. Nate grabbed his digital camera and followed the clatter of pans to the kitchen, which had a common wall with the servants' room.

"Stop working for a few minutes and come check out the house with me," he said, the sight of her wearing a starched apron reinforcing his homey image of her. He tucked his camera into a handy corner of the kitchen, a compact room that could be shut off visually from the combination living/dining room by closing bifold shutter doors installed along a pass-through counter.

The living room furniture faced a glass wall with a view of the beach and the Pacific Ocean beyond the rooftop of the house in front. The master bedroom enjoyed the same panorama, the bed positioned to take in the ocean vista, as well. A sumptuous master bathroom adjoined the bedroom and contained a whirlpool tub and an etched glass shower stall. The bathroom connected on the far wall to a home office.

"Do you really expect to get pictures of them, you know, doing stuff?" Lyndsey asked when they stepped onto a deck that stretched across the front of the house and wrapped around the living room.

Doing stuff? He almost smiled at her phrasing. "Not in bed, if that's what you mean. My best opportunity will be from the kitchen into the living room and out onto this deck."

"You think they'll be messing around in front of us?"

The horror in her voice finally did draw a smile. "People accustomed to servants don't notice them. They won't ask us personal questions. In fact, they'll probably ignore us altogether except for giving specific instructions about food or other comforts. If they notice us beyond that, we haven't done a good job."

"You don't set up surveillance equipment? No video or microphones?"

"Not my style. It's bad enough having to photograph what I *can* see."

"You really hate divorce cases, don't you? You implied it to Arianna the other night."

"I stopped doing them years ago. The firm accepts them, but not me."

"Is there a particular reason?"

"I've seen enough. So, how's the kitchen?"

Silence hovered between them as she caught up with his quick change of subject. "Well equipped. But if I'm cooking, what job does that leave for you?"

"Whatever else needs doing, particularly anything where I can gather information on them. It'll almost be a vacation for you, Ms. McCord."

"A vacation," she repeated wistfully, as if the concept were foreign. She turned away and leaned against the railing. "I love the ocean," she said, lifting her face and inhaling. "My mom took my sister and me to the beach a lot. It was cheap entertainment. We always had so much fun."

Her hair had coiled tighter in the ocean air. He let his gaze drift down her appreciatively, lingering on the neatly tied apron bow and the strings that trailed down her rear.

"What about the sleeping arrangements?" she asked, facing him.

"You sleep under the sheet. I'll sleep on top."

"Are you a right-side or left-side sleeper?"

"Take whichever you want. I'll adjust."

She pushed away from the railing and ambled toward him, then tapped a finger to his chest. "Marriage is full of adjustments, isn't it, honey?" she said, fluttering her lashes before strolling away.

He considered the privileges of marriage…the big glass shower…the very small bed.

Then he reconsidered his need to keep the job a job while pretending to be married to her. He had a feeling she wasn't going to make it easy on him.

Her unspoken challenge made him laugh. *Bring it on, Ms. McCord. Bring it on.*

From the kitchen Lyndsey heard Nate greet Michael Marbury and his assistant, Tricia. Lyndsey pressed her hands to her stomach and blew out a breath. *You can do this. You can do this.* The words tumbled over and over. She looked at the floor, took another breath and left the kitchen, almost crashing into Mr. Marbury.

"And this is my wife, Lyndsey," Nate said. "I'll be right back with your luggage."

He strode off, leaving her alone with the couple, neither of whom looked at her. Mr. Marbury seemed to be admiring the view out the front window, and Tricia stood staring at Nate. Well, really. She had a man of her own—

Lyndsey put the brakes on her thoughts. Possessive? Over a man she hardly knew, except in her fantasies? She couldn't blame the woman, however. His broad shoulders filled out his sage-green polo shirt; his trim waist and long legs were emphasized by perfectly fitting khakis. He was a sight to behold—her sight. For this weekend, anyway.

She set aside her surge of jealousy to debate whether she should direct her words to the man or the woman. Who was in charge? The fifty-three-year-old trim, gray-haired man with the air of authority or the twenty-five-year-old auburn beauty with an even more authoritative look? Since the man never made eye contact, Lyndsey spoke to his assistant, hoping to draw her attention as she seemed to be waiting for Nate to return.

"May I get you something to drink?" Lyndsey asked.

Tricia blinked. Her expression cooled. "We'll unpack first." She urged Mr. Marbury toward the bedroom. He went like a puppet. "Is dinner almost ready?" she asked over her shoulder.

Lyndsey ran a mental list. The salad was done except for slicing the avocado, and a fruit and cheese plate was prepared for dessert. She needed only to steam the asparagus, heat the sourdough baguette and grill the salmon. "Twenty to thirty minutes, or longer if you'd prefer."

"No. The earlier the better," Tricia said. "On second thought, we'd like ice water now. In fact, I need an ice bucket kept full in the bedroom at all times, so please make sure ice is always made. I'll fill it myself when it's empty." She followed Mr. Marbury into the master bedroom and shut the door.

"Right away," Lyndsey said to an empty room. A minute later she heard Nate pass through with the luggage then a low murmur of voices from the bedroom as she fixed a tray with an ice bucket, goblets and bottled water.

He came into the kitchen. "I'll take that to them. Nervous?" he asked quietly.

"A little. They're so…unfriendly, even to each other. I expected them to be joined at the hip."

"Then the job would be too easy," he said with a wink. "One of the things I like and hate about this business is that my expectations are rarely met."

He left with the tray, but his departing grin relaxed her, and she got caught up in the spirit of the experience. They were playing parts in an improvisation. She should just enjoy the adventure and not worry about the outcome.

She double-checked the table, which she'd set earlier with exquisite linens and china she found in a hutch, then gave a vase of yellow tulips a slight turn and stepped back. Perfect.

Twenty-five minutes later she served up four plates. Nate knocked on the couple's bedroom door and announced that dinner was ready. Lyndsey closed the shutters between the kitchen and dining area, and she and Nate ate standing at the sink while the couple dined more leisurely.

Tricia came unannounced into the kitchen when they were almost finished with their meal. She held up a hand as they came to attention. Her expression was a little friendlier. "We don't need anything. I just wanted to thank you for the meal. It was perfect."

"You're welcome," Lyndsey said, pleased.

"What is that wonderful smell?"

Lyndsey glanced at the oven. "Chocolate chip cookies. They weren't on the meal plan but—"

"Say no more. They make a great midnight snack."

"Yes."

"Michael and I were surprised to hear a couple would be filling in for Mr. Black, who had come so highly recommended. The job hardly seems to need two people."

"We're newlyweds. We don't like to be apart," Lyndsey said, the words popping out. She turned toward Nate, who came up behind her, his eyes conveying a fascinating combination of tenderness and heat. She swallowed.

"Oh? How long have you been married?"

"Three months on Sunday," Nate answered. He rested a hand on Lyndsey's shoulder.

Tricia leaned against the doorjamb, her arms crossed, her gaze settling on Nate. "How did you meet?" she asked.

"On a blind date," he answered without hesitation.

"We hated each other," Lyndsey added, embellishing, feeling Nate's fingers press lightly into her flesh. In approval? Or as in, *Don't get carried away?*

"Really? Hated each other?"

She nodded. "I thought he was arrogant. He thought I was flaky, didn't you, honey?"

"Pretty much."

"So what happened?" Tricia asked.

"Can't ignore chemistry," Nate said.

Lyndsey patted his hand. He entwined her fingers with his. She took a quick breath, caught off guard by his warmth. Chemistry, indeed.

Tricia's friendly expression faded. "Mr. Martin requests

that you retire as soon as the kitchen is cleaned up. We won't need anything else, and we'd like privacy until morning.''

Lyndsey hid her surprise. What happened to his wife's assertion that he would wake up the help to fix him a snack during the night? "Of course, ma'am. Would you like coffee brought to you before breakfast?''

She considered it. "You can set up the coffeemaker tonight. I'll turn it on in the morning when I get up, probably around six-thirty. We'll breakfast around eight.''

"I'll leave you some cookies on a plate,'' Lyndsey said.

Tricia waved a goodbye.

Nate put a finger to his lips before Lyndsey could say anything. In silence they cleared and washed the dishes. The cookies were baked and moved to cooling racks then plates. She poured two glasses of milk and asked him to carry a plate into their bedroom.

Their bedroom...

It was eight o'clock, the beginning of a long night.

Nate turned on the television in their room, leaving the volume loud enough to cover their conversation. She plunked her fists on her hips. He wasn't surprised at the first words she spoke.

"You said they wouldn't ask personal questions.''

He was as surprised as she, although he shouldn't be. This case wasn't following predictable patterns. "You improvised well,'' he said, and was rewarded after a moment with a smile that lit up her eyes, even behind her glasses.

"I did think you were arrogant, you know,'' she said, taking off her glasses and laying them on the table as she sat down.

"You don't now?'' He watched her shake out her curls with her fingers. She looked tired. Considering how little sleep they'd gotten the night before, it wasn't surprising.

She picked up a cookie and seemed to study it. "Maybe you just have excessive confidence. Did you think I was flaky?"

"Those were your words, not mine." He sat in the other chair. "I didn't know what to make of you. You were creeping around like you didn't belong there."

"I didn't want to interrupt, but surely you knew I worked there."

"I knew someone came in during the night to transcribe the reports. I'd even seen a car in the parking lot when I pulled in. But I was ticked off, so it didn't register. I apologize for not coming into the office since you were hired, and introducing myself, which I should have done. Arianna reminded me that I hadn't." He grabbed a cookie, took a bite then toasted her with it. He hadn't had a homemade chocolate chip cookie in a long time.

"I know your voice so well I felt like I'd already met you," she said.

"I imagine you know everyone's voice," he replied, curious at the faraway look in her eyes.

"What? Oh, of course I do. Voice *and* idiosyncrasies. For example, you rarely hesitate and almost never change your mind or insert something at the end. Sam and Arianna file good reports, too. You're all efficient."

"Have you met Sam?" Sam Remington was the third partner of ARC Security & Investigations. He, Arianna and Nate had met in the army, then opened their agency six years ago, after planning it for years.

"I've met him several times. He's the quiet one. He's got a way about him that makes you want to take a step back, you know? He's, I don't know the word exactly, fierce, maybe?"

"Intense."

"Yes. But once you get past that he's easy to talk to and really thoughtful."

"In what way?" Damn, these cookies are good, he thought, grabbing another.

She shifted in the chair, not answering him right away. "It'll probably sound silly."

Intrigued, Nate eyed her over the rim of his glass of milk. "I doubt it." *Sam* and *silly* weren't two words Nate would ever put together in a sentence.

"You know how analytical he is," she said. "Good with numbers."

"*Great* with numbers. And computers."

She nodded. "He has an old Rubik's Cube...."

"I've seen it in his office."

She cupped her glass between her hands, spinning it slowly. "Whenever he's in town he leaves it on my desk. I'm supposed to mix it up for five minutes then leave it on his desk. The next day he solves it and gives it back, along with a note saying how long he took to do it. His record is one minute and thirty-three seconds."

"How does that make him thoughtful?"

"It makes me feel like part of the office when I could easily feel invisible. When he's out of town I miss it."

"And Arianna? How would you categorize her?" he asked.

"Competent. Cool under fire yet warm. We connected on some level when she first interviewed me. I like her a lot. She's good about checking in with me a couple of times a week, either by phone or in person."

"I think I've just been criticized."

"Not at all. With you I was perfectly content just to fan—" She stopped, coughed, took a swallow of milk. "Excuse me. I was perfectly content to *tran*scribe the reports. I knew what the job entailed when I took it." She put her empty glass on the table and stood. "I'm going to get ready for bed."

He knew the situation was about to get awkward so he

focused on the television as she took sweatpants and a T-shirt out of the dresser and disappeared into the bathroom. He decided to take their empty glasses to the kitchen. Maybe he could hear or see something.

He eased open the door and moved quietly down the hall. Silence greeted him. No voices, no television, except from the servants' quarters. He waited a while. Nothing.

By the time he returned to the room, Lyndsey was in bed, the covers pulled over her shoulders, her back to him. He took his cell phone into the bathroom, called Charlie Black then Mrs. Marbury to give her a report, choosing his words carefully.

He joined Lyndsey a few minutes later. With the television and lights off, the room seemed even smaller. Like her, he wore sweats and a T-shirt. He smelled soap and toothpaste, different from his.

The only other woman he'd spent a celibate night in bed with was Arianna. Not that he hadn't been attracted to her, years ago, when they first met. Then they talked and he came to appreciate her intelligence—not to mention she could put a man in his place with just a look. She was no object. He was glad he'd caught on to that early in their acquaintance or he might have ruined what had become a solid friendship and a great business relationship. The sexual attraction was long gone.

This intimacy with Lyndsey was different. He felt naked.

Nate became increasingly aware of her, even though she didn't breathe audibly or move an inch. He wondered which one of them would give in first to exhaustion and fall asleep. Probably him, since he had a feeling she would stay awake all night if she needed to.

He slid his hands under his head and stared at the ceiling.

"Was that your girlfriend you were calling?" she asked into the quiet.

"The client."

"Oh. What did you tell her?"

"That they arrived, that they weren't talkative or demonstrative, and that they had retired for the night."

"How did she take it?"

"Without emotion. So, what do you think of your first undercover job?"

"I love it," came her instant response, then she rolled onto her back and turned her head toward him, tucking the covers under her chin. "It's fun."

"Fun?"

"Shouldn't it be? Nothing's going as predicted, which makes it kind of exciting."

He thought about it. While he loved what he did, he'd stopped acknowledging what made the job so appealing. "You seem to be a natural."

"I do, don't I?"

"Yeah. But don't get carried away with the role. It's easy to trip yourself up."

"You mean like those things I told Tricia?"

"Anything more would've been overkill."

"See, I knew that." The excitement was back in her voice. She turned on her side, facing him. "But she seemed to buy it all, didn't she?"

"I think so."

"She was jealous."

He had closed his eyes and was drifting a little, so her words didn't register for a few seconds. "Jealous?" he repeated.

"She checks you out all the time."

"She does not."

"Does so. She's hot for you."

He laughed.

"It's true."

"No, it isn't," he argued. "She's devoted to her boss. She's solicitous of his every move. I think she'd cut his meat for him if he'd let her."

"And what is it with him, anyway? He's supposed to be some big-shot executive, but he lets her make all the decisions. That man hasn't said two words in front of me."

"They stop talking in front of me, too. One box I carried from the car was paperwork, though."

"Maybe this trip is business, not pleasure. Maybe it's all a big misunderstanding."

"If that were the case, why wouldn't he tell his wife about it?"

She got quiet for a minute. "Oh. Right."

"I've learned to trust a spouse's intuition. Suspicions are usually justified."

"So Mrs. Marbury couldn't be overreacting?"

"It's unlikely."

"You said that nothing in this case is running to expectation."

She had a good mind, a logical mind. He appreciated it. "True."

"That doesn't lead you to think that Mrs. Marbury could be wrong, too?"

"Let's look at it from her point of view. She knows him like no one else does. He starts acting differently. She finds out he's going away for the weekend with his assistant, and not only does he not invite his wife along, he doesn't even tell her where he's going. Infidelity isn't new territory for him—a fact Mrs. Marbury knows, since she was his assistant before she became his second wife. She not only knows he's capable of cheating, she even knows how he does it. They probably had weekends away under the guise of business trips themselves."

He could almost hear her thinking. He closed his eyes, feeling his muscles relax and his body grow heavy.

"Why didn't they just have food delivered?" she asked suddenly. "We're potential witnesses."

Because they're used to being waited on, he thought but didn't say aloud. He needed sleep. So did she.

He made a sleepy sound as he rolled to his side, away from her. He heard her sigh.

"She does so have the hots for you," she whispered.

He grinned.

Three

——

Seeking the source of the heat behind her, Lyndsey wriggled backward until she felt a wall of resistance. Much better, she thought sleepily. Warm. Three seconds hadn't passed before her eyes popped open and she realized exactly what she'd snuggled against—a hard male body.

How could that be? He was on top of the sheet, she was under—

No, she wasn't. She didn't feel cotton against her bare feet but the textured weave of the blanket. He hadn't violated her space; she'd violated his.

How? Then she remembered. She'd gotten up around three o'clock and slipped into the bathroom to take off the bra she'd worn to bed as if it were armor. It was cutting into her. She must have gotten under the blanket instead of the sheet when she climbed back into bed. She was surprised she'd gone back to sleep so easily.

Lyndsey eased away from him. His hand came down on

her hip, stopping her. A few seconds later his whole arm slipped over her, trapping her against him. If he moved his fingers two inches higher he would touch her breasts.

Her body went on alert. She couldn't draw a full breath. Her breasts swelled. Her nipples turned hard and achy.

She should move. Instead she relaxed against him, welcoming the comfort of his body and the desire that flared inside her without apology. She angled her arm a tiny bit to see her watch. Almost five-fifteen. How much longer could she enjoy him until he woke up? In all her fantasies, she hadn't imagined this reality, this chemistry. This sense of rightness.

She knew the moment he awakened. His breathing changed, his body tensed. His hand flattened against her stomach, his thumb pressed into her breast. She waited for him to move. It seemed like an hour passed before he eased himself away, but it was probably only a few seconds.

Her breath released on a long shaky exhale.

"Lyndsey?" His voice was soft yet questioning.

"I'm sorry," she said, scrambling away, rubbing her arms against the chill of the morning—or was it embarrassment? Or, more likely, disappointment? "I don't know how I ended up on top of the sheet. I didn't do it on purpose, I promise. I wouldn't—"

"Stop," he said, interrupting. "It's fine."

She sat on the edge of the bed, her back to him. "But I violated your space. I—"

He made a sound she couldn't interpret. She looked over her shoulder in time to see him sit up against the headboard. He combed his hair with his fingers. "It's no big deal."

Maybe not to you, she thought, irritated at his blasé attitude. He probably woke up next to someone at least once a week. She never had. Not that she was inexperienced, but she hadn't wanted to set a bad example for her sister by having a man sleep over. She'd had few relationships through the years. Guys gave up on her when they realized how little time and attention she could give them. Her independence probably made them think she didn't need anything. She did. She just didn't know how to ask for it.

For all she knew, Nate had a girlfriend.

The thought depressed her. Of course he had one. He had everything to offer.

"Hey," he said.

"What?" She didn't mean to sound belligerent, but she knew she did.

"Don't sweat it."

"Okay."

He got out of bed. "I'm going for a run. I'll pick up a newspaper on the way back."

She climbed back under the covers until he left the room. Taking advantage of his absence and the early hour, she took a leisurely shower, not bothering to do much with her hair since it would only turn into ringlets in the damp weather.

By the time she went into the kitchen she was in a better mood. She turned on the coffeemaker then took grapefruit out of the refrigerator to section. Blueberry pancakes and bacon would complete the menu, but there was no hurry. She could set the table while the coffee was brewing.

Lyndsey used the white everyday china instead of the fancy dinnerware of the previous night. She found green place mats and napkins to contrast nicely with the yellow tulips and was humming to herself when the bedroom door opened. Tricia stepped out, shutting the door quietly behind her. She carried the ice bucket.

"Good morning," Lyndsey said, surveying her. Tricia had already brushed her hair and wore a black silk peignoir over a matching lacy nightgown that peeped out at her ankles as she moved. "The coffee's ready. Shall I fix your tray?"

"Yes, thank you. Cream and sugar, too." Tricia followed her into the kitchen. She dumped the melted ice into the sink then moved to the refrigerator to refill the bucket. "This is a beautiful house, isn't it?"

"It's wonderful. I love the view."

Tricia scooped ice into the bucket then set it aside and leaned against the counter, waiting. "I hadn't been here before."

Lyndsey just smiled, not wanting to say something she shouldn't.

"How do you like being married?" Tricia asked.

"It's also wonderful," she said as she pulled mugs out of a cupboard.

"And the view's not bad, either," Tricia said.

Lyndsey laughed as if she enjoyed the joke, but she didn't. Not one bit. How dare this woman ogle her husb— Her pretend husband? "Nate went for a run and to get a newspaper," she said, pouring the coffee. "He should be back soon."

"Good. Michael likes his paper early. So, is this what you and your husband do for a living?"

"Not exclusively. We only take weekend jobs. I'm still in college. He's in construction. It's slow right now." That would account for his tan, his streaky blond hair and his muscles, she decided.

"How long did you date before you got married?"

"Long enough to know he was the one."

"How does anyone know that?"

The question almost seemed rhetorical. Was she expecting an answer? "I guess if it's right you know."

"Don't you think everyone feels like that when they get married?"

"I can't speak for everyone, only myself."

"Do you think he'll be faithful?"

What was going on? Lyndsey focused on fixing the tray—first the mugs, then sugar and cream in beautiful porcelain containers. Spoons. Napkins. Was she supposed to engage in this conversation? Would she glean something that could be used against Mr. Marbury? "I expect fidelity. Wouldn't you?"

"I would hope for it."

Ah. The difference between us, Lyndsey thought. I wouldn't marry a man I didn't expect to stay faithful, to love me until death. Her biggest fear was that she would fall in love with someone who wouldn't stay when the going got tough. She hoped she'd at least learned something from her mother's mistakes.

She heard the back door open. Soon Nate appeared.

"Just in time," Lyndsey said, relieved to have him back. "You can add the newspaper to the tray."

He slipped the paper along the edge of the tray after giving Lyndsey a curious look. Was her discomfort with the conversation visible? She hoped so. She wanted him to step in and change the subject.

"Good morning," he said to Tricia, coming to Lyndsey's rescue.

"Good morning," she said in return, looking him up and down.

Lyndsey said *See!* with her eyes. Nate's took on a mischievous sparkle.

"I'm going to take a shower," he said to Lyndsey. "Unless you need me for something."

Do I ever. I need you to kiss me. I don't care that you're sweaty and need a shave. You look like heaven.

"I'm fine," Lyndsey managed while recalling the feel of his body along hers and his thumb on her breast. He winked.

''You can carry the tray into the bedroom first,'' Tricia said to him, grabbing the ice bucket and preceding him to open the door.

When he came back, he stopped in the kitchen long enough to yank Lyndsey's apron ties undone. She smiled as she retied them and blessed whatever hand of fate had put her in the office later than usual the night before last.

Hours later Lyndsey stood in the kitchen while Nate cleared the lunch dishes in the dining room. Mr. Marbury finally spoke, and it was with the authority she expected from a man of his position.

''Your wife told Tricia that you work in construction,'' he said to Nate. ''I have a job for you.''

Lyndsey clamped a hand over her mouth as she listened, horrified. She'd tripped them up, even after he'd told her about the dangers of overkill. She shouldn't have made up the story in the first place, but she should have told Nate about it, at least.

''The wood rail along the top of the balcony needs to be replaced,'' Mr. Marbury continued. ''The materials were delivered last week and are in the garage. I'll pay you extra, if you'll do the job today.''

His tone of voice indicated he wasn't asking but telling, no matter what his words were. There was no ''if'' involved.

''Yes, sir,'' she heard Nate say.

A few seconds later he brought the dishes into the kitchen, gave her a direct but cool glance and started loading the dishwasher while she finished the marinade for the chicken they would have for dinner. Her heart thumped in her chest in rhythmic torture. A minute went by. Then another. Two more. He finally came up behind her, put a hand on the counter on each side of her and leaned close.

"Was there anything else you forgot to mention?" he whispered.

He was angry. She was distracted by how close he stood, how his breath gave her chills, how the muscles and tendons in his forearms made her long to run her hands down them. "I'm sorry."

"I don't suppose you know how to replace a railing?"

She shook her head.

"Face me, please."

She swallowed and turned. He didn't budge. They were inches apart.

"Any ideas about how to get us out of this?" he asked.

"I could fake an appendicitis attack."

His eyes were as blue as the sky at twilight, giving her a glimpse into a dangerous side of him she hadn't seen before, one that thrilled her in ways she never would've imagined. She couldn't stop staring at him, trying to see deeper, to understand who he was. Because she really liked him. A lot. A whole lot. She needed to find reasons not to, because she had a feeling he could break her heart into tiny, slow-healing fragments.

Then it occurred to her how to get them out of the jam she'd gotten them into.

"I know how to use an electric drill." She set her hands on his chest, excited. Out of sheer necessity she'd learned the basics of home repair. "I can drive a nail in straight, too. I could do it, Nate. You just need to look like you're the one in charge."

His mouth twitched. He smiled. Then he dropped his head and laughed.

"What?" she asked.

"You. You're so sincere." His smile hadn't faded, although he still seemed to be regrouping from his anger reluctantly. "I know a thing or two about construction."

"You were toying with me? You let me be scared for no reason?"

"Most women enjoy being toyed with now and then."

Her breath hitched at the innuendo. "I'm not most women." She was proud that she could form words. Amazed, actually.

"No, you're not. You're—"

The kitchen door swung open. Lyndsey jumped. Nate merely turned his head. They must look as if they'd been caught kissing.

"Excuse me," Tricia said.

He backed away but slid his arm around Lyndsey's waist. "Is there something else, ma'am?"

"Michael says you'll find tools in the cabinet next to the washer and dryer in the garage."

"Thanks." He dipped his thumb into Lyndsey's waistband.

She didn't breathe. Tricia didn't move.

"I'll get right to it," he added.

Tricia left without comment.

"If I'd known my cover was going to be that I worked in construction, I'd have brought my pickup," he said quietly to Lyndsey. It was clear he was still irritated with her but was trying not to show it.

He hadn't moved his hand. She wished she could just lean into him and enjoy it. She'd made an error in judgment. Was he going to trust her to do a good job from here on?

"You have a pickup?" she asked, putting distance between them before she started wiping down the already clean counters.

"I'm a country boy at heart." His tension still hummed.

"Sure you are."

"I am. What'd you figure I drove?"

"Something sporty and convertible. And red."

"Got one of those, too. A Corvette. Different cars for different purposes."

"Any others?"

"A Lexus. You need a four-seater now and then."

"Because you double-date a lot?"

He grinned. He wasn't bragging about the cars, she decided, but being honest. She wondered what it would be like to have a vehicle that started up the first time you turned the key. Or had a working heater. Or tires with treads. She only had to hold on another four years, until Jess graduated and got a job. Lyndsey would treat herself to her first brand-new car then.

"This job is turning out to be one surprise after another," he said cryptically. "Let's go see what kind of carpenters we make."

"I can't wait to see you in a tool belt, honey," she said, batting her lashes, hoping to wipe out whatever remained of his anger.

He raised his brows. "Are you toying with me?"

"If you're like most men, you like it."

"Well now, I think you just shimmed me between a rock and a hard place. I don't believe I'm like most men, but I do like you toying with me."

Lyndsey wondered how they were going to get through another night in a bedroom alone after all the flirting and touching. The anticipation made her feel more alive than she could remember feeling. More feminine. More desired.

If this was a one-time opportunity, should she deny or encourage? Tempt or wait to be tempted? Was it better to satisfy her needs and have regrets or not satisfy them...and have regrets? She'd thought a fantasy fulfilled wouldn't be a good thing, but maybe she was wrong.

She had all afternoon to think about it. He'd be the biggest heartbreak of her life, no doubt about it.

* * *

Her chance to make up for her rookie mistake came without much warning later that afternoon. The railing had been replaced and looked perfect, but they were sweaty from working in the sun, so Nate showered first, then Lyndsey got in. Fifteen seconds hadn't passed before she heard his voice.

"Are you a fan of irony? They want me to go rent *True Lies* from the video store," he said.

Startled, she crossed her arms over her body. Through the steamed glass, she saw he'd barely opened the door and was talking through a crack.

"Okay," she said. What else could she say?

Instead of the door closing it swung open. He walked toward her, his hand covering his eyes. She stood frozen as he fumbled for the latch and pushed the shower door open.

"Come here," he said, low.

Hot water beat against her shoulders, her back, then her rear as she stepped toward him.

"They're looking comfortable out on the balcony. Get into the kitchen as soon as you can. You might snag a few photos while I'm gone if they think you'll be in here a while."

"Okay." Even though he'd sort of blindfolded himself, the idea that she was naked in front of him sent tornadoes of awareness whirling through her, touching down every so often in a new erogenous zone, gathering strength.

"You remember how to use the camera?" he asked.

"Of course." He'd shown her the day before.

"Good. I'll be back as soon as I can." He paused. "You know, I never figured you for a red nail polish kind of woman."

Lyndsey looked at her toes. By the time she raised her head he was gone. She didn't have a minute to think about it. She hurried out of the shower, dried off and dressed so fast that her clothes stuck to her damp body. Skip the makeup. Finger-comb her hair. Tiptoe out of the room and into the kitchen.

Mr. Marbury and Tricia were framed by the glass door in a perfect vignette, a beautiful pinkish sky behind them. She was seated in a deck chair, her head bent forward, her long hair falling over her breasts. Mr. Marbury stood behind her, his hands on his shoulders. He was giving her a massage.

Lyndsey snapped several photos. Then he leaned close to Tricia, his mouth near her ear. She turned toward him, smiling. Their faces were inches apart. Lyndsey kept snapping until Mr. Marbury straightened and stared right at her.

Caught.

Four

The camera was small. She tucked it in her palm, pretended to be brushing her hair from her face, then dropped it into her pocket. She was washing her hands when he appeared at the counter dividing the kitchen from the dining room/living room.

"What were you doing?" he asked.

"When?" *Nerve, don't desert me now.*

"Just now. You were watching us."

"No, sir. I was admiring the sunset. The sun was sinking into the ocean. I don't get to see that very often. Wasn't it gorgeous?" She smiled.

He turned to see the view she said she'd been admiring. Tricia waited, her eyes on them.

Lyndsey checked her menu. *Just forge on. Baffle him with innocence.* "I'm going to start dinner. It'll take about an hour, if that's good for you."

He looked bewildered. "What are we having?"

She read off the notes. "Tomato and mozzarella salad. Penne with spicy chicken, sun-dried tomatoes, shallots, Kalamata olives and feta. Lemon sorbet and Italian cookies for dessert. It makes my mouth water. Can I get you anything while you wait?"

"No." He eased backward for several steps before he turned around and returned to the balcony. After a moment of discussion he and Tricia entered the master bedroom from the balcony and the house went quiet.

Lyndsey leaned against the counter. She did it. She'd pulled it off. The rush was heady. She high-fived the refrigerator. "Yes!"

When Nate returned, she tossed him the camera. He took it into the bedroom to view. A few minutes later he joined her in the kitchen and swiped a few olives as she chopped them.

"Did they turn out okay?" she asked, anxious.

"They're clear. Do you think the client will be happy with them?" He kept his voice to a near whisper.

"There's no kiss," she said. "They saw me before they had a chance to kiss. But if I were married to him, I'd be furious and hurt that he was touching another woman that way. Looking at her that way."

"But is it enough evidence for Mrs. Marbury's legal needs?"

"I would say no."

"You'd be right."

"What now?" she asked, some of her triumph fading.

"We can't manipulate a scene to make it fit."

"I haven't even seen them hold hands."

"Neither have I. I got up a few times during the night and put my ear to their door. I didn't hear anything."

"That's creepy."

"Yeah. I really hoped we could end the investigation this weekend."

She looked up at the resignation in his voice. "What was so important about this job that you agreed to take it when you obviously didn't want to?"

"Charlie Black."

"The P.I. you took the case from?"

"Not *from. For.* We worked for Charlie when we first got in the business, until we qualified for licenses on our own. We grew his business way too fast, and he was happy and relieved when we opened ARC and he could go back to being a one-man operation. He's continued to send us jobs that are too big for him, and they often lead to others, but this one was his. Then his wife had a heart attack and he couldn't follow through."

"Oh, how awful. Is she all right?"

"They may do bypass." He leaned an elbow on the counter. "You're a nice person, Ms. McCord, to worry about someone you don't know."

"I think most people are nice."

"Hang around this business long enough and you'll change your mind. Very few people stand up to scrutiny."

She stopped dicing the shallots to focus on him. "I'm sorry you've lost your faith in people."

"You're restoring some of it," he said, his gaze steady.

She waited for a coherent thought to enter her head. "Well, I understand your being frustrated taking this case, but it seemed more than that."

He shrugged. "I was supposed to leave today on my first vacation in years."

"To?"

"Australia."

Australia. The word seemed magical. She hadn't even been as far as San Francisco. "Were you able to postpone it? You can go later, can't you?" *Were you taking a girl-friend?*

"Probably. I'll have to reschedule assignments again. Plus I'd planned to be there over Christmas."

"Alone?" The word came out without a second thought.

"Yes."

"How could you celebrate Christmas by yourself?"

"The point was not to celebrate."

"You…don't like Christmas?"

"And you do. I noticed yours was the only work space in the office decorated for Christmas."

He didn't make it sound like a good thing. She didn't know how to respond. She was sad for him, for anyone who didn't get caught up in the spirit of the holidays. "Do you know why I took this job?"

"Because I railroaded you?"

She hesitated. "Well. That, too. But mostly because I could use the money to bring my sister home for the holidays. This would've been our first Christmas apart."

"Where is she?"

"She's a freshman at Cornell. An architecture major."

"How does a Southern California girl survive the winter in Ithaca, New York?"

"Surprisingly well. She'd never seen snow before and she says she loves it. It helps that she lives on campus so she doesn't have to drive somewhere every day."

As she cooked she told him about how her mother died when Lyndsey was nineteen and Jess was eleven. That Lyndsey had just finished her freshman year at UCLA. How she moved back home to raise her sister.

Then she talked about how she never knew her father, that he'd walked out before she was born, then so did Jess's father when she was only six months old.

"Mom had a problem choosing men with staying power," she said, adding the penne to boiling water. "She was a great mother, though. Fun and free-spirited. Every day was an adventure. It's so quiet now without Jess. Who would've thought I'd experience empty-nest syndrome at twenty-six."

Nate put together the salad Lyndsey demonstrated. A slice of tomato, a slice of mozzarella, a large basil leaf. Repeat. Drizzle with olive oil. He worked close beside her so he could continue to keep his voice quiet. "Did you have to give up college?"

"No, but it took me longer. I got my master's in accounting in May, then I took the Universal CPA Exam last month. I'll have the results in February."

"I can't picture you as an accountant."

Her back went stiff. "What's wrong with it? It's steady work. Excellent pay. And I'm good at it."

Touchy, Nate thought. Protesting a little too much? "I wasn't insulting you. I'm sure you're good at it, but I do know several CPAs. They don't tend to be people oriented. You are. And you're observant."

"I'm detail oriented. It's a good trait for an accountant."

"And an investigator. So are you quitting us when you pass the exam?"

"When I get a job. It's not a secret. Arianna knows. I told her when she hired me."

"Of course you did."

"What does that mean?"

Touchier, still. She intrigued him. "You know that saying about someone having an honest face? You could be the poster child."

"I've been lying to—" She angled her head toward the door.

"You've been acting. There's a difference." He stepped away from the counter as a soft sound intruded. Their conversation had been barely above a whisper so he wasn't worried they'd been overheard, but it irritated him that Mr. Marbury, or more likely Tricia, was trying to eavesdrop.

"I'll be right back." He opened the door.

Tricia lifted her hand as if to knock. "I—I was wondering about dinner."

"Ten minutes," Lyndsey said.

Nate realized that Lyndsey's imagination hadn't been working overtime. Tricia did look him over like a piece of meat, but he wasn't sure it was born of passion. Her expression was more of a sneer. He kept quiet, putting the burden on her.

"Thank you," she said, her chin notching up. She left.

Nate waited until Tricia's bedroom door shut before closing the kitchen door again. He came up behind Lyndsey and said quietly, "You were right. She wants me."

"What'd she do?"

"Undressed me with her eyes." She was so easy to tease, he almost felt guilty about it.

She stirred the pasta faster, slopping water over the top. "I told you. Besides, she's already got a man of her own. She needs to leave mine alone."

Silence crash-landed in the room.

"I mean—" She fumbled the spoon and her words. "You know what I mean. She thinks you're a married man."

An unexpected wave of tenderness assaulted him. How did anyone that innocent survive in the big, bad world? "She's already with a married man, Lyndsey."

"But he's old."

Nate was still smiling when he served the first course.

Once again they were sent to their room right after dinner, except this time they weren't exhausted.

As dilemmas went, this was a big one. How to spend at least two hours in a tiny room with a man who'd filled her fantasies for months, then had become a pretty good reality, too. Situations like this didn't happen to her. It was like a movie or something: Lyndsey the Ordinary, who stands out about as well as camouflage, is lured into the world of espionage and becomes Lyndsey the Extraordinary. Nate the Great falls madly in love with her. She toys with him, driving him crazy. He begs to sleep with her....

She smiled at the scenario. Begging. Yeah, she liked that.

"What's so funny?" he asked.

He was trying to fix a broken zipper on his shaving kit, his back to her. She'd been enjoying the view as she spun her tale.

Her face burned at being caught. "Do you have eyes in the back of your head?"

He pointed to a mirror on the opposite wall over the dresser.

Oh. "I wasn't smiling at you," she said.

"I didn't say you were."

"Your voice implied it."

"You're reading between the lines, Ms. McCord."

She grabbed a cookie and munched on it, refusing to be drawn into a battle of words with him. Especially when he was right.

He tossed the shaving kit on the bed. "That's hopeless. How would you like to go down to the beach?"

"Now?"

"Why not? We've been dismissed for the night."

"But what if they change their minds and want something?"

"They'll have to wait."

"But what if they do something we should see? Shouldn't we—"

"Let's go." He grabbed her hand and pulled her up.

"You're bossy," she said, but she followed him out the

door, her hand held tightly in his, her pulse pounding at the adventure.

"I *am* your boss."

She kept forgetting that.

Five

There was nothing like a walk on the beach at night, Nate thought as they strolled along the shoreline. They hadn't spoken for the past ten minutes. They were barefoot, their pant legs rolled up. He watched Lyndsey lift her face into the breeze and shake her head. Her hair danced around her.

"We should probably head back," he said into the comfortable silence. He was tempted to put his arm around her as they walked back to the house. He wanted to feel her arm slip around his waist, and her head rest against his shoulder. But she kept a few feet between them.

He thought about how she had assumed her responsibilities, forgoing a time in her life when she should have been free to explore and experiment and raise a little hell.

"How did your mother die?" he asked.

She didn't answer for a minute. "She had an aneurysm. Jess found her in bed."

"And you not only had to deal with your grief, you had to become a parent. Did you resent that?"

"Not often. I knew how to budget money, probably because my mom was horrible at it. It came as no surprise that she only had a small life insurance policy. Along with Social Security payments for Jess, I stretched the money out until she turned eighteen. What saved us—what made it possible for me to keep going to college—was that the house was paid for. My mother had inherited it from her mother."

"You worked and went to college and raised a child. Jess worked, too, I imagine, when she was old enough?"

"No. It's hard to hold down a job and do well in school and have a social life. I didn't want her to miss out. She was already denied a mother. She ended up being valedictorian because she focused on her studies. She was homecoming queen, too."

"That's a hell of a double punch. Did you work while you were in high school?"

"Yes. But I wanted to."

Nate didn't believe her. She wouldn't have insisted her sister not work if Lyndsey had really enjoyed working herself. "What'd you do?"

"The usual. Fast food, sold tickets at a movie theater. Baby-sat. And yes I also got good grades."

"Valedictorian grades?" He looked over at her in time to see her smile.

"Close. Very close," she said.

"Did it hold you back, not being number one?"

"I got into the college I wanted to."

"Were you always an accounting major?"

"Nope. Theater."

He'd expected something different, but not that. "Why'd you switch?"

"Is that a rhetorical question? Look at me. Realistically what were my chances of making it as an actress?"

"I'm looking." *And liking what I see.* Why would she have any less of a chance to be successful in Hollywood than any other woman? "I don't get it."

She looked as if she didn't believe him. "I needed an income I could count on," she said, changing the slant of the discussion. "Everything worked out. I'll be able to pay for Jess's college."

He got it. She didn't want to talk about why she didn't think she was right for Hollywood. "Didn't Jess get scholarships?"

"Not full ride. It costs a fortune to attend a good university. And it's not only tuition and books and dorm room. It's all the other stuff you need. Scholarships and financial aid only go so far."

"Is she working?"

"Not yet."

"She's been there since August."

"I didn't want to push her. It's hard enough adjusting to college and your first time away from home, but especially three thousand miles away." She slowed her steps. "What's with the third degree?"

"Just killing time." He could see she was becoming annoyed at his questions, but he had an endless number of them.

"Well, it's not fair. You're learning everything about me, and I know nothing about you."

"Asking questions is my business."

"That was an interrogation. Now I have a question for you."

"Fire away."

"What did you mean the other night in the office when you said that I fit?"

"Just that. You fit. With me. We look like we could be

a couple.'' He stopped. ''Hang on. They're on the balcony.''

Lyndsey focused in the direction of the house. She could barely make out two silhouettes.

''Let's get closer.'' He took her hand and moved along at a good pace.

''Won't they see us?''

''Maybe.'' He stopped. ''They're looking our way. Come closer.''

He drew her into his arms, shifting their bodies so that he could see the house. After a few seconds she let out a long, slow breath and relaxed into him. His arms tightened. So did hers. She loved the feel of his body, the comfort of his embrace. She closed her eyes.

''Are they still there?'' she asked, not caring but hoping he would think she was still doing her job instead of thoroughly enjoying being held.

''Yes.'' He drew back slightly, bent his head toward hers.

He was going to kiss her.

Amazed and expectant she waited. Then she saw his eyes were still focused on the house. It was a ploy. Except…

His body was responding to hers.

''Sorry,'' he whispered, which struck her as funny.

She started to laugh. He was apologizing for flattering her. Or maybe he was just easy.

''This is supposed to be a romantic moment,'' he said.

She laughed harder. What an idiot she was, thinking he was really attracted to her. It was just an automatic reaction, that's all.

''Lyndsey?'' His tone asked if she'd lost her mind.

She had. Along with her common sense. She wished he wasn't the most fascinating man she'd ever met. Not that she'd been close to very many. Without a father around she hadn't had firsthand experience with the male way of thinking, only her mother's comments about their skewed logic, self-centeredness and lack of responsibility, especially the charmers—and Lyndsey's and Jess's fathers were both charmers. Lyndsey didn't think it was fair to lump all men into the description. To her mother's credit, she never seemed to be whining but was stating the facts as she knew them. She even spoke fondly of both men.

Nate was certainly logical and responsible. Self-centered? Not really.

But she couldn't ignore the obvious: he was charming. He was also sophisticated, attractive and successful, and he probably dated gorgeous women who were slender and equally sophisticated. Lyndsey, on the other hand, was a homebody who frequently forgot to wear makeup, whose curly hair was out of fashion, whose body proved she wasn't a big fan of exercise, and who struggled to make ends meet. Plus she worked for him. How many strikes did she need?

Yet he told her they fit. That they looked like they could be a couple. And he'd come to that conclusion when she was wearing her ugly old black sweater and jeans, no makeup, and her hair was a mess. What was he seeing that she wasn't?

"They went inside the house," he said, stepping back.

"Can we sit for a couple of minutes?" she asked.

He hesitated a few seconds. "Sure, why not."

She stopped trying to figure him out and just enjoyed listening to the surf pound the shore. Voices traveled, laughter, shouts. She didn't know where they came from, only that it meant they weren't alone. She closed her eyes and breathed the salt air, so distinctive, so calming. She pictured Nate on a beach in Australia. It would be summer there. Warm. Balmy. She envied him the opportunity to travel. Sometime she would travel, too.

She'd been thinking a lot about her future and what she wanted. Travel was only one goal. Her work goals were shifting, too. Becoming a private investigator wouldn't have entered her mind before, but the idea had taken hold at some point today and stuck. She was detail oriented, people oriented, and she loved a puzzle. She was tiresomely meticulous, which was why there was never an error in the reports she typed.

Nate interrupted her thoughts. "I can't figure them out," he said.

Lyndsey almost sighed. Back to business. "They don't act like lovers."

He didn't look convinced. "I don't know. There's a certain intimacy between them. I've been in groups of people where a man and a woman are on opposite sides of the room but I know they're together in every other sense. When people have been intimate, you know it, even those who think they're hiding it."

"But what kind of intimacy are you talking about? Aren't there several levels? My sister and I can sit together, our arms touching. There's nothing sexual about it, but it is intimate."

"If it's man/woman, I'm talking sexual intimacy."

"Always?" she asked.

"Ninety percent of the time."

"Maybe on the man's part. For women, intimacy comes from being comfortable, I think, whether it's with a man or a woman."

He looked skeptical. "So you have male friends?"

"Well…no, I guess not. Not close friends. Not someone I confide in."

"Because?"

"Are you just trying to be right? I'm only one woman. Poll a few thousand more."

"I'm interested in your answer. Why don't you have any male friends?"

Because one thing my mother told me I've found to be true—men don't have staying power. They take what they want, then they make a clean break. Not that she'd wanted it any other way. So far she hadn't met a guy she wanted to spend six months with, much less her whole life.

"I don't know, Nate. I guess I haven't met that many men who appealed to me enough to try to make friends."

"We need to go."

She sighed as she stood. She wouldn't soon forget this night, being on the beach with her fantasy man. She shivered at the thought.

"Cold?" he asked.

The man was far too observant. "A little."

He put his arm around her and drew her close. She intended to argue. Really, she did. But she wrapped her arm around his waist instead and let his body heat warm her.

"I think I should be remembering that you're my boss," she said.

"Let's agree for the rest of this weekend that we're co-workers, not boss and employee, although, frankly, I don't think you've given me enough respect anyway."

"Oh, you don't?"

"No. I think you're opinionated, and not deferential at all."

"Which makes me the perfect wife."

She waited for his comeback but none came.

Half an hour later their feet were washed clean of sand, they'd changed into their sweatpants and T-shirts and were lying on the bed watching an old episode of *The Cosby Show.*

"I've been thinking a lot about your sister," he said at the first commercial.

She groaned. "You are a bulldozer."

"Just hear me out."

"Like I have a choice?"

"You could tell me to shut up and go to sleep."

"Like you'd listen? You sure do talk a lot, for a man."

"You like the silent, brooding type?"

"I like the minds-his-own-business type."

He smiled. "Do you also like the he's-looking-out-for-your-best-interests type?"

"For now I'd like a man who doesn't put a question mark on the end of everything he says."

"You would?"

She shoved him. He fell onto his side, laughing. When she did her best to scowl at him, he changed positions so that he could face her and propped himself up on an elbow near her feet. He grabbed her foot through the covers and pressed into her arch. She couldn't help it. She moaned.

"You like that?" he asked.

She nodded.

"You didn't seem to mind that question."

"I'm fickle." She closed her eyes and eased her shoulders into the pillow. She made another sound of pleasure as he pushed his thumb into the pad of her foot.

"Put your feet outside the covers," he said.

Because she could and still keep her eyes closed, she did. She didn't want to see his face. She just wanted to feel his touch. It'd been so long since someone had taken care of her.

"Are you falling asleep?" he asked after a while.

"And miss out on this? No way."

"About Jess…"

She laughed and groaned at the same time.

"Lyndsey."

"Oh, all right. Get it over with."

"I realize I've never met your sister, so I'm basing my opinion strictly on what you've told me."

"Duly noted."

He stopped the foot massage. She grudgingly opened her eyes and pushed herself up to sit cross-legged. He sat up, too.

"I've seen it time and time again. The kids who are given everything by their parents end up the most screwed up."

"My sister wasn't given everything. She *lost* everything. She never knew her father. Her mother died when she was eleven. Eleven!"

"And you stepped in and did an admirable job. But she's an adult now, and you're not helping her grow up by giving her so much, by not making her work for what she gets. You made it on your own, even with the extra pressure of raising her. Jess could—and should—too. She'll not only appreciate what she earns, she'll learn how to take care of herself. That's important."

"You don't understand."

"Maybe not, since I haven't been in your position. But I do know there comes a time when letting go is the best gift you can give someone, even when that someone doesn't think she needs it."

It wasn't as if Lyndsey hadn't debated the issue with herself many times—and even come to the same conclusion. It was just that it was so hard to let Jess go. To let her make mistakes. To let her struggle or falter—or fail. Would Jess hate her then? She couldn't bear that.

She saw sympathy in Nate's eyes and resented him for it, without knowing why. "You're right. You haven't met my sister. You don't know what a terrific person she is. I haven't spoiled her. I made her crummy life a little better, and I will continue to. Because I love her. And because she's all I have." Her voice trembled. It made her mad.

"Don't cry." He said the words hard and fast, with something like panic in his eyes. Physically he retreated.

Lyndsey wouldn't have cried even if he hadn't reacted so violently to the possibility. She'd stopped crying years ago. Better to just suck it up and move on.

"I'm sorry," he said.

She didn't want him to apologize. She wanted him to keep pushing her until she accepted his help, because it would mean he cared about her, like he was encouraging her to do with Jess. But he wasn't pushing. He was apologizing. It infuriated her, she who rarely lost her temper, who always gave people the benefit of the doubt. "You have no right to tell me how to live my life."

"You're right, I don't."

She crossed her arms. "I've managed just fine for seven years."

"Okay."

"What's that supposed to mean?"

"I'm agreeing with you."

"I don't need any help."

"Everyone needs help now and then."

"Not me."

"Even you." Nate inched closer as she drew back. He knew she was so used to going it alone that she didn't know how to share the burden. He wanted to be her sounding board. He wanted to do something wonderful for her, something unexpected, something that would make her smile that glorious smile.

"Don't," she said.

"Don't what?"

"Whatever it is you're planning. I see it in your eyes."

He put a hand on her arm, felt her muscles bunch. "I'd like to help you."

"How?"

He resisted smiling at her continued belligerence. "What would make you feel better?"

"Nothing."

"So you're just going to stay mad at me?"

"That's right."

"Are we having our first marital spat?"

She tossed her head. "I guess the honeymoon is over."

"Maybe not. We could kiss and make up." Why the hell had he said that?

She stared at him for several seconds, hesitancy in her eyes. He waited for her to say no, to tease him a little about it. Instead she looked serious and contemplative.

He remembered the moment on the beach and his instant reaction to holding her against him. He wanted to finish what they'd started. *Just say no, Lyndsey.*

She nodded. How could he back down without hurting her feelings?

"Are you sure?" he asked. *Just say no.*

She nodded again.

A few choice swearwords swirled in his head. "Will you accept it as my apology?"

"Oh, quit asking questions and do it."

He smiled at her impatience. Stalling, he pulled off her glasses and set them aside, trying to slow himself down because, when she looked at him like that, with all that need in her eyes, he wanted to rush. And he wanted to run.

"You have the most expressive eyes, Ms. McCord. They're always saying something."

"You can't tell anything through my glasses."

"Is that why you wear them? To hide?"

"To see."

"You could wear contacts."

"Look, if you don't want to do this…"

"What's your hurry?"

"We're not supposed to go to bed angry." Her eyes dared him.

"I've always found that theory flawed," he said, running a finger down her cheek, along her jaw, across her lips. "It's better to go to bed angry than to say something you'll regret or can't take back."

"Do you ever shut up?"

He loved that she was irritated. Loved that he upset her equilibrium. Because she sure as hell was upsetting his.

He meant to kiss her lightly, just enough to fulfill the dare. But she made a sexy little sound when his lips touched hers, as if she'd been waiting for him forever. Her lips were soft, her tongue warm, her breath sweet. He wanted to devour her.

Slow down. Slow…down.

The commands went unheeded. He wrapped his arms around her and shifted her to lie under him, levering his weight off her with his arms. Her hair tumbled around her head. Her eyes were half-closed. Her mouth, her incredible mouth, was slightly open, her breathing irregular.

He dipped his head, touched his lips to hers tenderly. She whispered his name with such longing. He nestled more comfortably between her legs. She moaned, drawing her knees up, letting him closer. He hadn't meant for things to go so far but he couldn't seem to stop. He buried his face against her neck, kissed the tender flesh under her ear, moved his hips rhythmically against her. She tipped her pelvis, accepting him.

Then he stopped thinking. She rocked under him, lifted into him. He thought he would burst. A long, low moan came from her. He blocked the rest of the sounds with his mouth. Her climax went on and on, until he was sweating from holding back.

He wanted to bury himself in her—

"Did you bring protection?" she asked, her voice strained.

Nate froze in the arctic remnants of her words. What had he done? What the hell had he done?

He loosened his hold, rolled onto his side. "Lyndsey, I—no, I didn't bring protection." Which was a lie. They were in his overnight bag, as always, but this wasn't the time or place for them.

She came to awareness in a flash and backed away from him, eyes wide and cheeks flushed. "Oh, my God," she said. "I—I don't know where that came from." She slid off the bed and hurried into the bathroom.

Well, you pretty much screwed that up, he told himself. He shoved his hands through his hair, locked his fingers behind his head. He'd only meant to apologize for butting into her personal life. How had it transitioned into…that?

Hell. They barely knew each other. He was her boss. And he may be only six years older but he'd lived at least a lifetime longer.

He should've seen it coming. No one had looked so adoringly at him since…since his ex-wife. He'd made sure since then to choose women who didn't.

He looked blindly around the room. Hell, he could make split-second decisions about life and death situations, but he didn't trust his judgment about women like Lyndsey.

Nate eyed the closed bathroom door and wondered when she would come out. Deciding to make it easier on her, he went into the living room. He couldn't go onto the balcony since it connected to the master suite, so he stood at the plate-glass windows and watched the night.

A door opened. Tricia came out, wearing a long, lacy black gown. No lights were on in the house but enough spilled in from outdoors.

"What are you doing?" she asked sharply.

"I heard a noise. Just checking it out."

She moved closer. She was his usual type, he realized. Tall and slender, with a toned body and long, straight hair. His Barbies, Arianna called them. His reward for success, he countered back.

"Do you see anything?" She stood close to him. Close enough he could smell her perfume.

"No."

"I was just getting some cookies," she said, but didn't move.

He scanned the horizon, avoiding looking at her. Her nightgown was cut low, exposing a lot of breast. Lyndsey was ten times sexier in her T-shirt and sweats and those funky little glasses that her hair got tangled in. "Is there something you need, ma'am?"

She touched his arm. "Some advice?"

"I'm just the help." He took a step back, politely shrugging off her hand. "If you'll excuse me."

"Lyndsey…your wife said she expects fidelity. Do you think such a thing is possible in marriage?"

He clenched his jaw against the truth—*not in my experience*—but he believed that Lyndsey believed it. And since he was married to her—for this assignment—then he believed it, too. "Of course I do," he said instead, playing the role of a happily married man.

"I think I'm about to be proposed to. I'm not sure how to answer."

"I can't help you with that."

She sighed. "It's a complicated situation. He comes with a lot of baggage."

"Don't we all. Good night, ma'am." He couldn't get out of there fast enough.

The lights and television were off when he opened the bedroom door. He padded across the floor, lifted the blanket and climbed under. She was faced away from him. He doubted she was asleep.

"We both got carried away," he said to her back. "Let's not let it damage our relationship."

"Okay. G'night."

Okay. There was that word again. The word that meant nothing—or everything.

Six

The next morning Lyndsey waited until Nate left for his run before she opened her eyes. She was mortified. Not only had she assumed erroneously that he wanted to make love with her, but now he must also think she was easy.

She pressed her hands to her face and stifled a groan. He didn't know she'd been building up to this for months. She was primed to fall for him, but the fall had come harder and faster than she could have imagined.

He never should have offered sympathy and an available shoulder. She'd been too long without either. And how were they supposed to pretend to be the happy couple now? That would require dusting off every old acting skill she possessed.

The bedroom door opened, startling her. Nate strode across the room like a man on a mission and sat on the bed beside her.

"I thought you were going for a run," she said, bewildered.

"I was. I am. I figured you were stewing about what happened. I want to clear the air."

"Okay."

He smiled, but she didn't know why. He reached for one of her hands. "I like you."

"I like you, too." Geez, was that ever an understatement.

"You've not only been fun to work with, you've been professional. Considering you had no experience, you've done an amazing job."

"Most of the time I've just kept my mouth shut."

"That's a skill most people don't master. You got it right from the beginning."

"Oh, I'm so glad." Especially now that she was thinking of changing professions. She would talk to him about that later, though.

"Don't think that entitles you to a bonus."

She smiled because he did. Then she relaxed. She'd already gotten her bonus, last night in this very bed.

"Are we okay?" he asked.

"Definitely."

"Good. I'll be back in an hour."

When he returned an hour later he brought with him the substantial Sunday paper to add to the coffee tray then went off to shower. As Lyndsey prepared a zucchini frittata, toasted bagels and fruit, she hummed, almost dancing around the kitchen.

Her decision was made. She'd found her calling. She would make use of all her skills by becoming a private investigator. Surely her accounting background would be invaluable, as well as her acting ability. Plus, she loved the kinds of work it involved. Loved the challenge. She'd typed enough case files to know a lot of the job was routine, but a lot wasn't. There was always paperwork. Computer research. Phone calls. She was good at it all. However, she excelled in people skills. Because she blended into the background, she'd always been a people watcher and thought she understood human nature well.

When he took her home tonight she would talk to him about making a career change.

Should they also talk about what had happened in bed? She felt her face heat. She'd actually…lost control. With very little effort, too. With all their clothes on, too. That was a first. What had he thought about that?

"Lyndsey," Tricia said from behind her.

She turned around, putting a smile on her face. "Good morning. Isn't it a beautiful day?"

Tricia glanced toward the living room windows, where gray, overcast skies filled the view. She looked skeptical. "I guess."

"Your tray's ready. Just let me pour fresh coffee for you."

"You're making Cobb salad for lunch?"

"That's what the meal plan calls for. Is there a problem with that?"

"No." Tricia put her shoulders back a little. "Michael wants you to prepare the salads after breakfast and put them in the refrigerator. You and your husband can leave right after."

A few seconds of startled silence followed. "What about cleaning up?" Lyndsey asked finally.

"A housekeeping service does that. You were here to cook and run errands, if we needed anything. I thought you knew that."

"Of course we knew that," Nate said, stepping into the kitchen. "You're just catching us off guard, having us leave early."

"We figured you'd like some time together, given your busy schedules, and there's little left for you to do here, anyway. Happy three-month anniversary. Here, I'll take the tray myself today.''

Lyndsey stared at Nate. He shook his head a fraction.

"This is great," she said conversationally. "I've got that paper to finish for class tomorrow."

He nodded. "Anything I can do here?"

She wished there was. At least they could whisper about their early dismissal. "No."

"I'll go pack."

Lyndsey fretted. Had they done something wrong? Had she tripped up somehow? She thought over her conversations with Tricia. Nothing. They probably just wanted privacy. She still couldn't figure out why they just hadn't had food delivered. Much cheaper, and all the privacy they wanted.

She would never understand the rich.

Nate backed out of the garage. It was all he could do not to burn rubber as they left. He'd never done a job where he had accomplished so little.

"I don't get it," Lyndsey said after a minute.

"What's to get? They didn't want us hanging around any longer."

"I gathered that, but why aren't we staying nearby, like at the beach? We could take the camera."

"The chances of anything happening that's worth photographing are too slim to bother. At least this way we know we've got time before he goes home. We can see the client and show her what we have and talk about where to go from here."

"How do you justify your fee when you don't produce anything of value?"

"You do the job. Its outcome is out of your control." Like anything about this job had ever been *in* his control.

"Do you think you'll do more surveillance on him?"

"If Mrs. Marbury requests it. Getting results is rarely a one-time opportunity. Sometimes you work for months on a case before you come up with the documentation. Sometimes you never do." He rationalized his failure because he felt he should have gotten something over the weekend. A kiss, even a hug between the subjects. Something that could be offered as proof. Anything to wrap up the case.

"What if there's nothing to find?" she asked. "What if we're all wrong and there's no affair?"

"Look at the facts. Tricia was proprietary with him. Most men in his position wouldn't let a woman who wasn't his lover speak for him."

"She's also his assistant. That gives her a comfort level beyond the normal."

"Good point," he said. "But she also came out of the bedroom wearing a low-cut negligee."

"But we never saw evidence they were sleeping together. There's a couch in the office."

"You're really playing devil's advocate with that one."

"Well, it's possible," Lyndsey said. "She wouldn't let me in the bedroom to make the bed. I never set foot in the bedroom or the office except when we took our own tour before they arrived. Did you?"

"Just the bedroom briefly twice. The bed was never made." He drummed his fingers on the steering wheel. "He gave her a massage, and there was that moment where their faces were close. Too close for a 'just friends' relationship."

"I know." She sighed. "It's all very confusing. Too many mixed signals."

"Exactly."

"If you're interested in my opinion, I still say they aren't lovers."

"I'm interested in your opinion, Lyndsey."

"But you think I'm wrong."

"I didn't say that. Either way adds up. It's going to take more work to find the truth. Look, can we drop this for a while? The client's going to be interrogating me soon enough."

"Sure."

He appreciated her silence. Once again he noted how quietly she sat, her hands in her lap, her thoughts her own. She didn't chatter for no reason. She answered questions, and she kept up her end of a conversation, but she didn't talk just to fill the silence.

He was grateful, too, that she hadn't brought up last night, yet another screwup. He had to figure out something to say, however, sometime soon.

He phoned Mrs. Marbury when they were a few minutes away. Still she kept them waiting for fifteen minutes before joining them in the sitting room. She looked as if she hadn't slept since they'd last seen her.

"Why are you back so early?" she demanded.

"We don't know," Nate said. "There was little left for us to do."

"Were they suspicious of you?"

"They were guarded." He looked at Lyndsey. "We both felt there was more to their relationship than they showed us, but they maintained strict privacy and discretion."

"You said on the phone that you have a picture."

"Yes." He opened his computer and brought up the series of photographs. "As you can see, there's no real evidence."

She shrank a little with each picture, until she dropped into a nearby chair. Nate sat as well. "What do you want us to do?" he asked.

She straightened her back. "What are my options?"

"We can continue surveillance whenever he leaves his office. Has he been coming home at night?"

"Yes, but late. Very late."

"Does he say he's working?"

"He doesn't say."

And you don't ask? "Do you call him at the office?"

"Not often. He doesn't like me to. The only way I'll get proof is if you get it for me. I can't do it."

"You want us to continue, then?"

The door opened and Mr. Marbury strode in. Nate stood and moved toward Lyndsey. Her eyes went wide. She seemed about to leap out of her chair. He put a hand on her shoulder.

"Ah, the loving newlyweds. And my adoring wife."

"You weren't supposed to be home for hours, darling," Mrs. Marbury said, sounding bored. She leaned back and crossed her legs, bouncing one foot.

Nate was stunned by her level of control.

"I had them followed. I wasn't far behind." Mr. Marbury turned to Nate. "Tricia recognized you from a party she attended last year. You were playing personal bodyguard to Alexis Wells."

Not playing, but doing his job. The Oscar-winning actress had received death threats and needed protection. But, dammit, he knew that as the most publicly visible partner of ARC he had a chance of being recognized. He should've let one of the junior investigators do the job. Because it was for Charlie, he hadn't trusted anyone else. And he'd screwed it up more than anyone else could have.

"I hired them," his wife said, her gaze following him as he came up to the computer and looked at the image there, the one of him and Tricia almost kissing.

"Obviously." He clenched his fists. Only the mantel clock made any sound. Nate felt Lyndsey's tension in her shoulder. He couldn't do anything but wait and see what Mr. Marbury did, then react to it. The man dragged a finger across the image before shoving the lid down.

"I doubt that's good enough for your purposes, my dear," he said. "Not exactly flagrante delicto, wouldn't you agree, Mr. Caldwell?"

Nate said nothing.

"Trust, once broken, is irreparable," he said calmly to his wife, then he took measured strides out of the room. The heavy front door opened and closed. A car started.

Again there was only the sound of a clock ticking.

"So, there was never a chance of knowing the truth. We were defeated before we started," Mrs. Marbury said. "He gave you enough to tease you. And me."

Lyndsey hopped up and went to her. She knelt down. "I'm so sorry," she said, taking the woman's hands. "If it's any consolation, I don't think—"

Nate surged forward, stopping her. Her opinions were just that. "Let's go."

She hesitated. He put his hand under her elbow and pulled her up. To Mrs. Marbury, he said, "It's one of the risks of the business—being recognized. It's never happened to me before. It may never again. I'm sorry that it did, since it voids an investigation when the subject is onto the investigator. If there's any other way we can be of service, please let us know."

He swept the computer off the table with his free hand and pulled Lyndsey along with the other.

"Nate," she said when they got into the car.

"Not now."

Screwup. How many times had his father called him that. *Never amount to anything.* Even though there'd been truth to his old man's words when Nate was a teenager, he'd grown up and stopped needing to prove anything. There was no reason. He *had* amounted to something. He was among the top in his field, had garnered respect and admiration from clients and peers alike. Now this. This…screwup.

And Lyndsey had witnessed it.

* * *

When he insisted on carrying her suitcase and garment bag, Lyndsey didn't argue, since she wanted to talk to him about her future. If she let him carry her belongings it would get him through the front door.

Lyndsey was proud of her little home. Although less than a thousand square feet and having only two bedrooms, it was cozy and welcoming, the furnishings not overly feminine, and on the walls were her mother's art, bold and full of life. She had a passion for red, which was incorporated into every painting, if only her signature.

Nate was so quiet she hardly knew he was there.

"Would you like something to drink?" she asked as they stepped inside.

"No, thanks. Where do you want these?"

"You can put them on the sofa."

He looked around, taking in the boxes stacked on the coffee table and floor.

"My Christmas decorations," she said, apologizing for the mess. "That's what my plans were for the weekend."

He didn't just dislike Christmas, she decided from his expression, it had some kind of bitter hold on him. And painful. He looked at the boxes instead of the beautiful art on the walls. His jaw turned to granite.

Obviously this wasn't the time to grill him about the twists and turns of their assignment or about his profession.

He set down her luggage and turned to her. His eyes were blank.

"This was fun," she said, extending her hand when what she wanted to do was hug him.

He reacted automatically, accepting her hand. Why are you hurting so much? she wanted to ask him. How can I help you?

''You were great,'' he said. ''I'll see you.''

That was it. A moment later he was gone, and she was left with so many thoughts spinning in her head. She went into her bathroom and looked in the mirror, expecting to see something different, because she felt different. More self-assured. Stronger.

Prettier. How could that be? She was such an average looking woman with nothing in particular to distinguish her, but at that moment she looked pretty.

Chalking up the difference to the fact she was wearing makeup for a change, she retrieved her luggage and carried it into her bedroom. She checked her answering machine. No messages. Jess hadn't returned her call asking what day she could fly home and what day she would have to be back at school. Lyndsey couldn't make the arrangements without that information. She could e-mail her sister, except she rarely answered those, either.

Lyndsey hung up some clothes from the garment bag and tossed others into the hamper. Then she opened her overnight bag. On top was her pair of red panties and matching red lace bra, folded neatly.

Nate had packed her bag. It hadn't occurred to her....

She plopped onto her bed, the lingerie in her hands. Her face was on fire. He'd tucked one cup into the other in the same way she did.

Whipping off her glasses, she tossed them onto the nightstand. Well. The mystery was over before it began. He would know that she didn't wear cotton underwear and white bras, but bright colors and lace. She wondered what had gone through his mind as he placed them in her bag.

The phone rang. She dragged the receiver to her face. ''Hello?''

''I meant to tell you something,'' Nate said. ''Co-worker to co-worker, friend to friend. Before I turn back into your boss.''

She'd expected Jess, so she was doubly surprised to hear Nate—and to hear him sounding normal, especially after the mood he'd been in when he left not long ago.

"What's that?" she asked.

"If you're invited to a Christmas party, you should definitely wear the red."

A click followed. Her cheeks burned hotter. She dropped onto her back and stared at the ceiling. A smile tugged at her lips. So, he'd seen her underwear. He'd probably seen sexier. More sheer.

But it was your underwear.

So?

So he's going to picture you in it from now on.

Yes, he is, she thought, satisfied. Yes, he is.

Seven

"**W**hat do you mean you can't come home for Christmas?" Lyndsey almost yelled into the phone. "Jess! It won't put me further into debt. I earned some extra money. It's fine."

"I'm sorry, Lynnie. I am. We never planned for me to come home! You know everyone has to move out of the dorms over the winter break. I sublet an apartment for the month. I told you that."

"You did." Lyndsey rubbed her forehead. "But now you can come home."

"I can't. I signed up for winter session," she said, quiet and fast.

Shock snatched Lyndsey's breath. "Why?"

"Because there's a class I need to take."

"We mapped out your courses so that you wouldn't need to take winter session. It's so expensive." Lyndsey looked around her cubicle without seeing anything. She had just arrived at work when the phone rang, the one line she was supposed to answer at night.

"It's not just that," Jess said.

"Then what is it?"

Her sister didn't answer. Possibilities flashed in Lyndsey's mind, none of them acceptable. "You can tell me anything. You know that." *Just don't tell me you're pregnant.*

"I failed one class. I need to retake it now or I can't move on to the next level."

Lyndsey dropped her purse on her desk and finally sat, weighed down by disbelief. "You're still taking finals. How do you know you failed?"

"Because I do."

"I don't get it, Jess. You're smart without trying."

"This isn't like high school, you know."

"I've been to college. I know it's different. I also know you can handle it. What's going on? Are you partying a lot? You're hardly ever home when I call."

"I go out, just like everyone else. You don't expect me to hole up in my room all the time, do you?" She sounded both hurt and belligerent. "I know I have a job to do here. You drummed that into me."

"Then why aren't you doing it?"

"I am. It's just hard. It's not like I don't want to come home, you know. I miss you, Lynnie."

I miss you, too. She fought to maintain the parent role instead of the lonely sister. "How are the rest of your grades?"

"They're not great, but I'm passing."

Lyndsey knew about the freshman struggle, but she had expected more of Jess, who always excelled in academics.

"Do you go to class?" Lyndsey asked.

"Ye-es." The singsong answer was followed by a huge sigh.

"All of them?"

"Most."

Lyndsey closed her eyes. "Are you sure the winter session will solve the problem?"

"I'm sure. I'm really, really sorry, Lynnie. I'll be home in May, just like we planned."

We planned that before I knew how hard it was going to be not to see you for nine months. "Won't you be lonely?" Lyndsey barely got the words out.

"Lots of kids are stuck here. It'll be okay. Um, I'm gonna need some money to pay for the class. Good thing you earned some extra, huh?"

There went the car repairs, too. By the time she paid the extra tuition, nothing would be left. In fact, she would be even further in debt. Winter session fees were exorbitant.

"You can't do this again, Jess. I don't have money to spare. You have to stick to the program we set up. You have to pass your classes. You're more than capable."

"I know. I promise I'll do better."

"Have you had any luck getting a job?"

"Not yet. I guess I applied too late for Christmas jobs, and everyone will be laying off right after the holidays. People say it'll open up again in February or March."

The master plan had included Jess working full-time during the month-long winter break, even if it meant her taking two part-time jobs. Discouragement settled in. Lyndsey almost wished she hadn't earned the extra money, hadn't gotten her hopes up. "You need to find a job, Jess."

"I will. Listen, I gotta go, okay? I love you!"

"I love you, too," Lyndsey said to a humming dial tone. After a minute she hung up the phone, then her sweater. She noted the time on her time sheet, jumbled the Rubik's Cube for Sam then settled down at the computer, but the swing of emotions over the past few days took its toll. She struggled to concentrate on the reports she needed to type, which always required a great deal of attention.

Hours later she finished transcribing, surprised to find no report from Nate. Surely he needed to file something on the Marbury case.

Oh, who was she kidding? She didn't care about his report. She just needed to hear his voice. She'd hoped all day he would call. Another disappointment. But after the way she'd expected sex from him, she wasn't surprised. It was her own fault.

"You're pathetic," she said aloud.

"I am?"

She recognized the voice and was torn between being embarrassed and delighted that he was there. "I'm pathetic, not you. Although I might have included you if I'd known you were there."

Nate grinned. "Why are you pathetic?"

"There you go with the questions again."

"Occupational hazard. What's going on?"

"You didn't file a report."

"How does that make you pathetic?"

"It doesn't. I was changing the subject."

Nate grabbed a rolling chair from the next cubicle and sat knee to knee with her. "I'm working on it," he said. "The report," he added when she seemed confused. "I had something else to do today."

"Attend a cooking class?"

"Funny." He reached into his back pocket. "I talked with Arianna and Sam. We all agreed you should get your Christmas bonus now." He passed her the envelope.

"I didn't even know there was a bonus. What is it, a coupon for a turkey?"

"We're a little more appreciative of our staff's hard work than that. Take a look."

She pulled out the contents. Her face drained of color. "It's a plane ticket."

"It's a voucher for one, actually. You call the airline, arrange the flight and give them the number right there." He tapped the form. "Merry Christmas." The words didn't stick in his throat, for a change, because he was more concerned about Lyndsey's reaction. She should be flashing that awesome smile.

"Thank you. It's a wonderful gift, but you can keep it. My sister can't come home."

"Why not?"

She shook her head. Her throat convulsed. Don't cry, he ordered silently.

"She has to stay at school. Winter session."

"So use the ticket to go see her."

"What?"

That the idea hadn't occurred to her said a lot to Nate. He took her hands in his. "Sweetheart. Planes fly both directions."

She didn't say anything for a minute. "I've never flown before."

"Never? Didn't you go visit the campus with Jess?"

"We chose not to spend money on that. They have virtual tours online, and we chose by reputation, too." She flung herself at him, wrapping her arms around his neck. "Thank you. Oh, thank you so much. I won't even tell you it's too much for an employee who's only been here for three months."

"You're welcome." As she pulled back he cupped her face and studied her. She smiled. That was all he needed. He grazed her lips with his. His bed had seemed enormous last night after sharing one with her.

"I missed you today," she said against his mouth. "I shouldn't say that, but I did."

He remembered how she felt curled up against him the

first morning. Then during the night, the second night, he'd lain awake looking at her, touching her curls, finding them soft and springy.

He set his hands at her waist and deepened the kiss. She moved closer. He let his hands glide up her rib cage, felt her go still as he cupped one breast, then a sound intruded. Footsteps. He jerked back just before his partner Sam Remington came into view. Lyndsey looked away, resettling her glasses. She picked up a pen and tablet of paper and scribbled something.

"Burning the two a.m. oil?" Sam asked Nate.

"I hadn't filed the Marbury report."

Sam said nothing. He was taller than Nate, and broader, and he had a stern face, which rarely broke into a smile. That face had intimidated the hell out of a lot of people, and now he looked from Nate to Lyndsey and back again.

"How're you, Ms. McCord?" he asked, leaning casually against her entryway.

"Fine. Great, in fact." She tossed him his jumbled Rubik's Cube. "Thank you for the plane ticket. You don't know how much it means to me."

He was focused on the puzzle cube, twisting and turning, eyeing it, then twisting it again, his movements fast and sure. He gave her a brief glance. "Our pleasure. I hope you have a good time."

"Oh, I will. I'm going to see my sister in New York. She's at Cornell."

"I remember. What'd you think of your weekend assignment?"

"I loved it."

Okay, time to go now, Nate thought, standing, needing to get Sam alone. "Got a minute?"

"Sure," Sam said. "Hang on." A few seconds later he

handed the solved cube back to Lyndsey. "Are you done for the night?"

"Except for distributing the case files." Her gaze shifted to Nate. "Unless you want me to stay and type up your report?"

"It can wait until tomorrow. Give me the files. I'll pass them out."

She handed him the stack then fussed with the things on her desk, aligning her stapler, phone and notepad with precision. Sam didn't budge. Nate crossed his arms and looked at him. A tiny smile flitted across Sam's mouth.

"I see you're both wearing new jewelry," he said.

Nate touched his thumb to the wedding ring. He'd forgotten the damn thing. "I figured it was safer on my hand than in my pocket." He slid it off.

"Me, too," Lyndsey said, dropping her ring into Nate's hand.

The ping of gold hitting gold rang like a death knell.

"No scorch marks under that?" Sam asked Nate innocently.

Lyndsey pulled on her sweater and tugged her purse over her shoulder. "Well...good night."

Sam stepped out of the way. Nate touched her shoulder as she passed by. She slowed down for a moment then hurried off.

He wandered to the window overlooking the parking lot. Sam followed. Tinted glass prevented her from seeing them watching her. Her engine ground, coughed, then grabbed.

"What're you doing here?" Nate asked.

"I worked the Hastings party. Decided to pick up some files so I can sleep in and work from home tomorrow. Today."

They watched Lyndsey use a squeegee to wipe the moisture off her windshield, then Nate felt Sam's gaze on him.

"I don't think I've seen a guiltier look," Sam said mildly.

Nate slipped his hands into his pockets. "I'm sure you have."

"I wasn't talking about you. You've mastered the blank expression. I'm talking about Ms. McCord. What'd you do, kiss her?"

When Nate didn't respond, Sam swore.

"Not a good idea, Nathan."

"I know."

"Can't help it?"

Nate shook his head slowly.

"Well, it was bound to happen sometime," Sam said.

"What was?"

"You know what. You've protected your heart for a long time."

"My heart's intact."

There was a long pause before Sam said, "Then you'd better think long and hard about what happens next. First, you can't toy with an employee. You've investigated enough harassment cases to know that. Second, she won't rebound like other women. If you think she'll lose interest and patience like the others, you're dead wrong."

Sam pointed to the parking lot. "Look at her. She squeegees her damn windows. She backs her car out of the parking space even though she could just drive straight through the space in front of her. There's no car there. What does she think would happen?" He shook his head. "She's a rule follower. She'll expect you to play by the book. Her book. The one she's created for herself about men and life."

Nate wanted to tell Sam he would put an end to it, but the words wouldn't come.

"I know you've been burned, Nate. I know you don't

have faith in happily ever after. But she does. Remember that.''

''You're a fine one to speak.''

''I don't go from woman to woman.''

''No, you just stay hung up on the same one, year after year. I hear she's finally available. Why don't you go after her?''

''That's my business.''

''Right. And Lyndsey is mine.''

Sam drew a deep breath then rested an arm on Nate's shoulder. ''So, we gave her a plane ticket, did we?''

Sweetheart. He called her sweetheart.

A ball of fire surrounded her heart then spread heat through her body, which was a good thing, since her car heater had died. She had to squeegee her windows and hope to make it home without needing her defroster.

She was going to New York. She would fly in a plane. She would see for herself how Jess was doing. Her sister's decreasing level of communication since she left home was both understandable and frustrating as she spread her wings, but at least now Lyndsey could talk to her in person. She could watch Jess open her Christmas present, a gorgeous leaf-green sweater. They could drink hot chocolate and talk late into the night, like old times.

They had a Christmas Eve tradition of leafing through the photo albums of their Christmases with their mother. Lyndsey would pack them to take. The angel treetop ornament they put on the tree in honor of their mother would have to wait for next year.

This would be her first year without a tree.

She thought about how Nate hated Christmas and wondered why. People didn't hate the holiday for no reason.

He'd kissed her. In the office. More than once. Then he'd touched her, just barely. If Sam hadn't come by…well, that was probably as far as it would've gone, anyway.

It struck her then that she couldn't talk to Nate about her becoming an investigator, because she would be putting him on the spot, given their as-yet-undefined relationship. Why risk messing it up? There were other ways to get answers.

Lyndsey pulled into her garage. She admired the wreath on the front door as she let herself into her house. How did Nate handle Christmas cards, she wondered? Would he open one from her? She'd have to find a funny one.

She turned on her computer to go online to check flights, but before she logged on, her phone rang, startling her.

"I hope you weren't in bed yet," Nate said.

As if that matters. "No. I was about to check flights."

"That's why I'm calling. Since you haven't flown before, I'm volunteering to make the arrangements."

His voice seemed different to her now. No longer the smooth, efficient professional but the man who'd kissed her. Teased her. Satisfied her but not himself.

"I accept, thank you," she said. "I was figuring on an early-morning flight on Saturday and then a Monday morning return."

"Why so short?"

"What choice do I have? I'm not eligible for vacation—and don't you dare tell me to take extra time. That puts a burden on someone else in the office to do my job as well as their own. I won't do that."

"But—"

"I mean it, Nate. You've done enough already."

"*But*…didn't you get the memo about having Monday and Tuesday off?"

She was sure she would have remembered that. "No. I understand why we get Monday off, since Christmas is on Sunday, but why Tuesday?"

"Because the Christmas party is on Saturday. So that means you can come back on Wednesday and not miss any work."

Four days. "That's terrific. And I meant to ask you tonight—" *but I got distracted when you kissed me* "—about your P.I. friend's wife. How is she doing?"

"She had a quadruple bypass this morning, but she came through the surgery okay. Charlie's just barely keeping it together. I spent the day with him. That's the real reason I didn't get around to doing the Marbury report."

"Did you tell him about it?"

"Oh, yeah. Gave him his only laugh of the day."

He didn't sound like it was funny at all. Was he that upset that the case hadn't gone as he'd hoped? He probably wasn't used to things going wrong. "I'm glad she's doing well."

"Me, too."

She didn't want to hang up. She wanted to lie on her bed and talk for hours. She'd learned that sometimes when people weren't face-to-face, they talked about things they wouldn't otherwise. Like why he hated Christmas, and how she really did resent her sister's freedom a little, since Lyndsey had never had any freedom herself.

And that she was falling in love with him.

"Don't finalize the flight plans until I've spoken with Jess, okay?" she said instead. "I wish I could surprise her but I don't dare."

"I'll make reservations but put them on hold for twenty-four hours. Let me know after you talk to her. You have my cell number, right?"

"I do."

"Lyndsey, I really wish you would take some extra—"

"No. Thank you."

"You're stubborn."

"It's not a bad trait, you know. You just make it sound bad."

"How late do you sleep?" he asked.

"When I work nights I'm up by eleven at the latest, usually closer to ten. I'm in the office by seven. My sister's a little hard to get answers from, however. She's developed an independent streak that's hard to break through."

"I remember the feeling myself. Only I rebelled by joining the army. And before you say anything, remember I was eighteen. It made sense at the time. My dad was a Marine. If I wanted to tick him off—and I did—it meant choosing a different branch of the military."

Lyndsey did get comfortable on her bed then, hoping the conversation would last. "Why the military at all?"

"Rebellion, pure and simple."

"Did you regret it?" She hadn't had time for rebellion, although she'd felt it often enough.

"I don't regret it much. I met Sam and Arianna in the army, and life is good because of that."

"You didn't get to go to college?"

"I used to blame my dad for that, too. Now I just wish he'd acknowledge my success."

Grief welled inside Lyndsey at his words. Her mother would never be able to acknowledge her success, but had she lived, she would've been president of Lyndsey's fan club. "Lack of college hasn't slowed you down any," she said to Nate. "In fact, it doesn't seem like the firm could handle any more business."

"Maybe. But I wish I'd done some things differently. I admire you, raising your sister on your own, sticking with college."

"We do what we need to."

"I should let you get to bed."

"Okay." She heard him laugh quietly. "What's so funny?"

"I just enjoy you. Good night, Lyndsey."

"G'night."

It was hard letting him dictate the relationship, but she needed to let him. He was comfortable with her, that much she knew. He was attracted to her. She probably shouldn't read much into it. They'd gotten close because of circumstances. He'd probably slept with and dumped a million women.

But all the reasoning in the world couldn't stop the pitter-patter of her heart when she was with him. Or the daydreams. Or the secret wish that he might fall as hard for her as she had fallen for him.

Eight

Nate's cell phone rang as he jogged along the beach near his house. He didn't usually take the phone with him, so the sound jarred, even though he was expecting Lyndsey to call. He glanced at the screen, saw it was her number.

"Good morning, Ms. McCord," he said, not missing a stride.

"Hi."

Her voice was different. Forced. He came to a stop, tried to control his breathing so he wouldn't pant into the phone. "What's wrong?"

"I hope you can cancel the ticket without any penalty."

"Sure. Why?"

"Because my sister lied to me." Anger and hurt coated her words.

"About what?"

"She doesn't want me to visit. She never did want to come home, either. She's—she's going to Vermont to ski. With her boyfriend. I didn't even know she had one."

He started jogging toward home. "I'm coming over."

"No. I'm going out to buy a Christmas tree. I'm okay. I just wanted you to cancel the flight."

"I'm coming over. It'll take me forty-five minutes."

"It's not necessary."

"Do not leave before I get there." He disconnected before she could argue, then he sent a few choice words toward the East Coast.

Nate was beginning to understand her and her independence. She would go out of her way to show she didn't need him. Hell, he wasn't even sure why he was going there.

Maybe he didn't want to examine why too closely, either.

Less than an hour later he knocked on her door.

"I'm fine," she said without preamble as she held the door for him. "Honest."

He surveyed her as he passed by. She wore blue jeans, and a red blouse covered with smiling, leaping reindeer. Only the top button was undone. When had buttoned-up become such a turn-on for him? Maybe because of the prospect of unbuttoning it? He had a hard time reconciling this woman with the one who had held nothing back the other night. "I'll bet you told your sister you were fine, too."

"I'm glad you're here, but I don't want to talk about my sister."

"Or your disappointment?"

"That either."

"Just one question?" he asked.

She crossed her arms. "Choose wisely, Question Man."

He smiled. "Is Jess really signed up for winter session?"

"That much is true. But she has time off between the

end of finals and the beginning of the session. She could've come home.''

''In her defense, until yesterday she didn't think she could, so she took care of herself. That's good, isn't it?''

She narrowed her eyes at him then broke into a reluctant smile. ''Oh, quit being rational.''

He put an arm companionably around her shoulder. ''You wouldn't want her to sit around, lonely and bored, would you?''

''Like me, you mean?''

''I didn't say that.''

''Would you like something to drink?'' she asked when he stepped away.

''I thought we were going tree shopping.''

Lyndsey stared at him. Had she heard him correctly? ''*I* was. I didn't figure you'd be interested.''

''I brought my pickup.'' He dangled his keys.

She really didn't need a truck for the size of tree she would buy, but she wasn't about to stop him from coming with her, not when she'd been given an opportunity to change his mind about Christmas. ''That would be nice, thank you.''

''However, there is one condition,'' he added.

''There are strings attached?''

His gaze softened. ''Aren't there always?''

''No. Not from me, anyway.''

''Why doesn't that surprise me?'' He cupped her face, brushed his thumb along her cheek. ''I was only going to say, enough with the thank-yous.''

The tender look in his eyes erased any uncertainty she had. ''How about this instead?'' She twined her arms around his neck and pulled herself up on tiptoe, bringing her mouth near his.

''This is good,'' he said, gathering her close.

''This is dangerous,'' she said in return. They hadn't

kissed yet, but she could feel his breath, warm against her face.

His hands slid down over her rear and pulled her snugly against him. "You seem daring enough."

She would've laughed at the idea if she weren't so distracted by the feel of his body against hers. Daring? Not until a few days ago. "Please stop talking." *Before I lose my nerve.*

His kiss fulfilled dreams then promised even more, changing from soft and tempting to bold and demanding. He pulled back after a minute, looked entirely unsure of himself, then came back for more, slanting his head the other direction, asking more of her second by second. His hands went on a journey of exploration, dragging up her sides, his palms pressing into the sides of her breasts, awakening, arousing, urging. He lifted his head and she wanted to whimper. *Not yet. Don't stop yet.* He read her thoughts, kissed her again, deeper, hotter, demanding more. She stopped thinking as his tongue swept her lower lip then dipped inside her mouth to mate with hers in a fiery dance.

She felt him against her abdomen, hard and thrilling and flattering. Her bedroom was so close....

"You taste like cinnamon," he said, easing back.

"I—I just made Snickerdoodles."

"What's that?" His fingertips danced along her spine, low.

She arched. "Cookies," she managed to say. "Want some?"

"Do you know how sexy you are?" He nuzzled her neck.

Me? She was proud of herself for not saying the word out loud and incredulously. "I dabbed vanilla behind my ears. It's supposed to drive men crazy."

She felt him smile.

"Did you?" he asked, sniffing, sending chills through her.

"No, but the theory is supposed to be true." She wanted to stop talking and let things heat up between them, but she sensed a hesitation on his part. She wasn't going to make the same mistake as the last time and jump to conclusions. They would sleep together when—if—the time was right.

"I'll pack some cookies to take with us." She started toward the kitchen.

"Lyndsey."

At the serious tone in his voice she faced him reluctantly, her fears echoing in her head. *Please don't leave. Don't be afraid of what's growing between us.*

"Can you make that a dozen? I haven't had breakfast."

Relief flooded her. "I'd love to fix you breakfast." *Every morning.*

"You would?"

He so obviously wasn't surprised that she gave him a little shove, but it was like pushing granite. He caught her hands and pressed them to his chest, over his heart.

"As I said, you're a very nice person, Ms. McCord. In return, I'll—"

"Stop. I don't want anything in return. I want to fix you breakfast. I like your company. And we might as well get something else straight before we go, too. You're not buying me a tree."

"Hold on a second, Stubborn. I was only going to say that in return for you making me breakfast, I'll eat it."

Oh, he could put the most innocent expression on his face. She didn't know whether to believe him. "You were not."

"That's my story and I'm stickin' to it."

She didn't have a comeback, so she said what was on her mind instead. "Thank you for being here, Nate." *For cheering me up. For the hours of anticipation you gave me when I thought Jess and I could spend Christmas together, after all. I thought I was resigned to being apart, but I realize now that I wasn't.* She smiled. "I'm okay now. I've accepted that life is changing faster than it used to. I've caught up."

"Good."

He swept her into his arms, and he felt wonderful. Warm and safe. She ended the hug before he did. "How do you like your eggs?" she asked.

"Cooked."

"Ah. Just as I suspected. You're easy."

"You can't decorate a tree without a mug of hot chocolate," Lyndsey said. "It's tradition."

"We're having a heat wave. It's eighty-five degrees." He had situated the four-foot-tall Douglas fir in its stand and was untangling a string of colored lights while Lyndsey sorted through her ornaments.

"You don't have to help me decorate, you know," she said, eyeing him dubiously as he fought with the lights. The lights were winning.

"You worried my work won't pass inspection?"

He was teasing her, as he had while they shopped, calling her the Inspector General of Trees and telling her he'd seen parachutes packed with less fanatical attention to detail.

"I can always redo it after you leave." She smiled sweetly at him.

He grunted. "I still don't understand why people put so much time and effort into Christmas."

"Because it's a joyful time of year. People are happy."

"People always looked stressed-out to me."

"Then they're not celebrating it the right way."

"What's the right way? What was your best Christmas?" he asked.

The memory swamped her, taking her back eighteen years as if it were yesterday. "The year I was eight. Mom came home from the hospital with Jess a week right after Thanksgiving. She was such a good baby. She hardly ever cried, and I loved holding her."

He'd succeeded in untangling half of the strand and looked as if he was resisting the temptation to stomp on the rest so that he could just go buy new sets as he'd wanted.

"You have strong maternal instincts," he said.

"I liked girl stuff. Dolls and clothes and playing beauty parlor. Jess was my living doll." She grabbed the other end of the cord to help him straighten it. "Plus that year Jess's dad was living here. It was my first and only taste of 'real' family. There were lots of presents. I adored him. He was like a big kid, and my mom laughed all the time."

"And he just walked out?"

"Memorial Day. I remember because he was supposed to take us to a picnic in the park. He went to get some sodas. We waited here for hours. Finally Mom spread a blanket on the living room floor and unpacked the cooler right there. We ate. I went to bed. She found a note from him on her pillow when she pulled down the quilt that night."

"A man of honor, obviously."

She shrugged at his sarcasm. "Everyone's got their own burdens. You, too, I would guess."

"Actually, eight was a pivotal year for me, too."

"In what way?"

"*Star Wars* and Elvis."

"Sounds like a bad country song."

He grinned. "Well, my dog didn't die the same year or

it could've been. And don't you be maligning country music. It's better than opera.''

''What happened?''

''My dad was home on leave in June—he was, is still, a Marine—and he took me to see *Star Wars*.''

''You liked the movie, I gather.''

''Oh, yeah. But more than that, it changed my relationship with my dad.'' The lights were finally untangled. He started arranging the bulbs on the tree as Lyndsey kept the cord straight. ''We finally had something in common.''

''Why weren't you close before?''

''For one, he was gone most of the time. My mom refused to follow him from base to base, so we had a house in Baton Rouge, and he came home when he felt like it.'' He kept his hands busy and his eyes on the tree. ''My older brother, Greg, and I walked on eggshells around him. We weren't used to any kind of discipline from Mom, so we couldn't wait for him to leave. But that year I was eight was different. We'd finally found a connection. When he left I figured things would be different after that. Then Elvis died. My mother was fragile to start with, but his death was her undoing. She went into mourning so deep that she barely functioned, and she cried all the time. I mean, all the time.''

Lyndsey recalled his panic when he thought she was going to cry the other night. Now it made sense.

''I'd never heard my dad yell until he came home for Christmas that year,'' he continued. ''He was always a quiet dictator. The commands were in his eyes and his posture and his choice of words. Not this time. Everything he held against her came out. She had a complete breakdown. He put her in a facility, sold the house and most of the furnishings, then took my brother and me to where he was stationed in California.''

So, he associated Christmas with his mother being taken

away, and his father taking over after years as an absentee parent.

"I never forgave him for moving us away from home, especially away from Mom."

"You mean you never saw her again?"

"We saw her. About six months later she was released, and he made her come live with us. I thought it was cruel, but he wouldn't let her go. She functioned, but her spirit was gone. They lived in the same house until I graduated from high school. They got a divorce, then I got even by joining the army, as I told you."

"Do you see your parents?"

"Not often. Dad remarried. I've got nine-year-old twin half sisters. He's happy, I think. Mom moved back to Louisiana. She battles depression all the time, but she seems relatively content. I see her several times a year, but I don't stay long. We don't have much to say to each other."

Nate finished putting on one string of lights and reached for another. "I shouldn't resent my dad, I guess, because Greg and I didn't have any kind of discipline until he took charge, and we needed it, but he handled it all wrong. He was like our drill sergeant instead of our father. I hated him most of the time. According to him, I couldn't do anything right. We yelled a lot."

"I can't imagine you yelling."

"I don't anymore." He didn't invest that kind of emotion. Keep it light. Keep it simple. Keep it short-term. That was his motto when it came to relationships.

"Here," she said. "Let me show you how to untangle those lights without a fight." She gave him one end of the cord; she took the other and walked away. It unrolled easily.

"You couldn't have shown me that the first time?" he asked, grateful to end the discussion about his past. He chose not to look back, but to learn from his mistakes and move on. He didn't understand why he'd confided so much to her, since he'd never done that before, except once with Sam and Arianna, and that situation had been unusual— because they weren't sure they were going to live to see another day. The bond they'd formed that day while they faced death was the strongest he had.

Nate and Lyndsey stepped back a while later to admire their work. The tree sparkled and shimmered with mostly handmade ornaments and colorful lights reflecting off shiny red balls.

"Just needs two things," Lyndscy said. She tucked a red and green tree skirt around the base then opened a box, folded back some white tissue paper to reveal a delicate angel treetopper. "Jess and I picked this out the year Mom died, to honor her. It's always the last decoration we put on." She hesitated. "Would you close the blinds, please?"

She slipped it onto the top and straightened the white satin skirt, then her halo and wings. She stepped back, her arms folded across her stomach. Nate watched her a minute and saw sadness swamp her. He came up behind her, wrapped his arms around her. She leaned against him.

"You would've liked her," she said softly. In the darkened room the tree took center stage. "She was so much fun. Spontaneous and loving and generous. Young in her thinking. Daring. Just not very responsible."

"You made up for that."

"I guess."

"You guess? *Responsible* is your middle name." He enjoyed the feel of her hair against his jaw. One loopy curl fell into the vee of his shirt, brushing his skin. What was it about her that was so different? He should feel safe with her because she wasn't the kind of woman he was usually attracted to, but he didn't feel safe. And she wasn't overtly sexy, but that just made her sexier. She didn't hang on his every word, either, and flatter him unnecessarily. Nor did she want him to take care of her or help her out in any way—which made him want to even more. She was independent yet traditional.

And she never mentioned the Marbury case and how he blew it. He appreciated that.

"Are you hungry?" she asked. "I've got time to fix us dinner before I go to work."

"Let me take you out. Nothing fancy."

"Dinner out would be fun. I need to shower and change first."

"Go ahead."

"Make yourself at home."

"Is there anything I can do?"

"If you'd like to put the empty boxes out in the garage, that would be great. I won't be long."

He gathered the boxes then stacked them neatly in the attached one-car garage, maneuvering himself around her car, noticing the dings and dents and faded paint. He thought about his cars. Overkill. Outward signs of success that he needed for himself. Recognition mattered to him, especially since he didn't get any from his parents.

He looked around the orderly space, seeing her life and history in marked boxes. Lyndsey, school, one said. Jess, school. Mom. Grandma Joan. Great Grandma Alice. No wonder Lyndsey was so independent. There didn't seem to be a history of any men sticking around long enough to leave memorabilia, not even in earlier generations.

Dammit. How could he get involved with her when all the men in her life walked out? Or weren't they invited to stay? That was a possibility, too.

The problem was, he couldn't seem to stay away.

But Sam had made a good point. Nate dated women who understood the rules—simple and short-term. He always stepped back when the relationship turned serious, making it easy for a woman to walk away. He hadn't had to break up with anyone. He just forced their hand. No emotional scenes that way.

Nate returned to the house. He couldn't hear the shower running, but the bathroom door was closed. He pictured her in there, naked, damp, flushed.

The phone rang.

"Would you get that, please?" she called out.

He picked up the phone reluctantly. "McCord residence."

"Nate?"

Arianna. He swore under his breath.

"What are you doing at Lyndsey's?"

"Helping her decorate her Christmas tree." Did that sound casual enough?

Silence. Absolute silence. "This is Nate Caldwell?" Arianna asked finally.

"Funny, Ar. How'd you find me?"

"Your cell phone's turned off. I tracked you through the GPS."

Sam, Arianna and Nate had global positioning system on all their cars as a precaution. "What's going on?" he asked.

"I could ask the same of you. Your phone is never turned off. Never."

"I'm on vacation."

A brief pause. "She's an employee, Nate."

"I like her. And she could use a friend. What's up?"

"Someone took a shot at Alexis Wells."

He came to attention. "She okay?"

"Scared but okay."

"It's been a year since the last threat. We relaxed about it. Dammit. Where is she?"

"At home. She's leased a jet to take her to her place on Maui. She wants you to come along."

"Yeah, okay." He glanced at his watch. "Tell her I'll

meet her at the airstrip in an hour. She knows the precautions to take in getting there. Find out which LAPD detective is handling her case.''

''All right. Nate—''

''I'll call you from the jet, before we take off.'' He hung up, not giving her a chance to say anything more.

''Is something wrong?''

He turned around. Lyndsey stood in the living room doorway wearing a white terry-cloth robe and a frown. She looked dewy and fresh. And irresistible.

He walked to her. ''I have to leave town.''

''For how long?''

''I don't know. Depends how fast the police do their part of the job.'' He rubbed her arms. Her warmth seeped through the fabric. ''I'm sorry about dinner.''

''Is it dangerous?''

''Hard to tell yet.''

''Who's the client?''

''I can't say.''

Lyndsey drew back. ''I'll be transcribing the case files.''

''Not this one. Some clients demand premium confidentiality. Those files are handled differently. Filed differently. I'll call you when I can.''

''Promise?''

''Yeah.''

She stepped closer and flattened her hands on his chest, missing him already. ''Thank you for the beautiful day. I had fun.''

''Me, too.'' He stared at her mouth, lowered his head and found her lips, not gently but urgently, as sound and taste and sensation joined exultantly.

A volcano of desire flowed hot through her veins, weighing her down. If she seemed a little desperate, so be it. She needed him. She was a little afraid for him. The combination churned in her stomach, pounded in her blood, stoked a fire in her heart. She wanted to curl up inside his skin and go with him. How could that be? How could she feel so much for him after knowing him for such a short time?

"I have to go," he said finally.

"You'll be careful?"

"Yes."

"Promise me one other thing?"

"What?"

How could she think when he looked at her like that? Like she was something important or…precious. "Promise you won't revert to being Scrooge because I'm not there to reinforce the joy of Christmas. Look around. See how pretty the world is right now."

"I'll try, sweetheart."

He left, the endearment sitting there like a gift with a big red bow.

Lyndsey let herself into the office at seven o'clock and was surprised to find several people still at their desks. Occasionally one or two investigators worked late in the office or came in after hours, but never this many, since they worked in the field the majority of the time. She counted five, most of whom she'd never met. She introduced herself as she made her way to her cubicle, glad to put faces to names.

She put away her sweater and purse, signed in and picked up Sam's Rubik's Cube. The note underneath indicated he'd taken two minutes and forty-six seconds to solve the last time. He must've had a lot on his mind, because he rarely took that long. She always felt guilty about being paid for the fun of jumbling the cube, so Sam solved that by officially writing the task into her job description. She played with the cube for several minutes, finishing up as she walked toward his office to set it on his desk.

"Lyndsey?" Arianna called out from her office as Lyndsey passed by.

She stopped in Arianna's doorway and smiled. "How're you?"

"Good, thanks. Would you come in for a minute? Shut the door, please."

Arianna Alvarado was a beautiful woman with long, dark hair, intense dark eyes, flawless skin, and a figure that made men stare and stumble. Like Nate and Sam, she was thirty-two. Lyndsey had seen her turn on the charm full force for a client once and envied her ability to be professional and feminine at the same time.

"Nate filled me in on the Marbury case," Arianna said, settling into her leather chair. "What'd you think?"

"I think I'd like to become a private investigator."

Arianna's rare speechlessness made Lyndsey smile. "I caught you off guard."

"Well, yes."

Lyndsey leaned forward. "I can't tell you how much I enjoyed the assignment. I was revved up most of the weekend. It was incredible."

"It was new."

"Totally. But I was good at it…I think." *If you don't count my saying too much to the client and almost getting us into big trouble.*

"So Nate said. However, there's a difference between following instructions and taking charge."

"You don't think I could do it?"

"Don't put words in my mouth." She toyed with a pen. "It seems like a fast decision."

"Yes and no. I got my degree in accounting because of the job stability. I needed to know I could support my sister and myself. But I don't have a passion for it. I've been dreading doing it full-time to the point of not applying for many positions yet. The investigative work grabbed me and didn't let go, even though things didn't go smoothly, maybe even because they didn't. And I figure that my accounting background can only help. I know ARC takes on fraud and embezzlement cases. I figure the salary's got to be competitive with entry-level CPA."

"Do you know what's involved in becoming licensed?"

"I looked it up on the Internet. Three years of compensated experience in investigative work, two thousand hours each year, under the supervision of a licensed investigator."

Arianna didn't respond immediately. She drummed her pen on her desk and stared at Lyndsey until she squirmed under the scrutiny.

"Have you talked to Nate about this?" Arianna asked.

"No, and I don't want him to know."

"Why not?"

"Because I don't want him to have influence either way. This is my career. My life. It has to be my decision."

"He shopped for a Christmas tree with you today. And you—" Arianna cocked her head. "You're glowing."

Lyndsey hesitated. How much should she say? "We got close over the weekend. It's not surprising, is it? We spent all of our time together. It accelerated a…our friendship."

"Are you sure you know what you're doing?"

"No," Lyndsey said honestly, excitement building at the changes ahead. "I'm going along for the ride because I've never ridden anywhere like it before. Everything is happening at once, so I'm not trusting my emotions completely, but I'm sure about one thing. I love this work. I want to keep doing it. I want to get good at it."

"You're sure this career change has nothing to do with Nate? It can't have anything to do with him, Lyndsey. Nate's not—" She stopped, as if she'd said too much.

Not someone I can count on? Lyndsey filled in the end of the sentence. Maybe Arianna was right. But maybe Lyndsey could change it. Maybe she needed to take that risk.

"I really want to do it, Arianna." Was that a good enough answer? Evasive enough? She couldn't answer it with total honesty because she didn't know for sure herself. "I haven't been this excited about anything in a long time."

"Okay." Arianna closed her eyes for a moment. "Okay. Here's what I'll do. I'll work with you for a couple of weeks. I'll give you case files to study and we'll discuss them. We'll test your instincts, because the right instincts are critical, especially for a woman, because people look for you to fail. Most people find more comfort with a man guarding them. You do know we do security as well as investigation?"

"Yes, but does every employee? I'm not sure that's something I'd be good at."

"Everyone here does. We have a reputation to maintain. Frankly, I would require you to train in martial arts. It not only fine-tunes your body but it sharpens your mind and speeds up your reaction time. Then would come weapons training. Are you still sure about this?"

Lyndsey nodded. To a nonexerciser it sounded like her definition of hell, but she could do it.

"You'll also be assigned some of the most boring work you could ever imagine, Lyndsey. Some days, some months, it's just tedious. It's reading page after page after page of information looking for one key word or number. It's boring and frustrating. Then there'll be situations where you'll need to extricate yourself from predicaments by using only your wits. It's long hours and hard work. Sometimes it's scary work. Occasionally it's potentially life threatening."

"I'm a hard worker."

"I don't doubt that. Do you have guts? Are you fearless? I'm not saying you couldn't do an adequate job. A lot of it would be easy for you, but I have a feeling you don't want to just do the job. You want to be extraordinary."

Hope fluttered inside Lyndsey. A new dream took flight. "I want to be like you."

Arianna laughed. "I'm flattered."

"I mean it."

"I see that you do." She studied Lyndsey for a few seconds. "All right. I don't have time to spare right now. We're swamped."

"I know."

"You want a job here at ARC, I imagine."

"I want to work for the best."

"I can't guarantee a position. That's a decision all three partners make, and in the past we've only hired experienced investigators, ones who already have their licenses so they can work independently."

"I plan to do this, no matter where I have to go or what I have to do. You'd be missing out on a great employee."

"I expect you're right," she said with a smile. "For now let's just concentrate on finding out if you have what it takes. We'll start right after Christmas."

"Thank you. Thank you so much." Lyndsey stood and resisted the temptation to hug her. She got to the doorway and turned around. "You won't tell Nate?"

"I won't tell Nate. Or Sam, for that matter. First things first."

"Thanks. Oh, and thank you for the airplane ticket. You all are so generous." She almost danced to Sam's office to leave the Rubik's Cube. Her life was coming together in ways she'd merely dreamed of.

The only problem was, if she went forward with her

plans and stayed on at ARC, how would that change her relationship with Nate? He knew she planned to leave. What if she told him she wanted to stay? Would that change everything?

And for better or worse?

Nine

"Lyndsey, we hired people to do that," Arianna said above the din of the company Christmas party, where thirty employees were consuming large quantities of food and drink.

"I can't help it. It's the old caterer in me." She eyed the food table. "I see a serving tray and I have to pass it around."

Arianna dragged her away. "You're a guest. Enjoy yourself."

"I have been. It's wonderful meeting everyone in person. What an eclectic bunch."

"That's a nice way of putting it. What are you doing tonight?"

Christmas Eve. It was an odd day for a company party but the only day when most people could attend. The mid-afternoon celebration would finish early enough for family time.

"Christmas Eve is full of traditions for me," Lyndsey said evasively, watching the door, hoping Nate would walk through it—and hoping he wouldn't. She'd worn a red dress just for him, to show him what he'd missed. To prove she wasn't pining.

Arianna leaned close. "He won't be here."

The words hit her like a punch in the stomach. "I thought the case was over."

"Did he tell you that?"

"I haven't spoken to him since he left." How could he kiss her like he did, and look at her like he had and then ignore her? "But I'm guessing he was guarding Alexis Wells. Mr. Marbury's assistant remembered seeing them together last year—that's how she knew who Nate was. I heard on the news this morning that the man who'd shot at Alexis was caught yesterday near her house on Maui, so he'll have to be extradited. Is that why Nate won't be here?"

"No, that's police business. Nate never attends the Christmas party."

Disappointment swamped Lyndsey, which really made her mad. She was already furious with him for not calling. Why was she investing so much energy in a man who liked to keep her dangling?

She took a sip of mulled cider, tried to keep her voice level. "Is he back in town?"

Arianna didn't answer.

"I shouldn't have put you on the spot," Lyndsey said apologizing.

He'd been gone eleven days. Not one call.

Out of the corner of her eye she saw someone come into the room from the lobby. She clenched her glass, preparing to act as if she hadn't missed him for one moment.

But it wasn't Nate. It was an enormous Santa Claus carrying a bag over his shoulder. "Ho, ho, ho," he bel lowed, assuming the classic Santa pose, legs spread and boots planted, a fist propped on his hip and his belly shaking.

"Oh, no," Lorraine from payroll cried. "Run, ladies. It's Grabby Claus."

"C'mere, you," Santa said, catching her and dragging her to a chair. "Sit on my lap, little girl, and tell Santa what you want for Christmas."

Lorraine laughed while fending off his wandering hands. "I want the same thing as last year and the year before, Santa."

"Me in your bed?" he roared.

"Have you met Abel?" Arianna asked Lyndsey.

"That's Abel Metzger? Oh, I should've known his voice. I didn't realize he was so big."

"He can plough through a crowd like no one else. Abel does this every year. Just go along with him. It'll save you from being hunted down and yanked into his lap."

"Do you?"

"Are you kidding? He gives out Godiva truffles."

Lyndsey laughed as he enticed one woman after another to his lap. Then he crooked his finger at Arianna, who moseyed over, settled onto his thigh and looped her arms around his neck. Lyndsey noticed he wasn't as hands on with Arianna as he was with the rest of the women. His voice wasn't so huge, either, and his cheeks pinkened like the real Santa.

Lyndsey decided she could learn a thing or two about female power by watching her boss.

"Have you been naughty or nice, little girl?"

"Naughty. Very naughty."

"Ho, ho, ho! That gets you two boxes of chocolates."

Arianna kissed his cheek. "Thank you, Santa. I'll try to be even naughtier next year."

He looked relieved when Arianna stepped away, then

he zeroed in on Lyndsey. "And who's this vixen in the red dress?" He patted his lap. "Your turn, little lady."

For someone who wasn't used to being the center of attention it was a big step, but she took a page out of Arianna's book and approached him as if she was the one in control.

"Have you been naughty or nice, little girl?"

"Nice." She toyed with his beard, twining a long white strand around her finger.

"Can't earn your candy that way. What would you like for Christmas?"

"A chance to be naughty." She batted her eyes as everyone laughed.

"Ho, ho, *ho.* Got anyone in mind?"

She was about to say *you,* just to see him blush, but a silence came over the room. She looked around and saw Nate. He looked ready to turn and run.

And he looked gorgeous in his gray suit and black T-shirt.

"Got room here for you, little boy," Santa said, patting his other leg. "Even got you a present. This one's lookin' to be naughty."

"I think our harassment premium just went up," Nate said with a sigh, but he took a seat, his legs bumping Lyndsey's.

"So you got my letter, Santa," Nate said, giving Lyndsey a wink.

She could barely hear over the blood pounding in her ears. *Don't you dare be sweet. I'm mad at you.*

From nowhere, Santa produced a sprig of mistletoe and held it aloft. "Someone's waiting for a kiss, little boy."

Nate's smile turned decidedly wicked. Lyndsey held her breath. Here? In front of everyone? She let her eyes ask the questions.

He winked again then he turned to Santa and planted a

big, smacking kiss on his lips. Everyone roared. Nate and Lyndsey were shoved off his lap. Nate caught her by the arm before she stumbled.

"Cooties," Santa exclaimed, sputtering.

"You've got enough alcohol in you to kill the plague," Nate said. He stroked Lyndsey's arm with his thumb before releasing her.

Santa stood and whipped off his fluffy beard and hair. "Well, somebody get me a whiskey, straight up, anyway. Just to be sure."

Nate turned to Lyndsey. "You okay?"

She nodded. He couldn't read her. He might as well have been a stranger the way she looked at him.

"Welcome back," she said simply. "Excuse me." She headed to the bar, leaving him standing there, which was the smart thing to do in front of their co-workers.

He kept her in sight as he made his way around the room, greeting everyone. She got into an animated discussion with Julie, the receptionist. After a while he ended up next to Sam.

"So," Sam said, not needing any other words to convey his surprise at Nate showing up for the party.

"Yeah," Nate replied, not needing any other words to convey his own surprise back. They'd known each other too long and well.

"Good job on grabbing the shooter," Sam said.

"It was satisfying taking him down."

"Joe Vicente, the LAPD detective, told Arianna and me about the guy's apartment."

"Sick," Nate said. They'd found every inch of wall space covered with Alexis's photos, which wasn't all that unusual. But they'd also found instruments of torture. He'd never intended to kill her but to incapacitate her and drag her off to his place. "Speaking of Vicente, you met him, right?"

"When he came to look at our files from last year's threat. He and Arianna danced around each other a bit."

"No way."

"Could've knocked me over."

"He's a cop. LAPD, at that." Nate spotted Arianna talking with several of the investigators. "I liked him. But we both know *that* would be impossible. She wouldn't go out with him. Ever."

Sam shrugged. "So, have you got plans for tonight?"

He took a sip of merlot and sought Lyndsey with his eyes. "Why? What're you doing?"

"My usual Christmas Eve tradition. Put my copy of *It's a Wonderful Life* in the video and get quietly drunk. Wanna join me?"

Nate eyed him. "Do women get your sense of humor?"

"Sometimes." Sam cocked his head toward Lyndsey. "She's gotten a little more withdrawn every day you've been gone and trying not to show it. Arianna will probably ream you out about it."

People started coming up then, thanking them for the party, saying their goodbyes. Designated drivers were given their charges, the caterers packed everything and left. After taking Nate into her office and giving him hell for whatever he was doing to Lyndsey, Arianna took off to spend the evening with her family.

Apparently Nate had to make amends with Lyndsey, although maybe it would be best to let their relationship die a natural death now, while she was mad at him.

He noticed that she kept herself busy. She took down Christmas decorations, which Arianna had told him Lyndsey had put up, complaining that the office lacked spirit.

"That didn't have to be done today," Sam told her as she closed up the box.

"A lot of people don't like to see the decorations when Christmas is over."

"Well, thank you. Merry Christmas, Lyndsey." He gave Nate a "be careful" look and wished him Merry Christmas, as well.

"I'll walk out with you, Sam," she said abruptly. "Let me get my purse."

Sam raised his brows at Nate.

"Would you mind waiting a minute, Lyndsey?" Nate asked.

"I'm kind of in a hurry."

To do what? "This won't take long."

Nate waited for the front door to close behind Sam. She didn't move, didn't look at him, but stood there, her box of decorations in her arms, her purse over her shoulder.

"You're mad at me."

Her smile was brittle. "You have to care in order to be mad at someone. I stopped caring, oh, about five days ago."

"Why?"

"Why do you think?"

"I don't know." Not for sure, he added to himself. He could guess.

"Because you don't care about *me*," she said, her eyes cool, her mouth hard. "It's okay. Sometimes I'm a little slow when it comes to men. Must be in the genes. Can I go now?"

"I do care about you."

"You have a funny way of showing it."

She was right about that. He'd intentionally not called her, not only because of the job but because every time he was with her, he stopped following his own rules, like no serious relationships, no heartache, and no scenes.

Especially no scenes. He argued, debated, with Arianna but he hadn't argued with another woman for as long as he could remember. He didn't invest that much emotion, because he didn't want it in return. He'd learned from his mistakes.

He and Lyndsey were headed for a scene, and he didn't know how to stop it except to walk out. He couldn't do that.

"You're mad because I didn't call?" he asked, already knowing the answer.

She dropped the box on her desk and faced him, hands on hips. "Are you really that dense?"

"I don't want to make assumptions."

Her color was high. In heels she was several inches taller, which felt strange to him. She seemed to match his height.

"Yet you assumed I wouldn't expect a call from you?" she asked.

"I was working a hard case."

"In eleven days you never had a minute to say hi? Nate, you could've left me a message on my answering machine and I would've been as happy as a cat rolling in catnip. You said you would call." Her voice got softer and softer. "You promised."

"Do you think I didn't think about you?" he asked, heating up. *Don't you cry.* "I'm here, aren't I? I'm sure you heard I never come to the Christmas party. I tried to stay away. I couldn't."

"So now you're mad at *me* because I make you do things you don't want to do?" She scooped up the box again and started to leave.

He grabbed it and tossed it down. "Now who's making assumptions? Do you always walk out in the middle of a fight?"

"It's better to go to bed angry than to say something you'll regret or can't take back," she singsonged, parroting his own words at the beach house.

"I thought it would make you happy knowing that you

tempt me that much. That I have no willpower when it comes to you.''

''Not when it makes you mad. Why should that make me happy?'' She shook her head. ''I'm leaving. You're way too…too—''

''Screwed up?'' *Tell me something I don't know.*

''No.'' She looked at him oddly. ''Is that what you think about yourself?''

''I missed you. There. Does that make you happy?''

His blood was singing. He loved that she kept giving him hell. How idiotic was that?

She walked away.

''Lyndsey.'' He couldn't get any more words out.

She turned. ''I don't want to hurt you, Nate.''

''Then don't go.''

After what seemed like an hour she let her purse fall to the floor as she walked toward him, something unidentifiable in her eyes. She didn't stop but went right into his arms and kissed him. And kissed him. And kissed him some more. Nothing had tasted so good, so warm, so right as she did. Her lips were soft and busy. Her tongue as demanding as his. And all those throaty little sounds…

He maneuvered his hands between their bodies and unfastened the row of buttons down her dress, as he'd been aching to ever since he walked into the party. He slipped his hands under the soft fabric and molded her rib cage, moving her backward into her cubicle until she sat on the edge of her desk. Her eyes spoke volumes, but mostly they said yes.

He separated the fabric, revealing her bra underneath, and a lot of skin.

''You wore the red.''

''I can be very obedient.''

''When you want to be?''

She nodded. ''I missed you so much.''

The words burned him. Her eyes never leaving his face, she pulled his shirt free and shoved it up. Her hands, hot and curious, moved over his chest, his abdomen, and beyond, tracing his hard flesh with her fingertips.

He couldn't talk. It scared him, these feelings. Everything was going so fast. The physical chemistry was strong. Overwhelming. His head and heart were doing battle about who should be in charge, and now a more insistent part of his body joined the debate. There was no contest. He wanted her. Now. He dragged his tongue between her breasts, along the lace edge of fabric. Her fragrance, warm and spicy, assaulted him. He suckled her through the lace, her nipples hard and tempting. He couldn't wait to get her naked and writhing under him. He wanted to see her, all of her. Touch her. Explore her. Bury himself in her.

Find home in her.

He raised his head and kissed her again, all the while bunching her skirt above her hips, stepping between her legs, opening her wide. He sought her with his hand, discovered soft, silky panties that he slipped his fingers under, finding incredible heat and inviting dampness. She said his name—

The phone rang.

They jumped. As it continued to ring they stared at each other, breathing hard.

He swore. "We can't do this," he said, dragging his hands through his hair. She was already fumbling with her buttons. Her cheeks were almost as red as her dress.

"Let's—"

"Stop," she said, low and harsh. "Just stop. No one's forcing you."

She ran out.

He should've gone after her. She'd misunderstood. But maybe it was for the best.

Are you out of your mind? his sensible self screamed. Go after her.

He was too late. He got to the parking lot in time to see her drive off. He watched until the taillights of her car disappeared.

She hadn't backed out of her space but had driven straight through the one in front of her.

She'd broken a rule.

Because of him.

Ten

Barefoot, Lyndsey paced her living room. Her frustration and pent-up energy needed an outlet, and pacing was the only thing she could do inside her house, short of throwing or punching things. But then she'd just have to clean up something and replace it. And feel like an idiot.

He wasn't worth it. He was not worth all this grief. She'd been just fine before he came along and she would be fine again. She would show him.

Her doorbell rang. She picked up a bag she'd set on the sofa and opened the door. She tried to smile.

It wasn't who she expected, however.

"Don't you ask who it is before you open the door?" Nate asked, frowning.

"Not that it's any of your business, but I was expecting someone."

"Yo, Lynnie." Her nineteen-year-old neighbor, Benito Gonzales, came up the walk. His timing was perfect. He walked like he owned the world, dressed like a thug, and had been Jess's unpaid guardian through high school. Lyndsey adored him.

"Smokin' dress," he said, giving her the once-over.

She felt Nate's attention spike. "Thank you," she said, then introduced the men.

"Yo, man," Ben said, giving Nate some kind of secret handshake. Lyndsey gave him credit. He didn't fumble.

She held out the bag to Ben. "Merry Christmas."

He patted his stomach. "I'd already packed away those others you brought over. Thanks."

"You're welcome."

"Later," he said, waving a hand as he sauntered away.

"Those were your cookies," she said to Nate.

"Mine?"

"That's right. I baked them for you." She crossed her arms. "Why are you here?"

"You misunderstood," he said, looking serious and sincere. "Back at the office, when I said we couldn't. I meant that we couldn't do it there. Too many people have keys. What if someone walked in?"

"So what do you want now?"

"For you to accept my apology."

"Is that all?"

He nodded.

"Okay." She started to shut the door.

"No." He blocked it with his arm. "No, that's not all."

The ice around her heart began to melt. She could see how hard it was for him, telling her how he felt. This was not a man often in touch with his emotions.

He lifted his head and looked into her eyes. "I want to make love with you. I want to sleep beside you. I want to spend Christmas with you."

"Okay." She barely got the word out.

"Okay?"

She nodded, stepped back and held the door for him. He swept her into his arms, pushed the door shut with his foot.

"I'm sorry I hurt you," he said.

She tightened her hold on him until the urge to cry went away.

"You gave away my cookies," he said, lightening the moment.

"Only two dozen. I baked you ten."

"Ten dozen?"

"I packed them in freezer bags so you could keep them on hand for whenever you wanted them."

"You think they'd last long enough that I'd need to freeze 'em?"

He seemed to be stalling. She wondered if he was nervous. It seemed amazing that he would be, and even more amazing that she wasn't. Nothing had ever felt so right as this.

He won't stay around. Lyndsey ignored the caution calling out in her head, even though the truth stung. She wanted to sleep with him. He would probably break her heart, but she was going to risk it for the chance to be with him, to make memories, to feel cherished.

"I'd offer you a tour of the house but you've already been here," she said.

"I didn't see your bedroom."

Finally. She smiled before she lifted her head from where it was tucked against his neck. "Follow me."

He didn't budge. "I have to go to the car first."

"Why?"

He half smiled.

"Oh." Protection. "I've got some." At his raised brows, she rushed on. "Well, I was hopeful. I mean, unless you have to have your own. Some super jumbo size or…something…."

He looked as though he was trying not to laugh, then he held her hand as they walked to her room. She tried to see it as he might. An antique sleigh bed and highboy dresser that had belonged to her grandmother. Her mother's amazing art on the walls. A quilt of bold colors, which she tossed back, revealing white sheets. She lit a candle beside the bed and turned to him.

"Now, where did we leave off?" she asked.

"You were sighing," he said, taking a step closer.

"Was I?"

"Or maybe moaning." Closer still.

"Probably."

He undid the top button of her dress. Another. One more.

"What were you doing?" she asked.

"I was believing in heaven."

She waited for the last button to be undone. "You're shaking," she said in wonder.

"You should see what I'm seeing. Feel what I'm feeling."

He couldn't have paid her a higher compliment. She didn't feel the least bit shy or hesitant with him. This was right. Meant to be. Destined. He made her feel beautiful.

Soon her dress fell to the floor. He ran his fingers along her collarbones, over her shoulders, down her back. He unhooked her bra and pulled it away, tossing it aside, leaving her only in her red panties.

"Beautiful," he murmured, testing the weight of her breasts and the shape of her nipples. He drew one into his mouth for what seemed like forever, then the other even longer, until her knees started to buckle.

Still it was going too fast, she thought. Slow down. Savor. Remember.

He knelt in front of her as she stepped out of the dress then threaded her fingers through his hair, drawing him closer. His mouth touched her abdomen. He dragged the tip of his tongue down until he reached fabric, then he molded his hands over her rear and tugged her panties down and off. He didn't lift his head but cupped her from below, his thumbs stroking, opening, separating, arousing her beyond anything she'd experienced. Slowly, tenderly, he put his lips to her, touched her with his tongue.

"Now *you're* shaking," he murmured, his breath blowing hot against her. "Your bracelets sound like sleigh bells."

She made a sound she couldn't believe came from her. He nudged her until she landed on the bed. "Lie down."

"No."

"This is no time to be stubborn, Stubborn."

"I want it to be together." She reached for his belt, unzipped his pants, pushed them down. He got rid of them, along with his shoes and socks. She pulled his shirt over his head, learned the contours of his chest with her hands and her mouth, felt his muscles twitch. Finally she pulled off his boxer briefs and admired him.

"You're beautiful, too," she said softly, hardly able to believe he was hers. He was such an ideal, all broad shoulders and muscular chest and flat abdomen. Long, sturdy legs, strong arms. And that most masculine part of him, bold and powerful. She put her mouth to him as he had to her, tenderly, her tongue exploring gently.

He grabbed her head. "If you want this to be together, you need to stop doing that. God, Lyndsey. You're driving me crazy."

She felt strong and brave. She leaned across him, opened her nightstand and pulled out a condom, passing it to him.

For all that he normally talked a blue streak, it was strange that he was so quiet now as he eased her onto the mattress. But what he didn't say with words he said with his eyes and his hands and body. He slid the bracelets off her wrist one by one and set them aside. His kisses started soft, intensified, then overwhelmed. She'd never known that kind of passion, as if he'd been waiting for her for all his life. She knew she'd been waiting for *him*.

She let her mind go blank so that only this experience would fill it, nothing else. She welcomed him into her heart and her body eagerly, willingly, lovingly. He filled her, stretched her, took her. There was no time to go slowly, no time to build. He'd barely joined with her when they dug their fingers into each other, pressed closer, moved faster and found paradise in a quick, hard climb that went beyond the summit, bursting through the clouds. The sensation lasted seconds, minutes, hours. A slow return to earth, then collapse.

She refused to let him move off her but held him tight, tears threatening because it was so beautiful. She didn't dare cry—it had been so long since she had that she would probably have a complete meltdown. More important, he hated tears.

Finally he rolled onto his side, taking her with him. "I'm too heavy for you," he said, drawing back enough to look at her, brushing her hair away from her face.

I love you. She didn't say the words out loud but heard them in her heart. Even though they were whispered, they flooded her with hope and despair. It was too soon. She was superstitious. She'd heard the best way to lose a man was to tell him you loved him before he was ready to hear it. She had no intention of making that mistake.

So for now she would hide her feelings, a big task for a woman who apparently had an honest face.

"Are you hungry?" she asked.

"You are such a hostess." He smiled at her. "I had plenty at the office, but thank you. Are you cold? We can pull the sheet up."

She shook her head. She was a little chilled, but she

wanted to lie naked with him, to look at him, to have him look at her. *He thinks I'm beautiful.* She drew circles on his chest leisurely, still hardly able to believe he was there. With her. He'd made love with her.

He rolled away from her. "I'll be right back."

She heard water run in the bathroom, then she had the pleasure of watching him walk back into the room and get back into bed. It was only six-thirty. They had the whole night ahead of them.

At some point they moved from the bedroom to the living room. Lyndsey wore her robe. Nate had on sweatpants and a T-shirt he'd gotten from a gym bag he always kept in his car. The tree lights were on, Christmas songs played low in the background. He had his head in her lap enjoying a scalp massage and decided he would be hardpressed to remember a better night in his life.

"Would you prefer to open your Christmas present tonight or tomorrow?" Lyndsey asked.

"You didn't have to get me a present just because I got you one."

Her fingers stopped moving. "I—I didn't.... You got me a present?"

He opened his eyes and looked up at her, seeing that she was serious. "You don't know?"

"Know what?"

He sat up. "Did you think those tires appeared by magic?"

"Tires?"

"You didn't even notice?" He started to laugh. The joke was on him. He held out his hand. "Come on."

"Where?"

"To your garage."

She grabbed the lapels of her robe and tugged them closer. "I can't go out there in my robe. With you."

"Ah, the scandalous Ms. McCord. I'm sure you've given them plenty of fuel for the neighborhood gossip fire through the years. What's one more log on the fire?" he teased, pulling her out the front door.

"Well, old Mrs. Brubaker across the street will be more thrilled than scandalized. And Benito's been telling me for a long time there was nothing wrong with me that some hot sex wouldn't cure."

"Was he offering to play doctor?" He ignored the unfamiliar jab to his gut.

"No, he keeps trying to set me up with his cousin. Why, Nate. Are you jealous?"

"Not in my nature." *Usually.* He opened her garage door and pulled on the overhead light.

She crouched down, ran her hand over one tire. "It has tread." She looked up at him. "I knew something was different. I noticed it, night before last? But it was raining, so I chalked it up to that. I hadn't left the house during the day. You know, I leave for work in the dark and come home in the dark. But I should've seen them today. It was daylight. I didn't notice."

He waited for her to say she couldn't accept the gift. That it was too much. That she could take care of herself just fine, thank you very much.

"When I heard rain was forecast, I got worried," he said in his defense, beating her to it. "I didn't want you out on the road with bald tires."

She stood up, her eyes glistening suspiciously.

"Somebody needs to take care of you, Stubborn." He took a step toward her. "It's okay just to say thank-you."

She came into his arms. "Thank you."

"You're welcome." He tucked her closer.

"How did you manage it?"

"While you were working. The mechanic was supposed to park his van so that you couldn't see your car if you happened to look out the window.'' He paused. ''A man would've noticed them that night, you know.''

''I'm a woman.'' She fluttered her lashes.

''I never would've guessed.'' Hand in hand they returned to the house. ''I figured you'd fight me about it.''

''One fight a night is all I can handle.'' She lifted a large box from under the tree and gave it to him without comment.

He was never comfortable opening presents. What did you say? How did you act? He rarely gave traditional gifts, either, not wanting to watch people open them. When he gave a gift, it was offered unwrapped and casually.

He opened the box to find not one item but an assortment.

''Since you couldn't get to Australia, I brought it to you,'' she said, looking pleased with herself.

There were videotapes on the country, a piece of coral, a baggie of sand, sunscreen, a stuffed kangaroo, a bottle of Australian wine, and a bikini bottom. He dangled it from one finger. ''I hope this hot pink number is yours and not something I'm supposed to wear.''

She laughed. ''I heard there are topless beaches there. Just thought I'd give you a mental image.''

He pictured her in it. ''My house is a block from the beach. Would you like to go tomorrow? Wear this? With the top.''

''It's December. Not exactly bikini weather.''

''It's supposed to reach seventy-two tomorrow.'' *I need to see you wearing it.*

''That hot, huh?''

''It'll be nice in the sun.''

She sort of shrugged, but he couldn't tell whether she was saying yes or no.

''What's wrong?'' he asked.

''Nothing.''

He studied her. "Yes, there is. Tell me."

"It's just…being in a bikini."

"Yeah?"

"My skin is so white. And there's—" she fluttered her hands "—you know. My body."

He didn't know what to make of her. "What's wrong with your body?"

"Oh, never mind."

It struck him then that she was really uncomfortable. How could that be? "I've seen you naked," he said softly. "I like you naked." Which was an understatement. She had curves, generous but firm. Mouthwatering. There was nothing about her he would change.

The phone rang. Nate figured out from the conversation it was her sister calling to say Merry Christmas. Lyndsey's face lit up. Nate could hug Jess for calling Lyndsey tonight. He had a picture of her little sister in his mind, cute—he'd seen her photographs—a little selfish and self-centered. Typical eighteen-year-old discovering independence. But she needed to remember Lyndsey and how important Christmas was to her. So he was glad she called.

He wandered over to the Christmas tree while they talked. When they'd decorated it, he purposely hadn't paid much attention to the ornaments. Now he studied them, examining each of the homemade objects, some with their names on them, others with photos. He and his brother had made some ornaments as children, but that had stopped when his mother had her breakdown. His father had thrown out their box of decorations when they moved to California.

Christmas in the Caldwell household was only a slightly different day from the rest of the year. There were a few presents but no tree. A wreath on the front door so that the world would think they celebrated, but no decorations inside. He'd hated it. Hated pretending to be happy with the new socks and underwear and one game. He'd desperately wanted a bicycle one year and had badgered his father for months. He got one—secondhand and rusty. He was too embarrassed to ride it. His father was furious and hauled it to the dump without saying a word.

Nate never had learned to ride a bike.

Then when he'd married, he thought it would be different. He and his wife could start their own traditions. What a joke.

He had to get out of the house, let the thoughts blow away. "I'll be back in a few minutes," he mouthed to Lyndsey, then he went out the front door.

Lyndsey had been watching him while she talked to Jess. There'd been such sadness in his face as he'd looked at her ornaments. Beyond the fact his mother was taken away from him at Christmas, what else haunted him? If she'd never come home, Lyndsey could understand the bad memories he associated with the holiday, but his mother had spent more years with him.

"Are you alone for Christmas?" Jess asked over the phone.

"No. I'm with a friend."

"A male friend?"

"As a matter-of-fact."

"Tell me about him."

How could she describe him? "He's tall, blond and handsome. He's thoughtful and generous." *He puts my satisfaction over his own. His kisses make me dizzy.* "His name is Nate."

"Are you madly in love? You are. I hear it in your voice."

"I'm enjoying his company. Are *you* madly in love?"

"I'm enjoying his company," Jess teased. "And he's telling me I have to get off the phone so he can call his parents. I love you, Lynnie. Merry Christmas."

"Merry Christmas, Jess." A myriad of emotions bombarded Lyndsey when she hung up. Unwavering love for her sister, worry that she would get hurt by this boy, and pleasure that Jess seemed to be maturing and settling down.

Then there were her feelings for Nate. Secret love for him, worry that she would get hurt, and pleasure that her life seemed to be changing in such wonderful ways.

She tucked her legs under her and nestled into the sofa, waiting for Nate to return. When he came through the door, she smiled at him in welcome. He stopped, stared, then stuck his hands in his pockets and moved to the tree.

He touched a bread-dough ornament she'd made in third grade, her school picture glued to it. She always thought she looked like a poodle in that picture, with her wild, kinky hair.

"You were cute," he said.

He seemed exceptionally calm yet at the same time tense. "I was geeky," she said.

"But cute geeky. You should've seen me at that age."

"I can't picture you geeky."

"Oh, I wasn't. I was adorable. Like I said, you should've seen me." He grinned, but it didn't seem real.

What seemed real was when he came up to her, cupped her face and kissed her slowly. Sweetly. His nimble fingers untied her robe and pushed the fabric aside. His clever mouth found new ways to excite her. Within moments they were naked. She urged him down onto the sofa.

"Not here," he said. "In the bedroom. I want lots of room."

For what? she wondered.

Who cares?

He knelt beside the bed and pulled her legs over his shoulders, then used his mouth to make love to her thoroughly, exquisitely, selflessly. He knew where to touch, how to tease, when to torment by pulling back then starting over. She shook, she moaned, she begged. He pressed on, taking her over the top until she thought she would cry out from the intensity, then he rose up and plunged into her until she did.

They fell asleep in each other's arms, welcomed the morning with a slow, leisurely joining, then spent every minute of the next two days together. His house wasn't large but was in a prime location, being a block from the Santa Monica beach. His decorating style was simple. He didn't have much but wasn't home enough to care, he told her. When he had the time he would decorate. Until then, the basics would have to do.

The last evening they sat on his deck drinking wine and eating appetizers she'd thrown together. They were going out to dinner at some point but wanted to watch the sunset first.

"Do you ever take this view for granted?" she asked, settling her shoulders into the comfortable deck chair.

"Never."

Lyndsey hated for the day to end. Tomorrow it was back to work, back to real life. Nate was headed to San Francisco for a few days to do advance security for the arrival of an important politician from Asia. At least this time he would call her. She wondered how he would feel about Christmas from now on. Had his attitude changed?

She took a sip of merlot, savored it a moment, then turned her head to look at him. His profile was strong, like the rest of him. He must have felt her gaze on him because he turned, too, and raised his brows in question.

"Why do you hate Christmas so much?" she asked.

He looked away, took a swallow of wine then another. He was debating with himself, she decided, on what he would say. The truth, she wanted to shout at him. Just tell me the truth.

"On Christmas the year I was twenty-one," he said finally, "I found out my wife was cheating on me."

Eleven

———

Nate didn't watch her reaction, but he felt it—shock, and maybe even hurt that he'd waited this long to tell her he'd been married. He could use that old dodge that she hadn't asked, but he respected her too much for that. He'd purposely avoided talking about it.

"Your wife," she repeated calmly.

And she thought Arianna was cool under fire? Lyndsey should take a good look at herself. "My ex-wife. Beth."

"Would you like to talk about it?"

"Do you really want to hear it?"

"Of course I do."

He looked into his almost empty glass, swirling what was left. "There's not a lot to tell. We met when I was visiting my dad while I was on leave. I was nineteen and lonely. She lived up the street. We were both out jogging, she flirted, I responded. I was shy back then, especially with girls."

"I can't imagine that."

He wondered what she was thinking. Outwardly she was so cool. "Beth was a year older. She was my first sexual experience...but I wasn't hers. When my leave was up we stayed in contact. She pursued it more than I did at first, but I fell passionately in love." *I was too young and stupid to know it wasn't real.* "A few months later I found out I was being sent overseas as the Gulf War was heating up. I flew home at Christmas, married her, then went to war. I thought she was everything I ever wanted—and she probably was at the time. My father tried to talk me out of it. He backed down when he saw I would've gone to Las Vegas if I'd had to."

"It's hard to change a teenager's mind."

"Yeah. Long story short, I didn't get to come home again for a year. Christmas again. I was going to surprise her. I let my dad in on the plan, and he picked me up at the airport. On the way to our apartment he gave me an envelope. Didn't say a word. Inside were pictures of Beth, not just with one man, but several."

"At the same time?"

He was grateful for the momentary distraction of her reaction. "No."

"Your father took these pictures?"

"He hired a P.I."

"Not Charlie!"

"No. Some sleazy jerk who didn't mind getting up close and personal."

"I'm so sorry."

"Yeah, well, we learn our cruelest lessons the hard way, don't we? Crazy thing was, at first I was mad at my father."

"Shooting the messenger."

He nodded. "She wasn't who I thought she was." She'd

changed from sweet, adoring girl to provocative woman in a year. "I didn't want to believe she'd done it, despite the proof, but she didn't even try to lie. I was gone, she said. She had needs." The same complaints he'd gotten since then from women—he was gone too much. He was unavailable emotionally. He never took their relationship seriously. All of it true. Nothing had changed, nor would it, so he'd adapted. Keep it light. Keep it simple. Keep it short-term. No one gets hurt that way.

"And that's why I hate Christmas…and handling divorce cases, which I've seen far too many of," he said, then looked at her. "So, any ex-husband I should know about?"

She got out of her chair and settled herself on his lap, resting her head against his. "No."

He put his arms around her. He knew her body well now, every glorious curve, every freckle. He knew what heated her up in a hurry, what dragged out her climax, and that she was generous and eager to please.

And honest.

He'd effectively avoided women like her for so long, afraid of repeating the same mistake as he made with his ex-wife, but Lyndsey brought something to his life he hadn't known was missing. He couldn't put it into words. He only knew it existed.

Time to stop thinking about it. "Are you ready to go to dinner?" he asked.

"I'm hungry." She kissed his temple. "For you."

"I would've thought your appetite would be well satisfied by now."

"Is yours?"

"No, but—"

She pressed her lips to his, stopping his words. "Wha

makes me different? Plus, you're leaving tomorrow. I want to give you something to remember me by.''

Like there was any chance he'd forget. But his curiosity was piqued by the sexy promise in her voice. ''What do you have in mind?''

She whispered in his ear.

He found it fascinating that she was daring enough to propose what she had but couldn't say the words aloud. She was a remarkable mix of innocent and provocative, traditional and modern, courageous and cautious.

He whispered something back, just to see her blush.

Which she did, right before she proved she was a woman of her word.

''I signed up for tae kwon do lessons,'' Lyndsey told Arianna the next evening in the office. ''My first class is tomorrow.'' She'd figured out a way to pay for the lessons. Now she just had to make it happen.

''You're really serious.''

''Completely.''

''And it's because it's what you want. It has nothing to do with Nate.''

''If it weren't for Nate I probably wouldn't have even thought of it, but I think I'll be good at it. I've watched him in action. I've learned from you already. I know there's a reason I have to put in six thousand hours over the next three years—to get experience so that I don't make mistakes like I did on the Marbury case. I'll learn. I don't make the same mistake twice.''

Arianna leaned back in her chair. ''I've been thinking about you a lot. Your innocent look could either get you in trouble or get you answers to questions that no one else is able to.'' She turned her chair around and grabbed a small stack of files. ''Here's your homework. Read them thoroughly. Come in at six tomorrow night and we'll talk about them.''

''I can take them home with me?''

''Just don't lose them.''

''Of course not.'' Lyndsey tried not to be effusive in her gratitude.

''Don't thank me yet. A piece of advice, though?''

''Anything.''

''You might arrange for a massage after your tae kwon do lesson.''

''That bad?''

''Take my word for it.''

Lyndsey already ached from all the physical activity over the past few days. ''Thanks.'' She got up to leave.

''How was your Christmas?'' Arianna asked, her voice pointedly casual.

''Very nice. How was yours?''

Arianna smiled. ''You're already learning. Turning the tables is a good technique. Except I can tell by looking at you that it was more than nice. You carry yourself differently.''

''I do?''

''Straighter. Taller. There's an air of confidence about you that wasn't there. And I don't think I've ever seen you undo more than one button on your blouse before.''

She'd been daring enough to undo a second button. She really didn't think anyone would notice. After Nate dropped her off at her house on his way to the airport early that morning, she searched her closet, looking for ways to jazz up her wardrobe without spending any money. She'd found one solution—wear what she already owned.. differently. Mix different combinations. Unfasten an extra button, show off a little more skin, add a necklace

With the purchase of a couple of items, she could change her look quite a bit.

She didn't want to blend with the background any longer.

"You look happy," Arianna said.

"Which worries you."

"I won't beat it into the ground. You know the risks."

A few days ago Lyndsey had convinced herself that she didn't care if she got hurt. It was worth the risk, knowing that if she didn't let herself enjoy him, she would regret it for the rest of her life. Every girl had fairy-tale dreams. How often did they come true? Rarely, she was sure. But never, if she didn't try.

"I'm only worried about the repercussions here," Arianna continued. "I don't know if we could keep you. Our loyalty has to be to Nate, as the partner. He, Sam and I have worked too hard to stand by and watch our business falter."

"If it comes to that, I'll resign." She tried to sound businesslike but her stomach churned.

Arianna hesitated. "I could recommend you to another P.I....."

It finally struck Lyndsey that Arianna honestly believed Nate could not make a commitment. Ever. She knew him better than Lyndsey did. As well she should.

Lyndsey headed for the door, not wanting to hear anything else. "That would be great. I don't foresee any problems, though."

When Nate didn't call her the next day, she began to doubt.

The phone jerked Lyndsey out of a sound sleep.

"Did I wake you?" Nate asked.

Lyndsey clenched the telephone receiver, shoved her

hair from her eyes and squinted at her bedside clock. "Heck, no. I was doing naked aerobics."

He laughed quietly. "Thanks. I needed that visual to get me through the next fifteen minutes."

She pushed herself onto one elbow and leaned toward her bedside clock. Four o'clock. She blinked, shook her head and looked again. Still four o'clock.

He'd been gone since Wednesday. Now it was Saturday, New Year's Eve. He'd called her at work Thursday night for a short conversation, but that was all.

Oh, quit being selfish, she thought. This isn't high school. Welcome to your first adult relationship. Think about him, how tired he must be. "Have you slept tonight?" she asked sympathetically.

"I'm going to grab a couple hours now. Looks like I'll be flying home this afternoon. Alexis Wells invited us to a party tonight. Would you like to go?"

She sat straight up. The fact he issued the invitation so casually said a lot. He was used to stuff that like. Movie stars, powerful politicians. They were just clients to him. People.

And you'll get used to them, too. The idea made her smile in disbelief. What a turnaround her life had made in a few weeks.

"Are you there?" he asked.

"I'm thinking." There was nothing in her closet worthy of such an event. Plus, while the idea of attending thrilled her, the reality was she wasn't ready for such a leap. "Do you want to go?" she asked.

He yawned. "Doesn't matter. It's up to you."

"You wouldn't think less of me if I say no?"

"I'd think more of you. I'd rather spend the evening just with you, but I didn't want to deny you the chance to rub elbows."

Like she would have something to say to the actress and her friends? "That's not something I need. It would be fun to tell Jess, but that's all."

"Another time, then. How about dinner and dancing instead? I know a great little club. No frills. Just incredible steaks and good music. It'll be jammed, but it should be fun."

A date. A real date. And a guaranteed kiss at midnight to welcome the new year. "It sounds fabulous."

"I'll pick you up around eight. I'm sorry I had to wake you. It really was my only opportunity to call if I was going to give you any notice for tonight."

You can call me anytime, day or night. I'll always want to talk to you. She was proud of herself for not saying the words out loud, for protecting herself a little.

"I can't wait to see you," she said.

There was a long pause, then he said good-night. She snuggled under the quilt, tucked it against her chin. Sleep was impossible. Finally she sat up against the headboard, put on her glasses and pulled the phone into her lap. She calculated the time in New York. Seven-fifteen. A little early but what the heck.

She heard the phone being picked up, then the receiver bounced against something, then silence, then, "H'lo." Husky voice. Irritated tone.

"Happy New Year's Eve, Jess."

"Jeez, Lynnie." She groaned. "It's, like, the dead of night."

"You'll never guess what just happened."

"This better be good."

"I got invited to a party at Alexis Wells's house."

Long pause. "*The* Alexis Wells?"

"*The.*"

Jess screamed. Lyndsey screamed back.

"Ohmigod. Ohmigod. Tell me everything," Jess said, apparently wide-awake.

Lyndsey did.

"You said no? *You said no?* Are you crazy?"

"Maybe. Probably."

"You like this guy a lot, don't you?" Jess's voice softened.

"Yeah."

"He'd better treat you right."

"He got me invited to an Oscar-winning actress's house for New Year's Eve, didn't he?"

"I mean you. Lynnie, the person. You. He better treat you right."

Lyndsey's eyes stung. She loved her sister so much. "I have something else to tell you."

"I can tell I'm not gonna like this."

"You have to get a job, Jess." Silence. Lyndsey forged on. "I need some money to do some things that are important to me. I went on to your university Web site. There are on-campus jobs you're qualified for. If you work ten hours a week, you'll make what I send you in allowance. If you work fifteen, you'll have extra."

"But—"

"No buts. You have to do this. It's important for both of us. I'm cutting you off the second week of the spring semester, so you'd better get your act in gear."

"I don't have any experience."

"You'll get some. You'll do fine, Jess. You meet people well. Once they interview you, you'll have your choice of jobs."

"So you're saying this is for my own good."

"I know you don't think so, but it is."

"I finally got a boyfriend. I won't have time for him."

Lyndsey understood that feeling completely. "Budge-

your time. And put your education first. Show Mom you can do it. Make her proud.''

''Like Mom would know.''

''She knows.''

Lyndsey hung up a couple of minutes later. An iron anvil fell off her chest. After all these years of worrying about Jess, mothering her, guiding her, Lyndsey would put herself first now and then. Okay, so she'd used the make-Mom-proud card.

Desperate times called for desperate measures.

Twelve

Nate couldn't remember bringing a woman flowers before. He'd ordered them occasionally and had them delivered, but he hadn't personally brought a bouquet until now. He'd kept the florist shop open an extra fifteen minutes while he decided what suited Lyndsey, then tipped the clerk for her inconvenience, wiping the irritation off her face fast.

He'd already forgotten the name of the flower. They looked a little like daisies except their blooms were bigger and deep red-orange in color, a wild look that appealed to him and reminded him of her.

She opened her front door as he got out of his car. God she was beautiful. He shut the car door, then hesitated. She looked…different. She was wearing a plain black dress but there was nothing simple about it. It was cut low on top and the skirt landed several inches above her knees. I hugged her curves in a way that made his mouth go dry.

As if she couldn't wait for him another second she stepped onto her porch, then came up the walkway to meet him. Her blinding smile got bigger, brighter. Her eyes—

She wasn't wearing her glasses.

"Hi," she said softly, almost shyly, as she slipped her arms around his neck.

Her body felt amazing. "If I kiss you like I want to, old Mrs. Brubaker will definitely be thrilled."

Her eyes sparkled. "Then it's your duty to the neighborhood, at least."

He brushed her lips with his until hers parted.

"I missed you," she whispered against his mouth, her breath soft and warm.

He pulled her closer, deepened the kiss, felt her shudder. She moved her hips against his.

"So are you packin', Mr. P.I., or are you just happy to see me?"

A whistle pierced the night. "Yo, Lynnie!"

They turned their heads to see Benito saunter by.

"You been cured?" he called out.

"Definitely."

"Okay." He fixed his gaze on Nate. "That's a special lady."

Nate heard the threat in his voice. "Yes, she is," he said in return.

"Okay. Don't do nothin' I wouldn't do." He laughed and kept walking.

Nate handed Lyndsey the flowers. She buried her face in them. He didn't think they had much of a scent, but she sniffed them and smiled her thanks.

He followed her to the house and into the kitchen to find a vase for the flowers. "I almost didn't recognize you," he said, enjoying watching her move around the kitchen. Her legs seemed exceptionally long with the short skirt and high heels. "Did something happen to your glasses?"

"I got contacts."

"Why?"

"It was time," she said enigmatically. "You're the one who suggested it."

"I did?" Why would he do that? He loved her funny little glasses. He loved her in buttoned-up clothes, too. She was sexy as hell. Not that she wasn't now—hell, now he wanted to toss her on the dining-room table and make a feast of her—but it was a different kind of sexy from how she was before. The change made her seem different, not the Lyndsey he knew.

"The lenses are new," she said, "so I can't wear them the whole night, but for now I will." She stood back to study her arrangement. "The flowers are beautiful, Nate. Thank you so much." She kissed him as she passed by, carrying the flowers into the living room, empty now of Christmas decorations. She set the vase on the coffee table. "I told Jess I was cutting off her allowance when the semester starts and that she has to get a job."

Nate tried not to show how pleased that news made him. "How'd she react?"

"She was a little peeved, but she'll do it." She gave him a casual glance over her shoulder. "I started taking tae kwon do lessons."

Stunned was too mild a word for what he felt as she kept heaping on surprises. Sexy dress, contacts, giving Jess an ultimatum, and now tae kwon do? "Why?"

"Arianna raves about it, how it's helped her concentration and reaction time, and keeps her toned. I've been pretty sedentary lately because of my job at ARC, and before that I was studying for the exam."

"Okay, but tae kwon do? Couldn't there have been

something else? Pilates? Spinning? Tae kwon do is a long-term commitment.''

''I like the added bonus of self-defense. It seems sensible in this day and age.''

''There are classes specifically for that. Hell, I can teach you self-defense moves.''

She faced him, frowning. ''Does it bother you?''

It did, although he couldn't say exactly why. ''Why would it bother me?''

''I don't know. I hear you have a black belt in karate. I would think you would encourage others to learn martial arts.''

''I started when I was ten.''

''And I'm starting now.'' She came up to him. ''You seem a little out of sorts. Are you tired?''

Hell, no. He was exhausted. Maybe that's why he felt surly. But this was supposed to be a fun evening. He needed to change the mood, so he put his arms around her waist, slid his hands down her rear and pulled her close. ''You've taken the basic black dress to a whole new level. Let's go show you off.''

Hours later he peeled that dress off her after she'd teased him all night, leaning toward him at the table over dinner and drinks and some of the best jazz this side of New Orleans. She'd propped her chin in her hand, linked her fingers with his on the table and watched him intently as he talked. He was flattered by her interest in his work, but he seemed to do all of the talking because she kept asking questions, while he just wanted to strip her naked and make love to her right then and there.

He'd reached his limit by the time they got back to her house. The dress came off easily. She wore black lace lingerie that he almost tore he was in such a hurry. His need astounded him. He knew he was probably going too fast, coming on too strong. He didn't give her a chance to do more than be taken along for the ride, hardly letting her touch him, afraid he would explode before he satisfied her.

She was different, too, in the sounds she made, the urgent words she spoke, and her complete openness. Whatever traces of modesty she'd had before were gone now, and he welcomed it. Her body was perfect to look at, incredible to touch. Whatever he asked, she did, not just willingly but enthusiastically.

"Nate," she said once, drawing out his name. "Now."

"Soon," he said. But not too soon. Every time she neared the peak, he pulled back, until she turned into something wild. He urged her even higher, let her fall even lower, then took her up again. She clawed his back. Her body shook. He was thrilled by how she arched to meet him, then by the feel of her legs locked around him, and finally by the look on her face when she climaxed. He stopped holding back, drove harder and faster into her and found release in a burst of sensation so powerful he could scarcely draw in air. Worlds merged in a flash of light and thunder, leaving an eerie silence in its wake, darker than he'd ever known, deeper than he'd ever imagined.

He gathered enough energy to lift himself up, found she was breathing as raggedly as he was, and took her mouth in a long, thorough kiss until they breathed as one.

Then he slept, her breasts his pillow, her heartbeat his compass, guiding him home to rest.

Lyndsey wandered into her bedroom about every fifteen minutes. He'd slept through breakfast, the Rose Parade, and the opening half of the first Bowl game. He was so soundly asleep he seemed comatose. Sprawled across her bed and taking up all the space, he rarely moved. She kept checking to see if he was breathing.

He must have been beyond exhausted last night, yet he'd

still taken her out, wined and dined her, kissed her passionately at midnight and made love to her like a man just off a deserted island.

She'd never had this kind of physical relationship. The intensity amazed her. Her lack of modesty was new, too, as was her fearlessness. Her body ached contentedly.

She took a mug of coffee with her the next time she went into the bedroom. He was sitting up, looking groggy and adorable with his rumpled hair and scruffy beard.

"Why'd you let me sleep so late?" he asked, accepting the mug.

"You would've slept through cannon fire." She sat beside him. "You needed it."

He sipped his coffee and looked at her over the rim of his mug. "Would you like to go to the beach?"

"What do you usually do on New Year's Day?"

"Sam and I hang out and watch the games with a few other guys. We're not always in town at the same time, though, so it's not something we do every year. We wouldn't have this year since he's in Boston."

"I'll watch the games with you."

"You like football?"

"Sure."

He smiled. "No, you don't. So I'll ask again. Do you want to go to the beach?"

"We can watch the games today and go to the beach tomorrow."

"I have to go to Chicago tomorrow. I just got a call." He held up his cell phone. "That's what woke me."

How strange. She hadn't heard his phone ring. "What's the assignment? Or can't you say?"

"It's a corporate job setting up a security system for a client who's moving his business to Chicago from L.A."

"I thought Sam was the one to design the security systems. Panic rooms, things like that."

''He's got his hands full at the moment, and this client can't wait. I've got the basic skills, and the final plans will land on Sam's desk for his input. Anyway, I'll be gone two days, three at the most.'' He tossed aside the sheet, stood and stretched. ''If you've got some fix-it jobs I could do for you around the house, I'm pretty handy. Let me grab a quick shower first.''

He walked to the door, stopped there and turned around.

She caught her breath at the sight of him. He was hers. That gorgeous man was hers. For now.

He held out a hand. ''Yes, you can join me.''

How did he know she was about to ask him that?

''You keep looking at me like that and I'm going to get a swelled head,'' he said.

She laughed and flung herself into his arms. Love me, she pleaded silently. Love me.

Three nights later Nate let himself into the office after midnight. He stopped in the lobby, deciding how to approach Lyndsey. Their relationship had undergone a slight transformation in the past week. He could account for some of it—he'd become more tentative with her. He was waiting for her to walk away, not only because they'd been together for almost a month, the usual life span of his relationships since he never offered any kind of commitment, but because the signs were already there.

First, although she hadn't complained about his work schedule yet, she made comments about it under the guise of telling him he worked too hard. Second, she was changing, had changed a lot since he'd first met her, less than a month ago.

He wasn't surprised. She was experiencing freedom for the first time in years, and she was about to realize her goal of becoming a C.P.A. Her life was in transition.

It occurred to him that she was the same age he was

when he left the army and went to work for Charlie, a situation that had opened up a new life, one rewritten daily with every new experience.

No, he wasn't surprised at her changes, given the circumstances. He was just wary. Plus he liked her the way she was.

Nate didn't try to sneak up on Lyndsey. He called her name as he walked through the office. "I come bearing food," he added. He'd brought dinner with him, thinking if they talked at the office instead of at home they could have an actual conversation. At the office they couldn't just fall into bed.

He heard something fall to the floor, then the sound of paper rustling. She spun around when he walked into her cubicle. Her hands were behind her back. She leaned against her desk.

"You're back!"

Her voice was too bubbly, her cheeks too pink. She looked…guilty. Plus she didn't make a move toward him.

"Are we alone?" He looked around. He hadn't seen a car other than hers in the parking lot, but that didn't guarantee anything.

She nodded.

What was going on? "I don't get a kiss hello?"

"Of course you do." She came toward him, kissed him lightly, then tried to step back.

He drew her into his arms. She felt stiff. Over her shoulder he glanced at her desk, where papers and files were scattered. The times he'd seen her at work, her desk had been organized and neat.

"Is there something wrong?" he asked.

"No. Why do you ask?" She stepped back, blocking his view of her desk again.

"Did I scare you, coming in like that?"

She hesitated. "A little. It's okay. Mmm, that smells good."

He'd almost forgotten he was carrying the bag. "Spaghetti and meatballs from Angelina's. I'll get a chair."

"You know," she said in a rush, "my desk is a mess. Maybe we could eat in your office?"

"Yeah, we can do that."

Her smile was brittle.

"How much more work do you have left?" *When are you going to tell me what's going on? Why aren't you saying you missed me?*

"I'm done. I just have to clean up my papers and distribute the reports. In fact, I'll do it now while you set out dinner."

He left, but he didn't want to. It wasn't as if he could have called her predictable before this, because she frequently surprised him, but her behavior was so far out of character he didn't know what to make of it.

She seemed more relaxed a few minutes later when she came into his room. He had the food out on his coffee table in front of his sofa.

"What do you want to drink? I have water and I have water," he said.

"Water would be nice, if you have it."

"Good choice." He poured it into wineglasses.

"How was your trip?"

"Productive."

His tension built as she didn't make eye contact with him. And the blouse she was wearing had three buttons undone. And he missed her glasses.

Finally he put his plate down. "What's going on?"

"With what?"

"You."

"I don't know what you mean, except I'm happy." She stuffed half a meatball in her mouth.

"About what?"

"That you're back, Question Man. That I got my car heater fixed today. That Jess got a job."

"She did?"

"On campus. She even sounds excited about it."

Which wouldn't account for Lyndsey's unusual behavior, but he let it go for now. It was after two in the morning Chicago time. He was too tired to push her. Tomorrow, after he'd had a night's sleep.

"Are you coming home with me?" she asked as she helped clean up later.

"I'm pretty beat. I'll come by tomorrow afternoon, if you don't have other plans."

"Okay. See you then." She walked away.

He grabbed her arm. Now he knew for sure something was wrong. She hadn't kissed him. "Do you have something to tell me?"

"Like what?"

Guilty seemed to flash in neon in her eyes. He prepared himself for the worst. "Is this it for us, Lyndsey? Are we over?"

She looked stunned. "No! Absolutely not."

No guilt that time, and no lie, either. He was more confused than ever.

She moved in on him, pressed her lips to his. He didn't know what to think. What to do. She seemed desperate for him to believe her. After a few seconds he gave in, wrapping his arms around her, pulling her closer, kissing her. He drew back and stared at her. He wasn't sure he knew this Lyndsey.

"I'll walk you to your car," he said.

"That would be nice, thank you."

They stopped at her cubicle. She grabbed her sweater and...a briefcase?

"New purse?" he asked.

"What? Oh. No. I had a job interview this afternoon before I came to work."

His gut twisted. "How'd it go?"

"Pretty good, I think."

He turned out lights and reset the alarm. The walk to her car seemed endless. "So I'll see you tomorrow. Around one?"

"Perfect."

He watched her drive off. It wasn't until her taillights disappeared that it registered whose file was on her desk. Alexis Wells. Why? And how, since they were locked in a file cabinet that no one had access to except the partners?

Nate returned to the building and unlocked the cabinet. Wells was missing.

He went to Lyndsey's cubicle and opened drawers. No files.

She'd taken it with her.

He dragged his hands down his face and looked blindly around her work space. This couldn't wait until tomorrow.

Fifteen minutes later he knocked on her door. He saw her peek through the blinds.

"Just a second," she said. It took longer than that.

Getting rid of the evidence?

He was stunned by the depth of his anger. He'd trusted her more than any woman, even Arianna, because he'd shared his memories, his failings, his faults. He was trying not to jump to conclusions, but there weren't many possibilities.

Just when he'd let down his guard. Just when he'd decided to trust his judgment that this time he hadn't made a mistake.

The door opened. "What are you doing here?"

"I need to talk to you. Can I come in?"

She backed away. He scanned the room. No file. No briefcase.

"I want the Wells file back," he said.

She'd taken out her contacts and put her glasses on, but he could still see a range of reactions cross her face. Surprise, guilt, then resignation. Without a word she went into her sister's bedroom and came out with her briefcase. She set it on the coffee table next to the flowers he'd given her and pulled out the contents. Not one but five files.

He took them from her, glanced at the names on the tabs. All files from their locked cabinet. "Why do you have these?" he asked, barely able to contain his fury. If it had been anyone else he would've thought she was selling stories to the tabloids, but this was Lyndsey. Lyndsey with the honest face, the generous spirit, the passionate soul.

"I didn't want you to know yet," she said wearily. "Can we sit down?"

Blood pounded in his ears. His heart raced as he took a seat on the opposite end of the sofa from her. She sat like she had the first night, perched on the edge, her hands folded in her lap.

"I want to be a private investigator," she said.

It was so far out in left field he could only stare at her.

"Arianna's been helping me," she continued in a hurry, her eyes beseeching him to understand.

"Arianna has…?"

"She's been working with me the past couple of weeks. I read case files and we discuss them. She comes up with scenarios, and I'm supposed to figure out how I would handle them. She's testing me to see if I've got the instincts it takes. And the nerve. I know it's not the same as actual investigation but—"

He put up a hand, stopping her. "You want to be a P.I.?"

She nodded.

"Why didn't you tell me?"

"Because my decision couldn't have anything to do with you. And you would've been an influence, either way."

"Your decision is made now?"

"It is as far as I'm concerned. Arianna hasn't given me the thumbs-up yet." She pointed to the files in Nate's hands. "Those are my final exam."

He rubbed his temple where his head began to ache. "You expect to work for ARC?" The question came out more harshly than he'd intended, but he felt trapped. If she stayed on at the company she would be around, expecting something from him that wasn't in him to give. The relationship was bound to fizzle out, yet they would continue to see each other all the time. At some point she would have another man in her life. Get married.

Dammit. She was supposed to be safe. She was supposed to leave the company next month, putting a natural end to things. She would walk away, no scenes.

She lifted her chin. Her posture turned rigid. "I'd hoped to work for your company, but I understand that might make you uncomfortable. Arianna said she could recommend me to another P.I."

Arianna, what the hell have you done?

He stood, not knowing what else to say. The files were still in his hands. Take them or leave them? Arianna had given her permission.

"You can have the files," she said, her voice uncommonly quiet. "You're obviously uncomfortable leaving them. I wouldn't be able to focus on studying them, anyway." Her hands clenched, her mouth trembled. She pressed her lips together.

"We'll talk," he said, heading to the door. "Later."

"Okay."

He hesitated at the quaver in her voice but forced himself to keep going. And drove to Arianna's house.

* * *

Lyndsey didn't sleep, didn't even try to. She kept reliving the look on Nate's face when he'd asked if she expected to work at ARC. She'd obviously backed him into a corner, precisely what she'd tried to prevent by keeping her plans from him. She never wanted to put him in that position.

He wasn't pleasantly surprised by the possibility of her staying on at the firm. He was furious.

She sat on her couch all night, hoping he would come back to say he understood. To tell her she would make a great P.I., and that ARC would be lucky to have her. And that he wanted her in his life permanently, too.

Her phone rang at seven-twenty. She snatched it up. "Hello?"

"Lyndsey, it's Arianna."

She sagged. "Hi."

"Did I wake you?"

"No."

"Could you come into the office this morning?"

"Nate—"

"I know. He came over last night. We need to talk about it."

"I don't want to run into him until he's ready to talk to me."

"He's working from home today."

"Oh. Okay."

"I'm heading to the office now. Come anytime you're ready."

Arianna's businesslike tone gave away nothing. Lyndsey didn't have a clue what this turn of events meant.

But one thing was clear. She had to resign.

Thirteen

Lyndsey knew a lot more people in the office since the Christmas party. She got stopped several times as she made her way to Arianna's office. The last thing she felt capable of was idle chitchat but she had no choice.

Arianna's door was open. Lyndsey knocked anyway.

"Come on in. Have a seat. I'll be right with you." She was typing something into her computer.

Lyndsey looked around. Like Nate and Sam, Arianna didn't have photographs on her desk or anywhere else in her office. Were they such loners, then? Is that what her life would be like as an investigator?

No. Several of them at ARC were married and had children. But if you wanted to get to the top, did you have to forfeit a personal life? She didn't think she could do that. She wanted a family of her own someday. Not soon, though. She'd just gotten through raising Jess.

Arianna saved her document, turned her chair to face

Lyndsey, then got up and closed the door. She didn't return to her chair but leaned against the front of her desk.

"How are you?" she asked.

Lyndsey's eyes stung at the sympathetic tone. She blinked and swallowed. "I'm fine."

"Right."

Lyndsey handed her a sheet of paper, her resignation. Arianna glanced at it before setting it on her desk. She didn't rip it up, however.

"I shouldn't have asked you to deceive Nate," Lyndsey said.

"That was a mutual decision made for good reasons."

"He hates me."

"No. If he's mad at anyone, it's me. How did he find out, anyway? He was yelling so much last night I didn't get to ask."

"He was yelling?"

Arianna nodded.

"He never yells."

"I know."

Lyndsey thought about that for a minute. "Um, he found out because he came into the office about the time I was wrapping up. I didn't want him to see the files you'd given me. He knew something was wrong, then I kept making it worse. I never wanted to put him in this position."

"You know you'll face much worse situations as an investigator. You can't lose your cool, Lyndsey."

"I do fine with everyone but Nate. I can't lie to him. He *knows*."

Arianna returned to her chair and picked up the letter of resignation. "I don't want to accept this."

"You don't have a choice. We both know I can't work for him. It would be impossible. I'll stay until you find a replacement."

"You'll stay until you have a job. I know you can't afford to be without an income."

Lyndsey hated that she'd messed things up so badly. Look at what she was forfeiting. A great boss who understood. A wonderful group of co-workers. It was depressing.

"I'm really sorry. You tried to warn me." She must have inherited her mother's genes. She'd fallen in love with a man who didn't know how to make a relationship last. Better to find out now than be left with a baby, like her mother. "Will you still recommend me to another P.I.?"

"Let me think on it. I want the right person for you."

Her intercom buzzed. Arianna pressed a button. "Yes?"

"Sorry to interrupt, but there's a call for Lyndsey from a Mrs. Marbury on line one."

"Thank you, Julie." She pushed the phone across her desk. "You can take it in here or at your own desk."

"Here's fine." She took a settling breath, lifted the receiver and punched line one. "This is Lyndsey McCord, Mrs. Marbury. What can I do for you?"

"I'd like to talk to you. Just you. Could you come to my house?"

"If you can hold on a minute, I'll check my schedule." Lyndsey pushed the hold button. "She wants me to go to her house. Without Nate."

"Are you up to it?"

"I'm not an investigator."

"You're going to be."

The simple statement told Lyndsey everything. She'd passed the test. She couldn't take the time to wallow in it, however. She got back on the line. "I can come right now, if you'd like, Mrs. Marbury."

"Yes, fine. I'll be expecting you."

Lyndsey cradled the receiver. "I'll need to borrow a car.

I wouldn't be allowed in her neighborhood driving my old heap.''

"Take mine." She opened a drawer and pulled out a set of keys.

"I meant one of the company cars."

"I'm not territorial. It's the dark blue BMW. Have fun."

Lyndsey stood. The keys felt heavy in her hand, like a ton of responsibility. "I'll come straight back."

"I'm sure you will. Lyndsey?"

"What?"

"This isn't the time to take backward steps."

"What do you mean?"

"The night you met Nate you went toe-to-toe with him and held your own. Undo that second button again. Put your contacts back in. Show your confidence. You're doing fine."

Lyndsey kept Arianna's words in mind as she drove. By the time she'd been taken to Mrs. Marbury's sitting room, she felt in control again.

"Thank you for coming so promptly," the woman said, extending her hand.

She didn't look any better than she had when Lyndsey last saw her weeks ago. "How can I help you?"

"You started to tell me something when you were here before, but your partner stopped you. What was it?"

After a brief debate Lyndsey decided to be truthful. The poor woman's circumstances couldn't get any worse by what Lyndsey had to say. "I watched your husband and Tricia all weekend. I don't think he's in love with her."

Mrs. Marbury clenched the chair arms. "What makes you say that?"

"Because except for the shoulder massage there was no physical contact between them. Maybe there was a reason for that. It seems to me that it's all circumstantial evidence. Then the way he looked at the picture on Nate's computer screen and what he said about trust once broken being irrevocable…I don't know. It just doesn't fit. Why would he be angry at you about broken trust if he was the guilty one?''

''Are you saying there's nothing between them?''

''I don't know for sure. They were playing games, trying to trip us up, so who knows what was real. I can't even tell you for sure if she slept in his bed or on the couch in the office. What I can tell you is that he wasn't looking at her the way a man looks at a woman he's in love with. Or in lust with, for that matter.''

Mrs. Marbury broke down. She buried her face in her hands and started to sob. Lyndsey looked around the room, then finally went to her, knelt down and held her until she'd drenched Lyndsey's shoulder with tears. Empathetic tears welled up in Lyndsey's eyes, too. Her throat burned. She had her own troubles.

''I love my husband, Ms. McCord.''

''Lyndsey.''

She nodded. ''I did trust him—until he started acting secretive. He won't talk to me, not even on the phone. I need to talk to him. Please, can you convince him to see me just once? I need to explain.''

Lyndsey made a quick decision, not because Mrs. Marbury asked, but because Lyndsey believed there was much more to the story. ''I'll try. That's all I can say. I don't know whether he'll see me.''

''Make him. Please.''

''I'll try,'' Lyndsey repeated. She stood. ''Do you have children, Mrs. Marbury?''

''Lucinda. And, no, I don't. Michael does from his first marriage. I knew when he married me that he didn't want any more. I just always hoped I could talk him into it. If he loved me enough…'' Her voice trailed off as she cried again.

Lyndsey let herself out.

Arianna met her in the ARC parking lot as she pulled in. "Perfect timing," she said. "I've got an emergency."

"Should I wait around to talk to you about the Marbury case?"

"I'll call you at home when I get back in." She shut her car door and left.

Lyndsey thought about Lucinda Marbury while she drove home and decided she couldn't see Mr. Marbury alone. Lucinda had said before that he thought women didn't have any place in jobs he considered a man's domain, like private investigator. Plus she was part of a deceit against him. He probably wouldn't speak to her.

Even so, what would she be trying to prove? That she was a skilled investigator who didn't need help? She wasn't...and she did. Even if her instincts were good, she couldn't see the man by herself. This job belonged to Nate.

But she didn't want to be cut out of it, either. She'd been there from the beginning. She wanted to see it through.

Which settled it. She had to call him. They had to go together.

Nate sat in his deck chair, his laptop resting on his thighs, his gaze on the horizon. The security system for his L.A.-to-Chicago client was designed. In a minute he would e-mail it to work to be printed and put on Sam's desk.

He closed his eyes, worn-out, but all he saw was Lyndsey's face when he'd left her house last night. This morning. Whatever. He dropped the lid on his laptop and set it aside.

Her lips had trembled. Her eyes had darkened to almost black. He didn't know what it all meant. He couldn't believe she'd gone behind his back like that. If she'd talked to him instead of Arianna, he would've—

Hell. What would he have done? Discouraged her, maybe. Probably. He didn't want her around after their affair was over.

His cell phone rang. He hesitated when he saw it was Lyndsey.

Coward.

He pressed the start button, said hello.

"I'm sorry to bother you at home," she said, sounding businesslike.

"No problem." His pulse picked up tempo. He resented it.

"Lucinda Marbury asked me to come see her today. With Arianna's permission, I did. I want to report what happened." She went on to describe their conversation.

"We're not marriage counselors," he said, then was met with silence.

"Maybe this time we need to be," she said finally, coolly.

"What makes you think Marbury will see us?"

"Tricia."

"You talked to Tricia?"

"I got us an appointment at four o'clock, pending your availability."

Her efficiency prompted his first smile of the day. "I assume you would go on your own if I refuse? If I say you can't go, either?"

"Absolutely."

"That's insubordination."

"I'd tell you to fire me but I already turned in my resignation."

He sat up. "When?"

"This morning. Look, are you coming with me or not?"

She quit? "I am."

There was a long pause, then, "Good."

She quit? "How are you going to handle it?" he asked.

"I doubt Mr. Marbury would talk to me. You're the boss."

Was he? No one could tell that based on this conversation. "If you were going to handle it, what would you do?"

"If they had children, I would've played to the abandonment issue. But they don't, and it probably wouldn't have worked anyway because he has children from his first marriage and that didn't stop him from getting a divorce."

"Which leaves?"

"The fact she loves him."

"You think it really is love and not money that motivates her?"

"Yes, cynic, I do."

"And love conquers all."

"No." Her voice got quieter. "But it helps."

Time to end this conversation. "I'll pick you up at three-fifteen."

"I'll meet you in the lobby of his building at three-fifty."

The line went dead.

Fourteen

Lyndsey was worried about being late, so she arrived early, finding parking in the three-story garage attached to the Mar-Cal building. She signed in at the security desk then took a seat to wait for Nate.

When he walked in, she went numb. She'd seen him in action before, but not in this role, dressed in a suit and tie, looking powerful and in control. In charge.

She wore the only suit she owned, the one she'd bought for job interviews. Black jacket and pants, which she paired with a white silk shirt—with two buttons undone. She rose to meet him. *Steady. Steady. He's just a man. The man you have to stop loving.*

"Have you already signed in?" he asked as he approached the desk.

She nodded.

After Nate signed the register, the guard called Mr. Marbury's office for approval to send them up. They walked in silence to the elevator. Nate pushed the button for the eighteenth floor. The doors slid closed. Quiet descended. Sixteen hours ago he would've taken advantage of the opportunity to kiss her, she thought.

"You look very professional," he said.

"So do you."

He half smiled at that.

Stupid, she thought. So stupid. Of course he looked professional. Why wouldn't he?

She hated that she was nervous now that he was about to see her in a different light. He knew she wanted to be an investigator. She wasn't just his accessory, brought along to cook. He would be critiquing her words and actions. She couldn't afford to mess up, even if it wasn't a real investigation job.

As the doors opened she looked at him, admiring his profile. She missed him already. Missed touching him. Sleeping beside him.

Tricia greeted them at the elevator. Lyndsey was glad she'd already broken the ice over the telephone.

"He's on a call," she said, leading the way down the corridor. "He's upset with me for giving you this appointment. You won't find him pleasant or cooperative."

"Thanks for the warning," Lyndsey said. "I'm sure he won't be upset with you for long."

"It doesn't matter. I've already given my notice. Tomorrow's my last day." She held up her left hand, where a large diamond winked. "I'm getting married."

Lyndsey was swamped with something she decided was envy. "That's…wonderful news," she managed. "Who's the lucky man?"

"His name is Paul. Actually—" her voice got lower "—he's president of Mar-Cal's biggest competitor."

"He's who you were talking about at the beach house?" Nate asked. "The one with all the baggage?"

"He's been married twice. It made me reluctant. But I decided to have faith in his love, because I don't want to live without him." She paused before glass double doors. "Here we are."

Tricia left them standing in a luxurious office suite. A woman typed at a computer. Tricia's replacement? Lyndsey wondered. If so, on the surface she was a good choice. Older than Mr. Marbury, well groomed but not slim and beautiful. No potential as a trophy wife.

"Come this way," Tricia said, holding open the door to the inner sanctum.

Lyndsey met Nate's gaze briefly. Reassured by the encouraging look in his eyes, she relaxed. What was the worst that could happen? Mr. Marbury could order them out. They waited to be invited to sit, but he seemed determined to keep them standing.

Nate moved to a chair in front of the massive desk and sat. He motioned for Lyndsey to do the same.

"I'm not going to stand on ceremony," Nate said. "We aren't here as investigators."

"Why are you here?"

"Your wife wants to talk to you."

"I'm aware of that. She can talk to my lawyer."

Oh, he was a cool one, Lyndsey thought. He leaned back in his chair, his hands folded in his lap. He stayed focused on Nate, never once letting his gaze drift.

Nate leaned forward. "Before it comes to that, don't you think you owe her the courtesy of a conversation? You've got ten years invested in this relationship."

Startled, Lyndsey tried to keep a businesslike expression. How could he be so logical with Mr. Marbury and not with her? Didn't Nate owe *her* the courtesy of a conversation?

"I don't owe her anything. She thinks I cheated."

"Did you?"

He scowled. "No."

Lyndsey wished she could high-five someone. She knew he hadn't betrayed his wife. She knew it.

"If you talk to her you'll understand why she thinks you did," Nate said.

"She has a good reason? I gave her a reason to think that about me?"

He seemed stunned by that news. Lyndsey didn't think he was acting.

"Yes," Nate said.

He spread his hands. "I don't see how that's possible. I've always been faithful to her. Never even been tempted. Hell, I got my—" He stopped. "I still can't believe she thought I would stray."

"I can't emphasize enough that she did think that," Nate replied.

Lyndsey put a hand on the edge of the desk. "You got what for her?" she asked, having seen something in his eyes.

He looked at her, then at Nate. "Is this conversation confidential?"

"Of course," Nate said.

"Lucinda wants children. I had my vasectomy reversed as a surprise for our tenth anniversary."

Lyndsey sat back, floored.

"You'd had it done that day we met you?" Nate asked.

"That morning."

"Which would account for your lack of activity. And the quantity of ice." Nate winced and shifted in his chair.

Lyndsey almost smiled.

"To keep the swelling down. I was so doped up when we got there I didn't know or care what was going on. Tricia recognized you right away and told me. We had to completely change our plans."

"How?" Nate asked.

Mr. Marbury got up from his desk and moved to the window. ''I had intended to go to the beach house alone. I didn't need anyone fussing over me, and I couldn't tell Lucinda without spoiling the surprise. Plus, I didn't want to get her hopes up until we knew the surgery was a success. Then I got the opportunity to buy a company I've had my eye on for a long time. Problem was, someone else was also interested, and I only had that weekend to put together a report to present to my board. It's a formality since I own fifty-one percent of the company, but it's good business to get their approval and support.

''Without Tricia I couldn't have done it. That's all we did in the bedroom—work. The ironic thing is, I thought you were corporate spies sent to get a copy of the bid I was proposing. I'd arranged for that Charlie person to cook for me, then he suddenly has a change in plans and can't come, but he found a replacement. I bought it—until I learned you were a P.I.''

He glanced over his shoulder. ''Tricia and I spent our time trying to act like we were vacationing, when in fact we were working feverishly to assemble the report and keep you from knowing.'' He gave a bitter laugh. ''And you didn't know or care. Irony.''

He shook his head and looked out the window again. Lyndsey raised her brows at Nate.

''I hired someone to follow you when you left the beach house,'' Mr. Marbury continued, ''hoping you would lead me to whoever was competing for the buyout. Instead you drove to my house, which baffled me. It wasn't until I saw the picture on your laptop that I realized Lucinda had hired you because she thought I was cheating.''

His voice broke on the last word. Lyndsey started to plead a case for him to go to his wife, to bare his soul. Nate put up his hand to stop her.

''Sometimes pride needs to be set aside for something

more important.'' He joined Mr. Marbury at the window. ''Go to your wife. Listen to her. Confide in her. You both made assumptions and mistakes.''

Lyndsey would've added something about forgiveness and love, but otherwise she thought Nate said the right things. He angled his head toward the door, indicating to Lyndsey that they were leaving.

''Goodbye, Mr. Marbury,'' she said.

They stopped to wish Tricia good luck before they left the building.

''Where are you parked?'' he asked.

''On the second floor, near the stairs.''

''I'm on the third.''

Which meant they would walk to the garage together.

''Do you think he'll go to his wife?'' Nate asked when they got off the elevator.

''He's probably on his way now.''

''You think so?''

''He wanted someone's permission—or kick in the butt—to get him moving. He wouldn't have poured his heart out if he wasn't dying to go to her.'' She paused. ''That thing you said to him about pride? That was perfect. It was exactly what he needed to hear.'' *And what you need to take to heart, too.*

They left the lobby and took the stairs to the second parking level. An ache began to spread from the middle of her chest. Was this the last time she would see him? She was sure he would avoid coming into the office at night until she left ARC. She supposed there weren't such things as P.I. conventions, where they might meet up again at some point, get drunk and sleep together one last time. She at least wanted closure.

Okay, so that was a lie. She wanted him to be as reasonable with her as he'd been with Mr. Marbury.

She wanted a lifetime.

They stopped beside her car. She unlocked the door and tossed her purse inside. *Stop me from going, Nate.*

"I'll see you get paid for your extra hours," he said.

The pain in her chest intensified. "We got sent home early that Sunday, with full pay. I've already been fairly compensated," she said, offering his own words back as if she were teasing—or maybe not teasing but using her own irony.

The attempt at a joke fell flat. "You'll get paid," he said.

That did it. "To hell with getting paid," she said, her fury clawing its way up from the pit of her stomach. "Be honest with me, instead. Do what you told Mr. Marbury to do."

"What?"

She threw up her hands. "That's it, Question Man. I'm outta here." She started to climb into her car. If this was the way he wanted to leave it, fine. She wasn't hanging around for more heartache.

He put a hand on her door. "I'm not ready for this to end," he said. His eyes said more. They begged.

She couldn't let him get away with giving her a piece of the pie. She was starving for the whole thing. "For what to end?"

"You and me."

Her body reacted to his words. You and me. It was what she wanted. So why wasn't she flinging herself into his arms and saying okay. Me, too. Let's go to my house.

Because it wasn't enough anymore. "Am I supposed to wait around until you are ready?" She was proud of how she got the words out, even though they killed her.

"I didn't mean it like that."

"How did you mean it?"

"I don't understand why you're leaving. Why you quit the company."

"You want me to stay until you get me out of your system? Then what? I'm supposed to be able to keep working with you? How do you think I could work for you after what we shared?" *Figure out a way, Nate. Make it happen.* "Our relationship was a mistake. I told myself the only reason I didn't stop it was because I would be leaving in two months, then we could continue without having the boss/employee issue between us. But the truth is…I let it happen because I couldn't help myself."

She couldn't read his expression. She hated how he clammed up when his emotions were involved. Any other time she couldn't get him to stop talking. She pictured him speaking to Mr. Marbury, heard his words, his understanding. Until now she'd been so worried that he would feel obligated to her in some way that she hadn't shared her feelings. Not this time. He wouldn't have the excuse of not knowing how she felt. She was not letting him off the hook.

"You made some assumptions about me," she said, her head high. "I'm not a sophisticated woman who has a fling then puts it out of her head. When I was with you, I—" She stopped, drew a breath, then blurted out her feelings. "I found myself. And I like myself. I'm proud of what I've accomplished and excited to be heading in a new direction, whether you like it or not. You did that for me.

"I didn't change your life like you did mine, I guess. I didn't open up worlds and give you confidence and treat you better than anyone else ever has. All I did…all I did was love you."

She got into her car, started her engine and drove away. In her rearview mirror she saw him just standing and watching.

Somehow she made it home before she fell apart.

Fifteen

Nate looked at his watch for the third time without registering the time. The staff meeting seemed endless. He had no patience for the recitation of case reports by the various investigators, and he contributed nothing in return. Most of the time he drummed a pen on his notepad until someone either threw something at him or told him to knock it off.

When the meeting broke up, he scooped up the notepad and headed to the conference room door.

"Nate," Sam called. "Hold on."

The last of the staff filed past him. No one talked to him.

"Shut the door, please," Arianna said. "We need a partners meeting."

Sam pointed to a chair, meaning Nate should sit. "What're you trying to do, run the business into the ground single-handedly?"

"What the hell does that mean?" Nate asked.

"I mean every day for the past two weeks someone has complained to Ar or me about you. You're surly. You're not available to brainstorm a case. You're ignoring basic courtesies, like please and thank-you. It stops now."

Nate knew he was guilty. He'd intended to fix it every day, but every day he got worse. "You're right. I apologize."

"An apology isn't enough this time," Arianna said. "Sam and I are ordering you to take that trip to Australia you postponed. Get out of here. Get your head together."

"By the time you get back, Lyndsey will be gone," Sam added. "That should help."

Nate looked sharply at him. "She's not already?"

"She doesn't have a new job yet. Ar promised her she could stay until she found something."

"I've put out some feelers," Arianna said. "No bites yet. I think she started applying for C.P.A. jobs again, just to get away. Anyway, that's not your problem. Your problem is you. Fix it. I'm sure you can find some willing Barbie from Down Under to help." With that unsubtle gibe at him, she left.

"Arianna should learn to speak her mind, don't you think?" Nate said conversationally to Sam.

Sam sat opposite him. "We've both been holding back, hoping things would change."

"I know." Nate looked at his friend, saw understanding in his eyes.

"Why don't you just give in to it, Nate?"

"I can't."

"Because?"

"Because what if it doesn't work? You know what will happen, what always happens. She'll start resenting the time I'm gone. She'll want a commitment. The Marburys getting back together is a rare happy ending. I can't hurt her again. What kind of man would that make me?"

"I can give you a list of good marriages, starting with Charlie and his wife. You're exaggerating because it justifies avoiding Lyndsey."

He couldn't deny it. "How is she, anyway?"

"Not gonna answer that, Nathan. You wanna know, you find out for yourself. You know what watching you has taught me? That lying to yourself is as bad as lying to someone else. And next summer when my high-school class holds its fifteen-year reunion, I'm going. I'll face my past."

"Why wait until then?"

"For a lot of reasons." Sam looked at his watch and pushed himself up. "Ar and I have to get to that meeting with the mayor. Book your flight."

Half an hour later his travel agent called with the new flights and hotel reservations. He wasn't leaving until eight o'clock that night, which gave him hours until he had to be at the airport. He might as well go home and pack, because he sure wasn't going to get any work done here.

The intercom buzzed. "Nate? You've got a call from a Roy Gordon on line two."

"Did he say what it was about?"

"No. He just asked to speak to one of the owners about an employee. Arianna and Sam are gone."

"Okay. Thank you, Julie," he remembered to add before picking up the phone. "This is Nate Caldwell."

"Good morning, sir. I'm Roy Gordon from Rasmussen, Gordon and Culpepper Accounting. I'm calling about a Ms. Lyndsey McCord. She's applied for work with us and listed your firm as a reference. Could you verify her employment for me, please?"

An accounting firm? Hell, no, he didn't want to verify

her employment. *Do you give up that easily, Lyndsey?*
He'd expected more of her.

That he'd had a hand in her situation almost killed him.

"I can confirm her date of hire," Nate said finally, forcing himself past his anger and resignation.

"That would be September seventh?"

Nate didn't know for sure, but he knew Lyndsey wouldn't lie. "That's right."

"She's a transcriber?"

"Yes." *And she types flawless reports and hasn't missed a day. And her kisses are hot and sweet and generous. And she makes love like it's as necessary as breathing.*

"Would you say she's an honest person?"

The man's nasally voice grated on Nate. "By law that's the only information I need to give."

"You aren't going to answer because she's not honest?"

Nate barely stopped himself from swearing. "She's extremely honest. You would be lucky to get her."

"So, you're recommending her?"

No. Hell, no. "Yes."

"Good. That's good. Now, just between you and me, did she cause problems with the men in your office? We've got a lot of men and, you know, she's pretty hot."

It was exactly what Nate wanted—a reason to get mad. A reason to vent his frustrations. He stood. His chair crashed into the credenza behind his desk. His fists clenched. "Expect charges to be filed against you and your firm." He had the unadulterated pleasure of slamming down the phone. He couldn't catch his breath for several seconds. Fury snaked through him, doubling in strength, tripling, until it reached the point of no return.

He left his office, not looking right or left, not answering anyone's query. Nothing could stop him. He was going to make damned sure Ms. Stubborn McCord didn't work for that bastard. If she hated his guts because of it, who gave a damn? How much worse could it get?

Lyndsey set the timer for twelve minutes and started to fill another cookie sheet for the next batch. If she wasn't careful she would gain five pounds in two hours.

Her doorbell rang. And rang. And rang.

She hurried through the dining room and to the front door, then hesitated. "Who is it?"

"Nate. Open up."

She groaned. Of all days. She was wearing her stupid old black jeans and sweater again. She hadn't put on any makeup. Her hair. Well, she didn't want to think about that.

"Open up!"

She jumped, then unlocked the door and opened it.

"You are not going to work for that…Gordon. Where is your sense, Lyndsey? He's a sexist pig. You with all your great people skills can't see that?"

His jaw was rigid, his eyes bright. Lyndsey didn't know what he was talking about.

"And what the hell are you doing applying for an accounting job when you want to be a private investigator? Are you giving up your dream that easily? It makes me question your commitment."

Fascinated by his anger, she just stared at him. She hadn't applied for an accounting job. She didn't know a Gordon.

Arianna. Lyndsey would bet this was Arianna's way of intervening, of forcing him to talk to her. How had she manipulated it?

"Well?" he said.

"Well what?"

"Are you giving up?"

Was it crazy that she liked how he'd lost control? If she wanted to learn the truth, did she need to keep him out of control? *Ah, Nate, I know you so much better than you might think.* "That's none of your business," she said calmly.

His scowl deepened. "It is my business. I care about you."

"No, you're being paternal. You can't order me around."

"Paternal?" He filled the doorway with his fury.

"Yes." She crossed her arms. Her heart pounded hard and fast. "Haven't I made enough sacrifices? If I want to work for Mr....Mr. What's-his-name, I will. What gives you the right to tell me how to live my life?"

"What gives me the right?" He stepped into the room, backing her up. *"I love you."*

She took another step back. He'd yelled at her. Yelled. That he loved her. She wanted to throw herself in his arms. Instead she crossed hers again. "You have a strange way of showing it."

"Because it scares the hell out of me," he said, the words like sandpaper on metal. "I love you. I've been miserable without you. Ask anyone."

His misery shouldn't make her this happy. "Maybe you'd better shut the door."

"Lyndsey, I've never missed anyone before. Not like this."

His eyes were filled with agony. He shut the door with a quiet click, as if his energy was completely gone, then he walked to the sofa and sank into the cushions, subdued. His sudden mood shift confused her. She sat in a chair across from him so that she could look him in the eye. She had to see for herself that he was telling the truth. She couldn't survive another two weeks like this again.

"I've barely slept," he said.

She believed him. She hadn't slept much either.

"I knew you were different. I just didn't know how different." He rested his arms against his thighs and leaned toward her. "I liked you from the beginning, then you started to change. To, I don't know, to blossom. I kept expecting you to leave me behind, like your glasses. Then when you confided in Arianna instead of me about wanting to become a P.I., I figured you didn't trust me. I didn't blame you," he said, when she started to interrupt. "Women have had good reason not to trust me. I haven't made a commitment since my divorce. I never wanted to. I want to now.

"I'm begging you, Lyndsey. I've been an idiot. You have no reason to trust me. But you turned my world upside down, and I didn't know how to function in it. I need you. You make me happy in a way I never thought anyone could, because I didn't think I would ever let anyone even try. You tested every belief I had about women and loyalty and trust. You broke down barriers, brick by brick.

"If you'll give me one more chance, I'll prove it."

Lyndsey swallowed the painful lump in her throat.

"Please," he said, leaning closer.

Her throat closed. She nodded, saw something much bigger than relief on his face.

"Have I told you," he said, his voice shaking, "how I love the way you sit like that, right on the edge of your chair, your hands in your lap like some Victorian lady?" He moved to the side of her chair and slid in behind her, wrapping his arms around her waist, pulling her close, his body trembling. "I want to do this every time I see you sitting like this."

Her back cushioned by his chest, she rested against him. Tears burned her eyes at the tenderness in his voice.

"I want to hold you forever, Lyndsey McCord. Just like this. I love you."

"Nate—" A shrill series of beeps interrupted the moment. "My timer," she said, trying to get off his lap.

His arms tightened more. "Ignore it."

"I've got cookies in the oven."

She felt his hesitation, then he said, "Let 'em burn."

If that didn't prove his love, she didn't know what did. "They could catch on fire," she said. "Smoke. Flames. Firefighters. No sex for hours because we'll have to clean up."

He went still, then he buried his face along her neck, his breath ragged. "Does that mean you forgive me?"

"Yes." A tear trailed down her cheek, then another. "I love you."

He turned her around, settled her on his lap, facing him. Somber, he swiped his thumbs across her cheeks.

"I'm sorry. I know you hate crying," she said, suddenly crying more.

He kissed her as the tears flowed. She kissed him until they stopped. They held each other until they smelled food burning, then ran into the kitchen just as the smoke alarm went off, singing a duet with the timer.

"How would you like to go to Australia?" he shouted over the noise.

"When?" She tossed him some pot holders.

He snatched the tray of charred cookies out of the oven and dumped it in the sink then opened a window. "Tonight."

"I have to work tonight."

He laughed. He reached up and punched the reset button on the alarm. She turned off the timer. Smoke filled the room. The quiet roared in her ears.

"I don't have a passport," she added.

He took her into his arms. "Then for tonight, how about

I take you to paradise instead? You only need a photo ID for that.''

   ''Let me get my wallet....'' And then she kissed him.

* * * * *

TWO SPARKLING CHRISTMAS ROMANCES...

...full of the joys and warmth of the season

Twelfth Night Proposal
by Karen Rose Smith

Rescued by the Magic of Christmas
by Melissa McClone

Available 7th November 2008

www.millsandboon.co.uk

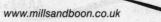